The Undoer

Melissa Cunningham

Clean Teen Publishing

clean teen PUBLISHING

ISBN: 978-1-63422-199-3
Cover Design by: Marya Heiman
Typography by: Courtney Knight
Editing by: Cynthia Shepp

M

YA content disclosure

For more information about our content disclosure, please utilize the QR code above with your smart phone or visit us at www.cleanteenpublishing.com.

Prologue

They call it *The Door to Hell.* A blackened crater that never stops spewing up poisonous gas. It burns, toxic and bubbling, from the bowels of the Earth in the middle of a barren wasteland. But gas isn't the only thing coming from that crater…

They slither out, those malevolent souls—demonic filth that wreak havoc and destroy lives. They don't even pretend to hide…

1

Brecken

I'm not a demon anymore. I defected. The demons hate me. I'm a traitor, and they'd love nothing more than to serve my head up on a platter.

But now I've been given the illustrious responsibility to close *The Door to Hell* and deal with the demonic "problem" that is infiltrating Earth. The higher-ups figure I'm perfect for the job since I was a demon… before.

I sit at a glass table in Raphael's office, which is located in Elysium's administrative building. As usual, wide windows let in a blinding amount of radiant light. Soft, white couches and chairs are arranged around the room, and beautiful artwork hangs on the walls. I feel out of place and uncomfortable. I don't belong here. I know this at a gut level, but I don't know how to fix it.

Closing my eyes, I soak in the light, knowing it could be the last time and hoping it might cleanse me. I'll miss the friends I've made here, but I'll fit in better on Earth, which looks darker and more dismal in comparison.

Raphael leans forward, a clever glint in his cool, green eyes. He seems relaxed, his hands clasped, a smile on his face, but his taut shoulders give away his true anxiety. *The Door* is a huge problem. No, not a problem. A catastrophe. Raphael's concern radiates around him like smog, infecting me with his same worries. All of Elysium is in a panic about it, and guardian angels have been pulled back from Earth as their charges are overtaken by demons.

Like mice, the demons are reproducing and are vomited into Earth's realm to find a body. Whatever plan we decide on has to work. And I'm in charge. The stress is overwhelming. Crushing.

I wait to hear Raphael and Michael's plan, because I can't think of one. If it works, maybe it will also clear my reputation as someone who "undoes" everything. Hence, my demon title, *The Great Undoer*. It's something I am stilled called, even today. I hate it.

"We have everything planned down to the very last detail. Down to every contingency." Michael reclines, his golden hair pulled back and tied at the nape of his neck. It's strange to see him in normal clothes—white robes and bare feet. I'm used to his gleaming armor and the power it radiates as he leads the armies of heaven into battle.

"Of course," I answer. Has he ever done anything halfway? I doubt it.

I once pitted my strength against his when I was a commander in Perdition's armies. I don't think Michael has forgotten. His gaze is cold and unfriendly when he looks at me. He doesn't think I belong here, but if not here, then where?

"You'll need help with this," Raphael adds, leaning forward and glancing over at Michael. "It can't be done alone."

I'd already figured that. I've thought of nothing else. Angels haven't been able to get *The Door* shut, and they were overwhelmed by the sheer number of demons coming through.

"Anyone in mind?" There's no one qualified except those well-trained soldiers who obey every command given them by Michael. *The Avenging Angels*. Battle-hardened warriors who have fought evil throughout history. Who fought *me* throughout history. They aren't peace-loving, celestial beings who stroke harps on pink, fluffy clouds. No, these guys take down the real enemies. I've had many close calls with them myself. And even they haven't been able to close *The Door* on their own.

They won't want to fight *with* me. I am more likely to receive a sword in my back than a sword of defense at my side. I want to trust them, but they still see me as a demon. As a liar. As *The Great Undoer*. I can't imagine who Michael and Raphael will find to assist me.

"They're called The Cazadors," Michael says with a wry grin.

He folds his arms over his massive chest and leans against the desk, crossing his ankles. He's enjoying this, which makes me feel like the joke is on me. "They're a group of kids who joined together to hunt demons. They can actually see them inside their human host. They train regularly, they have holy weapons, and you will be their new leader."

I can only stare at him. "You think *humans* can help me? This is not a job for mortals. Even the Avenging Angels haven't been able to fix this. We're overwhelmed and outnumbered."

Michael's eyes narrow, but he doesn't say anything.

"It's perfect. They'll never suspect a thing," Raphael says.

"Who? The demons or the humans?" Still, I just sit there, trying to figure out how this could possibly work.

Raphael chuckles. He's the only one with a sense of humor. "The demons, of course."

"And these Cazadors are already trained? By who?"

"By one of their own. This is why they need you." Raphael watches me, waiting for a reaction. He's thoughtful, which makes me wonder if something else is going on here. "They are already killing demons and sending them back to Barathrum, but the group needs a true leader to bring them together. They have the potential to be a force to be reckoned with."

"A force to be reckoned with." I shake my head in disbelief and slouch in my chair. This is a suicide mission. Are they trying to kill me? Is that the plan? I know Michael and his army hate me, but would they go to these lengths?

And then I realize something. If they send me back to Earth, I'll have to have a body. A physical body. I can't be the Cazador leader without one. Maybe… maybe this is my chance at redemption. If I can close *The Door* and stop the demon infiltration… I'll be forgiven. I'll be with Alisa again! Maybe this will be enough to redeem me. Suddenly, it sounds like a fantastic idea.

Michael shifts and releases a sigh. "You'll need a different name."

"Why?"

"Well, you can't go by your demon name. You'll be recognized,"

Raphael says.

It will also make me more of a target.

"Or by your old mortal name, Brecken." Michael smiles as if he knows something, but then he glances away and his grin disappears. I've never been able to read him. I never know what he's thinking. His face becomes a blank page without much emotion, and I try to hide the fact that I like him about as much as he likes me.

"What aren't you telling me?"

They give each other knowing looks. Raphael just shakes his head. "No one can know who you really are. You can't tell anyone."

"Okay."

"We mean anyone. It could destroy the whole plan before you even have a chance to get started. Promise us you won't reveal your true identity."

Who would I even tell? The only people who know me are my family. I've already been told not to search them out. "Sure. Fine." *Whatever.*

2

Dean

Darkness thrives, thick and heavy in shadow. Not even the slanted beams of light from the streetlamps illuminate the murky sidewalk. A chill slithers over my skin. They're coming. I can feel it.

Jag crouches at the end of the alleyway, poised and ready to dart into the street at the first sign of life. Not human life, but the other kind that has taken up residence on our dying planet. I hide behind him. He holds his knife loosely, fearless in his stance. A figure ambles down the middle of the street toward us. The guy mumbles and stumbles, drunk, a shell for the creature inside.

I see the demon clearly from where I crouch in an alleyway—a gray, ghostlike wraith, stretched and elongated inside its stolen home of flesh and bone. It comes from the underbelly of hell, erupting into this world in a burst of ash and fire, rather than amniotic fluid and blood. This is the part we care about—the form on the inside. The vaporous aura.

I tense, clutching my backpack, waiting.

When the demon stands directly across the street, Jag darts forward, leaping into the air to clear a car parked in his way. His right foot slaps against the hood, propelling him farther, like an acrobat twisting through the air. His dagger glistens in the lamplight as he slashes down, the etched runes on his steel blade glowing blue.

Watching, spellbound, I never take my eyes from the scene, my heart twisting in envy. I can't do what Jag does. I can't kill the phantoms inside their stolen bodies. Even holding the runed knife brings bile up from my stomach and makes my eyes water with terror.

The demon never has a chance to fight back. Jag's knife cuts through its skin and tissue, through its fleshly body, like butter. It explodes in an eruption of russet ash, and then the flesh and bone disintegrate, leaving a pile of dust on the road, a gold wedding band lying at the center.

Jag picks up the ring and drops it into his pocket. We'll pawn it later and order pizza. It sounds cold and harsh, but this is the reality we live in. We can't afford to consider the human side of it.

Well, Jag can't.

He is my best friend. I admire him more than anyone else, but he doesn't feel remorse after his massacres, and I can't stop feeling remorse just watching him. I hate that we kill people, even if they are possessed. I made the mistake of asking Jag about his lack of conscience once. He didn't speak to me for three days. Maybe he does hate it.

It would be nice if the demons could be exorcized through other means. We've tried, only to have the crap beaten out of us by the demon. We also lost a friend, who died in the process. The only way to get rid of the demon is to kill it while it resides *in* the body. They can't be killed—that we know of—any other way. Which is why Jag has to be fast, and I have to be frustrated. All I can do is watch because I refuse to stay at home alone.

The demons have to be stopped because they are killing people and committing horrific crimes, like torture and rape. Some demons have even found top leadership positions in the governments around the world.

Only a gifted few can see them inside the human. There aren't many of us. We call ourselves *Cazadors*. Demon hunters.

I want to be useful, but I only have one talent. I draw. Well, sketch. And not just in charcoal, but with any medium. My favorite is watercolor. But I can't paint a demon to death. They won't die just because I get their likeness down on paper. So I'm not that useful.

I *can* remember the details of their expressions and appearances though. They are not all alike. I'd hoped to someday work as a sketch artist. Maybe for the police. For now, I do it for free on darkened, dangerous streets so we can keep track of the demons we've sent back to hell and the ones that come back. Because they do.

Drawing as fast as I can, I contour and shape, shade and blend, until the image looking back at me gives me the chills... just as the actual demon does.

Jag still stands in the center of the street, searching. Listening. Are there more? Is there one hiding in the shadows around the corner? I swirl around, positive there is one breathing down my neck, poised to stab me in the back. Adrenaline darts through my veins and my pulse pounds, but no one is there.

I'm alone in the shadowed alley.

We've been jumped more times than I can count, and the demons don't always travel alone. In fact, more often than not, they roam in packs, fighting like wild dogs to be the alpha.

Wiping his knife on his pants, Jag saunters back over to me, his hair glowing gold in the one streetlamp that shines. He keeps it pulled back in a ponytail and refuses to cut it. He likes it long, thinking it gives him strength, like Samson.

"Dang! What a rush!" He re-sheathes his knife and rakes a hand through his escaped strands of hair. "What was my time?"

"Five and a half seconds," I answer. "You shaved off a half second from the last one. Good job."

"Did you get his face in time?" He gazes from me to my notebook page.

"Yeah, for the most part. I'll have to finish at home."

"You okay?" He hands me my backpack, which lies at his feet.

"I'm good." I try to sound honest, but he always knows when I'm lying. That comes from living together for so long. We are close, like brothers. Not in some sissy I-need-someone-to-take-care-of-me way, but in a *Dude, you're my bro* kind of way. We've known each other our whole lives. And like I said, there is no one I trust more.

I toss my notebook and pencils inside the pack, slinging it over my shoulder. I'm beat and ready to go home. Working nights is exhausting. I can't wait to fall onto my bed, which is really a sleeping bag… on the floor, but it's better than nothing.

A movement to our right catches my eye, and I freeze. Two demons, wearing high-class business suits, saunter around the corner. They stop as soon as they notice us—which is pretty quick since there really isn't anyone else around at two in the morning. The demon on the right smiles, like he knows who we are—or rather, who Jag is. He must know I'm harmless because he doesn't give me the time of day.

"Hello, young Cazador."

I grip the dagger in my belt even though I've never used it and probably never will. Sweat beads along my upper lip and my fingers tremble. Jag doesn't even blink, and he certainly doesn't take time to chitchat. He whips his blade out and stabs it into the chest of the demon closest to him—the one on the left—before it can open its mouth. It explodes in a cloud of cinnamon-colored ash. No metal falls to the ground, so he isn't carrying any money or wearing jewelry.

The demon on the right, the guy with the ugly smile, is quicker. He feints as Jag lunges, and then ducks under Jag's arm, spinning around so he's behind me. He grabs me around the neck and squeezes my windpipe with his elbow, cutting off my air.

I grasp his arm, but there is no way I can break his hold. My pack falls from my fingers and I struggle for freedom, my face growing hot and probably as red as my new Vans sneakers, which, by the way, are my favorite shade of vermillion.

"Now, now," the demon drawls. "There's no need to be so quick to judge. Why assume I'm here to hurt you? Look what you did to my friend." He points to the pile of ash while keeping my neck tight in the crook of his arm.

Jag glares. This fiend will have no compulsion about killing me, and will feel no regret or guilt after.

I try to catch Jag's eye, but his gaze never leaves the demon's.

"What do you want?"

"What all of us want. To live in peace without people like you ruining a good thing."

I beg Jag to hurry. My fingers and toes grow numb and my vision grows splotchy.

Jag's tone remains calm. "So, you want me to just leave you alone to live in peace?"

"Yes. Exactly. You don't hurt me, and I won't hurt you."

"Like you could."

"I could."

"Doubt it."

By now, I can hardly follow the conversation. I'll pass out any second, and my last thought will be of how pathetic an excuse I am for a Cazador. I can't even protect myself, let alone anyone else.

"Fine. You can go," Jag answers. "This is your one free pass. And I mean your only one."

"How kind, my young friend," the demon sneers, loosening his grip on me ever so slightly. I suck in a huge breath and my brain comes back to life.

"You have one second, jack-nit," Jag growls, his fingers curling into fists.

The demon lets his second tick away. "You don't even want to make a deal? I know who you are, young Cazador. I know things that could help you."

I wonder for one stupid second if the demon is telling the truth, but I never get the chance to find out. He pushes me into Jag's arms, throwing him off balance, and takes off, running the other way, escaping around the corner before I even have a chance to fall down on the sidewalk, which is exactly what I do.

Jag lets the demon go, but I swear to remember its *true* face—its demon face—for the next time… if there is a next time.

"You okay?" Jag stands before me unharmed.

I gasp, sputter, and clutch my throat. "Yeah. Just dandy." I rise to my knees, still shaky, and breathe deeply before standing up all the way. "That guy is strong."

"Did you get a good look at him? Enough to draw him?"

"Yeah." I'll never forget his face. Either of them—the human or the demon one. There'd been a touch of gray at his temples, and his blue eyes had crinkled when he smiled. He'd worn a dark suit and a long coat of gray wool. A professional. Not like the other demons we've met so far. The demon on the inside had sported a smooth, slate-colored head, a jagged mouth with cadmium-yellow teeth—not one of my favorite colors, and deep cobalt-blue eyes—endless pits of hopelessness.

I can't help but feel bad for the actual owner of the body. His world had disappeared in seconds when the demon took over. Had the man done something to allow the demon inside? Did he leave a family behind?

"Come on, then." Jag turns to head down the deserted street. "That's enough excitement for one night."

3

Dean

Jag and I only have each other now. We live in a rundown church at the end of an abandoned street. It's a small, white clapboard building with a chapel and an insignificant preacher's office off to the side. Plus a basement.

Home, sweet home.

I push open the door and step into the darkness, exhausted and ready to lie down on my ratty sleeping bag in the basement. Utilities were cancelled years ago, so there is no electricity, but that doesn't bother us. Jag lights a candle, and I follow him down the stairs. He plops onto his bedroll with a tired sigh, closing his eyes.

We only killed seven demons tonight, not including the one Jag let go. A slow night. I pull out my notebook. Touching up my drawings, I get down the last guy's face while I can remember it. The creak of the wooden beams above my head is a familiar song and soothes me, but how much longer can we do this? Sleeping during the day and prowling the streets at night. Our whole world centers on locating evil beings and dispatching them to hell… day after day… for how long?

Jag turns to me, propping his head up on his elbow, studying me while I draw. I can feel his gaze boring a hole through my chest, so I finally look up. "What?"

"Are you happy here?" He sighs, and I get the feeling he might not be. In this world, happiness is not the goal. Survival is what matters.

"Happy enough."

"I don't believe you."

"Don't be stupid." I go back to my drawing. I don't really

have a choice to be happier. I have nowhere else to go. My parents and sisters are dead. Killed in the Rift. So many people died… so many. Jag lost his family too. We're stuck with each other.

He laughs and lays back down, crossing his arms over his chest. His muscles flex and stretch under his ratty, black T-shirt. I try not to compare them to my flaccid, thin arms, but it's impossible not to. He looks like a Greek god and I look like Shaggy, only I don't have a Scooby Doo. I *am* the Scooby Doo in this relationship. Jag moves like a samurai without even trying and all I can do is wield a pencil, the sharper the better. It's not my fault. It's my genetics.

Jag turns over to face the brick wall. One candle is lit and glows in the dim, cement room. It gives my sketch an eerie, haunted appearance, and I repress a shiver. After finishing, I lie down and stare at the ceiling, thinking about our night. I'm getting tired of standing back and watching while Jag does all the work. I hide while he puts his life on the line. Jag would do anything for me, including die for me, and I'll never forgive myself if that ever happens.

"So…" My voice is barely a whisper. "Tomorrow, I think I'm going to do it. I'm going to kill a demon. After what happened tonight, I need to. I'm a weakness. The weak link. And you're not always going to be around to protect me. I don't like it when you have to."

He rolls back over to face me. "Dean. It doesn't bother me."

"It bothers me."

"You haven't even touched your knife since I bound it with runes," he says. "You can't stand to look at it." He frowns, and it irritates me. I have no comeback. He's right, and the determination I feel burning in my chest melts away. I can't help the scowl that replaces it.

He shakes his head and glances away, looking at nothing. "I'm sorry. But we've had this conversation before. You don't need to kill demons. I don't want you to. We need your talent for drawing. It's just as important as anything else." He gazes at me earnestly, as though it will reinforce his words, but I want to stay mad. I need to. My place in the Cazadors isn't like anyone else's.

I don't pull my own weight. They try to make it seem like my drawings matter, but they don't. Not really. Who cares if we come up against the same demons more than once? We kill it either way.

"Don't placate me." I roll over and face the opposite wall.

"I didn't mean it like that." He tries to backpedal. "I meant there are a lot of other things that are just as important for you to do. Just because you can see the demons doesn't mean you're supposed to kill them." He waits for my reaction. I feel his eyes on my back.

I sit back up and lean against the wall, running my fingers through my hair. It needs to be trimmed but isn't nearly as long as Jag's. "It's not important, whether I'm good at it or not."

"It is!"

Before the Rift, I'd been a promising artist. I'd had lofty goals, but I don't want to talk about it anymore. "Where were Doug and Owen tonight? Have you talked to them lately?" They are the other two Cazadors in our group. They live with their families a couple of miles away. They actually still have theirs. We're all just a bunch of teenagers, amateur demon slayers, but we're good at it. Last week, we all had a major disagreement. Doug and Owen walked out. I haven't seen them since.

"Not since the argument." He grunts and rolls over.

It was all about a girl… of course. The rest of us want her to join the Cazadors—me most of all. She's incredible in a million and one ways, but Jag refuses, as though he can make all the decisions and we have to obey. I'm not sure we are even still a group.

I don't know why he is so adamant about it, but maybe it's because he feels responsible for us, and he can't let go of that while we're out hunting. Our safety distracts him. He feels the need to protect us, mostly me, which has almost cost us our lives a few times. And I am no help on the sidelines. Add a girl to the mix… and well, I can see why it eats at him.

Jag blows out the candle. Because darkness always makes me feel like I should whisper, I lean closer. "What happens now?" I bump into his back, my lips next to his ear.

"Dude, get back." He shoves me away.

"Sorry." He's weird about personal space. I'm just curious about what's going to happen. I don't think we should split up. We're better together. Strength in numbers. "Maybe if we trained more often..."

"No."

"Why not? It's fun having Doug and Owen around." Jag's irascible nature makes him less than entertaining at times. I like being around happy, easygoing people once in a while, and Doug and Owen are cheerful. I plow ahead and bring the sore subject back up. "Heidi has been begging to join for the last year."

Only a few months older than I am, she is everything a hunter should be. Tough as a she-bear and nearly as stubborn. She's in great shape and has been training all year. She also has that long, dark hair and those unforgettable blue eyes I can't stop seeing every time I close my own. I've never divulged this information to Jag because he describes her as a bad smell that has attached to the bottom of his shoe and won't go away.

But I want her around. All the time.

He's quiet for a moment, his breathing soft and deliberate. "It's easier if it's just you and me. Plus..." He doesn't finish even though I give him plenty of time.

"What?" I ask, finally.

"Never mind. It doesn't matter."

"It matters to me." I was the first one to call us a group. I was the one who came up with the name. I like the fact that we have purpose. I like it being organized. We can all see the demons. It only seems logical. Jag never wanted any of it, but he did assume leadership easily enough.

There is only one way to deal with his stubbornness. "Don't you *like* girls, Jag?" I let my voice get low and slow. "Is there something I should know since we live here together... all alone?"

He reaches over and punches me, pounding my shoulder with his fist. "That's all you need to know!" He tries not to laugh, I can tell, but one chuckle escapes as he gives me his back once again.

I grin and pull my sleeping bag up over my shoulders, ready for sleep. I'm good for him to have around. Even in the midst of all this misery, I can still see the lighter side of things, and Jag needs that. He needs me to make him laugh.

Because he only sees darkness… everywhere he looks.

4

Brecken

Raphael and Michael leave me standing alone on a dark street somewhere in southern California… in the middle of the night. The asphalt glistens after a recent rainstorm and stars peek through the clouds that move silently across the sky.

I take in a long, slow breath, reveling in the scent of ozone. It's a heady perfume I associate only with Earth. It's good to be back.

I have been away for five long years and yet, it feels like yesterday that I walked these streets. I can't believe I'm here again… in a body of flesh and bone, but I don't get to keep this body and stay here. That's fine. I don't need to.

Michael gave me a runed weapon, making me recognizable as a Cazador, but I still have my Nephilim blade, which will kill anything… permanently. Not just send them back to whatever spiritual realm they're from, like the runed dagger.

I turn in a circle, eyeing my location. They haven't dumped me in a completely foreign location. I know vaguely where I am. Downtown L.A. Or what used to be Downtown L.A. There's a bar across the street. A prime place for hunting. I'm supposed to let the Cazadors catch me killing demons as my way in to their elite group. The plan sounds easy enough.

Glancing up at the sky, I study the stars. I guess it's about eleven o'clock PM. I walk over to the bar and pull open the heavy, wooden door, striding inside. A cute, blonde bartender glances up and grins. A rush of adrenaline shoots through me as I take in her tight, black tank top, ample cleavage, and toned arms.

At one time, sex appeal had been one of my greatest weapons. One I'd wielded with pleasure… as a demon. I still feel the draw to use it now. It would be so easy, and I'd have a warm bed for the night. The fact that this thought even enters my mind tells me how far I've come.

Not far at all.

I'm already in love with the perfect woman, after all. She's waiting for me, and that is enough to motivate me to keep my gifts to myself.

I sit down on a stool and lean against the counter.

"What'll it be?" The bartender moves closer while wiping glasses and setting them on a towel.

"I'll have a coke." I smile, but I don't use the one that makes women weak in the knees.

Best to keep that one hidden.

"A coke?" I know what she's thinking. Why the crap am I in here if I don't want a beer or something stronger? I can't tell her the truth—that I'm hunting. That a demon is bound to sneak in to search for a new body—possibly hers. Human bodies don't last very long with a demon inside, so they are constantly looking for a replacement. I need to be sharp when I meet one face to face.

"Yep. Just a coke. I'm waiting… for someone."

She shrugs and pours my drink. "Whatever." She turns to deal with someone else, not even giving me a second glance.

Whoa. That feels weird. When was the last time I was ignored by a woman? It stuns me for a second, but I shake it off and swivel on the stool to search the room while I sip my drink. An older gentleman lounges at the other end of the bar, nursing a beer and minding his own business. He's human. No demon lurking inside him… yet. He looks worn and tired, his graying hair curling out from under his ball cap.

Demons are easy to spot. They have no aura. They do, however, leave a smoky residue that trails in their wake, like Pig Pen from Charlie Brown, their filthiness puffing out around them in a cloud. Most people can't see it, but I'm not most people. I turn back to the bartender and tend to my coke, waiting patiently.

I sit there for only a few minutes when I feel the temperature drop. It's subtle at first. I almost miss it. I've forgotten that a physical body makes it more difficult to detect things of a supernatural nature. It takes effort, and I'm a little slow on the uptake, having to focus harder.

Leisurely, I spin on my stool, searching the room. There. In the corner, not far from the door, the disembodied form crouches, surveying the bar for its next victim.

I called them *gray men* during my mortal existence—that I never got to finish—because of their smoky appearance and their long, thin arms, and hollow eyes. Their mouths had seemed huge to me, gaping and able to swallow me whole. I was only a kid then, and they terrified me.

I'm not afraid anymore.

I can kill it quickly before it enters a body. I have the Nephilim dagger that will do the trick—actually *kill* the demon's soul. That way, a mortal won't have to die also. That is always preferable, obviously. But there are too many people in here. Too many eyewitnesses. Too many questions to answer, because they can't see the demon, just me thrusting a knife into thin air, looking like a serial killer.

I have to make a choice. How fast can I escape? I'll take my chances rather than kill an innocent bystander.

Nonchalantly, I slide off my stool, slapping a few dollars down on the counter, acting as if I'm ready to leave. As I draw close to the door, I reach behind my back, wrapping my fingers around the hilt of my dagger, which is tucked into my belt. It's solid and cool in my grip. Familiar in my fingers. I've had it a long time. I'll use it over my runed dagger any day.

The demon watches me as I near, probably assuming I'm just a normal person it can possess. I never look at it directly, but I'm ready. Without missing a step, I lunge. The knife slides easily into the gray man, through its right eyehole. It erupts into a cloud of pewter ash that the patrons in the bar can't see.

When I glance up, they are all staring at me *and* the knife I hold. Smiling sheepishly, I straighten and tuck it into my jeans.

They continue to gape. Surely, they think I'm crazy or dangerous. Before someone calls the police, I dart into the night.

A darkened alley lurks across the street, so I hurry into its shadows, leaning against the brick building, breathing heavily. I shouldn't have done that in front of so many people. It was stupid, but at least I saved someone from becoming demon fodder. The bad side is, there weren't any Cazadors in the bar to see me do it. At least, I don't think there were. I'm not even sure who I'm looking for. Raphael said I'd know them when I saw them, and that it's my job to earn their trust and become their leader.

Yeah. That's going to be easy.

With my heart rate under control, I step from the alley. The bar door opens and the man who'd been sitting at the end of the counter stands there, searching the darkness. He looks a little tipsy, and I have the feeling he is probably searching for me. He's going to try to be a hero; I just know it. He wants to take down the crazy guy with the Bowie knife.

I spin back into the shadows and wait, determined to avoid a needless argument. That's when I see them. Seven misty bodies floating down the street, heading toward the bar. I should have waited inside longer.

The lead demon makes a beeline for the guy in the doorway, unaware of the danger. It becomes a race with his cronies. I jump from my hiding spot and dash across the street. The demon beats me there.

Faster than I've ever seen before, it plows through the startled man's open mouth. His eyes widen and he stumbles back against the door, knocking the back of his head with a dull thunk. The demon enters him completely. As soon as the rest of the pack sees me, or more importantly, my Nephilim dagger, they turn and flee.

I raise my knife, but the newly possessed man is quick... and no longer drunk. He blocks my thrust with his forearm and smiles, and then gives me a quick punch in the face. Pain explodes behind my nose, and my vision goes dark and blurry. I stumble back a step to give my eyes a chance to stop watering. Oh, the pain! I forgot how much a human body can hurt!

The demon laughs, low and throaty. "You're new at this."

"Not that new." I can see the gray man beneath the façade as he grins manically at me.

"You can't kill me so easily, human."

"That's still up for debate." I grab my other knife—the runed one—and drive it into the guy's belly. "Give Bas Iblis my best."

The demon's eyes widen at my reference to one of his nefarious leaders—the one who hates me most right now—but he doesn't have time to react. He explodes into a cloud of dust that floats to the ground. This time, the ash will be visible to mortals... the part that was human. The guy's wedding ring clinks to the ground and rolls in a circle before it comes to rest.

Oh. I forgot that would happen. I can't walk away and leave something as personal as a wedding band lying on the ground like garbage. I glance around, hoping no one saw what I did. Granted, violence is a part of everyday life here on Earth, but I assume it's still illegal to murder.

The guy hadn't been old, maybe in his mid-forties, fairly fit. He was somebody. He mattered, but once the demon is inside, there is no other way to deal with it. At least, that's what Raphael tells me. Exorcisms aren't working. The demons have found a way to make the possession stable until the body gives out.

I lean down and pick up the gold band, a symbol of this man's loyalty to someone else, and roll the ring in my fingers. Life here is so fragile. Much more fragile than it used to be, it seems.

With a sigh, I look for a place to stay. More than anything, I want to go home and climb into my own bed in the basement of my family's house. It's been five years, and thanks to Raphael's magic, no one will recognize me. My room has probably been turned into storage.

My sisters don't like to go down there, with good reason, considering all the spirits that appeared to me there. Heidi and Sophie thought it was haunted, and they were kind of right. My heart warms when I think of them. Heidi has to be eighteen now and Sophie about fourteen, I think. The desire to see them grows.

I pull my hoodie up, stuff my hands deep into my jacket

pockets, and head down the street like a thug. I doubt I'll find my groupies my first night in town, so I search for a motel. My funds are limited, but Raphael gave me enough money to get me through the month. By then, I'm supposed to be one of the Cazadors. Hopefully, they'll feed me.

For the next three days, I plague the bars. They're hotspots, but I've yet to meet anyone that looks like they're in a club of demon hunters. I sleep during the day and prowl at night, falling into bed in my cheap motel room as the sun rises over the eastern hills.

The city is hardly recognizable. Everything looks so different and the destruction is unbelievable. Whole regions have been leveled and others thrust up to become hills. Millions of people were killed in the earthquakes—what people are calling the Rift—and the ones who are left survive on spurts of electricity, limited food, and an unstable government.

After three days, I can't take it anymore. I have to make sure my family is okay. I need to see my house and confirm it's still safe for them to live in. To hell with my promise.

Since I don't have a vehicle at my disposal, I choose the next best thing. A taxi. They are few and far between, but I manage to flag one down. We take the backstreets and alleyways, as there is rubble everywhere. Some streets are completely blocked off and only the most important ones have been cleared. The taxi gets me as close to my neighborhood as possible before dropping me off on a lonely sidewalk. I pay the driver, my jaw slack and my eyes wide.

There's nothing left.

I hurry down what used to be my street to find the houses all folded in on themselves. Mine is the last one, bumping up against the park, which miraculously, still stands, but my house is pretty much leveled. The roof sits on the ground as though the whole thing dropped twelve feet.

With a wrenching heart, I make my way around to find a way in. A hole in the back wall goes underneath the roof, but only a small dog or cat would be able to fit through. There's nothing here. My life as Brecken Shaefer is truly and officially over. Gone. Totally and completely. Where is my family?

My dad must have taken them somewhere. Maybe to his sister's place? She lives an hour north, but it would take two days of walking for me to get there. I've already spent too much money on the taxi, and I can't afford another fare. I probably shouldn't rekindle my old habit of hot wiring or stealing, but there aren't a lot of options. I can stand here, mourning my old home and my old life, or I can get on with my job. The sooner I start, the sooner I'll finish.

That's when I see him. A kid, barely out of high school, wearing a black denim jacket and jeans. His blond hair is pulled back into a ponytail with a rubber band, his skin pale, but it's the look in his dark eyes that stops me. Resolve. Anger. Ache. Grit. I find him so interesting that I wait to see where he goes next.

He scans the street, his gaze studying every corner, every shadow, every movement, as he waits outside a little corner grocery shop. A moment later, another kid, about the same age, comes out of the store and joins him, handing over a Snickers bar. He's shorter, slender, and has bright eyes and a ready smile. The first boy seems to wear his scowl as a permanent fixture. They're relaxed and comfortable together though. It's obvious they've been friends for a while, but it's the angry one who intrigues me. He's a predator. I can feel it. What is he scouring the street for?

I follow the pair, curious.

The sun begins to set and will soon fall behind the ocean. Darkness will reign and I'll become a hunter, but I still have time to kill.

5

Heidi

Everything went downhill after the Rift, including me. The Earth groaned, barfing up lava and belching ash through volcanos I'd never even heard of. Earthquakes leveled not only *my* town, but also half of the US. I still wake up screaming, the dreams alive and vivid.

In other words, I don't sleep much.

So many nights I've lain awake in my bed—a cot shoved into a corner of my aunt's basement because there aren't enough bedrooms—with my eyes scrunched closed. If I can't see the figures, maybe they aren't real, or at least they'll go away and leave me alone.

I call them ghosts, but they aren't ghosts. They're something else. Dark. Gray. Hideous and terrifying. When I first started seeing them, I could only see them out of the corner of my eye, as though they were shadows. But shadows aren't supposed to be able to move on their own.

What I know for sure is they want inside me, like a cancer. I'd quit believing in God... until the gray men came. If *they* exist, then surely, somewhere, there is a benevolent being—who also exists. Yin, yang, and all that. Opposites in all things.

But there was no rapture after the Rift. Neighbor turned against neighbor, gangs murdered whole families just for the food in their cupboards, and children were abandoned—all while the whole world caved in on itself... and I lived through it. I'm still here. I'm still alive. Kind of.

The first phantom I ever saw appeared at the foot of my bed, staring at me with a jagged mouth, its smile a grimace. It held onto the metal bar at my feet, the basement darker than dark. My little sister, Sophie, was lucky to share a room upstairs with cousins, so I had to face this nightmare alone. Slowly, I'd brought my knees up to my chest, my heart pounding so forcefully that the only thing I could hear was the whoosh, whoosh, whoosh of my own pulse.

And then, as suddenly as it appeared, it left.

That was the first time.

Now it happens *all* the time. I have no peace… unless I'm with the Cazadors.

The jagged leather on the tattoo chair scratches the back of my legs. I sit as still as death, the needle darting beneath my skin a thousand times a minute like an African killer bee—almost too quickly for my mind to register. I close my eyes and breathe… the stinging pain a gift. It makes me *feel,* and it will definitely be worth it when the tattoo is complete.

When finished, the tattoo will be a dagger between my shoulder blades, stretching four inches from top to tip, sacred runes etched on the blade in iridescent glory. I drew them carefully on a piece of paper so the tattoo artist can't get them wrong. It has to be exact. It has to be perfect.

With my head bowed and my thick hair creating a shield from anyone watching, I let a tear of healing trail down my cheek. This is a moment of catharsis. Of rebirth. It brings up long-buried emotions of heartache and powerlessness.

I am powerless no more.

I am leaving all that behind—leaving my painful childhood to step into womanhood.

I haven't had a close friend in ages, but this tattoo will bring me one step closer to the group of friends I want. That I need. I'll have protection at my back and they will too… even if they don't know it yet.

During the Rift, I learned it's better to not have ties. But the

Cazadors are different. And I'll be one of them… officially.

For the last year—since I discovered them—I've been practicing. Honing my skills with daggers, knives, and anything else considered a weapon. I will finally be a demon hunter, but I won't be alone. Not anymore. It's too dangerous to hunt alone, and I'm not stupid enough to keep trying. I've won a few skirmishes, but I've also had some close calls. Too close.

An especially sharp sting—like the queen bee taking aim over one of my vertebrae—brings me back to the present, and I hiss in reaction, gripping my thighs, my nails biting into my skin. I can do this. Pain is my companion. It always has been, whispering into my heart, its claws always flexing. It taught me to endure and be patient. This physical pain is just another test I will pass. It will be over soon, and I'll have a talisman I can draw strength from… for the rest of my life. However long that is.

"You're almost done," the tattoo artist says, still bent over my back. I can feel his warm hands balanced against my skin, and I picture him as he speaks, with his white, shortly cropped beard and his head covered in a navy-blue bandanna. Tattoo sleeves cover both of his arms, but his hands are steady. He smells like garlic and onions, but there are worse odors.

I don't answer him, focusing instead on the runed dagger in my bag at my feet. I stole it from Jag, the leader of the Cazadors, the last time I visited the church. I feel bad about doing it, but not bad enough, I guess. He always has a spare, and it seemed like fate. I've been asking for one for ages, and he keeps refusing me. I got tired of fighting with him and took matters into my own hands.

It was almost as if he had left it for me on purpose.

He's probably noticed it missing by now. But there is no way I can fight demons without one. They can't be killed any other way. The knife's magic is real, but I haven't used it yet. I want someone to have my back when I do, just in case.

My new tattoo will change everything. Already, it gives me courage I've never felt before—like a fire being stoked in my belly, growing and begging for more oxygen. The burn of battle lust increases inside me. Just the thought of thrusting the runed blade into a demon… its eyes widening in surprise, the poof of ash that will follow… brings goose bumps to my arms.

"Are you cold?" the artist asks.

I shake my head and hide a smile.

He changes position, wipes my tattoo with disinfectant, and then hands me a mirror. I angle it until I can see my prized creation, glittering in gold. A gilded dagger that glows with an ethereal light.

"It's perfect," I breathe in awe of the artist's workmanship. "I can't believe it."

"Believe it. It's gonna cost you."

I laugh, already having planned on that, but I have some money stashed away. Some of it came from a trust fund my mother set up before she died. And then Dad gave both Sophie and me a huge chunk of Brecken's life insurance policy, which I hadn't even known existed. Who has a life insurance policy at eighteen?

Originally, I planned to use the money for college, but that is a distant luxury now with the way the world is. I'm not even sure colleges still exist. The world needs warriors, not lawyers and accountants. Plus, I want to do something useful, something that matters.

After paying the tattooist, I head out into the sunshine, my new talisman burning like dry ice on my back. It focuses me on why I got it in the first place… proof of my commitment to my new calling. Demon huntress.

I stop at a reflective shop window and turn to get another look. The hilt of the dagger peeks out above my black tank top. The skin is raised and screaming-red, but as I take in the beautiful artistry, a smile curls my lips and the tiny diamond chip in my nose winks in the sunlight. Never before have I felt so beautiful or so strong. No one can take this away from me. It's etched into my very skin.

All the Cazadors have this same tattoo. Well, not this exact same one. Mine is by far the most beautiful. I made sure of that. But in my heart, it makes me one of them. A symbol of the ability to rid the world of evil.

With a happy sigh, I continue down the hot, dusty street, stopping to buy a hot dog from a vendor. I doubt the food's clean—because nothing is disinfected or washed well these days—but I stuff it in my mouth anyway. The tang of mustard slaps my taste buds, and I moan in delight. There are few things that truly make me feel alive. Food is one. I love food, the smell of it, the look of it when well prepared, and if street food hasn't killed me yet, it isn't going to.

Once upon a time, I actually thought about going to culinary school. Yeah. That probably won't happen now.

I could go home to my aunt's house to eat. I love my aunt Jenny—who took us in five years ago—but she is restrictive and suffocating. I grew up without a mother, and to suddenly have one telling me what to do and when to do it is stifling. On the other hand, Sophie has thrived with our new "mother". She soaks the attention up like a wilted flower being watered for the first time.

For me, it has been a different story. The fights started with my nose piercing—which I think is freaking awesome—and then morphed into arguments about my wardrobe. My aunt tells me I can't dress the way I want to—which is usually in black from head to toe. It got so hard that finally, I left. I check in every so often so she knows I'm alive, but I seldom go home. I'm eighteen. I don't need a mother.

I need to be a Cazador.

I need a release from the drowning rage that has consumed me since my brother drowned in a bathtub. There is something very suspicious about that whole deal, and my dad won't discuss it. Yeah. He's still alive, but he's a subject I won't discuss.

It was a few years after that gloomy and horrific time that I first met Jag, his dark eyes also full of rage and defiance. I felt a connection to him immediately. In the darkness, with only one streetlamp glowing, I'd watched him, spellbound, as he battled a gray phantom under an overpass. It managed to get away unscathed—Jag was only fourteen at the time, after all—and I'd tried to strike up a conversation, but the fact that I'd witnessed him fail had only made him angry. He stormed away, but I'd followed him... and his goofy friend, Dean.

My life changed that day and would never be the same.

6

Brecken

I follow the two boys into a park where people are dancing to rhythmic music and visiting at picnic tables. Slender cigarettes dangle from the revelers' fingers and red solo cups are gripped in their hands. Music thrums through the open doors of a pub across the street, and my senses go on high alert.

Enflamed clouds bathe the partiers in gilded light and ocean waves break just over the rise. I stay back in the shadows, watching and waiting to see if the devil will arrive at his party.

The boys stop to sit on a bench and proceed to eat their candy, watching the fun. I ease into relaxation for a moment and hope that I won't have to kill anyone tonight. Maybe I can just hang out, listen to songs I haven't heard before, and watch beautiful women sway to the beat.

This is just what I need. An evening off, surrounded by happy people and music that stirs my senses. Although this is the perfect place to watch for my dark, slithery friends—and they will surely come—I pretend I'm living a normal life, sans demons.

Every so often, I glance over at the two boys I followed. They pique my curiosity. Why are they here? They don't seem the partying type, and they aren't trying to sneak the overly available assortments of alcohol. Nor are they trying to buy any other illicit drugs. They just sit on the bench, watching and waiting, just like me.

I focus on the last vestiges of the candy bar the blond boy is shoving into his mouth. Dang, it looks good, and I haven't had chocolate in years. Pushing away from the wall, I saunter over to the corner shop. A cute little mom-and-pop spot with sodas in the back fridge and every form of sugar available in all its varieties. It's kid heaven, plain and simple.

I snag a couple of chocolate bars that look good and then a coke from the fridge, setting them down on the counter by the cash register. I'm second in line, so I take the time to peruse the store. Bright curtains hang over the windows in flouncy scallops. The walls are painted a bright lime green with black trim, going for an old-fashioned soda-shop look, but it comes across as more of an overdone seven-eleven.

"Evening," the cashier says when it's my turn. He glances at me over a pair of tiny, wire-rimmed glasses, and then goes to work, ringing up the numbers on his old-fashioned register with only his pointer finger. Graying hair curls over his ears and he wears a white apron over his clothes. He seems nice in a Santa Claus kind of way, and I'm glad his store was undamaged in spite of the earthquakes and marauding gangs.

"Evening," I answer. "Quite the party going on out there." I glance out the window at the bright lights and then back to the old man.

"Yep. It'll be like this every night for the next week. Rift Week and all that. Good for business," he says, handing me my change.

"Rift Week?" That's one holiday I'm unfamiliar with.

"You know. Five year anniversary of the Rift."

Funny they'd celebrate such a dismal day, but young people look for any excuse to let loose and party. They are still hopeful for the future, I guess. But for demons, they are perfect candidates for possession. Their bodies will last longer than an older model. And once again, I'm glad I'd followed the two boys here.

I leave the store with my bag of goodies and find my own bench in the plaza. A young couple sits at the other end, but they don't notice me. Their faces are glued together, the slurping and sucking turned up to full volume. I try not to watch, but it's like a train wreck. Hard to look away from.

The evening wears on, and as the hour grows late, the mom-and-pop store closes down. People become more raucous and rowdy. The exuberant atmosphere, which was lively and fun at first, goes downhill fast. Arguments erupt, guys fight over girls, girls smack the fighting guys, and there are even a few people passed out from drinking too much.

It's time. The demons will surely show up. This little plaza has become the perfect brewing ground. Once a human is high or drunk, they no longer put up any resistance. The door is wide open, and the demons walk right in.

I've seen it over and over.

And as though my thoughts are enough of an invitation, they come, their dark, murky souls crawling across the lawn and over benches like spiders.

I set my coke down and reach for my Nephilim dagger inside my jacket. I'm still, waiting until the last second to launch my attack. But just as I'm about to pounce, the blond, angry boy leaps from his bench and dives for a demon that has funneled its way through the top of a guy's head. The boy reaches the demon as the last bits of its smoky form are absorbed. Without hesitation, the boy drives a dagger through the man's heart.

I stop short. It happens so fast. With no hesitation. And I try not to be sickened at how methodical the kid is. For a moment, I can only stare, wondering if I look as cold and ruthless as I slay demons. Still frozen in surprise, I glance over at the blond boy's friend. He has a notebook on his lap and is scribbling furiously with a pencil. Why is he sitting there drawing? It seems so bizarre.

Shaking myself out of my stupor, I hurry over to help before the demons can get inside anyone else, but my hope is short-lived. There are just too many of them.

People who aren't possessed run screaming from my slaughter, probably thinking a bunch of mass murderers have escaped from prison. In the last five years, the murder rates have skyrocketed. It's all over the news, and it surprises me that people are stupid enough to go out at night when they could be safe at home.

I slash and stab, rake and slice, into the ghostly demons as fast as I can. My body moves without me having to think about it. This is what I am made to do. I don't see any demons I recognize, and I keep waiting for the day I come face to face with Andras or Lamia. I wouldn't mind ending their miserable lives.

I happen to glance up and notice the two boys frozen and staring at me. I haven't killed any humans yet since I can kill the demons before they get inside, but I don't have time to stop and answer their questions.

The blond boy's lips curl into an astonished smile, but he immediately goes back to work. The other boy—who sports a darker shade of sandy-blond hair—sits back down on the bench and continues to draw. I pay them no attention until I finish my work and there isn't another fiend to be seen. The park is empty and covered in ash.

I lean over in exhaustion, my hands on my knees, my dagger gripped in my fist, and heave in huge gulps of air. I ache all over. This must be what it feels like to run a marathon, although I bask in the feeling of having a physical body. When I straighten, the boy with the ponytail ambles over, his dagger held loosely in his fingers.

"How did you kill the demons before they took a body?" he asks before anything else, eyeing my Nephilim dagger, his brow furrowed. No dilly-dallying here… or introductions.

I decide to start with what's easiest. The truth… simplified. "I have a special knife." I hold it up for him to see. In the human realm, it radiates an ethereal light, bright in this darkened plaza, especially next to his runed dagger. My Nephilim blade was blessed by the Avenging Angels to do this work, and the runed daggers are nothing in comparison. Plus, they only send demons back to hell. The Nephilim blade kills them permanently.

He reaches out for my dagger, but hesitates, glancing into my eyes to make sure it's okay for him to touch it.

I nod. "Just don't touch the edge. Even a scratch will kill you."

He lifts it from my fingers, holding it hungrily and running his thumb across the smooth, shining cheek of the dagger, just above the grind. He's careful to stay away from its sharpened edge.

"It's beautiful," he whispers with a sigh. "Where did you get it?" His friend comes up and gazes reverently at the dagger. From the look in his eyes, he aches to hold it also, but he doesn't reach out to touch it. Ponytail boy even offers it to him, but Artist boy shakes his head and steps back.

I ignore Ponytail's question, not wanting to explain. If I'm not mistaken, these boys are the Cazadors. "It was given to me."

Ponytail boy hands it back. "Who are you? I haven't seen you around."

Sirens blare in the distance and are headed our way. There isn't time to answer his question. "The police are coming."

The boys follow me as we run a few blocks and then slow, hiding behind a garbage bin. "My name is Bre—t. Bret." I kick myself—figuratively—for my near blunder. "And you are?"

"I'm Dean," Artist boy says, smiling, "and this is Jag." He points to his scowling friend.

I put my hand out toward Jag, but he doesn't take it. He keeps his on the hilt of his sheathed dagger. Dean shakes my hand as though we're old friends.

"Dean and Jag. Nice to meet you and nice work you did here. Thanks for the help."

"The help?" Jag repeats, almost choking on the words. "I think it was the other way around. We've been working here for years." His eyes narrow as he studies my face, my clothes, and my weapons—including the runed dagger. His gaze flies back to mine. "Who are you really?"

"I told you. My name's Bret. And I'm new here. I didn't mean to move in on your territory or anything. I was actually looking for other people to hunt with." If all else fails, stick to the truth.

"Any people in particular?" Jag asks, his hand still resting on his knife. A move that is not lost on me. "Not many people have the guts for this job." He's trying to intimidate me, but it won't work. I'm way past pissing contests. I've led the armies of hell, after all. This kid is headed for disappointment if he thinks I'll cower or beg. I'm going to take his place, which will probably not go over well. But he's not my enemy, and I don't want to start our relationship feeling as if he is.

"I'm looking for a group called the Cazadors." I study them closely, monitoring their surprised expressions.

Before Jag can silence him, Dean blurts out. "That's us! We're the Cazadors!"

Jag frowns and grits his teeth as he slowly turns to glare at his friend.

"Oh, sorry," Dean says, noting Jag's disapproving glower.

Jag crosses his arms over his chest and spreads his feet solidly apart. "Why do you want to know?"

"I plan to join you." I smile and match his stance. "Take me to your leader," I say with bravado.

Dean's lip twitches as he fights back a chuckle, but Jag's frown intensifies. "*I'm* the leader of this group, but it's a *secret* group. No one's supposed to even know we exist." His statement is directed at Dean, who grimaces and glances away.

"Hmm. Well," I say. "Should we go back to your clubhouse and talk about it?"

"Our clubhouse?" Jag repeats slowly, one eyebrow rising in an arc. "Are you serious? We aren't a *club*. We're *assassins*. We kill demons. That's our *job*. We don't get together for parties, eat treats, or do projects. We aren't a club." His voice is deep as he explains all this slowly so I'll understand. I hear him loud and clear.

"Well, we kind of are," Dean says. "I mean, we do like to meet when we can."

Jag throws him another glare. "No, we don't."

Dean's mouth snaps shut as he gives Jag an annoyed expression. "And we do eat pizza."

"And we aren't hiring." Jag glances again at my Nephilim blade. I can't stop the slow smile that spreads across my face.

"Really?" I stuff my hands in my pockets and lean against a building's rough, brick wall. "You can't use someone with my experience, who knows how to get rid of demons before they inhabit a body?"

Jag grinds his teeth.

"Listen. I'm not here to cause trouble. I just want to help." And with a flip of my hand, I turn and walk away.

Dean whispers furiously behind me. "You can't let him leave! We need him. That knife. We need that knife."

I hear a growl of frustration, but I'm walking fast and they'll have to make an effort to catch up.

"Wait," Jag calls out. "Maybe we can do a trial run or something."

I hear the fury in his voice as he's forced to include me. But he's obviously a decent guy with morals, who doesn't want to keep killing people. My dagger will solve all their problems even if his pride is taking a serious dip. I stop, a smile hiding just behind my lips, but I make sure it isn't visible before I turn around to face them. "Are you sure? I don't want to make waves or anything. This is your "turf" as you pointed out." Do I sound condescending? Yes. I think I do. I don't even feel bad about it.

My comment is rewarded with another glare from Jag—I've stopped tallying them up—but Dean's smile widens. "Awesome! I'll get the guys together. We'll have dinner tomorrow night at seven. Meet us at the chur—"

"On the corner of Spruce and Ivy Lane," Jag interrupts.

"Right," Dean says, still smiling. "Spruce and Ivy. See you tomorrow."

"Got it." I wave and then head off around the corner. There is no way Jag will meet me tomorrow, and I doubt he'll let Dean. But one thing is sure…

I'm in.

7

Brecken

At precisely seven o'clock, I'm at the corner of Spruce and Ivy Lane, where I'm supposed to meet Jag and Dean. Just as I suspected, they aren't here. I wait a polite ten minutes before jogging the few blocks to the abandoned church I followed them to last night.

All is quiet on that lonely, mostly uninhabited, dead-end street. It's a perfect place for a hideout. The windows of the abandoned church are boarded up and the steeple stretches to a point, high and dirty white. Quaint. I like it immediately. At the end of the long block, a few kids ride old, rusty bikes in the sunset and one plays Kick-the-Can by himself.

Someone will notice me loitering, so I knock on the front door of the church. I only stand there for a moment before I hear rustling and heated whispering from the other side. The door is yanked open and there stands Jag, eyes flashing, one hand stretched across the doorway to block my entry. He looks like he just might slam it back in my face. He's speechless at my audacity.

A serene smile stays plastered on my face as I peek over his shoulder at Dean, who waits behind Jag with a wide grin.

"Hey, Bret! You found us," Dean blurts, trying to slip under Jag's arm.

"Of course he did," Jag mumbles, but he doesn't step out of the way or invite me in.

Dean pushes Jag's arm up and ducks beneath it. "We ordered pizza, but not everyone is here yet."

Reluctantly, Jag moves out of the way.

I lean back and survey the church, admiring the construction.

"Yeah. It wasn't too hard to find." I glance back at Jag with a wry smile. "I had a feeling you might forget to meet me, so I said a prayer and an angel pointed me in the right direction." I take pride in my comedic wit. It took eons to hone.

He doesn't answer, but his eyes narrow in obvious dislike.

I'm stumped at why he hates me so much. He doesn't even know me. Sure, I'm about to steal his place at the top, but only for a little while. I won't stay here indefinitely. Only until the job is completed and *The Door to Hell* is closed.

"Hey, guys!" someone calls from behind me. Two teenage boys saunter up the walk, one tall and thin with shaggy, brown hair. The other is short and stocky with military-short black hair and skin the color of mocha, his teeth gleaming white in his wide smile. Skinny carries a bag of pretzels he munches on.

"Dude, did you order the pizza?" Stocky asks. "I'm starved."

"Yup," Dean answers. "Should be here soon."

Jag turns to stare at Dean, his expression incredulous. "You gave the pizza place the church's address?" His eyebrows pull together into a scowl, and I can tell he's itching to say something more. Probably something about Dean's stupidity, but he holds it in. Remarkable. I had expected him to let loose with a violent temper or something. I guess he *does* know how to control himself.

"Well, yeah. I didn't think it mattered," Dean says. "The pizza guy isn't going to call the police. Like they care if we live here." Dean turns from Jag and glances at me, stuffing his hands in his pockets, looking perfectly chastised.

With an angry growl, Jag shakes his head and stomps back into the bowels of the church, not even bothering to greet their friends.

Dean shrugs and points to Skinny. "This is Owen." Then gesturing to Stocky, he says, "And this is Doug."

"Nice to meet you both," I say. "I'm Bret." The boys acknowledge me with a nod and Skinny goes right on munching pretzels.

"Bret wants to join the Cazadors," Dean says. "You should see him in action."

Doug looks me up and down, but he must be unimpressed. "Really?"

"He has a dagger you wouldn't believe." Dean points to my waist. "It kills demons *before* they take a body!"

"Really?" Owen's bored look turns to slightly admiring, but he seems to be withholding judgement. He holds the pretzel bag out to me. "Let's see it."

"How about we go in?" I point to the church.

The boys head inside, and I follow them into the chapel. Only a few pews remain and are pushed over against one wall. The building has sustained some damage and looks pretty dilapidated. The ceiling is cracked, and huge chunks of sheet rock and plaster are missing. The room is shrouded in shadow, but a lone pulpit stands at the front, waiting for a preacher. Dusty choir seats are arranged behind it, slumped like old men, their feet nailed to the floor. A few pieces of stained glass litter the floor beneath the windows, glowing in the evening light that threads through the cracks.

The boys have built a fire pit in the center of the room over a mosaic of tiles, but the design is too far gone to tell what the picture was. The pit doesn't look like it's been used in a while. Owen drags one of the benches over, and Doug pushes another. He isn't a huge kid, but he's strong. The benches look solid and heavy.

There's plenty of room for all of us to lounge and wait for the pizza to arrive. I have to admit that I'm hungry. I'm glad they ordered dinner.

These boys are a team, but I have yet to see the easy camaraderie I expected, so I wait for the ambiance to warm, to see them interact as a group. I sit down on a pew next to Dean, who chats happily, asking the other boys what they've been up to the last few days. Jag re-enters the chapel and leans against the far wall, his arms crossed over his chest. His annoyance casts a dark pall over the room.

Does he ever relax or loosen up? What is he so angry about? How does Dean stand being with him all the time? Is Jag abusing him? Man, I hope not. I want as little drama as possible while I'm here. I just want to get my job done and leave. The sooner I finish, the sooner I can be reunited with Alisa. This is my final exam, and I plan to pass with flying colors.

"So, you don't live here?" I ask Owen, trying to change the subject. I don't really care who lives where. I just want to get them talking.

He scowls, his thick eyebrows pulling down and his thin lips tightening. "Dude, we don't *get* to." He tosses a pretzel into his mouth and chews angrily. "Jag likes living alone. It's stupid if you ask me. I'm tired of having to walk here every time we need to meet. It's far, man. Like three miles." He flips his head to the side, and the hair on his forehead flops out of his eyes.

"So, only Jag and Dean live here then?" I didn't mean to bring up a sore subject, but now I'm curious. I glance over at Dean, and he is the only one nodding. Jag is suddenly nowhere to be found.

"We live at home with our parents." Doug gestures to Owen and himself. "We're neighbors. We went to Hill Valley High together. Jag went to Ocean Side. He was a year ahead of us."

"Hey!" Jag interrupts, coming up a set of stairs by the front door. "This isn't group therapy. We don't share everything. Some things are private. We don't know this guy well enough to know what we can tell him." He sinks down at the end of the opposite pew, splendidly pulling off the predator look as he gazes at us from under his long eyelashes, his jaw flexing.

A tentative knock echoes on the front doors. Jag holds out a small bag to Dean, who grabs it. It jangles with change when he runs for the door. The pizza guy stands there, all dopey and confused as he studies the address. He holds a red, insulated bag in one arm, and the smell of cheese and pepperoni wafts clear across the room. I almost moan out loud.

"You guys order pizza?" The guy tries to peek in.

Dean keeps the door mostly closed and pays him in quarters, nickels, and dimes, most likely taken from dead demon dust piles. "Yep. Thanks." He shuts the door before the guy can say anything else. When he places the boxes by the fire pit, we all dig in. Tomato sauce, cheese, and the tang of hot pepperoni assault my taste buds. My mouth waters as the explosion of flavor nearly lays me flat. My eyes close as I revel in the pleasure of something so simple. Hot. Gooey. Pizza. I chew slowly, relishing every bite.

"Dude, you act like you've never had pizza before," Owen says, his eyes laughing as he gazes at me.

"It's been years," I answer, reaching for a second slice.

"That's crazy," Doug says, talking with his mouth full. "I couldn't go for more than a couple of days without it. It's my main staple. I'd die without pizza, and it's the only fast food that still exists… almost." He takes another huge bite and smiles as if he's just eaten the sun. I like him and want to know him better. Anyone who loves pizza as much as I do is an instant friend.

Jag has yet to say much of anything. He eats quickly, methodically, just like he fights. He watches his friends, but he doesn't participate in friendly conversation. He lounges, but the tenseness of his shoulders tells me he's ready to jump at a moment's notice. He's all contradictions.

The evening grows dark, and soon, no light makes its way through the wooden slats over the windows. Night comes, and it's time to go to work.

"So, where should we hunt tonight?" Dean asks, already getting his backpack together. He drops in pencils and a pad of paper, but no weapons. "We haven't worked together in over a week. Can you believe it?" He directs his question toward Doug and Owen.

"Yeah, I can believe it," Owen says, casting a sour glance at Jag, who completely ignores him.

Instead, Jag looks up with a glint in his eyes. There's something slightly deviant about his expression, and I know that whatever comes out of his mouth won't be good.

"I thought we'd head over to the Down Quarter," he says.

The boys regard him in surprise, and Dean inhales sharply, clearly reluctant. "But… we don't hunt there. It isn't safe. Even for us."

A slow smile spreads across Jag's lips, and he swivels to face me. "But we have a magic weapon now."

I haven't been briefed on this location, but I'm not too worried about it. Either Jag truly knows I can do what he can't or he wants me out of the picture and is willing to get me killed. Nice kid. At least I'll get to kill some demons.

The boys look over at me, hesitant questions in their eyes. I feel confident, so I smile in response. "So what's the Down Quarter?"

"It's only the most dangerous place in the state," Doug says, eating another slice of pizza, which has now grown cold.

"Huh." I close my eyes, trying to picture such a place.

"So, you ready?" Jag asks, walking over to a narrow table where he has set his many weapons. Only one is runed, but he straps on at least five others, one by one.

"Yep." I've had eons of time dealing with devils, demons, dark spirits, and fallen angels. If I'm not an expert by now, I don't know who possibly could be.

"Great," Jag says, his lips pressed into a tight, grim line. "Feel free to take the lead."

I smile. That's just what I plan to do.

8

Dean

I run next to Jag as we head toward the Down Quarter, our companionable silence comfortable, natural, like always. We're in our element. I know how Jag is, and his posturing doesn't bother me. I blow it off… like always.

He and I are at the back of the pack, and Bret jogs at the front with Owen and Doug, who are setting the pace.

"I doubt Bret is even his real name," Jag mumbles. He doesn't speak loud enough for anyone else to hear, and he doesn't bother looking at me as he speaks. "He's trying to worm his way into the Cazadors. We just have to figure out why."

"Maybe it's to kill demons," I suggest.

He gives me a dubious look. I shrug because I figure we're lucky to have him. But Jag isn't finished yet.

"We're just a ragtag group of teens," he continues. "Why would he want to join us? No one even knows about us. How did he find us?"

"That's a lot of questions. Maybe we should just be happy he's here to help."

Another deprecating glance. He keeps his thoughts to himself for a while, and we run in silence. It feels like the Bataan Death March. I'm just about ready to stop when the DQ—as I like to call the Down Quarter—comes into view.

It's a dismal place. Gray, dusty, and abandoned. It's also a place we never go. *Ever*. Besides being so dangerous, it brings up too many terrible memories. Memories that torture Jag at night, making him wake up screaming.

They revolve around a girl named Lily. I can still picture her face, delicate and porcelain white, with fine, snowy-blonde hair lifting in the breeze. She was tiny and seemed more fairy than human, ready to float up on transparent wings. Her whole family died the day of the Rift. Jag found her in the rubble after the earthquake, under the Coronado Bridge, which now lies under water. He'd heard her soft voice, pleading for help from beneath a slab of concrete. She'd broken her leg and had dislocated her shoulder.

We nursed her back to health, right in our church—the only other person to ever live here with us. She and Jag grew close quickly and would steal kisses when they thought I wasn't looking. It lanced me through the heart, because… I loved her too. I wasn't stupid. I'd known what was going on, but I never told anyone. Jag was better for her. He was brave, strong, and could protect her. Back then, he was charismatic and exciting. Why would she want me over him? It was stupid to even think about, so I'd lived with the heartache in silence.

And then… Lily died.

It was an accident.

I let the memories flood my mind and rip my heart while we run. Sometimes, it feels good to ache like this, to miss her, the memories becoming fresh again, fueling my impotence for things I can't control.

It was the result of a tussle gone wrong with some really evil demons, and being in the wrong place at the wrong time. She was supposed to be waiting for us at the church. Instead, she'd followed us to the hunt. She couldn't see the demons inside their human host like we could. And she had walked into the middle of an ambush.

She died in Jag's arms, her life blood seeping into the grass beneath her body. I watched the light in her eyes fade, watched her last breath leave her chest, her face fall into stillness, while Jag held her. He'd kissed her eyes, her cheeks, her bloodstained hair, and all the while, I'd watched, wishing it could have been me holding her that last time.

After that, Jag became quiet and cold, deadly and ruthless.

He changed, and I guessed I did too. The world seemed dimmer, more evil and dangerous. Our old selves no longer existed. In this world, we became something else. I gave him the nickname Jag, after the big, black, ferocious cat he reminded me of. It fit. It stuck. We never used his given name again.

We come to the outskirts of the DQ and look down the dark, uninhabited street. A light breeze blows, but not enough to lift the dust. The air is heavy, moist, and pregnant, bursting with anticipation. We carry flashlights that cast beams too dim to really penetrate the darkness, and the belly of the beast lies just beyond. After our marathon, I don't feel capable of handling the DQ. I just want to go home, go to bed, and cry for Lily.

"Doesn't look like much is going on." Bret glances at Jag. "Maybe it's a slow night."

"Oh, they're there. Trust me," he answers.

The rest of us hold back, no one wanting to go in first. Bret slips his magic dagger out of his belt and holds it in his right hand, the runed knife in his left. "Well, let's check out that building down the street at least, and then go from there."

"Fine with me," I answer, as though my opinion matters, which I know it doesn't.

Owen and Doug grip their runed daggers, but I don't even bother to get mine out. Instead, I pull out my real weapons. A small pad of paper and a pencil.

Reluctantly, I follow my friends across the street to an abandoned apartment building, rising four levels. Squat, ugly, and rectangle. After entering, a case of stairs rises immediately before us. There's no elevator. Darkness cloaks the corners at the back and creates imaginary phantoms in my peripheral vision. It's quiet. Too quiet.

I take a deep breath, knowing I won't cause any damage to a demon with my eight-inch, number-two, sharpened pencil. The most I can do is poke an eye out. Bret stops with his hand up for us to wait, listening. Nothing.

He takes the stairs first and Jag follows, trailed by Owen, Doug, and then me. We come to the first door at the top of the stairs, Bret and Jag flanking the opening. My heart thumps, the anticipation being the hardest part. My eyes actually tear up… from terror.

Three years ago, I saw a group of demons gang up on a guy, but not to inhabit him—they already had meat suits—but to tear him apart. Each one yanking on an arm or a leg until they dismembered him. I'd watched, hidden, hearing the man's terrified and agonized screams, knowing I was next. Jag hadn't been around to save me that night, and the guilt of not even trying to rescue the poor guy plagues me.

This is *my* nightmare. The dream that wakes me at night. It happened right before my eyes. And happens to people all the time. That, and worse things I don't want to think about.

The door to the apartment is ajar. Jag peaks in. There's no movement or sound coming from inside. Bret taps the door with his toe, and it opens the rest of the way. He slips in and scurries to the first bedroom, glances inside, and gives the all-clear sign. Jag jogs past him to check out the next room's door. Owen does the same at the third door, which ends up being a bathroom.

I wait by the front door, hating myself for my unwillingness to kill. I should have stayed home rather than suffer this humiliation in front of everyone. They know I've resolved not to murder people—demon possession notwithstanding—and they seem to appreciate my resolve to hold true to my convictions, Jag being the only one who really *gets* it, but that doesn't change the fact that I still feel like a wuss.

The apartment is clear.

On to the next one. We repeat the program. I hate hunting like this. It's labor intensive and time consuming, like digging up earthworms that don't want to be caught. Waiting for demons to come to *us* is much easier. Just look for the closest frat party and you have your night scheduled. In coming here, Jag is trying to make a point, but no one seems to grasp what it is. Least of all Bret. And the fact that he's putting us all in danger pisses me off.

Not one apartment in the whole building has a demon hiding inside. This is highly unusual and disappointing… to everyone else.

"Where are they?" Owen asks, his frown deepening into frustration. "What a waste of time."

I shrug, trying to keep an expression of indifference even though I'm jumping for joy. "What time is it?" I ask Doug, who is wearing normal clothes tonight. Jeans and a T-shirt, navy-blue vans, and a denim jacket. It's odd seeing him out of costume—his black military uniform—and I wonder why he's dressed this way. If there is one thing I can say for Doug, he marches to his own tune. He doesn't care what people think. He does what he knows is right. He'd make a good leader if anything happened to Jag... not that anything would.

He's also our dedicated timekeeper. He wears two watches, one on each wrist. "Eleven thirty-five," he answers. "Why? Got somewhere else to be?" He smirks, his midnight eyes crinkling, assuming—I'm sure—that I am in a hurry to get out of here, which I am, but I also like to keep track of how long these excursions take. For my logbook/journal.

We leave that building and head back the way we came. The desolate streets remain silent, not a soul to be seen, evil or otherwise. Bret stops suddenly, squinting down a side road.

"What is it?" I ask.

Bret glances back at us, his head cocked and his eyes narrowed. "I thought I saw something. Now I'm not sure."

"Well, they're hard to see at night, especially if they don't have a body," I say.

"That's how I want them." Bret creeps down the sidewalk, sticking to the shadows.

Jag swears under his breath and takes off after him. The rest of us follow because that's what we do. We're the wingmen. We pick up the slack if Jag ever needs help. Well, Owen and Doug do.

Owen is amazing when he fights. Being so tall and thin actually accentuates his abilities, those gorilla arms reaching out with a dagger... A chill runs over my shoulders just thinking about it. Doug fights like a ninja, darting and dancing around—almost as though he is flying—small and deadly.

I catch up to Bret as he stops to glance around another corner. "Anything?"

He puts a finger to his lips and motions for us to follow. We sneak around a dilapidated building and the street grows even darker, if that's possible. There are no streetlamps that work here. Shadows thicken and everywhere I look, I swear a ghostly apparition is waiting to jump me. I don't know why I keep coming along on these expeditions. It's not like they need me. I'm more of a hindrance than a help.

The more I think about it, the more discouraged I become, my feet dragging along the crumbling sidewalk. I don't like being pathetic, but I hate killing more. Yet, I have the gift. I can see the demons. What is my purpose if not to kill them?

Jag sidles up next to me and crouches down. "I think he's leading us into a trap. What better way to get rid of a bunch of demon hunters? Or better yet, take over."

"Dude. That's ridiculous."

"I know he wants my spot as leader. I feel it deep in my bones. I'm not going to hand it over easily, and I'm certainly not going to just lay down and die so he can take it." He shakes his head, watching and waiting, his mouth in a thin, grim line. "I still haven't figured him out, but I'm not going to trust him until I do."

"You're the one who brought us here. What did you think would happen? This is the worst idea you've ever had. This is the worst part of town. And you *know* why. It's not just the demons that live here." I shake my head, tired of this paranoia where Bret is concerned.

Jag doesn't have a chance to answer as Bret motions us forward.

"There," Bret says, pointing down the block to an alley on the opposite side of the street. A huge garbage bin is turned on its side, and garbage is strewn all over the ground. No one will ever come here to clean it up. There's movement in the alley behind the bin.

"This is it," Bret whispers. "Wait for my sign." And with that, he darts down the street. Jag isn't about to be left behind.

Indecision burns in my chest, but I don't have time to be wishy-washy. I pull my pack tighter and follow behind Doug and Owen, who are already halfway across the street. Sweat beads along my forehead, and I feel it dripping down my back. This is so stupid. We shouldn't be here. My heart races. Hyperventilation isn't far behind. What am I doing?

Bret vaults over the garbage bin and disappears into the alley. Within a millisecond, I hear the wretched screeches of the damned as he dispatches them to hell where they belong… unless he's using his magic knife. Then they'll be dead forever.

Curiosity gets the better of me, and I can't *not* see what's happening. I crouch-run up to the dumpster where Doug and Owen hide, watching wide-eyed and open-mouthed at the incredible display.

Bret is a whirlwind of fury, slashing and stabbing, running up the sides of the building—crouching tiger style—and then doing backflips off, to stay out of the way of the demons while he systematically kills them. Even Jag just stands there agog, staring and speechless, his dagger hanging loosely in his fingers.

"I've never seen anything like this." I'm not speaking to anyone in particular. Just talking out loud. For whatever reason, there are over a hundred demons in the alley, crouched and hiding in the darkest corners as though they knew we were coming for them. A few fight back, but most try to flee… unsuccessfully. Bret gets them all. Even a *scratch* from his dagger makes them disintegrate into dust.

"That, my friend, is the grace of God." Owen glances at me, his face filled with the same kind of wonder as my own. But his expression is also filled with admiration and maybe even a touch of envy.

"That knife… we need that knife," Jag says.

It's over quickly, and Bret is back out of the alley before I can even register it. Not one demon is left.

"Wha… what was that?" Jag sputters. "Who the hell are you?"

He has asked that question before, but Bret has never really answered it. He's not human. He can't be. No one in this world can fight like that. I'm starting to wonder if Jag is right. Maybe Bret is a demon… or an angel. Would a demon come here to kill other demons?

My mind keeps trying to piece the whole scene together, but there is no answer for this. I've never seen anything like it. Ever. None of us have.

"I'm just a guy who kills demons," Bret says in a matter-of-fact tone, like it's no big deal at all. Like he does this every morning after breakfast. "Just like you."

"No. Not like us," I say, not even realizing the words are coming out of my mouth. "They were afraid of you. *Afraid*… of *you*."

He shakes his head and frowns, as though blowing it off. "They're just afraid of this knife. I told you before. I'm just someone who wants to help." Bret slides his daggers back into his belt and rubs his hands together. "Let's get something to eat. I'm starved."

"No," Jag snarls. "Answer our questions! You appear suddenly out of nowhere. You carry a weapon that can kill demons *before* they take a body. You jump into that alley with no thought at all… Who are you?"

Never have we come up against someone like Bret… someone better at killing demons than Jag is. There is no one anywhere who knows as much or has as much practice as the Cazadors. Not on this continent. We've been at this for almost five years, and yet this guy comes along and makes us look like a bunch of amateurs.

Bret stares into Jag's eyes as though he can see right through him, and maybe he can. "I'm not your enemy."

They're at a standoff, Jag's hands in fists, his jaw flexing. "I want you out. I want nothing to do with you, and even if you do kill demons, I don't trust you."

Bret stares right back, but he's not upset, not even a twitch of his eye registers anger. He's as calm as a summer morning, his shoulders relaxed and his body loose. "I belong in the Cazadors."

"We'll see about that," Jag says in a growl.

None of the rest say anything at all.

Jag moves up beside me, always keeping Bret in his line

of sight. He leans over and whispers, "Don't turn your back on this guy. There's only one way to explain what he can do. He's a demon." He sees my uncertain expression, nodding furiously. "Yes, he is." Jag grabs my arm and we start running out of there, Doug and Owen following close on our heels.

Jag glances at me, his eyes frightened. I haven't seen that expression in years. It terrifies me. "I might not be able to see the gray man inside him, but it's something I can feel, and I'll kill him before I let him hurt any of you."

9

Brecken

Jag could go up against a demon any day. He's fearless, but for some reason, he's afraid of me. I have become the enemy. I've done everything I can to avoid it. But here we are. What did I do wrong?

On some silent and invisible signal, we turn, leaving the Down Quarter behind us, our feet slapping the pavement, having accomplished what we came for, not that I am even sure what that is.

"We're heading back to the church," Jag says. "We need to figure out what happened here."

I don't even know what happened here. I hope he doesn't intend for me to do all the explaining. He'll be waiting a long time. I don't know why the demons were all bunched up at the end of that alley. I don't know what they were waiting for, but when they saw me, they seemed to know who I was.

Jag would love nothing more than to leave me behind, but I stick with them as they jog away from the Down Quarter and find a bus home because, well, it's my job and I'm determined to see it through, whether I feel welcome or not, which I don't.

We're lucky enough to get dropped off at the end of the church's street. To my surprise, a long-legged girl sits on the front porch, her chin resting in her hands. Long, dark hair covers her face like a veil until she lifts her head.

"Took you long enough. Where've you been?" She stands and smooths her black jeans, continuing to glare at Jag, who mostly ignores her, but I'm frozen to the sidewalk, unable to step forward or say anything at all.

She glances my way, giving me a quick appraisal, and then goes back to regarding Jag, waiting for an answer.

"Heidi!" Dean muscles past me and throws his arms around her in a welcoming hug. "We missed you tonight! Why weren't you here?"

She smiles warmly and hugs him back. I'm still standing there, frozen. Absolutely at a loss for words. My *sister* is right in front of me. My sister! What is she doing here?

"Hey, Dean," Heidi says. "Maybe because I'm never invited." She bumps knuckles with Doug and Owen, and then they all go inside the church together, Dean talking nonstop and peppering her with questions. It's as though she's a normal part of their community. They all know her… and like her.

My mind whirls a million miles a minute. What am I missing here? Heidi is at the church… with Jag. I had not anticipated seeing my sister. Although she doesn't seem to recognize me, or even care, from the look she gave me.

I shake off my surprise, hoping Jag has forgotten his fury, and step inside the condemned building. The musty scent of moldy wood and old fire permeates the air. I kind of like it. They are lounging on the chapel pews, and naturally, I go straight for Heidi, who has one leg thrown over the end of an armrest.

I stand there staring at her, unable to reconcile it in my mind that this beautiful girl is a girl no longer, but a young woman… all grown up. I can hardly believe she's right in front of me. Her sapphire eyes shine… just like the diamond chip in her nose that my eyes are drawn to. "You have a nose piercing?"

She frowns at me, and then my words register. Not really the best way to start a conversation with someone you supposedly don't know.

"Sorry, uh, I'm… Bret."

"Hey." She goes back to visiting with Owen and Doug, who are relating our story in the DQ and the amazing feat of killing all the demons in the alley.

But all I can think of is that it feels like I'm looking in a mirror. The shade of her irises, the mahogany color of her hair, the slope of her nose… everything… we could have been twins. Do none of the others see this? My heart races with panic as my gaze darts to each person in the room. Surely, they can see the resemblance and will start asking questions. She alone should recognize me, although Raphael told me no one would. But this is my sister! How can she not?

I'm ready to scoop her up in my arms and scream for joy. I want to hug her and tell her it's me. That I'm back! That she's no longer alone. I'll take care of her.

Her eyes lock with mine, and one slender eyebrow lifts along with the edge of her lips. "Take a picture, buddy. It'll last longer." With a snort, she shakes her head and looks away, laughing.

"Wha… what?" It feels uncomfortably like high school. Everyone turns to look at me, and all I can do is stare with my mouth gaping open.

Jag makes a derisive sound, shaking his head, and then Doug says, "Dude, she doesn't like to be stared at. She's a girl, not pizza. You've never seen one before?"

Slowly, my gaze shifts to him, and I scowl too. It's been a long time since I was mocked, and I've forgotten how debilitating it feels. I was The Great Undoer. I was second in line to be King of Hell. Not that it matters now, but the heat of their judgment zooms into me like darts hitting a bull's-eye. It's the first time in years that peer pressure has the power to unnerve me. All because of one person. My sister… who sits three feet away from me.

My first reaction is to put her in her place, like I would have done before I died. She's being a brat and who better to tell her than her older brother? As it is, I have to stand there, acting as if she's a stranger, like she's nothing to me.

I was strictly instructed not to reveal my identity. So, since I look stupid already, I stick out my hand. I'm not going to let an opportunity like this disappear by doing nothing. I want to know her, to know the woman she has become. "I'm new to the Cazadors. It's great to meet you." I smile like an idiot, waiting for her to shake my hand.

"No, he's not." Jag throws her a glance.

She stares at my hand for a moment, ignoring Jag, and then raises her hand with a chortle and a nod. "Me too."

"You're not in the Cazadors either." Jag propels himself from his bench in a huff and storms out of the room, stopping at the top of the stairs to glare at me. "I want you gone when I come back up." He doesn't wait for a response, but he expects me to obey.

I glance back at Heidi and can't help the stupid smile that stays plastered to my face. I am staring at my sister… one of my closest friends. Well, at times, one of my closest friends. We've argued more often than not. She was a bit of a snob in her junior high years, but we got past that… or had started to when I died.

I heard she took my death hard. I wish I could have somehow come back to see her, but it hadn't been allowed… for me. "So how do you know these guys?" I ask her, gesturing around the circle. "And do you hang out with them often?" What a stupid question, but it's too late to take it back.

"Maybe. I haven't seen you around."

I sit down next to her, hardly able to tear my eyes away, and I suddenly feel protective. "So, you're a Cazador then?" I dread her answer, but I school my expression.

"Not officially," Dean says as he smiles at her, adoration in his eyes. "But hopefully soon."

I let out a silent sigh of relief.

"Not ever," Jag answers from the stairs.

"Not necessarily," Dean says with a wink and a grin, lifting his pointer finger.

The other boys laugh and don't seem to mind the back and forth bickering. I pick up on the fact that they don't argue with Jag, whose shoulders tighten. The expression he gives Heidi isn't much better than the ones he gives me. There must be something about my family he doesn't like.

"Maybe we should have tryouts," Owen jokes, tossing a pretzel into his mouth. He must carry them in his pocket. He isn't holding the bag.

"Yeah," Doug chimes in. "It'll make it more official."

"No." Jag shakes his head as though we're stupid little children he has to explain things to over and over. "We're not taking applications." He turns and stares at me, his mouth in a hard, thin line, his eyes narrowed as he regards me. "Right now, I'm more interested in getting some questions answered. If you think we're going to let you stay without those explanations, you're more stupid than you look." He folds his well-muscled arms over his chest, waiting.

I could totally take him. "Right." My eyes dart to Heidi. "Ask away."

"First of all," Jag says. "Where are you from?"

I'm not sure what to say with Heidi sitting right next to me. I can't very well tell them I grew up only a few miles from here, in one of the many demolished neighborhoods they are probably familiar with. Heidi will try to figure out which house and will wonder why she didn't know me when we look the same age.

"Oh, I'm not from any place in particular. I bounce around a lot."

A scowl darkens Jag's expression, and he takes a predatory step closer.

"Wait!" I sit straighter in my seat, my hands out to placate him. I don't want to start a battle right here in the church. I'm supposed to their friend and leader, but that train has derailed. "I'm… from here."

"You are?" Doug asks, studying my face.

"Yeah, um, my family moved here literally two days before the Rift. I didn't really get to know anyone. That's, uh, why I say I bounced around. I did. After the Rift, I mean. I left California for a while, went to… uh, Arizona and even Oregon for a while. I've just come back." I smile and shrug, hoping my fabricated story sounds sincere.

"Explain how you could kill all those demons by yourself," Jag says.

"You did what?" Heidi twists around and sits up straight. "I thought you all killed the demons in the DQ."

"There was an alley filled with demons who *weren't* in human bodies," Owen explains. "Bret went in there like the Terminator and killed them all by himself while we watched."

"You killed them as demons. Not in bodies?" She searches my eyes, confused.

"I'm Superman, I guess." I try to lighten the mood, but from their expressions, it doesn't work. "But I'll take the Terminator too." It's typical banter for Heidi and me. This was how we joked around when we lived together. It comes out naturally, just being around her.

Her mouth opens, and that familiar glint comes to her eyes. I can tell she's tempted to joke back, but she doesn't. Instead, she turns to Jag. "I believe him."

"I don't care what you believe," he tells her. "You aren't even a Cazador."

"Not from what I can see," Dean says with a chuckle. "Nice tat, Heidi."

She hurries to pull her jacket up higher, but it's too late. Everyone gathers around and tries to see her newly forged tattoo. Jag is the only one not hovering for a glimpse. His countenance falls into one of dismay, and he stomps back to the basement.

"Fine!" she finally says to her snooping friends who are trying to pull off her jacket. "I'll show you." She slips her arms from the sleeves, allowing the boys to stretch her tank top down in the back.

I push closer too, and sure enough, a virgin tattoo rests between her shoulder blades. "You got a tattoo? Are you freaking kidding me?" Anger—like a bolt of electricity searching for a rod—flashes through me, all the way to my toes. Even my fingers tingle, and I feel a lecture aching to burst from my mouth. How can she be so irresponsible? Does she not know how easily these things become infected nowadays? How did she pay for it? Not to mention she's too young! I doubt our dad gave her permission. "How much did it cost?"

"Seriously, dude. Back off. Are you my mother?"

"Yeah, seriously." For the first time, Dean actually glares at me too. Owen and Doug look at me with surprised expressions.

She has said those very words to me—*are you my mother*—

so many times that I almost answer back with my automatic response of, *yes, I am your mother. And your father—since ours was always gone—and your babysitter, and your tormentor.* She would glare and I'd smirk, and then we'd both bust up laughing.

The words are right on the tip of my tongue, dying to slip out. I stare at her oh-so-familiar face and rein in my raging emotions. I'm acting like a lunatic. I have no right to tell her what to do, stranger or not.

"It's totally awesome," Doug murmurs, running his finger along the newly minted blade. "It's runed."

"And how did they get it to glow like that?" Owen asks. "It's so cool."

"Special ink." She smiles proudly.

I know that look. It's the expression of someone who has reached the top of Mount Everest, who has finished a marathon. She wants to be a Cazador and has proven her fearlessness by going under the needle. She has the tattoo to prove it.

I stand, pacing, holding my tongue, wondering when the hell my baby sister started seeing demons. She would have told me if it was back when we lived as a family, so it had to have been since the Rift. What other supernatural anomalies has the cataclysm caused?

I end up at the top of the stairs that lead down into the basement. It's totally rude of me to enter Jag's domain without permission, but we should talk, and I don't trust myself around Heidi at the moment.

At the bottom of the stairs is a small, cement room about twelve by twelve with no windows. Jag squats in front of an old army trunk, tossing things this way and that, searching for something. His eyes shift, and he notices me standing at the bottom of the stairs.

"What are you doing down here?"

"I'm just looking around. Figured it was storage." The room is cool, but not terribly cold. Two sleeping bags lie on the floor next to a low table with candles, a small radio, and other odds and ends.

"Well, this is my private room, so get out."

"I wanted to talk to you."

"There's nothing to talk about." He stands, his shoulders tense, like he's ready to throw me up the stairs if I don't go on my own volition.

"Jag… I'd like us to be friends. It doesn't have to be this way, us at each other's throats all the time."

"We won't be at each other's throats because you won't be around."

At this point, it's obvious the conversation will go nowhere. He's not ready for me yet. "Fine." I head back up to the chapel.

The boys are still admiring Heidi's tattoo, comparing it to their own. They each have a dagger etched in black on their upper arms. I've never noticed before. Theirs aren't anything special, so seeing how Heidi's radiates with shimmering, golden light, they are amazed and probably a bit jealous. Should I get one? That would be a big hell no. I won't have this body for long anyway.

Heidi's eyes meet mine as I step closer. She pulls her jacket back up, ending the marveling once and for all. "So, Bret. You want to be a Cazador too?"

"Uh, yeah."

At that moment, Jag appears at the top of the stairs, holding onto both sides of the doorframe as though he needs it for balance. He's out of breath and his lips are pulled back into a snarl. "Where is it?" He glares at each Cazador, searching their expressions accusingly. He stops on Heidi. "It was you, wasn't it?"

"What?" Her eyes grow wide as though she knows exactly what he's talking about.

"My spare runed blade. You took it."

Jag looks every bit the predator, dressed in black, his lips pulled back in fury, ready to pounce. And Heidi is definitely the mouse. Trapped. Caught beneath his gigantic paw of accusation. I can tell from the guilty look on her face that she has what he's looking for. This will not end well.

"Give it to me." He stalks toward her with his hand out.

The brother in me takes over. This rage-driven boy, who looks ready to take her head off, is not going anywhere near my sister. I jump up and take a stance between them, my arms outstretched. "Hold on just a minute."

"Get out of my way." Jag knocks my arm away and plants himself before Heidi, practically growling. "Give it back."

Heidi just stands there, her mouth working without any sound. Jag thrusts his hand forward, palm up. But she surprises me and shoves him back. "No. I have every right to it. I see the demons too. I am not going to sit home knitting while you all go hunting."

"Okay, wait just a minute," I say, trying to placate them.

"Shut up," they both say in unison.

Okay. Fine. I'll sit this one out, but if he dares lay even one finger on her...

"It's *my* dagger," Jag shouts, poking a finger at her for emphasis.

"As soon as you runed it, it became anyone's dagger who can see demons. You already have one. You've made one for everyone here!" She screams the words, her eyes wild, frustration and anger spilling out. "I need one too. Everybody here wants me to join, and you can't keep me out any longer! You don't get to make all the decisions. You're not everybody's boss!" She shouts directly into his face, inches away from his nose.

We used to go at it all the time in the old days, but seeing her righteous anger and flashing eyes... I have to admit, I'm siding with her. It will take a force of nature to hold her back. Jag doesn't stand a chance.

"I say we take a vote," Dean says, breaking in. "All in favor?"

Jag stares at Dean in astonishment. Everyone raises their hand but Jag and me. I don't bother because I won't count anyway. Dean's hand comes up, like a slap in Jag's face.

"This isn't a democracy," he snarls, his teeth clenched. "I *am* in charge. *I* made this group. *I* get to say who joins or not."

"Why?" Owen steps forward, his long, slender body stretching up straight and confident. "We should all get a say in who joins... and who leads us for that matter. I want someone in charge who is fair and will let us help."

"Well," Dean interjects. "To be fair, Jag does a really great job and he has kept us safe."

We all just stand there, waiting to see who will be brave enough to speak next.

10

HEIDI

From the moment I walk into the chapel, I can feel a bizarre change floating in the air. First, there's this new guy. There hasn't been a new Cazador for ages, and Bret seems to have appeared out of nowhere.

I watch him for a minute, a crazy twist in my stomach. There's something about him and the way he keeps looking at me. No, the way he keeps *staring* at me. Like stalker staring. Something isn't right, but I can't put my finger on it.

Jag stands before me, furious. More angry than I've ever seen him. His eyes are narrow and ice cold. I glance over at the new guy to see his expression. He has moved away to stand by the windows, one beam of light shining through the boards into his bright blue eyes, which are wide and worried. For someone who wants to join the Cazadors, that doesn't bode well.

Jag stands with his hand thrust out, waiting for his dagger. *Please let the floor open up to swallow me.* If I admit I took it, I'm a thief. If I lie to cover it up, I'm a liar. They all stare, knowing. I have *insidious* written all over my face, and I hate that feeling.

I almost bow in defeat, but something sparks inside my chest. Indignation. I stole from Jag, true, but he is denying me my God-given right to battle evil. The heat of righteous anger fills my heart and a boost of awesome shoots through my veins, overpowering my mortification.

I stand up straight and shove Jag back with the confidence of a glamazon—something my brother used to call me. A powerful woman with a dash of panache. I'm not afraid of Jag, and it isn't an act. He always bulldozes over me. He does it with pretty much everyone. To his cronies, he's a god. To me… I'm not sure what he is.

Doug puts his two cents in. "Dude," he says to Jag. "Just let it go. We all have a runed dagger. You weren't even using that one."

Slowly, Jag turns until he faces Doug fully. "This is not a discussion. You don't get to say anything about it. You don't have a vote. If you don't like it, get out."

Doug wilts, and I feel terrible for him. Today, it changes. Today, I'm different. Today, I'm strong. My new tattoo still burns like a son-of-a-bitch, reminding me of that fact.

"The answer is no," I say. "I need a weapon. I can see the demons the same as any of you. I've trained to kill them, same as you. You are keeping the dagger *from* me, and I'm done being shut out."

Incredulity settles on his face, and his eyes grow wide and round. Nobody talks back to Jag. Ever. For a moment, he's frozen, and then his expression thaws. "How about we fight for it?"

"What?" He would enjoy that. But he's stronger than I am, faster too. My heart sinks at what I know is coming. I don't want my time in the Cazadors to start out like this. Do I want to be one of them so badly that I'll subject myself to this kind of ridicule and humiliation?

"No, I don't want to fight you. For once, I just want you to act like a normal human being. Would that really be so hard? Would it really be so terrible to have a girl in the gang?"

Miracle of miracles, Jag has nothing to say. I can see it in his eyes. He expected me to fight fire with fire, and instead, I turned it around, making him look mean and heartless. Most of the time, he wouldn't care, but today, we have an audience, including a new recruit. Jag won't want to seem weak, but he also won't want to seem cruel. I know he has a heart in there somewhere… buried deep.

"Fine. Keep it. It's old and dull anyway." He turns away and walks out onto the front porch.

I just stand there, frozen in the weighty silence that follows, everyone's eyes on me. Jag gave in. Somehow, today, I won. I let the smile stay on my lips as this information sinks in. I file the feeling away so I can pull it out later and relish in it when I'm alone.

A moment later, Owen clears his throat and wipes his mouth of pretzel crumbs. He looks over at the new guy, who just stands there watching our drama as though he can't believe he even wants to join.

"Here's what I think," Owen says. "In case anyone wonders, because yeah, my opinion is valid here. I have a say in things too. I think Bret should be in. We need him. Anyone who can kill so many demons at one time deserves our trust." He sits back down on the bench and begins cleaning his fingernails, his lips pursed as though he doesn't have a care in the world.

Jag steps back into the church and leans against the front doorjamb, clearly having heard Owen's statement. Dean looks ready to speak up, but he doesn't. Instead, he stares at his feet as they shuffle on the dusty floor, probably not wanting to offend his best friend. Whatever. Just once, I wish he'd stand up to Jag. Someday, he might. I hope I'm around to see it.

"Maybe a tryout *would* be good." Doug looks around, and all of our eyes are on him. He puffs up, pleased to be the center of attention. He's not alpha, but he has valuable insights. Jag listens to him… sometimes. "We could see how Bret does against Jag in a mock battle. You know. To see if he's up to snuff."

The Cazadors have done this before, for fun, to see who the top dog really is. Owen and Doug hold their own against Jag, but nobody can actually beat him. I've never even tried. That would only serve to prove how pathetic I really am… at least against him, and that isn't something I feel the need to advertise.

I hope they don't ask me to fight him too. I've already said no and being close to Jag is a dangerous idea. Even though he is cold and prickly, there is something about him I'm drawn to—as sick as that sounds—even fascinated with, and I can't figure it out.

He's an itch I can't scratch. A thirst I can't quench. Maybe it's his drive, the way he pursues his goals, the way he's so single-minded. It can't possibly be the way his muscles flex beneath his clothes or the gleam of sweat on his brow when he's fighting. There are times when I stare at his mouth. Not because his lips look soft, but because his breath always smells of Oreo cookies and I love that.

I glance over at him. Maybe it's the way his hair falls from its tie at the back… just a few long, blond strands in his eyes… No, those are things I refuse to notice. Nothing good could come of thinking about Jag in this way. Plus, being near him is like touching an exposed live wire or watching a poisonous snake ready to strike, but not being able to move. Exciting to anticipate, but you know it's going to hurt… a lot.

"I'm up for that," the new guy says, a slow smile spreading across his face.

I study him like I just studied Jag. Bret's dark, shaggy hair curls at the base of his neck and dimples crease his cheeks. Physically, he's got it all. Bright twilight-blue eyes, and a rockin' hot body, but there is something odd about him. Shaking my head, I can't escape the feeling that he seems familiar, but I would remember that face if I'd met him before.

"Well, Jag?" Dean asks.

Jag kicks the old pizza box across the floor, cursing under his breath. With his hands on his hips, he turns away. We wait. His back is rigid, but expanding as he breathes. When he finally turns around to face us, his eyes are calm and there's a smile on his lips. "Let's do it."

He unstraps his belt and tosses it to the floor, then shakes out his arms, ready and waiting. I lean against the wall. Time slows as Bret and Jag angle closer together, their eyes watchful. Dust motes halt in their descent, suspended in a ray of candlelight, and even my breathing pauses in heightened anticipation.

They circle one another, feral animals ready to demonstrate their prowess. I've seen Jag fight many times. I've studied him. I know his moves. When he battles demons, it's with a single-minded grace that I yearn to duplicate. His body, while loose and supple, can twist and turn, bend and weave, in and out—almost like a ballroom dancer—faster than anyone else I've ever seen. I watch him, mesmerized.

Jag is the first to lunge, his shoulder slamming into Bret's gut, but rather than being bowled over by the inertia, he rolls with it, coming out on top instead. He pins Jag and then leaps back, smiling wickedly.

With a growl, Jag jumps back to his feet without pause. They circle again. This time, Jag waits. Bret reaches out repeatedly, play smacking, teasing, and taunting. Jag doesn't fall for it, but the fury in his expression grows dark and malevolent.

Bret attacks, his leg swiping low, snagging Jag's foot, but Jag catches his balance easily, like the cat he is, landing on his feet. Then Bret rams his elbow into Jag's chest with enough force that Jag flies back, crashing onto the floor, gasping for breath. He rolls over and comes to his feet, a new and unusual look in his eyes. One I haven't seen before. *Alarm*—the realization that he has come up against someone he might not be able to beat. And it looks to me like Bret is going easy on him.

Jag dives for Bret and they go at it, grabbing, pulling, restraining, and shoving. It seems that neither of them will give up, but a sheen of sweat begins to condensate on Jag's forehead. I lean forward, squinting to be sure. He's tiring.

But not Bret, who fights like a boss. He didn't seem that big at first glance—only a few inches taller than me—but watching him, it's impossible not to be affected by his sheer force of will, like an otherworldly power is at his back. I want to laugh, cheer, and clap my hands all at the same time. If there is anyone built to beat Jag in a brawl, it's this guy.

Dean sidles up beside me, matching my stance and crossing his arms. "So, who's your money on?" His smile deepens, and his sandy-blond hair curls endearingly around his ears.

I shove his shoulder with mine. "Bret, of course."

He laughs and shoves back. "You're in now, you know. There's no going back."

A smile creases my lips even though I'm trying to keep a straight face. "What makes you say that?"

"Just a feeling."

"Yeah, I have the same feeling." I should feel more excited, but the knowledge sits like a weighted stone in the pit of my stomach. This is what I've wanted for so long and now that it's here, it feels anticlimactic.

Conversation grows quiet as Bret and Jag grunt and breathe. And then they both step away from each other at some silent signal, their chests heaving, both sweaty.

"I'd say it's a draw." Owen tosses another pretzel into his mouth.

It isn't a draw. Bret could have beaten Jag and done it in the first five seconds. He let it last so Jag wouldn't lose face or feel undermined. I don't know how I know this, but I do, on a gut level. I glance at Bret, and he's looking at me too. He winks. It's quick, but it's mingled with a sly smile. He knows that I know.

"So," Bret says between ragged breaths. "Am I in or what?"

Jag wipes his face, wearing a scowl. "Or what." He hasn't technically lost, but he didn't win either, and that has to rub the wrong way.

"Hey, we had a fair fight and you didn't beat me." Bret wipes his face with a rag, his jaw hanging slack with a half-smile.

"And you still haven't told us anything about you." Jag stares right back, his jaw clenching. "Why should we let you in when we know nothing about you?"

"Ask me anything." Bret slouches to the floor, his back against the wall.

Owen speaks up before anyone else has a chance to. "Where'd you get the knife? The one that actually kills demons."

Bret drops his chin to his chest, chuckling. "From an angel."

Before he has time to even defend himself, Jag pounces and throws a punch that lands square in the middle of Bret's face. Bret rolls away, one hand covering his bleeding nose. But Jag isn't done. He leaps on top of Bret, his arm raised to punch again, but Owen and Doug race forward and grab him around the chest, pulling him off before his fist finds home.

"You think your high and mighty attitude is going to help you here? You think your lies will be believed? We're not a bunch of morons!" Jag lets his friends pull him away, but he shrugs from their grasp once he is standing.

Bret rises up on an elbow, wiping his face with the sleeve of his other arm. "Ow. That hurt."

Talk about odd man out. If I were him, I'd just leave, but then, I *was* him not so long ago, and I didn't leave. I'm curious to see what he will do now.

He exhales deeply and then looks Jag in the eye. "I'm not lying. I got the knife from the Archangel Raphael. It's called a Nephilim dagger. Nephilim weapons kill for good. If you are even scratched by one, your soul will cease to exist."

"Prove it." Doug crosses his arms over his chest, those dark, fierce eyes demanding an honest answer.

We all glance at Doug with expressions of disbelief. Including Bret.

"Dude, he said a *scratch* would kill you. Are you volunteering?" Owen shakes his head and pulls out a new, unopened bag of pretzels from an inside pocket of his jacket. He never stops eating. I have no idea where he puts it all.

Bret glances at the floor and smiles sheepishly. "I swear, I will never lie to you. I can't always tell you what you want to know, but I *was* sent here to help. That's all I can say. Will you let me help?"

Jag curses and wears a beaten expression. "And how do we know you aren't a demon yourself? Because that's what I think you are. In fact, I *know* it."

Bret's wounded expression makes me want to put my arm around him and tell him everything's going to be okay

"We'd be able to see the gray man inside," Doug says. "And I don't see anything."

"Me neither," Owen adds, holding the pretzel bag out to me. I shake my head, not at all hungry… unless he were carrying barbeque potato chips. Why can't he have those stashed in his pockets once in a while? Or better yet, chocolate.

"I don't see one either," I say, crouching down next to Bret. I turn him toward me and keep my hands on his arms as I look deeply into his eyes. If he were a demon, I'd know. I'd feel it in the pit of my stomach like acid or an ulcer. I feel nothing of the sort. As I gaze at him, a familiar warmth fills me from my toes all the way up to my belly, like a yummy, tingling bubble of sparkling apple cider. I close my eyes and inhale, swearing I smell the scent of pine. "He's no demon. That much I know."

"And you're an expert?" Jag asks me.

"Yes, as a matter of fact, I am." I stare him down, prepared to win this staring contest, but he shakes his head and escapes down the stairs to the basement. Dean jumps up to follow him, but I grab his arm, "Let him go. He needs to cool off anyway."

To his credit, Dean nods, knowing I'm right, but he can't let Jag feel bad all by his lonesome. He shrugs an apology and pounds down the stairs.

I turn back to Bret. "I guess I don't get my turn at Greco-Roman."

I lie on the church pew in front of the cold fire pit with only my coat thrown over me for warmth. Everyone's asleep, catching up on rest before we go hunting again tonight. It's quiet and my back aches, trying to sleep on this hard bench. It's moments like these when I miss having a real bed, a real bedroom, and my little sister Sophie jumping on me in the morning.

I can't live here with Dean and Jag—not that I'd want to—but even so, there is no invitation. In fact, if anything, the message to go away rings loud and clear. Dean feels sorry for me—he's admitted that much—but Jag doesn't. He wants the church all to himself. He doesn't play well with other children. He can have it. I hate it here. I swear it's haunted, and it has always given me the creeps. I would never sleep here by myself.

Some might think this is the life. Free. Independent. Exciting. Living with friends and killing demons. But this isn't a TV show, and we aren't Sam and Dean Winchester. Our lives are hard and often miserable as we eek out this tiresome existence.

Rolling over, I watch Bret sleeping on the pew across from

me. He stayed after Jag went to bed, not even bothering to ask permission. He doesn't have a blanket either, and his arms lie loosely over his chest. He seems younger in sleep and more at peace, with his lips slightly parted and his sooty lashes resting on his cheeks.

One of his eyes cracks open. I can't help but smile at him, with his hair all mussed and sleep in his eyes. I like him, I admit it, and the urge to tease him about his bed-head is almost irresistible.

"Morning, Heidi," he mumbles, rolling over to face the back of the pew. His words are muffled and soft, but I swear the next thing he says is, "Can you get Sophie some cereal?"

"What?"

But his mumbling has stopped, his eyes are closed, and he is already snoring again. I heard him wrong. He doesn't know me, let alone my little sister.

A half hour later, I'm heating up instant oatmeal over a fire I built all by myself in the fire pit. Yeah, I have skills. The instant cereal isn't the best, but it fills my belly. It's my main staple. I always keep a few packs in my bag.

"What are you doing?" someone yells from the stairs. Jag is standing in the doorway to the basement, a caustic frown on his face, looking directly at me.

"That's going to become your permanent expression if you don't start smiling once in a while." I grin at him, but he doesn't smile back. *Jerk*. Some days, I just can't stand the guy.

"You can't have a fire in here."

"Hello? Fire pit." I point to the metal pan with flames in it that sits right in front of me. It's been here for as long as I've known them… which is a long time. Kind of. I know they built it when they moved in, so what's the big deal?

"We don't use it. The smoke." He points to where the smoke twists and circles in the exposed rafters above my head. "There's no chimney."

"Ah." I hate the logical way he says things, and then the stupid feeling that erupts inside me after. I'd figured with how drafty this place is that it didn't matter.

"Plus, someone might see it," Bret adds. He has woken up and is watching me with sleepy eyes.

I hate the way they both look at me, as if I'm too stupid to figure it out on my own, and the heat of shame flushes through me. "Whatever."

Jag glances at Bret, his jaw flexing and his dark eyes shining, but he doesn't say anything to him. I sigh and dump a cup of water over the tiny flames. My mush is done cooking anyway.

"You should get that figured out." I point to the ceiling.

"Yeah. I'll get right on it." Jag walks over to my bench and plops down beside me, glancing at my breakfast. "Don't suppose you have any more of that?"

I shake my head. "You need a kitchen or at least something to cook on."

"That's a good idea." He rolls his eyes, and then I remember he has a camp stove downstairs in his private lair. "So, are you ready?"

I glance at him while chewing my pasty, tasteless mush, trying to figure out what he's talking about. "Huh?"

"You haven't tried out for the Cazadors yet." His evil grin grows, and I groan inwardly.

"Are you serious? Right now? I'm eating."

"I'll let you finish." He folds his arms over his chest, and the one ray of sunlight that happens to infiltrate the church lands on his face, making his skin glow and his hair look the color of sugar cookies. It's tied back at the nape of his neck, but a few strands escape and frame his face. He's alarmingly appealing and I exhale, surprised I'm holding my breath in the first place. He wears a tight, black sweater and smells of soap and damp skin. He showered? Where? Probably from the bucket he keeps by his bed. I've bathed that way hundreds of times.

Bret stretches and yawns. "You're going to spar? Now?"

"Is there a better time?" Jag looks directly at me. We're close enough that I can see every gold speck in his eyes, every crease around his eyes, each individual eyelash. He searches my eyes earnestly enough that I can't say no. For some reason, I don't want to.

"Alright." I set my half-eaten bowl aside and stand, slipping off my jacket. I still wear my black tank top and jeans from the night before, and I need a shower. I ignore the noxious odor coming from my armpits and hope Jag will too. He notices everything though, so I'm probably out of luck there. Guess I won't be distracting him with my womanly wiles. I move away from the fire and wait for him, my hair hanging over my shoulder in one long, messy tail. "Ready, cowboy?"

He saunters over, a smile on his face. He wears combat boots and cargo pants. Easier to move in than my jeans, which gives him an advantage. Jag is a couple of inches taller than I am, and he's stronger. Strength would be nice, but to win, I have to be quick. At least quicker than him, which considering who I'm up against, will be challenging.

I have to believe I can win.

We circle one another, moving slowly, with no one to witness but Bret, who is now sitting up on the bench, rubbing his disheveled hair.

Jag lunges, quick and lethal, but I anticipate that move. I know him well. He's sleek, but I dodge and knock the back of his head with my elbow when I pass under his arm. His head snaps forward, but he doesn't lose his focus or balance. He recovers smoothly and turns to face me, his smile widening.

I let my eyes soften, taking in every detail of him, from the movement of his feet, to the twitch of his fingers. He has tells, and I know what they are. I wait in fighting stance. He crouches and thrusts his arm toward me, like he's trying to smack my face, but I pull back. He grabs my braid instead and yanks me forward.

The move takes me by surprise, and I can't stop my sudden yelp of disbelief. I lose my balance and fall to one knee, and then he has me. He leaps on top, pulling my arm out from under me. My face slams against the cold, mosaic floor, the dust gusting away as I lie gasping.

He holds me down, his legs over mine, his chest smashed against my back, my arms helpless. Frustration springs to my eyes, and I fight back tears. Not because I'm hurt, but because I'm embarrassed. He pinned me so quickly, and I thought I was a better fighter than this. Faster than this. How did I even think I could compete with Jag when he can take me down in less than a minute?

His breath is warm against my ear. "Is this what you want? To be helpless? You can't even move. I could do whatever I wanted to you. Anything. Demons are as strong as I am, if not stronger. They're fast. Deadly fast. Do you *want* to die?"

I shove against him. He lifts off me and sits back, breathing hard, his eyes searching mine, but not with malice. I can't read the emotions that flicker there, and I don't want to. I turn away, not wanting him to see how vulnerable and weak he's made me feel. I don't want him to see the moisture that is collecting in my eyes. I keep my face aimed at the floor. "It doesn't matter. If we don't get rid of the demons, none of us will have a future. We'll all be dead or wish we were." I stalk over to my jacket and grab it from the dusty floor.

Jag draws himself up and brushes off his pants. He throws me a glance before walking out. One that has too much in it for me to decipher, and I'm not about to Sigmund Freud him in front of Bret.

"That's true," Bret says, suddenly beside me, his hand on my shoulder. "When did you start seeing them? The gray men, I mean."

I look up, and his smile turns soft. Kind. A smile that makes me want to trust and confide, but if I give into that emotion, a torrent of tears will thunder through the dam I've erected.

"After my brother died." I take the cup of water he offers and gulp it down.

"Really?"

I shrug and try to rein in my frown, a barb of sarcasm on the tip of my tongue, but it isn't his fault I lost the match. I'm itching to take my frustration out on something. "What does it matter?"

"I guess it doesn't," he says. "I was just curious." He grabs his backpack and follows me out the front door. "You're pretty good, but you lack discipline. Jag is quick, but you could be quicker."

"Gee, thanks."

"I just meant I could help you, if you want."

I stop on the front steps and turn to him. It's late afternoon, and the sun is still bright. The dry, bland odor of dust floats in the beams of sunlight, reminding me of the park by my old house. Parched, brown, and gasping its last breath of abandonment. I miss home. *He* makes me miss home for some reason… the smell of pancakes on Saturday morning. "Are you serious?"

"Yes. I'd be happy to train you since you're so bent on taking this route anyway. I'd rather you go to college, but if you're going to be stubborn…"

I realize he's teasing me, and the warmth I felt with him before rushes back, filling the craggy holes that were quarried by Jag during our wrestling match. "Okay."

We walk down the street, our arms accidentally touching once in a while, but it isn't weird or uncomfortable. Being with him feels natural, and I find myself wondering what it would be like to spend more time with him. I'm not against finding out.

11

Brecken

Teaching my little sister—who I do not want hunting demons—to hunt demons, is not part of my plan. I still think of her as a thirteen-year-old with braces, someone I need to take care of and protect. The only fighting I've ever seen her do is hair pulling—girl style—and slamming the bathroom door in my face. Although there were times when a cereal box exploded if neither of us would let go.

It seems serendipitous that we are reunited, and yet, we are still strangers.

I remember her fuzzy, leopard print pajama bottoms that she swore were good luck, and the pounding bass drum of her favorite rock group as it thumped its way down to my basement bedroom. I remember the hours she spent in the bathroom, and how she put milk or juice back in the fridge even if there was only a tablespoon left. But most of all, I remember sitting on the couch, visiting for hours and watching movies late at night.

Once, she asked me how she looked before she went out with some friends. I'd told her that she had on too much makeup. I didn't think she should wear makeup at all at her age, but I didn't mention that. Her eyes had narrowed and fear had stabbed through my chest—because you didn't want to be on Heidi's bad side—but instead of freaking out, she went back into the bathroom and removed some of the Lady Gaga.

Those moments hadn't happened often, but they were clear in my mind. I missed out on the last five years of her life, but I am intent on making up for lost time. I can do that and the job I've been enlisted to do.

But first, I need to find a place to live. Jag is not going to throw open the doors of welcome, so I pull out the newspaper I picked up yesterday and turn to my only friend on the planet. "So, Heidi. You want to help me find a place to live?"

"You aren't going to stay with Jag and Dean?" She winks playfully and chuckles.

Oh, she is adorable. So sweet and naïve. I love her so much. "Uh, no. I'm not getting any warm fuzzies from Jag, or did you not notice?"

She breaks out in laughter. The good, old-fashioned kind that bursts from your stomach and makes anyone close by want to laugh too, just for the infectiousness of it. This is how I remember her. Laughing. Eyes sparkling. Lips wide apart and teeth showing. I gaze into her eyes with a newfound appreciation of what I lost when I died, and what she's gone through these last few years. How many times has she laughed like this since I've been gone?

"Sure. I'll help."

We saunter down the street, in no hurry, toward the closest listing I've found. I want to be near the church, but after seeing how those two boys live, I opt for accommodations that are more modern. Well, as modern as you can get these days.

Our first stop is five blocks away in an old yellow-brick building with an iron front door. Solid, but not aesthetically pleasing. I don't care. We knock on the manager's door, and he shows us to an apartment on the fourth floor. There's no elevator, but there is electricity and running water, so already it's better than the church.

The manager unlocks the flimsy door, which I'll change if I move in, and we step inside. From the far corner to the front door, it's wide-open space. A studio apartment with whitewashed walls and the only room with a door is the bathroom. The floors are scuffed hardwood, and the whole west wall is floor-to-ceiling windows with a few years' worth of grime I can't see through.

"I'll take it."

For three hundred a month, it's a steal. I don't even check out the other listings. Our next stop is a small mom-and-pop furniture store where I order a used double bed—because who wants to sleep in a twin?—and other miscellaneous objects like a nightstand, lamps, and a trunk to keep my stuff in. It's obvious I'll need more money than what Raphael gave me. I'll have to hit him up for a bit more, but by that evening, I'm moved in and enjoying my view of the slums.

Heidi stands before the windows, the evening sun washing her in gold. She looks so ethereal and angelic.

She turns slightly to glance in my direction, her eyes wide and her expression soft. "I love it here. I'm so jealous. This is the perfect apartment."

"Yeah. It totally is." And I can't imagine Heidi walking out and going anywhere else. Jag isn't about to let her live at the church. And here I am in this awesome apartment… It doesn't seem right to make her go. "So, this isn't going to come out right, so bear with me, because I know we don't know each other very well, but this place is plenty big enough for two people… We could share rent."

She has no idea who I am. I could be any Joe Blow off the street, and here I am, asking her to live with me. Will she be reckless enough to say yes? I hope, in this instance, that she is.

She turns slowly to face me, her mouth opening, her eyes huge—like a tarsier holding onto a tree branch for dear life—but she holds back, not answering. Looking the place up and down, she surveys the wide-open space, its lack of privacy… and walls… and furniture.

I take in her stance, slightly insecure, but hopeful. She's bending, wanting to say yes, but still not convinced. Our dad would freak if it was any other guy, and I wonder where he is and why he isn't talking her out of joining the Cazadors. He and I never saw eye to eye. He did try to kill me once, but that's another story. He adored Heidi and Sophie. He'd never hurt or abandon either of them.

"You don't even know me. You have no idea what kind of person I am, and you want me to live here? To sleep in the same room?"

She's considering it. She wants to be a Cazador and live close to the gang. She is no more welcome at the church than I am. Here, she won't be alone anymore.

"Are you hitting on me?" she asks, matter of fact, and it is so off base that I can't think of anything to say. At least I don't respond with *yuck or gross*, which is what I'm thinking. "Heck no! No way!"

She frowns and draws her arms up over her chest, her gaze dropping to the floor. She glances out the windows. Her expressions are so easy to read, and I'm immediately aware that I've humiliated her. In my rush to convince her that I'd never hit on her, I made it clear she isn't attractive to me. Immediately, I try to U-turn. "Not that any guy wouldn't want to hit on you. Seriously, you're… totally hot. Really."

Her eyes widen and she takes a step back, her brows rising in something akin to astonishment and maybe a bit of hope. Okay. Maybe I said too much. I feel the need to backpedal in the other direction, but instead of opening my mouth and vomiting up anything else that might make the situation worse, I laugh and throw my hands up in the air. "Nothing is coming out right."

Still chuckling at my inability to phrase anything appropriately, I walk over to the window and stand beside her, staring out over the roofs below me. Most are shingled, but some are covered with corrugated tin. This is a poor neighborhood and getting poorer. "I shouldn't have asked you to move in. It's not appropriate anyway. Your parents would freak."

"Wait!" She reaches out in an effort to stop my train of thought from pulling into the station and uninviting her to live here. "It's okay. It's fine. I get it. And yes, I totally want to live here. If you were a dirt bag, I'd already know it by now. I can help with rent." She smiles, a blush creeping up her cheeks while she plays with something around her neck. A half-heart pendant with blazing flames on the curve. There is an identical, second half to that blazing heart. My sister, Sophie, wears it… or at least she used to.

I feign innocence and ask, "What's that you have there?"

She glances down and shrugs, wiping all emotion from her voice. "Nothing. Well, something that reminds me of why I do what I do." She tucks the chain inside her tank top.

I let it go and wish I could see Sophie too. "So…" I get excited about the idea of her moving in. "We'll cordon off that corner for your room." I point to the south east end of the apartment, which has lots of space and will still leave plenty of room for the training equipment I intend to buy for the living room. Who needs couches?

"Seriously?" Her eyes grow wide, and a smile forms that brightens the entire room. "That would be fantastic! I would love that."

I already know what living with Heidi is like, and it won't be a piece of cake. She never washes her own dishes and she leaves all sorts of girl things on the bathroom counters, but she's my sister, my family, and I am overjoyed to have found her. It will be just like old times.

She bounds back from her side of the room and throws her arms around me in a joyful hug. I hug her right back, burying my face in the familiar scent of her hair. Suave shampoo. Coconut.

"The first thing I'm gonna do is shower!" She grabs her backpack, which hopefully has clean clothes inside, because not only can I smell her hair, but the rest of her too.

I'm feeling generous and excited to have even part of my family under one roof, so I plan to get her some furniture of her own, to make her want to stay, because she sure as heck isn't going to sleep with me, not that she'd want to.

When Heidi opens the bathroom door, steam wafts out in a cloud and the mirror is frosted over in dew. Gazing at me from her reflection in the mirror while towel drying her hair, she asks, "So, are you on your own? Do you have family? How old are you?" She rubs her damp tresses with a ratty old towel.

"Family? No. But I had a rich old uncle who died and left me everything." It's an old joke, like everything else, between us, because Heidi and I were hardly ever serious with one another. We were either joking around or arguing. It's what made us close. The

Urban Dictionary says so.

"Shut. Up!" She swirls around and stares, her mouth agog. "That cannot be true! That's exactly what happened to me. That never happens in real life." Laughter bubbles up from inside her, and she drops down next to me on the bed.

"You had a rich uncle die and leave you money?" I ask, already knowing we didn't have an uncle, let alone a rich one.

"Not exactly. Tell me *your* story."

"Well, okay." I can think of absolutely nothing to say. If you want something to sound real, steal from the truth, but everything that's true for me is also true for Heidi. We had the same parents, the same extended family, and the same neighbors.

"You know what? I'm dying for something to eat. Are you hungry?"

She studies me with a wry smile. "Fine. Be a baby. I'll tell my story first." She crosses her legs, Indian style, clasping her hands before her. Her hair is still damp and looks almost blue-black in the waning twilight. "But I'm warning you. My story isn't a happy one."

"Tell me."

"It starts with a father who kills his only son."

12

Heidi

It feels like the sun has finally come out. Not only have I finally, unofficially, been accepted into the Cazadors, but I have a place to pitch my tent also. Bret's proposal takes me by surprise, but it settles well in my stomach… after the shock dissipates. I don't get the feeling he is trying to put the moves on me—which, truth be told, stings my pride—but it also means that I won't feel like I have to sleep with one eye open.

I want to tell him my story… a story I haven't told a single other person… not even my aunt. I don't confide in just anyone, and it amazes me that I'm about to do it with someone who is pretty much a complete stranger. But there is something about Bret that screams *trust me!*

And I do.

I'm not sure what to think of that. I don't trust easily, but he fascinates me. I can't explain what draws me to him, but something does. Taking a deep breath, I begin. "You're going to think my family is nuts."

He watches me, his eyes open and receptive. "All families are nuts."

With a snort of agreement and a roll of my eyes, I stifle a chuckle and start my tale of woe. "I'm not sure of all the details exactly. But it started before the Rift. My brother was in the hospital. He'd almost drowned, and we were all worried he'd have brain damage. It didn't look like he'd ever come out of his coma." Even still, the ache of those days in the hospital twists my heart. I fight to keep the emotion out of my voice and the tears out of my eyes. I can*not* cry right now. Not with him watching.

"One day, I walk into my brother's hospital room and… and he is on the floor. My dad is on top of him, holding a knife to his throat." I can still see it so clearly. Brecken's hospital gown up around his hips, his white legs, and the fact that they looked so thin. It's weird what details go through your mind when your brain refuses to grasp the truth. Brecken's expression had been twisted in agony and he'd looked pathetically weak, trying to hold back my father's knife.

I glance at Bret to get a read on his thoughts, but the only thing I see is his reaction of dismay, his mouth slightly open, his eyes looking more like a child's, begging me to stop talking.

"Sorry. Maybe I shouldn't have told you all that. My dad didn't kill my brother that day, right in front of me. He waited until later."

Bret continues his horrified stare, and I plead with him in my mind to take all I've said with a grain of salt, like it's just a bad movie rather than the stock I came from. Surely, he wonders if this kind of craziness runs in the family. Will he rescind his invitation for me to live here? I fiddle with a scrap of paper I found on the floor, folding and unfolding it until it's more like soft cotton than paper.

"Oh, Heidi… it sounds like a terrible… maybe… maybe he didn't kill him. Maybe…" He reaches out and draws me in, petting my head as if I'm a golden retriever, and yet, I don't pull away. I press closer to him, squeezing my eyes shut to keep the moisture back that threatens to fall. It feels so good to be held, to be comforted. I haven't felt that in such a long time, if ever. Not when Brecken died, not after we moved to my aunt's house, not from any friends at Brecken's funeral, and not after our dad left us.

Then I let it happen… for the first time in over five years. I let the tears of regret and ache fall. I let the abandonment I feel from Brecken, from my father, and even my mother, explode out of me in the form of wracking sobs that I can't hold back or control. The cathartic moment lasts forever, and Bret's strong arms hold me while I cry, my tears wetting his shoulder and arm. When I realize I need to blow my nose, I pull away, keeping my head turned. I dash to the bathroom and shut the door behind me.

Staring into the mirror, I gaze at the girl with swollen, red eyes, and then straighten my shoulders. I'm not a child anymore. I can't be trapped by the past any longer. Crying on Bret's shoulder has made that abundantly clear. I'm ready—and possibly able—to let go of the hurt and anger, the rejection and loneliness. I'm ready to let go of Brecken and my dad. I'm ready to move forward, to be a Cazador.

The store delivers our furniture in an old pickup truck. Two burly guys help us carry our new crap up four flights of stairs. I set up my room with a scarf over the lamp, and it all feels very Bohemian to me.

I haven't said a word about what happened yesterday, and neither has he. I'm determined to let it go and bask in the amazingness of my new life. I lie on my bed, cozy as a kitten, reading a book I found at the used bookstore around the corner, realizing I haven't felt this happy or at peace in years.

Bret stands over in the kitchen area, frying eggs, surprisingly domestic. We didn't demon hunt last night, but took the time to catch up on sleep instead, which we both desperately needed.

I watch him from the corner of my eye—the practiced way he flips the eggs—and the twist of his wrist. Maybe he was going to be a chef in his last life—before the Rift. He wears a contented smile that says he feels as "at home" as I do. It brings a rush of warmth to my heart.

While the eggs fry, he goes to work slicing an avocado. I drop my book and sit up straight, staring as he slices off the top of the avocado, cuts it in half, and makes slices down the meat. He then smacks the blade against the seed, twisting it—just so—to pull it out. He has no idea I'm staring. No idea that my heart is flipping over in summersaults or that I've stopped breathing.

I haven't had avocado with eggs in a long time. Not since I made them with my brother, Brecken, years ago. I don't know anyone else who even eats them this way… eggs, sunny-side up, with sliced avocado on the side. People eat avocados in an omelet, yeah, but messy? With the yolk smearing the green flesh? It's a *thing* in my family. To think there is someone else in the world who likes it the same way. How crazy cool.

"Breakfast is served!" he says with a flourish, setting our plates on the counter. We don't have a table with chairs, but I don't mind. I like it this way, the two of us sitting on our stools at the island counter.

I poke my eggs with a fork. There's nothing better than yolk-covered green goodness sliding over my tongue. I can't believe he made it for me.

"I hope you like this." He speaks with his mouth full, casual, not caring what I think about his bad manners. "I've been craving eggs. I used to eat them like this all the time, but I haven't had them in years."

He hasn't had eggs or avocados in years? He digs in like a starving waif, and all I can think of to say is, "Why?"

"Oh." He laughs and waves my comment away. "I don't know." He holds up a glass of orange juice. "To our new crib!"

I tip my glass to his, the clink ringing through the room, the commencement of a new chapter in both our lives. I don't know what today will bring, let alone the future, but for the first time in ages, it looks bright.

Bret and I set up the workout equipment in the wide-open space where a living room set should go. It's used and worn, but we don't care. My part of the machine—the bench and leg lifts—comes together slowly, but perfectly. When Bret is done with the arm and shoulder press, he has three screws left over. The whole dang thing is going to come crashing down while we are working out.

By the time we finish, there has been plenty of bickering back and forth. He doesn't read directions, acting as if the information has been downloaded automatically into his brain. I follow the directions meticulously.

Bret stands next to our finished project, all smiles. He places one hand on a steel bar and pats it like a beloved pet. "So, what do you think?"

"It looks ridden hard and put up wet." It's something my aunt used to say, and I like it. It fits.

Bret laughs and eyes the equipment like it's the best thing since peanut butter.

"I think this must be your first apartment."

His eyes flick to mine and then back to his new baby. "It is, actually… my first place."

"Did you just graduate then?" He looks about my age, but he seems older. Feels older. I can't believe he asked me to stay here with him. It should feel illicit and dangerous, but it doesn't, and I like that. The thing that worries me is that I'm perfectly aware of my faults and weaknesses, and on more than one occasion, my family has accused me of being high maintenance. I hope he doesn't regret his offer.

"From high school?" He coughs so I smack him squarely on the back.

"Unless you want to claim you already have your PhD, yeah. From high school."

"Well, actually, I didn't graduate. I… uh… got sick and had to quit."

"Meh. Graduating is highly overrated anyway." I file that piece of information away to ask about at another time. If he's insecure about it, I'll have to make sure he knows I couldn't care less. "So, about your family? I already told you about mine."

He looks up so slowly I actually stop what I'm doing—which isn't much—and give him my full attention. As he gazes into my eyes, I swear he's about to divulge some terrible secret, but then he walks over to his bed and flops down, crossing his ankles. He still has his shoes on. Shaking his head, he says, "Don't have one. Not anymore."

That's it? No other information? Why so secretive? Another thing to ask about at a later date, when we're better friends.

So many people have lost their families. I'm not surprised he's alone, and I count myself lucky to still have mine, disconnected as it is. I have an aunt, a sister, and a boatload of cousins. I don't count my dad. I hate him and will never forgive him for what he did to Brecken.

"Tell me about your aunt. How is she doing?" he asks as though he just read my mind.

Weird, because I can't remember even mentioning her to Bret, but maybe I did. With everything that's happened in the last few days, and with how tired I am at the moment, everything is blurring together. "She's fine, but I don't live with her anymore. She's too strict, and I have more important things to worry about."

"Like what?"

"Like training to be a Cazador." I punch him in the arm, but not too softly. Don't want to seem like a wimp. Hopefully, he'll take the hint and change the subject. I love my family and miss them terribly, but I can't think about them without heartache ensuing. That would make me a useless Cazador.

"And your dad? Because of what happened, you don't see him at all?"

Okay, now he's digging. It's not like I'm too dense to notice. In this world, the thing that keeps people alive is privacy. People don't share personal information, and nobody asks. That's how I like it. "What's up with all the questions?" I walk over to my side of the apartment and fall down on my bed, hoping to send the signal that I'm done playing get-to-know-you.

He releases a breath and nods. "I get it. I didn't get along with my dad either, so I was just curious about yours."

"It's not about getting along. It's about him murdering my brother." The heat of tears presses against the back of my eyes. That's the whole reason I don't want to discuss it. I will *not* cry.

Bret lies there, staring, his jaw slack, and then a terrible look of aching fills his eyes. There are no words he can say that will make it better though. I've already cried a thousand tears over this. I've already replayed it in my mind, over and over. I wish I could put my dad out of his misery, like he did to Brecken.

He convinced the police that Brecken had died of complications from leaving the hospital early, but I know the truth—that he waited until they were alone so he could do the deed without prying eyes. My dad left the next day and never came back. Not even to check on us.

I hate him.

All I want now is a place to call my own, with friends who love and accept me as I am. I never dreamed it was possible until I met Bret. He makes me feel like there's no secret I can't tell him, no flaw he won't accept. He seems like the perfect guy, and for a moment, I actually entertain the thought that maybe he could be.

I shake my head, pushing that train of thought away. "Well, I'm going to read for a bit."

Grabbing the folding divider that leans against the wall, I open it up to give myself some privacy. Once I'm back on my bed, tears spring to my eyes and I bury my face in my pillow. I don't make a sound. I can't show Bret how horribly it hurts to think about my dad. I've built a wall where he is concerned, and I'm not about to let it come crashing down now.

As hard as I try, I can't control the hiccupped sobs that escape. A few moments later, the mattress dips and a heavy weight presses against my side. He places a hand on my back, but I don't roll over. Crying in front of him—again—feels too raw and exposing. I can't let him see into my heart this soon into our relationship. Especially after last night. Surely, he already regrets his offer to let me live here.

"Shhh," he whispers kindly. "It'll be all right."

The warmth in his voice turns me against my will. There are tears in his eyes also, and my heart catches. I reach out and wipe the tears from his cheeks, wanting to comfort him even though I tried to deny him the same thing. In the next moment, I'm in his arms, and mine are wrapped tightly around him.

The moment of catharsis has no frame of time. It just is. We exist inside our own bubble of time, our hearts aching for all we've lost and all we've endured. I hold onto him as though he is the only thing keeping me from falling over the precipice of insanity, and truth be told, maybe he is. I've had no one for so long, no one who really loves me, that I've forgotten what it's like when someone does.

The fragile moment lingers.

If I move, it will shatter into a million pieces of glittering glass. Closing my eyes, I will it away. That moment when we'll part and I'll feel the frigid draft of loneliness again, wrapping me in its isolating arms. I squeeze my eyes shut, keeping those foolish feelings at bay. Oh, to stay in this place forever, where I only feel loved and wanted—that fairy-tale land where everyone has a loving mother, father, brothers, and sisters. Nobody is sick, and nobody is alone. Everyone has what they need, and there is only kindness.

But that place isn't real. Not even in my dreams anymore. My mind refuses to let me dwell there. I have to come back to the real world where people are capable of beating someone within an inch of their life just to take their loaf of bread. Where women are raped and children are abused because that's what demons do. I came back to this world because I have to stop the evil from continuing, creating nightmares for other children, like my sister Sophie.

I'm a barricade.

I am a Cazador.

I pull back even though I don't want to because if I don't, my heart will turn to mush.

Bret smooths my hair away from my tearstained face, and the adoration and delight I see in his eyes can't be denied. Does he truly care for me so much? My heart swells and I lean forward, pressing my lips to his.

13

Brecken

Stunned beyond belief, I freeze, my sister's lips pressed to mine. In my wildest dreams, I never imagined anything like this happening. All this time, I've only thought about how cool it would be to live with family again. I never suspected I'd give the wrong impression, and I mean a *really* wrong impression.

I pull back gently, trying to mask my horror. But from the look in Heidi's eyes, she can see it plainly in my expression.

Her eyes widen and her face drains of color, and then it turns a bright shade of crimson. She jerks away with a screech of dismay and jumps from the bed, grabbing her jacket as she flees the apartment, the door slamming behind her. She doesn't even let me explain. No wonder she has trouble with boys.

I sit on her bed, immobile, wanting to shriek myself, the wheels of my mind grinding, trying to pinpoint the exact moment when it all went wrong. I heard her crying even though she'd tried to hide it. Her sobs had broken my heart, and I'd felt the pull to comfort her, like I have so many times in the past. I can't stand to see her in pain, and I'd wanted her to feel there was someone who cares, someone who loves her.

I groan, rubbing my face in frustration, picturing her expression in my mind, the pure joy glowing in her eyes just before she kissed me. I am so stupid. Beyond stupid... *will she come back?*

I leap from the bed and run to the door, throwing it open. Heidi is nowhere in sight, nor can I hear her sneakers beating down the stairs. Leaning over the railing, I search down the four flights. She has already disappeared.

Pulling the door shut behind me, I go in search of her, around the block and then to the church because it seems a likely place for her to go. The Cazadors are her only friends that I know of. Who else would she run to?

I fight the urge to grow frantic. I don't want to lose Heidi just when I've gotten her back, gotten her to trust me. I mean, it was only a kiss. It's not the end of the world. And just because I was surprised doesn't mean anything. She has no idea why I reacted the way I did. She doesn't know she's my sister. She doesn't know if I have a girlfriend or not. Maybe I can tell her I'm gay. I can fix this.

I run the few blocks to the church. Dean sits on the front porch steps, a gray pillar supporting his back, his pencils spread out beside him as he draws, a rainbow of color in a depressingly drab landscape.

"Hey!" I call as I run up, out of breath. "Is Heidi here?" I lean over, resting my hands on my knees, trying to fill my lungs.

Dean glances up and shrugs, frowning and shifting his hips. "Haven't seen her."

He looks pretty dejected with his lips turned down and his shoulders slumped. Even the church seems to sag with his melancholy.

"What's wrong?" I slouch down next to him on the rough and worn cement. If Heidi isn't here, I don't know where to look. She'll have to come back on her own.

Dean continues to draw, sketching the tree that struggles to grow on the other side of the street. The twist of the gnarled branches and the quivering leaves are caught in still life by his gifted hand. His talent is remarkable, and I find myself envious. I would have loved a talent like this. As it is, all I seem to be good at is getting into trouble and seducing women, which can be thought of as the same thing.

That talent has backfired big time.

"Jag," he mumbles. "Ever since he heard Heidi moved in with you..." Dean's gaze darts to me and then back down at his drawing. He shrugs again, and it all becomes clear.

"He doesn't want her to live with me?" Dean is a year or so younger than Heidi. Sixteen, if I remember right, but he is a good guy. He's the kind of friend who will keep her grounded, and he'll always care about her, no matter what. I can see that. But this strange reaction leaves me stumped.

He shrugs again. There's something more here, but I doubt he'll confide in me, at least not right now.

"And neither do you, I take it." I lean back and rest my shoulders against the doorjamb, shaking my head in wonder, but before too many thoughts are able to form, Dean grabs a fistful of my shirt and jerks me forward. He's stronger than I gave him credit for. He doesn't say anything at first, just stares into my eyes with his jaw working as though he wants to spit something out. It's the first time I've seen such fire in his eyes, his emotions blazing, and I have no doubt about his sincerity. If only he'd be as passionate about killing demons.

"If you hurt her, I swear… I swear…"

"Dude, I get it." I gently shove his hands away and straighten my shirt. "I don't even like her that way."

A determined scowl draws his eyebrows into a V, and I swear I hear him growl as he grinds his teeth. "And why not? Is she not good enough for you?" He looks ready to attack again, so I hurry to put my hands up in surrender. If I doubted his loyalty to my sister before, it's no longer an issue.

"It's not that." I can't believe how this day is turning out. And it was so good just a half hour ago. I can't seem to win in any direction. I tilt my face to the heavens, willing Raphael to ignore what a mess I've made of things.

"She's perfect. Or can't you see that?" Dean sits back, deflated, and picks his sketchbook back up. "You're such an idiot."

"That's true."

With a snort, he starts drawing again, his pencil moving hastily, with angst. The slope of a jawline forms on the paper, and then the shading of dark hair around an oval face. Full lips and dimples materialize, and then dark eyes with long lashes, full of longing, with such depth of feeling… all done in black and white.

Heidi.

There's no mistaking her. The rendering is filled with humor and ache all at the same time. He has caught her perfectly. It's stunning. How did he do it so quickly?

"Wow."

"Yeah," he answers.

"Well, if you see her…"

"Yeah."

We sit in uncomfortable silence, probably hoping the other will leave first, and then when I am finally about to get up, the door behind us opens. Jag steps out, his eyes jerking to mine in unexpected surprise.

His demeanor isn't much different from Dean's, his gaze drilling a hole through me. I brace myself for an attack because it doesn't take a genius to figure out I'm not wanted here. I rise to my feet and dust off my pants.

"Why are you here?" he barks, straightforward and right to the point as usual. "Your own place not exciting enough?"

"Hey man, we're on the same team."

"You'll never be on my team." He elbows past me, shoving his hands deep into his pockets, his shoulders hunched as he stomps to the sidewalk. Stopping suddenly, he turns around. "You can call yourself a Cazador, but do it on your own. I don't want you with me. I don't trust you."

I know his words came from a place that isn't only jealousy, but also wounded pride. He thinks I'm a demon, and he's not totally wrong. Do I still give off that vibe? I'm not perfect. I haven't totally proven myself. I'm not redeemed yet, not an angel, or even heavenly material. I still make mistakes, am tempted to lie at times, and I have no compulsion about killing… bad guys anyway, but I am still employed by heavenly angels. That has to count for something. That has to show a little bit.

I haven't dwelled on my decision to defect from the demons in a while, but my heart clings to that choice. I don't belong with them anymore. I want goodness in my life. I want to *be* good, but my choice didn't change me overnight. I still have tendencies, urges, and habits. Habits that are hard to break. But Raphael believes in me. Alisa believes in me, and she's waiting for me. I won't disappoint her. So if Jag still sees or feels a demon inside of me, there's nothing I can do about it. I'm doing my best.

But the way he stares at me now… it's as if he *looks* for reasons to hate me, and now he has found another. He doesn't want to include Heidi in his gang, but he doesn't want me to include her either.

"That's totally fine. Heidi and I will start our own group, and you're more than welcome to join us whenever you'd like." I say this mainly to Dean, but I doubt he'll take me up on the offer. Not if he wants to stay in Jag's good graces. But there's a flicker of interest in Dean's expression even as he shakes his head.

"Well," I say. "The offer is always open… to both of you."

Stepping down from the porch, I walk away, knowing they are both staring at my back. I don't know what more I can do. Raphael and Michael want me to charm my way into the Cazadors. So far, I've made everyone hate me.

I don't really pay attention to where I'm going. I don't need to get home, and nightfall is still a few hours away. The rumble in my stomach demands attention, so I cross the street and head toward a busier part of town.

I stop at a hot dog stand and buy two, the tangy scent of pickles and onions making my stomach sing and my mouth salivate. There is no one at home to cook for tonight, so I take the easy way out. Loading up the buns with catsup and relish, I sit down on the curb to scarf my ultra-unhealthy meal… alone.

14

Heidi

I hear their whole conversation as I hide inside the church, just on the other side of the door, and the fact that Bret came looking for me softens my resolve just a little. I'd vowed never to go back to his apartment, my humiliation too consuming. I don't know if I can possibly face him again.

I saw the look in his eyes when I kissed him, felt the stiffness of his arms and lips. He'd been stunned and mortified, and when that realization had finally sunk in, so had I.

I've never been so embarrassed in my life. I've also never been so forward either. Not ever. It wasn't my first kiss, but was it so awful? Does my breath smell bad? Does he find me repulsive? Does he think I'm loose? A slut? Or worse?

How will I face him? But I have to. All my stuff is at his apartment.

Bret gave nothing away as he visited with Dean on the front stoop. He didn't confide in him or ask for advice. He kept my humiliation secret, and for that, I could kiss him again.

Jag had come upstairs and saw me crouched there, hiding like a coward. He'd stood there, watching me, waiting for me to look into his castigating eyes. If there is one thing he can't tolerate, it's a chicken. Groaning inwardly, I'd looked away, but he didn't say anything. When I did chance to glance up at his face, his expression wasn't one of condemnation, but pity, which is worse. His lips parted as though he might speak. I was sure he was going to gloat because I'd come here in tears, hours after moving in with Bret. He could tell me, *I told you so.*

"I'm sorry," he said instead, his eyes filled with sympathy… for about one second. He didn't ask why I hid there, what I was doing at his church, or when I was going to leave. He'd just opened the front door and left me in peace.

And here I sit in utter disbelief. Jag skipping an opportunity to embarrass me? That is a surprisingly kind act. I'd heard it was possible, and I know he's kind to Dean, brotherly even, but I've never seen him in an act of benevolence myself. I slump against the wall, letting these thoughts percolate in my mind.

After a moment, I peek out of the long, thin window by the door. It's mostly obscured by dirt and dust, but I can see that Bret is no longer out there. Standing, I dust off my pants and open the door. Jag is nowhere to be seen either, so it's just Dean and me.

I like Dean. He's the little brother I never had. Kind, patient, caring, and would give you the shirt off his back, even if it's ratty and see-through. I trust him, which is more than I can say about any other males of the species.

Plopping down, I take Bret's vacated spot with a sigh. Dean glances up, but he goes right back to drawing. He keeps the pad turned away, so I can't see what he's working on, but I'm not curious anyway. I'm too consumed with my own problems at the moment.

"So, you want to tell me what that was about?" he asks.

"No." The last thing I want to do is admit my stupidity, even if Dean is the only person who probably won't judge my poor decision-making skills.

"Oh, come on. It can't be that bad. What could make the Mighty Heidi fall?" He laughs and then says, "What did Bret the Brave do now?" I love Dean's penchant for doling out nicknames, and I've always enjoyed the one he gave me. It makes me smile.

The crook of his lips tells me he's watching me from hooded lids. I roll my eyes, glancing away.

"Come on. Tell me."

Taking a deep breath, I debate what to do. It wouldn't hurt to have someone to confide in, and Dean is as close to a girlfriend as I have at the moment. Maybe he can give me some sound advice.

"Fine. I kissed Bret, and he acted like I had the plague." I chance a furtive glance to gauge his reaction, which is one I don't expect. I'd expected a chuckle or good-natured ribbing, like I was one of the guys. What I get is completely different.

"Wha… what?" He stares at me, his forehead creased in dismay.

"Dean, is it that surprising? It's not like I don't like boys. Geez."

"No, uh… it's not that. I just can't believe—uh… he's an idiot," he says finally, a blush creeping up his neck like mercury in a thermometer.

"Yeah. I guess." He isn't helping me feel any better.

"Any normal guy would give his right arm to have a chance to—uh… to kiss you." His pink cheeks grow a deeper shade of red, and his ears join in the traitorous reaction. I doubt he's ever even kissed a girl, and it doesn't surprise me that it embarrasses him to say the word *kiss* out loud. He blushes as easily as taking a breath. It makes him sweet. It makes me protective.

"Guess he's not normal," I say with a chuckle, wishing it were true. "He's probably gay."

"Yeah," Dean says, a little more animated.

He looks a little too satisfied and I shrug, not wanting to get attached to this explanation in case, somehow, it isn't true. Because if Bret turns out to be straight, then it *is* just me he can't stomach.

"So, if you're uncomfortable going back to your place right away, you can totally stay here with me. We can hang." His words come out in a drawl, his arms out, and his fingers in *hang loose* signs. His smile stretches, radiating, his front, crooked tooth endearing rather than distracting. I can't say no to his offer. Since the Rift, my life has been isolated and lonely. I can't bring myself to leave him, sitting here alone like a waif on this dilapidated porch.

"I'd love to spend the day with you." I reach over to hug him around the neck as I would a lost puppy. "What should we do?" There are a million things I can think of. Most of them I'd rather do alone… like go to the used book store and browse for a new book, take a long, relaxing bath in Bret's new bathtub, find some new clothes to hunt in, maybe some new weapons.

Dean isn't really into shopping, which is obvious from the outfit he wears—ratty jeans with holes in both knees, a plaid, button-down shirt that is so thin it's see through, and shoes that are wrapped in duct tape to keep them together. I make a mental note to anonymously buy him a new outfit. He won't take it otherwise.

"Hmm. Well, I'm supposed to go to the park and draw. It's my job now, you know." He winks and I smile, knowing how much money he is bound to make doing that. "Or… we could go to the park and get a hot dog, and then go to the river and soak our feet in polluted water. Nothing is too good for my girl." He flashes me an ardent grin. "Or maybe we could go down to Main Street and listen to music, but there's music in the park too."

"How about we go back to my place?" The one I'd vowed never to return to. "And then I can show you our new workout machine. It's totally cool. You'll love it! I could show you some exercises, and then you could spot me or something." Even though it's still cool outside, it will quickly warm up and tar will soon be oozing on the asphalt. The thought of being outside when the heat wave hits is less than exciting. My idea is sounding better and better. Plus, Dean needs to build muscle and put on a few pounds.

"Do you think Bret will mind?"

"It's my place too, and he likes you." I wink at him, and he throws his pencil at me. I catch it in the air. Yeah. I'm that cool. "It's a good thing this has a dull point or I'd have to kill you. Nobody stabs me without punishment."

"Well, at least I can go to my death saying I tried." He stuffs the notebook into the backpack at his feet.

Growling in mock rage, I jump at him, but he's quick and already sprinting down the sidewalk. I chase after him, but the only thing I catch is the sound of his bubbling laughter as he leaves me in his wake.

15

Dean

A change is coming. I can feel it deep in my bones—like the way my grandad's arthritis acts up when a storm is on the horizon—or used to… when he was alive. I don't know if I should be scared or excited.

The Cazadors are splitting into two groups, and I don't like it. I want to include Bret and Heidi in ours. Owen and Doug do too. Will they drift over to Bret's group, leaving Jag and me on our own? Jag would probably like that better, but we need to stick together. That's also a feeling I have. I need to somehow convince our dark leader to let Bret and Heidi stay with us. I am probably the only one who can do it. He doesn't listen to anyone else.

But I don't want to think about Jag now. I want to think about Heidi. She's a soft breeze over a calm, summer ocean, the crispness of a warm, spring morning. I jump at the chance to spend time with her.

But the thought of her kissing Bret… there just aren't words to describe the stab of jealousy that goes through my chest when I hear those words. That, too, is a bone-deep ache, so I plaster on a smile to prove it doesn't matter.

We reach her apartment, and I follow her up four flights of stairs. I can't imagine hauling groceries that far. I had that job for a while, and now, wherever I go, I think about it out of habit. It makes me grateful for where I live now, even though it's a total dive. I like our church. It's conveniently located and feels safe. It's God's house and I feel Him there, like He's watching over us or something. Maybe it's just a habit. My parents were deeply religious. I'd like to believe they went somewhere better when they died, and that I'll join them someday.

I am also grateful for my new job of drawing pictures for people in the park. I charge a couple of bucks per picture, and that keeps us in food without having to steal. I'm tired of stealing.

Jag wasn't thrilled with the idea, but then, he never is thrilled with my ideas. He acts as if he has to protect me at all times, like I'm a child or something. I'm done relying on him to pay my way through life.

Heidi's apartment door is locked, and it takes a full minute to unlock it with all the extra deadbolts Bret installed. Talk about paranoid.

With a flourish, she throws open the door and steps inside, inviting me to follow. It's wide-open space, with huge, wooden beams and metal girders crossing the ceiling. The borders are wood paneling, painted white, and one wall is floor-to-ceiling windows.

I love it immediately, and another stab of jealousy twists through me. This is way better than the church, but there isn't enough room for a third person, not that I'd ever leave Jag anyway. The corner, across from the front door—that could easily be considered part of the living room—has to be Heidi's. I doubt Bret would place hot-pink scarves over his lamp or a Robin's-egg blue—my favorite shade—comforter over his bed.

A black-and-white, four-paneled shoji screen leans against the wall, and I exhale a breath I didn't know I was holding. At least she'll have a modicum of privacy when that's up.

It's one thing to share an apartment with a guy, and another to share one with no walls. All sorts of thoughts run rampant through my mind, and I pray that Bret really is gay. Can he see through that screen if the lights are just right? I hold in a groan and make my way over to her corner.

"Heidi, this is awesome! I love your… your room?" I raise my eyebrows in question, gesturing playfully to the eight-by-eight corner.

A furry rug lies beside the bed, and a cheap copy of Monet's *Water Lilies* hangs on the wall above the head. A scuffed armoire that has seen better days stands against the wall at the foot of the bed, and the whole thing screams *Heidi*. Where did she find the money to do this? As far as I know, she's as poor as I am, which is dirt poor. Maybe Bret paid for it.

She stands at the foot of her bed, the windows illuminating her skin with natural sunlight. The look on her face catches my breath as her lips curl into a smile. With her thick, mahogany hair tumbling over her shoulders and her eyes crinkling in happiness, I have to capture her. Just. Like. This.

Immediately, I pull out my pad of paper and plop down on her bed. Her laughter bubbles when she realizes what I'm doing. "No! Stay there, just like that," I command. "This'll be quick. I promise."

She moves into a supermodel pose, and then lifts the back of her hand to her forehead as though faint. Letting herself fall, she sprawls on top of the bed. Seeing her there, so beautiful, so comfortable, smiling up at me… I would give anything to be able to throw my pencil down and press my lips to hers… a kiss that would last all afternoon. I can picture the taste of her mouth. Raspberry lemonade, like the Chapstick she always wears. My mouth waters at the thought, and I hide my face so she can't see.

The moment stretches until my heart is near bursting, my hand racing to catch the light… and then our reverie is shattered the moment the door bursts open. Heidi and I jump, as though caught doing something clandestine, our eyes riveted to Bret's, whose are wide with surprise and relief.

"You're back?" He's out of breath and panting. In three long strides, he is at the foot of her bed. He grabs her arm and pulls her up, wrapping his arms tightly around her. "I'm so glad you came back. You have no idea."

Heidi's arms come up and wrap around Bret's back. He doesn't let go and for a moment, they just breathe, frozen in that scene of tenderness. I've stopped breathing completely and all I can do is stare, wishing I were the guy who held her, who felt the softness of her cheek pressed to mine.

In the split second before anything else happens, I imagine in my mind what will come next. She'll continue to hug him, dramatically mewling into his neck like a kitten, saying something about never leaving him again. They'll gaze into each other's eyes like actors in an old, sappy, black-and-white movie, and then he'll kiss her. Long and deep. Their bodies pressed together in passion.

My stomach twists, and the ache I feel inside is all consuming. I think I might actually die of a broken heart. Or throw up.

Before either of them can say anything, I rush to gather my things, to throw them into my pack willy-nilly, not even caring if they break or smear against each other. The pencils roll across the bed and onto the floor, prolonging my agony.

I know the truth in my heart. He is someone she could love. Someone courageous, valiant, and strong, who doesn't flinch at killing demons, but goes in with both guns blazing… or runed daggers blazing, whichever the case may be. He's powerful and passionate on so many levels. The reality of it slaps me in the face.

I will never be that.

And that is what she wants.

Not an artist.

I can't be here. Not with Bret, at least. He has changed the whole ambiance of the room. That fast. Like a dark cloud, heavy with rain, he has ruined my day. You can't paint in the rain.

"No! Don't go yet." Heidi's eyes entreat me, but it feels too weird, and I feel too pathetic.

"I'll come back. Promise." I give her my best smile as my heart wrenches inside me, trying to keep some semblance of pride as I hurry out the door. I shut it quickly behind me, breathing deeply and taking the stairs two at a time, my shame and humiliation wafting behind me like a stench I can actually smell.

I know now how she felt being rejected by Bret, putting herself out there and then having him trample her heart. I didn't do that exactly, but it feels like it. She has to know how I feel. She can't be that blind. Surely, she is pretending not to know, to spare my feelings. That makes it even worse.

I slam out of the main door of the building, reliving it all in my mind once again. Their embrace, Bret's fervent words of adoration… I even add a passionate kiss, just to torture myself a little bit more. I groan out loud, not even paying attention to where I'm going until I crash into the chest of a huge, burly man who catches me by the arms to steady me.

A wide, slimy smile spreads across his lips as he gazes down at me, not releasing his grip. I recognize him immediately. He had my neck in the crook of his elbow not long ago. We should have never let him go—not that we had much of a choice. The odor of decay permeates around him. His body is already starting to decompose. He must be pushing it hard to make it weaken so quickly, and he isn't wearing his snazzy business suit today.

"Hey. I remember you." His smiles widens, and his hands squeeze tighter on my biceps.

It's moments like these when I wish I worked out.

"Where have you and your hunter friend been hiding?" He draws me closer.

Once again, I am in the wrong place at the wrong time. "Dude, let go," I demand, yanking on my arm to no avail. His hold is an iron clamp and his fingers overlap his thumb because they are so long. It can't be that my arms are so alarmingly thin.

"Oh, I don't think so," he drawls. "You have a debt to repay. Your partner killed my friend. Remember?"

Adrenaline races to my extremities and my pulse pounds in my head, making me feel lightheaded and hyperaware. How could I have been so careless as to let this happen? I yank my arm again and study the face beneath the face. The gray outline of the very thing I've run from and refused to kill for the last five years. Even in the bright sunlight, I can see him. The *real* him. The dead, black holes of his eyes, the slits for his mouth and nose, the grayness of his form.

Dread seizes me, heavy and thick, right there on the street in broad daylight. What is he doing out during daytime hours anyway? My stomach lurches, and nausea bubbles inside me. I have to get away. I throw a clumsy punch with my free hand and drop my pack, but it's the least of my worries because Brutus has me by both arms and is dragging me down the street. Like a child in his grasp, it doesn't seem to matter how much I scream, kick, or punch. It doesn't faze him.

And nobody comes to my rescue.

He shoves me through a service door at the end of a nearby alley. There is no one around to see me slump into near unconsciousness when the guy's meaty fist slams into my face… three times.

"Shut up!" he growls, towing me like a rag doll down a set of cement stairs into a basement cellar, my shoes thumping on each step. A lone, dull lightbulb swings from the ceiling, making me feel like I'm on a roller coaster going around and around and around. Dizziness overwhelms me, and my nausea comes to fruition all over the front of me. He doesn't care, and at this point, neither do I. My vision is beyond fuzzy and my face throbs.

He drops me onto a cot in some back room that's about the size of a closet. The pain in my face blossoms, and blood flows freely over my lips and into my mouth. The metallic taste triggers my gag reflex again.

"Great," he mumbles, walking away and trying to wipe his clothes clean. But then he stops by the door and turns, looking at me. The light behind him creates a silhouette, and I only see a gray outline, resembling the demon inside him. "You'll be a rare treat, boy. A rare treat. Get some rest. You'll need it."

"Wait… what?" This can't be happening. I can't really be here, held hostage by demons. I roll over and face the wall. A foul odor pervades the room, or maybe it's the pillow, soured by other sick and bloody victims. I try to breathe through my mouth, but the sick feeling remains… in my stomach and in my heart.

16

Dean

Waking up is like clawing through a thick web of spider silk. Sticky and difficult, not to mention exhausting. I almost give up my adventures as Frodo and go back to sleep, too tired and in pain to keep trying, but I feel lucky to have woken up at all.

I don't know how long I've been out, and my face still throbs. I'm sure I have a concussion from the three punches to my face. My nose, which is swollen and tender to the touch, is probably broken.

I have never been attacked like this before. *Ever*. Jag has always protected me. I wish he were here now with his strength, bravery, and his ability to find a solution to any situation. The only thing I'm capable of is drawing a picture of this cell, but I've lost the tools of my trade. They lie on a sidewalk somewhere outside Heidi's apartment if they haven't already been stolen. How will I ever replace them?

Could this really be chalked up to being in the wrong place at the wrong time? Does my belief that *everything happens for a reason* still stand in my mind? What reason could there possibly be for this?

My cell lets in only a minimal amount of light through the small window on the door. There is no handle on the inside, so I'm not getting out unless they want me to. With a colossal amount of effort, I roll from the cot to my feet, almost losing my balance as dark explosions dance in my vision. The pounding in my head reaches a pinnacle of pain.

Stumbling to the door, I press my face into the opening

and strain to see down the hallway in either direction. Darkness shrouds everything at both ends… at least as far as I can tell, which isn't far. There are no windows, so I have no idea if it's morning, noon, or night, but my body screams for sleep, so I guess it's still night.

There are at least six other doors in the hallway. All of them with a cutout window not big enough to escape through. I'm not sure if the other rooms are occupied, but I hope to find out.

"Hey!" My voice is rough and scratchy from too much blood and phlegm. Immediately, a coughing fit ensues and the hacking is eye-wateringly painful. Did I get hit in the throat too? I don't remember. The pain all blurs together, and I yearn for one tiny sip of cool water as I rest my head against the door.

There's no answer from the dark rooms in the hall. I'm alone. What a dismal thought. Not that I wish this kind of hell on anyone else, but this place looks used, like they bring people here regularly. There's dried blood and puke on the floor and walls. Some of it is probably mine.

Why do they bring people here anyway? For torture? For experiments? Once again, I pray for a miracle that Jag will find me. As soon as he notices I'm missing, which will be immediately—because we always hunt together—he'll set out to find me, although he will have no idea where to look. He'll try the park first, thinking I'm there, drawing faces of bored old men and demanding children. But I won't be, and it will get dark. Then he'll worry.

With a tightness in my chest that is even more pronounced than before, I make my way back to the cot, falling onto its stiff canvas with a grunt, my brain bouncing off the walls of my skull, new black stars bursting in my vision. Groaning and dizzy, I let my body relax into sleep once again. I don't have the energy to wonder about tomorrow.

Letting my eyes close, I let thoughts of Heidi envelop me. Maybe, if I let myself dream of her, these walls won't seem so close and smothering, and my throat won't feel so dry.

I picture her sitting beside me on this smelly, old cot, telling me to buck up and stop dwelling on the negative. Her face swims in my mind, her eyes bright, and her mouth close to mine.

With a slow and heavy-labored effort, I awake, maybe hours later. I'm not sure. I know right where I am before my eyes even open. An ominous sound has awakened me—a screeching, like an unoiled metal door, or maybe a cot scraping across the cement floor.

With a groan, I roll over, my bruises screaming in protest. I almost go back to sleep, hoping to forget where I am. But I drag myself to the door. There's a fresh, new odor I can detect. Metallic. And it coats the back of my throat when I breathe.

"Hello?" I call, but I get no answer. Someone has to be close by. I didn't imagine that sound. Still, all the cell doors are closed and the hall is dark.

Slinking back to my cot, I lie down, folding my arms around me and squeezing my eyes shut. For the millionth time in the last twelve hours, I'm afraid. Bone-deep terrified. What do the demons want with me? Is there any chance of escape? Are they going to just leave me here to starve to death?

If I know anything about demons, it's this—they'll do whatever it takes to break you or watch you scream. They don't care about killing as much as *enjoying* death. If they can't possess, they'll experiment to figure out what makes you immune to their influence.

I pray—again—that Jag will find me. It can't end this way. I can't die as a plaything for demons.

17

Brecken

I strap on my gear, my Nephilim dagger in its sheath, a runed dagger in my boot and another strapped to my thigh. I'm dressed in black, hoping to be harder to spot in the shadows.

Heidi waits on the other side of the room, also dressed in battle gear. After Dean left, we stared at each other for a moment. She wouldn't let me explain or apologize. We haven't discussed the kiss, which is fine by me.

She has her one runed dagger strapped to her hip. The one she stole from Jag. She faces the windows, staring out at the newly rising moon as she braids her hair into one long, dark plait. It hangs almost to her waist. As much as I hate to admit it, she should cut it off. Jag proved that point pretty well. With a determined expression, she grits her teeth, unaware that I watch her.

What is going through that complicated mind right now? Is she afraid? Anxious? Excited? As though she can sense my stare, she turns, glancing over at me, one slender eyebrow rising in question.

Slipping the runed dagger from its sheath on my thigh, I walk over and hold it out to her. "I'd like you to have at least two. You know. One for each hand."

Her eyes lift to mine, dark, ocean depths of surprise. "Seriously?" She reaches out reverently and takes the dagger from my fingers, examining its length, the carvings in the blade. "Why?"

I can't very well say, *because you're my sister and I worry about you*, so I say, "I have a ton. You'll actually be helping me by taking this one."

"Thank you."

I shrug it off, trying to act like it's no big deal. But it is. I can't stand the thought of her going ninja on a demon. I want to command her to stay home. To stay safe. "Sure. Not a problem."

She glances into my eyes, smirking, and then gestures to my weapon-covered body. "Are you sure you can spare it?" She goes about tucking the blade into her belt on her other hip.

"I'll manage." I stand there smiling stupidly at her, our old camaraderie having returned. She forgives easily, which I'm amazed and grateful for. It's something she didn't do well when she was younger. I'm proud of who she has become. Not only is she beautiful on the outside, but she has a warm, loving heart on the inside, which, considering her circumstances, is highly unexpected.

"Ready?" I walk over to the door. My hand is on the knob when a furious pounding from the other side startles me. I actually jump in fright, squeaking in surprise like a little girl. Recovering quickly, I hide my embarrassment by raising my finger to my lips to motion to Heidi to be quiet.

I slide my Nephilim dagger out and stand to the side of the door. It's probably an overreaction, and it's just Dean returning for some unexpected reason, but I'm not about to make a mistake. There are only a couple of people who even know I live here, after all.

With a flash of my fingers, I throw the door open, ready for a fight. Jag's arms are splayed out on either side of the door, his chest heaving with the effort to breathe, as though he dashed here at full speed without stopping. "Is Dean here?"

The surprise of seeing him stumps me for a moment. I never pictured him coming to my home, or even knowing where it is. His eyes flick to Heidi, who still stands by her bed, her mouth open and ready to speak. In a fraction of a second, Jag surveys our entire living space, ending with the two beds on either side of the studio apartment. His gaze comes back to mine, but I don't miss the sting in his expression. I don't understand why he even cares.

"Dean?" Heidi repeats, her brows pulling down into a frown. "He left a couple of hours ago. He didn't go back to the church?"

"Have you seen him?" Jag asks me pointedly, his face pasty white in spite of his exertion.

I shake my head. "Not for a few hours."

"He was supposed to be home a long time ago. We were going hunting. I've searched everywhere. He'd never leave like this."

"Did you check the park?" Heidi hurries to the door and pushes past Jag to look down over the stairwell. "We should split up and search."

"I'm sure he's fine. He's probably drawing or something." I'd seen his face when I walked in on him and Heidi. Adoration had been written all over it, too plainly to ignore. He loves her, just like everyone else, and I interrupted whatever had been brewing. I'm not sure how I feel about that. Dean is nice and everything, but I don't see Heidi ending up with him.

"He never stays out alone after dark!" Jag shouts at me, panic edging his voice. "Never! He's afraid of the demons. He can't even kill them."

There's an undeniable ferocity in his eyes, but not just that. Devastating fear and loss also. However, I still think he's jumping to conclusions. Dean is probably fine, holed up somewhere, nursing his wounds, thinking I won something he can't have. It's ridiculous really.

There's a possibility Jag is right though. We live in the hood, and demons prowl these streets at night. But when Dean left our apartment, it was light. What could have possibly happened in broad daylight? The demons hide in their holes until darkness comes. The light actually repels them. I remember the painfully itchy sensation from my old demon days, and a shiver runs through my body at how real and alive those recollections are.

"He could have gone to visit Doug or Owen, or even other friends," I suggest. Surely, he has other friends besides the Cazadors. He's social and vivacious. Positive about life and the future. He's the only one of us who is.

"He didn't. He wouldn't." Jag seems to deflate as he says these last words. Hope disappears in his eyes like a lightbulb being flipped off. He falls against the wall, his hands rubbing back through his hair, frustrated. "We have to find him. Please, help me," he says directly to me, pleading with me, as though he even has to ask.

"Of course." I lock the apartment door behind me. Heidi is already a couple of stories down, and we follow her, bursting out of the building's door together.

Night has fallen completely, and only a few streetlamps are lit. Most of the neighborhood is quiet; the only sounds are car horns or doors slamming.

We take off down the street.

Three hours later, we're back on the front porch of the church. Dean has not returned and we've searched every park, plaza, and mom-and-pop store that's open. It's almost one in the morning, and no one has seen or heard anything. Dean has disappeared. Truly and completely.

Jag slumps to the front steps, his head between his knees, his hands behind his head, his face hidden. He doesn't move or even twitch. He barely seems to be breathing, but when he finally lifts his face, it's twisted in anguish and filled with torment. "We have to find him. Someone took him. I know it."

Heidi and I stare down at him, unable to argue. It looks like he's right. My gut tells me the demons are behind this. Was it an innocent possession or did they know who Dean was and who he travels with? If news has spread of my arrival, *I* could be their true target, but I keep this information to myself.

"What should we do?" Owen asks. When they heard about Dean, there was no question who we'd be searching for tonight.

"Think back," I say to Jag. "Over the last few weeks, did anything unusual happen? Did you meet anyone strange or someone who might have seemed too interested in you and Dean? Has there been anyone hanging out by the church who you don't know?"

Shaking his head emphatically, he growls. "No! I told you already. There was nothing weird going on. Nothing strange." As he springs to his feet, his hairband slips from his ponytail and the long strands fall forward, hanging in his face. He starts pacing, his frustration a tangible energy around him.

"We'll find him," Heidi whispers, stepping close to Jag and placing her hand on his arm. I can't believe she's brave enough to try it. I expect him the snap at her like a wounded animal, but he stops and turns his face to hers, his eyes swimming with guilt. He places his hand over hers before walking into the church alone.

The rest of us stay on the porch, shuffling our feet, not knowing what to do. Doug kicks a rock across the street, his black Vans covered in dust, his hands stuffed deep into his pockets. The tightness in his face and shoulders knots his expression, his ebony skin glowing with perspiration in the moonlight.

Owen is still and quiet, staring up at the moon. He doesn't talk or offer ideas. He's just sad. And in his black Cazador clothing, he looks like a long, thin shadow, something I wouldn't want to meet in a dark alley. These boys really care about Dean. I can see it clearly. They're a family, and Dean is a central part of it.

With nothing more to say, I follow Jag into the church. He isn't in the chapel, so I take the stairs down to the basement. He's kneeling before his open trunk, holding a picture Dean drew of Jag and some girl. A candle flickers in the almost pitch black cellar, but I can tell the portrait is done in black and white, in pencil or charcoal, and is slightly smeared. Jag brushes his fingers over the aged, somewhat crinkled edges.

"He drew this a few years ago. Her name was Lily."

I step up behind him, leaning over his shoulder to get a better look. "She's beautiful. A friend, I take it?"

"Mm." Jag doesn't nod or shake his head. I sense he isn't reminiscing about the girl, but thinking of Dean and how he might never draw again.

Jag will never stop searching for Dean. He will learn the truth if it kills him.

18

Heidi

I'm so tired. So bone achingly tired.

We search almost the whole night for Dean, and when we are too exhausted to take another step, we head back to the church. After an hour there with Jag, the adrenaline leaves me, I can't stay awake for another moment. I don't want to leave, but we'll be no good in the morning if we don't get some rest. I let Bret take me home.

But sleep will not come.

I lie in my bed, reviewing my last moments with Dean before he left my apartment, how his whole demeanor had changed when Bret came in. His expression of happiness had fallen, and the light in his eyes had disappeared. He hadn't been able to escape fast enough.

I should have run after him. I shouldn't have let him leave alone. He is one of my dearest friends, and I feel like I betrayed him. I can't even imagine what happened, but my imagination puts up a good fight. Scenarios run through my mind, one after another, each one worse than the other.

Gangs run the streets, not just demons, and someone could have attacked him, mugged him, or even killed him. But in my heart, I know… I know what my mind won't accept… that Dean has been taken by the one thing we are most afraid of. Otherworldly beings we don't understand. Beings with no conscience. Beings that use and throw our human bodies away like refuse.

What will they do to him? Has one possessed him somehow? Could he be walking around the city right now, a meat suit to some bigwig fiend? Groaning, I roll over. I haven't slept in a normal bed for a year. My mattress has been hard cement or grass, my blanket, a coat. *This* bed—which should be wonderful and comfortable—keeps me awake with its plushness. And I can't enjoy it knowing Dean is shivering in the dark, alone and frightened, or worse...

Moonlight glows through our wall of windows. Looking over to Bret's side of the apartment, I see the outline of him in his bed, the ridge of his shoulder and hips. He's faced away, his breath slow and even.

How can he sleep so peacefully? Why isn't he tossing and turning like me? But then, he doesn't know Dean like I do. He doesn't have a history with Dean like I do. I've known Dean for a few years. Watched him grow and mature. I've seen him laugh and cry, pout and argue. He is my brother in the truest sense of the word. I can't even imagine what Jag is going through right now. He's alone at the church. There is no way he is sleeping right now.

And since I can't sleep...

Slowly, I slip from my bed and pull on the clothes I wore the day before. They're on the floor and easy to spot at the foot of my bed. The hard part will be unlocking all the dead bolts without making a sound.

I strap on both my runed daggers—the one I stole from Jag and the one Bret gave me—and then tiptoe to the door. Quietly, while holding my breath, I turn the top lock. It clicks back with barely any sound at all. The second one is a little stiffer and takes some muscle, but it too pulls back softly. The third lock is stiff in its slot and harder to turn. I put some grit into my efforts and it clunks back so loudly that I freeze, not even daring to breathe as I wait for Bret to awaken. I stare across our tiny apartment at his still form.

He doesn't move.

Now for the chain. Slowly... oh, so slowly, I unhook the brass nob and set it gently against the wall. So far, so good. Brushing a strand of hair back behind my ear, I let myself inhale for one moment, my pulse pounding in my chest and throbbing in my forehead. Surely, Bret can hear me hyperventilating. He'll stop my flight to the church for sure. I just know it. Even though

I hardly know him, he acts like a… a big brother.

A strange rush—like chills—erupts at that thought. I glance back over at him and then shrug off those crazy feelings.

Grasping the door handle, I hesitate. I can't remember if it's noisy or quiet. I've come so far, undoing all these locks. Will this last turn of the nob be my undoing? Will it squeal and bring Bret out of his slumber? I hold my breath and twist… It turns without a sound. The gods are smiling down on me.

Releasing the breath I'm holding, I rest my head against the doorjamb for a moment. I can't believe I made it this far. Pulling the door open only a fraction, I slip out silently, locking it behind me. I can't leave Bret here without any protection at all. The deadbolts won't be set, but there is only so much I can do.

I have no idea what time it is, but my guess is that it's around four AM. The moon is full, and it lights the streets almost as bright as any streetlamp. A lone girl at night is a target. *Always.* And just because I have skills doesn't mean I'll stand a chance against a group of thugs, so I stick to the shadows. I'm not stupid… but I am afraid. I don't love being out here alone.

All is quiet, and I arrive safely at the church. Standing on the darkened porch, I wait, not sure what to do at this point. Should I knock? What if Jag, somehow, has finally fallen asleep? He needs it, and he has to be exhausted. I shouldn't wake him up. I try the handle. It's locked. I glance down the street both ways, realizing what a stupid mistake I've made. I shouldn't be here. What would I say to him anyway? He doesn't like me. He probably, in reality, will tell me to leave.

I turn around, resting my hand on one of the peeling, wooden pillars by the front door. Yeah, this was definitely a mistake. I'll go back home and chalk this up to crazy female hormone fluctuations. Just when I'm about to step off the porch, the door opens behind me. It's so unexpected that I can't stop my automatic reaction of screaming and striking out.

Luckily, Jag has quick responses too. He grabs my wrist, instantly holding it away from his face, but not letting go.

"Heidi?" His brown eyes are wide in the darkness and

shadows hollow out his cheeks, but his hand is warm on my arm and his bare chest glows in the moonlight. Seeing him like this… open, vulnerable, human… he seems… beautiful.

Something deep in my heart lurches, and I can't swallow. I stand there like an idiot, staring at his disheveled hair. My mouth is open and empty, just like my brain. What would he do if I threw my arms around him, held his cheek to mine, and told him I cared and understood?

"Why are you here?" He looks down the street before pulling me inside the church. He locks the door behind us and picks up a glowing candle that sits on the sill.

"I… um… I was worried about you and thought… well, I thought maybe you wouldn't want to be alone. I figured you wouldn't be able to sleep." I shuffle my feet on the dusty floor and glance everywhere but at him.

He frowns, but he still hasn't let go of my wrist. "And Bret let you come here alone?"

I pull my arm away and rub my wrist that he was holding too tight. "He's not my dad, Jag. I don't have to ask his permission, and I'm certainly capable of taking care of myself."

He releases a tired sigh and sinks down onto one of the benches. "I don't want to fight, Heidi."

Neither do I, but it's what we do best. We can't be in each other's presence without bickering, competing, or wanting to throw punches. "Sorry. I just wanted to see if you were okay."

He smiles up at me then, patting the bench beside him. I sit, bewildered at what to do or say next. Jag and I have never really been alone together. Dean was always there to fill up the awkward silences. I don't know how to talk to Jag. I hadn't thought it through this far. We sit quietly for a few moments, playing with dust on the bench or invisible threads on our clothing.

"You should probably get some rest," I say finally. "Morning is coming, and you're going to be too tired to function." I smile, feeling unbelievably shy. I don't know what I was thinking when I came here. That Jag would suddenly turn into a different person and like me? That because of Dean's disappearance, we'd connect like never before? I guess I'd hoped these things would happen, but life never works out that way for me. Ever. I start to stand, but he stops me with a hand on my thigh.

"Please stay." He looks into my eyes with an expression I've honestly never seen on him before, the candle creating a halo of light around us. "You're exhausted too."

He can aggravate me more than anyone else, and yet, I feel drawn to him in a way I can't explain. Maybe it's animal magnetism or the way he makes me want to be better at everything. Or just being close to him in the dark. Maybe it's that we're alone for the first time ever.

The old church is silent around us, harboring deep shadows in every corner. If I were here alone, it would have totally creeped me out, but he is with me and it makes all the difference. He chases the phantoms away. Literally.

Jag takes my hand and stands. I rise with him, wondering what we're going to do next. He leads me down into his dark, makeshift bedroom in the basement cellar. His and Dean's sleeping bags lie on the floor, and he draws me down next to him.

I feel ill at ease, sitting with him on his sleeping bag like it's normal for us, and the thought that Jag doesn't even like me keeps screaming in my mind. The basement is even darker than the chapel, and the dusty cement walls look black in the candlelight. I keep my gaze on Jag and try to rein in all thoughts of ghosts and goblins. I'm safe with him. Nothing can hurt me here. He can protect me. He protects everybody. For some reason, the thought that I can protect myself never enters my mind.

He sets the candle on the chest behind him and then lies down, his head resting on his hand. His face is shrouded in shadow and the candlelight shines through his blond hair, outlining the edge of his jaw. He's smiling as he reaches out to take my hand again. "I'm glad you came over. I didn't feel like being alone."

I can't believe he would admit this to me. The great and powerful Jag doesn't want to be alone?

"What's wrong?" he asks.

He notices my nervousness. Of course he does. He notices

everything. Always. I laugh, embarrassed, unable to stop myself. I don't know how to act around him, and laughing is always my go-to reaction. And being alone like this on his bed...

"Nothing. It's just..." I look around at the unfathomable and haunting shadows. There are too may dark corners I can't see. How does he stand it?

I lie down since he's tugging on my arm to do so and scoot a bit closer, trying not to let my eyes dart toward the monsters that aren't there. The darkness plays tricks on my eyes, so I close them and just breathe. Some Cazador. Afraid of the dark.

Jag whispers, "Don't worry. Nothing will happen to you here."

"I know," I say just as softly.

"Come here." He pulls me closer, the scent of his hair and clothes surrounding me like a comforting blanket. I lay my head on his shoulder, and he wraps his arms around me. Being with him like this feels like a dream, like I've finally found the place I'm supposed to be. I'm suddenly grateful Bret didn't want a romantic relationship. It would have been a mistake. I know that now. There is definitely something strange and cool about Bret, but this feeling with Jag is different. It's always been there at the back of my heart, hidden. I see that now. Maybe that's why we fought so much, and why Jag resisted me too.

The fact that he wants me *now*, after rejecting me for so long... What changed? Was moving in with Bret the catalyst? Maybe that's what it took for Jag to realize he felt something more for me than annoyance.

For me, it was Dean's disappearance. I couldn't stand the thought of Jag being here alone with no one to love him, and I did... oh... no... I would never admit that out loud. *Ever*. I have strict rules about relationships. I've kept myself separate and alone on purpose. Every person I love seems to either betray me or die.

But this thing with Jag...

Now it doesn't matter how dark it is, or how scary the world has become. I feel safe in his arms. Taking a deep breath, I inhale the scent of *him*, earthy and male, still unable to believe I'm here with him… alone.

"What are we doing, Jag?" I don't want to ask. It will ruin the moment for sure, but I can't stand not knowing. Am I being played? Are his feelings as sincere as mine? I just don't think I can stand it if they aren't.

He's silent for a moment. I almost wonder if he is going to ignore me, but then he releases a sigh. I expect him to pull away, the moment destroyed, but instead, his arms tighten and he holds me closer. "I don't know. Do you want to go?"

I pull back just enough to look him in the eyes. Our faces are only an inch apart. The fact that his lips are so close to mine is enough to send my heart pounding.

I want him to kiss me.

And more than anything, in that moment, it feels like something will break inside me if he doesn't. "I don't want to be anywhere else."

His eyes soften, our hearts beating in unison. He leans forward, our mouths a breath apart, and yet he hesitates. But I feel the warmth of his skin, the heat of his touch as he waits… just like I do. When it seems I can't take the anticipation any longer, he closes the distance, his lips touching mine, feather light. So soft that I can do nothing but ache for more. But instead of deepening the kiss, which I know we both want, he groans and then rests his chin on my head, inhaling deeply. I snuggle into his chest and close my eyes, feeling safe for the first time in ages. He doesn't try anything else, even though he could have… and I would have let him.

I'm nowhere near rested when I wake, but finding myself alone in the basement, I quickly jump up. I have no idea what time it is, so I hurry up the stairs, feeling the stares of a thousand ghosts.

Light is streaming in between the board-covered windows. It's morning and late at that. With aching muscles, I fling open the front door. Jag had better not have left me here alone.

He sits on the front steps, drinking coffee from a Styrofoam cup. He hands me a second one that sits beside him. I'm not sure what to say to him, with my chest heaving and my expression post-alarm. *Good morning, and thanks for the awesome night? Why did you leave me alone in the pit of despair?*

In the light of day, it's weird between us, and I wonder if it will always be this way. I can't envision a future where it is otherwise. Last night was a miraculous interlude. An anomaly.

"Just in time," he says, handing the cup to me.

"Thanks." I sit down beside him, wondering why he looks so calm, as though our moment in time has not evaporated with the dew, but lingers like a mist. "You seem calm this morning."

Jag sighs, staring down at his hands.

I hurry to add, "I didn't mean it like… you weren't worried. I just thought you'd be panicking about Dean. You seem very relaxed."

He nods, taking a gulp from the Styrofoam cup in his hands. "I did wake up panicking. And I left early, searching the park until I found a demon."

"Really?" I take a sip from the cup he offers me. The coffee is hot and black. I prefer cream, but that costs more and Jag doesn't have much money. "Did you learn anything from it?"

"Not much. Only that a demon can be tortured for longer than I thought."

I don't want to picture that, so I keep my mouth moving. "So you came home?"

"I knew you'd be awake, and I didn't want you freaked out. I know you hate it here." There isn't any malice in his words. For the first time ever, I see the smile in his eyes. He's never been this easy with me. With Dean, sure, but not with anyone else. I keep waiting for the bubble to pop.

"So, are you ready to start searching again then?" I ask.

"No," he answers. "Not yet. Bret will be here any moment… as soon as he realizes you're not tucked safely in your bed."

But he isn't here yet. "Maybe he's a late sleeper."

"Let's hope."

I steal a glance at him through the long veil of my hair, and he is watching me, smiling when he catches my eye. I still can't believe he's looking at me like this, so… sweet and boyfriendly.

"So, why *did* you come over last night?" he asks, staring at his coffee, unable to meet my eyes. He doesn't like being vulnerable either.

"I told you." I brush my hair back behind my ears. "I thought you'd be worrying yourself sick. I was… um, worried too, I guess." I shake my head at the irony of it all. He should be running around, frantic, and I can't wrap my mind around the fact that he came back for me. He was worried about *me*, and he didn't want me to be afraid and alone in the church.

"I am worried." He holds his cup between his knees, his hands looking larger than I remember. And then I picture them holding my head against his shoulder and stroking my hair like he did last night. The heat of a blush creeps up my neck and cheeks.

Jag's eyes close for a moment, probably picturing the same thing, and he inhales deeply. "Dean was taken during the day. That means the demons are getting braver."

Okay. So he isn't thinking of me. "So where is this demon you found now?"

"Dead."

"Dead?"

"Yep." He takes another long gulp of coffee. No wonder he seems so calm and relaxed. He's already gotten his frustrations out, but he isn't being very forthcoming with the information he learned.

"So…?" I ask.

He turns to me, his smile widening. "There's a network of demons we never knew existed. And a hierarchy of leaders." He shakes his head. "This demon was a peon and didn't know any details other than the fact there was a big, secret powwow during the night and only the important demons were invited. I know it has something to do with Dean. I feel it. We just have to find this demon lair and get rid of them all."

I think about this and nod, sipping my breakfast. "So now what?"

"We find *another* demon. See if it knows more than the last one." He smiles, and I get the feeling he's going to enjoy hurting the bad guys. Torturing demons might be Jag's new calling.

I shiver.

19

Dean

The clanking of keys rattles outside my cell door. I've been lying here for a while, my throat growing scratchier as the minutes tick by. "Who's there?" I call, but it only comes out as a croak.

The door squeaks open and Brutus—the guy who kidnapped me—steps in. Yeah, I gave him a nickname. It's my thing after all. A dim light shines on him from behind. He looks bigger than before, if that's even possible.

"Time to get up," he says with a smile in his deep, resonating voice.

When I don't move quickly enough, he grabs me by the arm, yanking me from the metal cot. I bang my knee on a steel bar and barely find my feet before he starts hauling me out of the room. At the end of the hall, we pass through the storage room with the stairs that lead out to the alley.

We don't go out that door though, but skirt through the storage room that's lined with shelves of canned goods. Between two of the tall shelves, we stop at what looks like a cement wall. Brutus reaches behind some canned peaches and flicks a switch. The cement wall screeches, sliding open to reveal a long, black corridor.

The oppressive darkness in that space stretches its inky fingers and wraps them around my quivering heart. Like suffocating liana vines, squeezing the life out of its host tree, the life leaches out of me just thinking about what lies beyond this door.

"I'm not going in there." I dig in my heels, pulling back.

Brutus stares at me, his smile wide and his eyes crinkling in humor. His dark hair is slicked back with gel. He looks more like a Mafioso each time I see him. "You'll be entertaining. You show such defiance! I almost can't wait."

As I glare back at him, my fingers curl into fists. Next to him, I look like a pathetic wolf pup rather than something fierce, but I want to hurt this guy. "I'm not your toy."

"No," he says. "You won't be. You'll be the plaything of someone else." With an effortless yank of his arm, I fall into the dark corridor. The cement wall closes behind us, leaving us in utter blackness. Brutus hauls me along the dirt path as it angles downward, not too steeply, but enough that I can tell we're heading farther underground. His hand clamps down like an iron shackle on my arm, and my bare feet scuff along the floor.

Reaching out with my free hand, I try to find a wall since I'm lurching blindly along. Brutus drags me with untiring strength, but there is no wall to lean on. I don't know how he can see where we're going, and I'm completely at his mercy, unable to make my eyes focus on anything.

"Where are we going?" I ask finally, out of breath, my aching body screaming out in protest. I want to lie down so badly, and my stomach rumbles in hunger. How long has it been since I've eaten? It seems like days.

"To hell," Brutus answers with a devil's chortle rather than a man's, and a chill slithers down my back. Every step I take, I wonder how much farther, and when it seems I can't take another, we stop before a heavy, metal door.

He knocks, and it scrapes open. I'm introduced into a huge ballroom, glowing with a thousand candles. It's similar to a church chapel, complete with a cross, except it is hanging upside down. Chills ripple through me again, and the hairs on my arms stand on end.

Chairs line the walls, and an obsidian throne sits at the head of the room in front of the cross. A long table runs along the back wall, which is where most of the candles are, creating a haunted glow at that end of the room. A hundred golden goblets, filled with a dark, ruby-colored liquid, sit on the table waiting to be picked up.

In the light, I see how disheveled I look. My clothes are torn and bloodied, my feet are bare—and have been since I arrived—and my knuckles are bruised and cracked from the fight I put up—to my credit. I can't imagine what my face looks like. It still throbs and has not healed at all yet.

I saw a kid with a broken nose once. He had two black eyes for a week. I reach up to finger the bruises, to see if I can tell if it's broken or crooked. It hurts too much, so I give up, not wanting to subject myself to more agony than I have to.

Even though there are at least a hundred chairs lining the walls of the room, there are only a few people in attendance so far. One guy in particular keeps me riveted because he is unlike anything I've ever seen before. He sits at the front of the room on the throne, lounging, relaxed. He's a demon, but he isn't like the other demons.

He doesn't come close to looking like the things we kill every night, nor does he look like any of the pictures I've seen in my studies. Jag and I took a vast amount of time to learn about our enemy before we were brave enough to kill one. There were encyclopedias at the library, but our true education came after we'd gone into battle… or at least, Jag had.

Pale, russet skin covers this demon, and he wears no clothes. Long, black spikes grow from his fingertips like icepicks, and two twisting horns spring from his forehead, curling back over his leathery skull. His lips are blood red. When he smiles—which he did when I came in—his yellow, jagged teeth glisten in the candlelight.

"Welcome," this terrifying creature says, his words a low, thunderous rumble.

As I'm led forward, I just stare, all the horror stories I've ever read rushing back to my mind. If I ever wondered if monsters lived under the bed, I know now. They do. And they feed on unsuspecting, helpless people.

"Tell me your name, boy," the beast commands. His abysmally deep voice is impossible to describe and is filled with the screams of the damned. Like the roar of a rogue tidal wave, I feel it to the depth of my bones, not just in my ears. He is something that can call forth the legions of the underworld. I know it instinctively.

I don't answer. I can't… for a moment. I tremble, searching the room for other anomalies like him, but he is the only one so hideous. His wicked smile widens, and with a blink of his eyes, he morphs instantly into a normal, human-looking man. He wears a gray, pinstriped suit and his white-blond hair is slicked back. Blue eyes sparkle beneath dark eyebrows and his teeth are white and straight. He's handsome. Movie star handsome.

"Is this better?" he asks, his arms stretched wide as though he is performing, which he probably is.

Still, I remain silent, watching him carefully as he saunters closer.

One of his hands rests over his chest as though he is humbled and pleased to meet me. "I'm very happy to make your acquaintance," he says. "You may call me Coem." He bows slightly, never taking his eyes from mine.

He's so striking, so different from before. "Are you Satan?" I ask in a whisper, realizing quickly how stupid that sounds. He bursts out laughing, his amusement seeming more like the cheerful chuckle of a friendly neighbor than a terrifying monster.

"No, no. I'm not Satan. He was a weakling who couldn't get the job done. No, I'm from a different world altogether. There are many unseen worlds out there in the Big Black. Did you not know this?"

I shake my head, my lips slack and numb. Is this something people learn at church? I didn't go much with my family and I feel stupid, thinking it must be something from the Bible.

"The people of Earth are so ignorant and uninformed," he says.

There is no way out of this and I pray to die quickly, with as little crying and begging as possible. I have a feeling that whatever torture they have planned for me won't be over for a while. My heart races when he reaches a finger toward me. If he touches me, a trail of fire will welt on my skin. I just know it.

"Does it amaze you how stupid the people of Earth are?" he asks Brutus, who laughs and nods his head in agreement.

"But that is neither here nor there," Coem continues. "You're here now, and we are in for a treat." He runs his finger down the side of my face and under my chin. His touch is cool and smooth. No burning at all. I close my eyes.

"Come." He takes my hand and leads me to the center of the room, where I stand like a child, submissive and afraid… and then he shackles me to the floor. I don't notice the cuffs and chains until they are clasped around my wrists, and then he walks away. I tug on the chains. They are at least an inch thick, and I'll never be able to break away.

"Hey! Wait!" I call, confused, but Coem ignores me. The room begins to fill. All sorts of foul beings enter and find a spot to sit. At least half are gray men, like I am familiar with, a few others are human-looking spirits, and some look similar to Coem before he turned himself into a man, but none are as hideous or terrifying.

The creepiest of all are the men who aren't possessed at all. Mortal men, who are here of their own accord, drinking wine and conversing with the many devils in attendance. I don't understand their relationship to the demons at all.

I call out to them. Surely, they'll have compassion on a fellow human being. "Please! You!" I catch one man's eyes. "*Help* me!" I yank on my chains to show him I'm a prisoner, stupidly thinking it will matter in some way. He glances at me, like a few others, and then turns back to his conversation. How is this possible? I can't wrap my mind around it, and my heart sinks.

Coem sits down on his throne and places his arms on the armrests at his side. He smiles, and a shadow of jagged teeth—like the negative picture of film—shows over his human-looking teeth. He yells, "Let the games begin!"

20

Dean

I always thought the demons came here to run rampant, to cause havoc. But now I know they are controlled and organized. They have leaders, a hierarchy. This makes it worse than before.

As I stand there, chained to the floor, surveying my underground prison, I realize these aren't mindless fiends bouncing from one stolen body to the next, but an army, directed and commanded by their leaders to overtake our world.

The demons fill the room, packed into corners, and they don't seem to mind being jostled for space. Their savage smiles are wide and expectant as they gaze at me with what can only be described as hunger. Some are disembodied, their gray, sinewy arms and legs slithering and twisting like smoke.

Coem sits on his black, stone throne, gazing out over the horde, his expressions morphing from one moment to the next. Smiles. Frowns. Glares. He looks completely out of place in his dark, pinstriped business suit, despite the fact that he is their king.

I am court jester. And they won't stop until my heart does.

My pulse pounds and my face grows hot. It becomes hard to breathe in this stuffy, overcrowded room, and I wonder stupidly if I've just developed asthma. My body continues to tremble as I begin to hyperventilate. I keep a constant strain on my chains in the hopes that they will miraculously release if I just pull hard enough, but my arms are cramping and shaky.

The scent of candle wax permeates the air, but instead of a calming balm, like it is in our church basement, the acidic fumes fill my nostrils and turn my stomach sour. The candles seem to grow and breathe with my terror, the room becoming brighter as I become more frightened.

When the doors at the back are closed and locked, my heart just about stops. It's beginning. Silence reigns where there were once voices and a cacophony of laughter. The only sound I hear is the clinking of my chains and the ragged breaths I inhale.

"Welcome all, friends and fiends," Coem says, still sitting casually on his throne. "Welcome to my home! For tonight's entertainment, we have brought you… a Cazador! A killer of demons!"

The room erupts in a roar, their leering faces hateful, calling for my destruction. My eyes jerk to Coem's. He knows who I am! Or who I'm supposed to be. Actual Cazadors are able to kill demons. So am I one really?

"I'm sorry," I call, desperate to think of a way out of this. "I'm not whatever you just said. I don't even know what a cazadory-thing is!"

The room grows quiet again.

"What's that you say?" Brutus asks. He stands beside Coem's throne with his meaty arms crossed over his chest. He raises one eyebrow in question.

My eyes water as my mind grasps at something intelligent to say.

"You say you are *not* a Cazador?" Coem repeats, leaning forward, his visage shifting from human form to beastly as he concentrates on my face.

"No, I'm not. I don't even know what that is. I'm just a normal person." The lie comes easily, which surprises me. I've never been a very good liar.

"Really?" Coem stands, his hands clasped behind his back as he makes his way calmly toward me, a slight smile adorning his handsome human face. "Mephistophilis!" he calls to Brutus. "Come here."

When they stand side by side, Coem glances at his subordinate, his smile cold and his eyes narrow. I don't know how to read this guy, but if I were Brutus, I wouldn't trust him. He'd probably stick a shiv into your side when you're not looking. I almost feel sorry for Brutus… until I grimace and the bruises on my face scream out.

"You said you caught a Cazador. Did you?"

Brutus' gaze shifts between his commander and me. His eyebrows pull down into a worried scowl, but he sticks his chin out and holds his ground. "He is one. I know it. I ran into him and his partner when they were out hunting. They killed Nybbas right in front of me. He runs around town with the one they call The Jaguar."

Coem looks Brutus up and down, taking his time to answer. His eyes seem to see right through him, assessing him, and I wonder if Brutus is coming up short. "Well, we shall test him, and then we will all know for sure."

He turns back to me, still smiling. "Does that sound fair? Everyone came here tonight for the sole purpose of seeing a Cazador brought to his knees. It would be unfair to disappoint them. And you're here to entertain us anyway." He turns in a slow circle, his arms raised like a circus master. The audience shouts in agreement and cheers him on. "It's settled then. We will put this boy to the test. If he is an imposter and not a Cazador, well… he'll just be dead, which will be just as much fun. Weth! Come forward!"

A tall, lithe woman rises from a red velvet seat along the front row of the far wall. I can see through her, so she must be a spirit only. Making no sound, she floats toward me, ethereal and beautiful. Her wide, blue eyes are the color of sapphires and long, blonde hair falls over her shoulders and down her back. When she stands before me, a soft smile graces her porcelain-hued face. She seems very angelic and out of place here.

Coem bows to her in a gentlemanly gesture. She nods her head to him, and then steps up to me.

"What is your name?" she asks as softly as a warm breeze. My eyes close, and I take a long, slow inhalation. She smells like cinnamon and apples, and I feel my muscles relax along with my anxiety, as though I've just been filled with a summer day. This woman doesn't feel mean or cruel. She doesn't seem like someone I should be afraid of. A small part of my brain screams for me not to fall for her enchantments, that she is more powerful than I can imagine, but I push those thoughts away and draw in another breath of apples.

"This is Weth," Coem says before I can answer. "She is the highly revered and beloved demon of anger. You will see." He steps back, the smile never leaving his face, and walks with sure steps back to his black throne. He rolls into his seat and rests his chin on his fist as he watches Weth work her magic.

Her gaze returns to me, and her eyes soften as she looks deeply into mine. She can't possibly be a demon of anger. She is too calm and lovely, relaxed and serene. "Your name?"

"Dean," I answer as she raises her hand to my face, tracing, feather light, the bruises on my cheeks.

"You are wounded."

"Yes."

Her hand cups my cheek and my eyes close, her fingers cool and healing. How is it possible that I can *feel* her when she doesn't have a physical body? I have no idea, but I don't question it.

"It must have been terrible, to be hurt in such a way. Mephistophilis is a horrible, wicked beast. He has no compulsion about causing pain."

I feel a stirring with her words, and heat begins to well in my chest. She continues to speak, condemning the abominable Brutus for his scheming and physical abuse of me. Each sentence paints him as a darker, fouler creature than the last, and the fire in my belly grows to a burning flame.

"You should kill him," she whispers in my ear, too softly for anyone else to hear. "You could do it, and I could help you. I hate him also. More than you could possibly know. You would be doing the world good."

I feel the power in her words, and I believe her. I could do it… with her help. I could finally kill a demon. I could kill Brutus, and everyone would know that I really am a Cazador. It's a dream come true in a way. Even though I love being a peacemaker and not a killer, there is a realization deep inside me that I am weak. I am inferior. It comes bursting to the surface, and shame fills me. I need to kill Brutus to prove I am strong. I am someone who can fight and win. I am someone Heidi will want!

Weth continues to strengthen the fire inside me until I am near bursting, straining on my chains, the veins in my arms and neck bulging with the effort. And yet… there is a microscopic piece of my mind that tells me this isn't real.

But that doesn't matter as she worms her way through my mind like a cancer. She keeps fanning the flames, and even though the emotions aren't real, they *feel* real. She seems to read my mind as she stokes the embers of jealousy for Jag. Of his fearlessness, his fierceness. As my anger grows, so does another emotion. One I haven't felt in a very long time.

Hate.

For Jag.

I know, deep in my heart, that I am every inch the jaguar that he is. I, too, can be ferocious, wild, and a terrible force to be reckoned with. With uninhibited abandon, I growl, searching for a victim. He stands along the side wall, ugly and vile, his arms crossed over his chest, his lips turned up into a half smile.

Mephistophilis.

I hate him too. More than I've ever hated anything in my life. Like a jagged crevice of magma exploding out of the earth, the raw enmity boils so forcefully that I can think of nothing else. I want to kill him. I *have* to kill him!

The very next second, when I open my mouth to shriek out my loathing for Brutus, Weth swirls, like a gray tornado of smoke, straight into my mouth and down my throat, burning her way to my lungs and stomach with the bite of dry ice.

Everything stops as she barrels into the depths of me, my arms and legs stiffening and becoming frigid and immobile. I can't move, let alone think straight or understand what is happening. Ice fills my veins, and I shiver uncontrollably.

A cramp grips me around the middle, like a knife has slashed across my abdomen and my innards are falling out. Weth is cutting me apart from the inside out. I fall to my knees, retching. Weth explodes back out of me like the rancid vomit she is.

I fell for her lies completely. I believed her ugly words and hate-filled sentiments. I felt the hatred growing in me like a solid oak tree, its roots digging deep into my soul. And I *liked* it. It had made me feel powerful. Vengeful. Righteous.

The grayness of Weth slowly molds back into the form of a woman, and she pulls herself from the floor, weak and spent, barely able to support herself.

"Well?" Coem asks, his eyebrows raised in question when she doesn't answer immediately.

"He… is not… possessable… at this time." She stumbles back to her chair, no longer with the grace and elegance she previously exhibited. "Some innate element repels me."

"Hmm. Interesting." Coem taps his lips, thinking and staring at me. I fall to the floor, exhausted. As soon as Weth leaves my body, so does the frigid coldness and intense anger. I just want to lie down and die. Never have I felt so tired. Okay, maybe I felt this way after getting beaten up, but still, this is pretty bad too.

"Please, just let me go. I don't know what you want."

"I don't think so." Coem flicks his wrist at someone on the opposite side of the room and I don't bother to look at who it is. What's the point? A gray man walks, or floats, up to me, his mouth a black, jagged line. Like all gray men, his eyes are black slits of endless darkness. This is no soul. It's a fragment, the bare pieces of a damaged spirit, and the only way it will ever feel complete is to meld with another body.

Without thought, my body recoils. My fear of this being is greater than the others so far. This is the kind of demon I see every night when Jag and I go hunting. These are the intruders of the bodies we are forced to kill. This is the face of evil in my nightmares.

His dark maw stretches unnaturally into a grimace. A migraine begins, and I resist a sob of hopelessness as I try to stand. I will not go down without a fight.

This gray man doesn't speak, but Brutus does. He calls out

across the room, "Vi-dar, Vi-dar, Vi-dar." The crowd joins in, chanting the demon's name. Again and again, the words throb through the room like a mantra, weakening me and strengthening him.

Vidar places one giant hand on the top of my head. His fingers are so long that they reach all the way to the top of my neck. Our faces are only inches apart, his eyes fathomless pits of misery. I cry out when his fingers begin to squeeze. My knees give out and I fall, crying out when it feels like a nail is being shoved through my left eye socket.

I've had migraines off and on my whole life, but this is a pressure without source. An ache that hurts everywhere at once. My neck crackles as I try to wrench away. He presses harder, the agony increasing, and I'm sure my skull will be crushed. Screaming fills my ears, and then I realize it's me. My breathing comes in hitches and I grab for the gray man's hand, but he's as wispy as Weth and I can't get a grip.

I'm growing numb, and I thank God for this miraculous reprieve. When I open my eyes, I learn the truth. Vidar has let go of me and stands facing Coem, bowing slowly. He walks back to his place along the wall, never saying a word the entire time. I'd felt intimately connected to him, as though he could read my thoughts and memories. How is it possible to be violated in such a way? Could this fiend see into my soul and know my secrets? Will he now go after my friends who are my family?

I can't let that happen. I can't let them break me. I have to find a way out. Jag and the others might not be able to find me, and if they can't, then what? I realize in that moment that it's up to me. I'll have to save myself.

"It looks as though you are a difficult body to inhabit," Coem states, rising to his feet and strolling over to crouch beside me. I lie on the floor, the cement cool beneath my palms. I don't care what Coem or anyone else thinks. My mind finds it almost impossible to comprehend this horrifying experience.

"Please… let… me go." I refuse to cry, even though tears press against the backs of my eyes. My head pounds and even the candlelight feels too bright.

He tsks and lifts my chin with his finger. "We are not finished. The night is still young."

I don't bother to keep my head raised. Two demons have pitted themselves against me so far, but they haven't won… yet. I'm not sure I can survive another one of these strange onslaughts though. If they are going to kill me, I wish they would just get it over with.

21

Brecken

When I wake, I stretch and roll over, expecting to see Heidi sound asleep on her side of the apartment. She is *not* there, and her bed is a mess. I glance over at the bathroom, which is only a few feet from the foot of my bed, but the door is open and the lights are off.

I lurch to a sitting position. She wouldn't leave without telling me. But then, yeah, she totally would. It's not as if I'm her dad. She doesn't have to constantly check in with me, but I really wish she would.

Hopping out of bed, I hurry to get dressed, scraping a comb through my tangled hair. I leave the apartment with a sigh as I lock the numerous deadbolts I placed on the door. Heidi hadn't locked any of them when she left.

It's a ten-minute walk to the church. Before I even get close, I see her and Jag visiting on the front porch. A strange twist reverberates in my chest, seeing them together. I don't know why it bothers me, but it does. It stops me for a second, and it's at that moment that she looks up and notices me. An expression of surprise flashes in her eyes, but it is soon replaced with a smile.

"Hey, Bret!"

I wave back, trying to figure out why they don't seem to be in a rush to scour the streets for Dean. I would have thought Jag would be out, knocking doors and turning over every stone. He nods toward me, but that's it.

I stop before them, my hands in my pockets. "Any news?"

Heidi tries to speak mid-gulp and chokes. Her eyes are wide and excited. "Yes!" She wipes spilled coffee from her chin. "Jag went out early this morning and interrogated a demon."

I figure if the news were dire or imminent, they would have already spit it out, so I keep my gaze on Heidi, not wanting to deal with Jag so early in the morning. Maybe I need coffee too.

"How come you didn't wake me when you left? We could have come together." I sound parental and want to kick myself. She's wild and untamable. Always has been. But as her older brother, I want to rein her in and keep her safe. There's nothing she'd hate more. She'd rebel before I could blink. I know her well.

She steals a quick glance at Jag, and he smiles as if he knows he's won something I've lost. I grit my teeth. Something's happened between them, and I can't dig it out without looking like a jealous suitor.

"Oh, I woke early and you looked wiped. I didn't want to wake you," she says with eyes downcast. She can't even look at me? I can read her without even trying hard. She's lying right to my face!

I turn to Jag to keep from saying anything I might regret. Taking a deep breath, I focus on what Heidi *has* told me. That Jag interrogated a demon. He wouldn't have gotten much. Even if he threatened to kill it, it wouldn't have cared. It would just go into a different body because Jag doesn't have the kind of weapon that will make it stay dead permanently. But if he tortured it first… that could be a different story. No creature likes to endure pain.

"What did you learn?" I ask.

"Not much. Only that the demons are organized, like an actual army."

He doesn't meet my gaze either, but casts a glance at Heidi. I have to really focus to keep from grabbing him by the neck and smashing his head into the wall. If he's done anything to her…

I look back and forth between them, how close they're sitting to one another, the familiar way Heidi glances at him when she thinks I'm not looking. The comfortable way Jag's knee rests against hers. All sorts of things go through my mind. None of them good.

As far as the organization of demons goes, I already know

about that. I comment offhandedly since it's the only safe thing to do. "Yeah. They are set up well. Generals, lieutenants, levels of advancement. The whole shebang."

They both stare at me, gaping.

"How do you know that already?" Heidi asks.

"You knew this and didn't tell us before?" Jag asks at the same time.

If they want info on demons, I can give them everything, but how to do it without making myself look suspicious or guilty… which I've just done? "You aren't the only ones who know how to torture demons." I stare back. "So," I ask, intent on steering the conversation in a different direction. "Get any good info?"

"Well." Jag stands and crumples his Styrofoam cup. "I was hoping to learn if the demon knew who had taken Dean and what they'd done with him."

"And did it?"

"No," he says. "It only knew that something big was going on, but he hadn't been invited to the party."

No, a low-level wouldn't have been. They aren't privy to important meetings. But if that is what happened… if Dean was taken by important demons and they are holding him for information… I wrack my mind for a solution.

"We were going to try to find another demon to see if it has any more info to go on," Heidi says, also rising and tossing her cup toward a huge garbage pile across the street. It's overflowing, and no one has bothered to empty it for ages. The cup only makes it halfway across the street. Swearing under her breath, she saunters over to pick it up. She takes it all the way over and stuffs it inside the dumpster. It's a mountainous pile that's starting to stink.

"You should really get that taken care of," I say to Jag.

He shrugs and starts walking away. Heidi hurries to catch up with him. Once again, I am left behind.

"What about Owen and Doug? Are they coming?" I call after them.

"I don't know what they're doing," Jag says. "But I'm not waiting around for anyone."

Exhaling, I follow. We walk the few blocks into town, to the plaza that is surrounded by little shops and eateries. I grab doughnuts for Heidi and me. She flicks her eyes toward Jag and I receive her message grudgingly, buying Jag a doughnut too. He takes it and gives me a nod of acknowledgement.

We sit down on the bench and wait, watching each passerby with a practiced eye. It isn't ten minutes later that I elbow Jag and point to a guy on the corner of the plaza. He stands under a copse of trees, wearing a black leather jacket and leaning against a tree, smoking a cigarette. He watches the plaza also, but he hasn't paid any real attention to us yet.

"I'll circle around," I whisper, hurrying in the opposite direction, hoping to catch the guy before he gets suspicious or leaves. I trust Jag to watch the front. There's an alleyway off to the side, but Heidi will block it. I don't like the idea of her being there at all, but obviously, I have no say.

I creep close, the trees just ahead. The demon hasn't noticed me yet. I move slowly, quietly, my Nephilim dagger at my side. It glints in the sunlight. In one swift motion, I have the guy around the neck and am pulling him into the shadows.

Heidi and Jag spring forward, searching the guy for weapons. They find a pocketknife, which they confiscate.

"Hey!" the demon cries out. "I didn't do anything!"

I slap my hand over his mouth, keeping my dagger at his neck. "Make one sound and I swear I'll slit your throat. It's Nephilim, so I'd stay quiet if I were you."

The guy's greasy, blond hair hasn't been combed in a while, and a foul smell wafts up from his unwashed body. Demons are so stupid when it comes to protecting and taking care of their stolen meat suits. They let them waste away quickly, all in the attempt to experience every awful thing they can before the body dies.

"Who are you?" our prisoner asks in a panicked whisper.

"It doesn't matter," I growl back. "What's your name?"

"I don't have a name. They call me The Dog," he says with a whimper.

I've heard of him. A lesser demon who survives on the scraps of his superiors. How sad that the dregs of the underworld are allowed to come through *The Door*. "You demons have something that isn't yours, and I want it back."

The Dog's eyes are wide and terrified, and when Jag pulls out his runed dagger, Dog goes limp in my arms. "I don't know anything. I swear. They don't tell me nothin'."

"I don't believe you," Jag says, leaning in close. "I think you know plenty, and if I don't hear the truth right now, I'll cut off every one of your fingers one at a time... slowly."

Jag's eyes, which always seem a little cold to me, are downright icy with hate, his teeth clenched. The chords in his neck stretch taut, and it seems to take everything he has to hold himself in check.

"Jag, I got this," I say, growing uneasy at his abrupt reaction.

My legs suddenly grow warm and my stomach knots. Disgusted, I swear under my breath and smack The Dog on the side of the head. He peed on me! Now I'll smell like urine all morning. And even though I'm sure he's terrified, The Dog smiles.

Jag scowls until he notices the growing wet streaks on the guy's stained and soiled khakis. A smile grows on Jag's grimacing lips also. "Sorry."

I don't think he means it.

The Dog sags against me as Jag presses the tip of his dagger into his chest. The demon screams in agony and starts to cry like a baby. "Please don't kill me. I just got this body!"

Jag actually laughs in The Dog's face. "Like I care how long you've had it."

The demon, although terrified, has the guts to actually spit in Jag's face. That is the wrong move on a variety of levels. The saliva drips down Jag's cheek before he wipes it away slowly... with a smile. He doesn't say another word, just plunges the dagger deep into the demon's chest.

"Great," I say as the body disintegrates into ash. "We needed him. Now we'll have to find another." I stand there staring at my filthy clothes, glaring at Jag. I'm pissed at having to work with someone so hotheaded and angry. I can't depend on him to keep his cool. He doesn't think a demon's life has any value. He hates them. No questions asked and no excuses.

I hate demons too, but for different reasons, because I know something Jag doesn't. Demon lives have purpose. The world needs what they bring to the table. It's all about opposition. Ying and yang. There can't be good if there isn't bad. But there are rules for both sides, and the demons are breaking theirs. They aren't supposed to completely suppress the human's soul. They aren't supposed to take over and kill their host. There are a certain number of evil spirits and demons that are allowed in this realm at one time, and they aren't following that particular regulation.

"It's fine," Jag says. "They're everywhere."

I know they are, but now, we'll have to spend time catching one. Most often when daylight comes, they go underground like vampires. Only the stupid ones stay out. Maybe we'll get lucky and run into another stupid demon.

But I doubt it.

22

Heidi

It's almost noon and sun shines brilliantly overhead. I wish I'd worn my old baseball cap to keep the scorching rays off my head. I'm a soggy mess, and my hair soaks up a ton of heat.

We sit in the park, moving from park bench to park bench, waiting for another demon to rear its ugly head, but none do. We eventually mosey down the street a few blocks to catch a bus to the Down Quarter. There has to be a fiend or two there, since it is their stomping ground.

I slip into a window seat and slide the top half of the window down, letting the warm wind blow my hair back. It feels so good. I wish I could take off my shirt and let my whole body be enveloped by the breeze, but sitting on a bus in only a sports bra will bring unwanted attention. Plus, I'm not brave enough to do that in front of Bret, let alone Jag.

"So, what time did you leave this morning?" Bret asks, sitting down next to me and leaning close so he doesn't have to speak too loud. He already asked this question, but I'd deftly avoided answering. I guess he's trying to pin me down. Is he jealous? For some reason, that doesn't give me the thrill I thought it would.

I glance across the aisle at Jag, who stares out the opposite window, a somber frown on his face, his expression cold and unreadable. One of his hands rests on the dagger at his hip, the other on his thigh. He looks tense and ready to spring from his seat at the least provocation.

Bret is still gazing at me with an uncomfortable intensity. I squirm, unnerved, and don't want to confide in him. It's too soon since our kiss. "Early," I answer, and then I go back to looking out the window.

"I don't mean to pry. I was just worried." He gives me a dejected smile, and my heart breaks just a little.

Releasing a pent-up breath, I whisper, "I know. I'm sorry. I just feel… so stupid." That little confession feels monumental, and I chance a glance into his soulful eyes. I find compassion in his gaze and maybe even a bit of forgiveness. But for what? I haven't done anything wrong. Just kissed a really cute guy. My feelings for him have changed though—after everything—and I am no longer crushing on him, but there is still a strange, deep connection, and I *want* to be close to him. It's impossibly confusing, considering my rapidly awakening feelings for Jag.

At that moment, Jag glances over. One of his eyebrows lifts as he takes in Bret's close proximity and our covert conversation. If he's curious or jealous, he doesn't let on. He goes back to looking out the window.

"It's okay," Bret says. "You didn't do anything wrong. Really. It's just… well, I've already given my heart to someone else." He grins, but it's more of a grimace, and his words do anything but soothe my wounded pride. He's already in love.

"To… who?" I ask before I can stop myself. The dread of knowing slams into me and squeezes that pumping muscle in my chest. For some reason, I still want to be important to him. I want to be someone he wants.

"She was… someone who died. Her name was… well, it doesn't matter." So he isn't gay. He loves a girl. A dead girl. She probably died in the Rift like so many others, but that was a long time ago. Isn't he ready to let her go and love again? "And you don't want to move on?"

He shakes his head and wears an expression of hopelessness, his brows rising and his lips pressed tightly together. "I can't move on. I'll never be able to. She stole my heart and took it with her." He laughs as though he knows how corny it sounds, but to me, it sounds heavenly. Would any boy ever utter those words about me?

I try to picture that phrase coming out of Jag's mouth, but

then I laugh to myself. That will never happen. He'd liked a girl during the Rift, but I don't know much about it. He won't talk about her and neither will Dean.

Jag stands up and bangs on the ceiling. The bus pulls to the side of the road, and we are left on a dusty, deserted street. I consider my two cohorts and then down the street we go, searching for any signs of life in the DQ.

I don't come here. Ever. Some buildings are crumbling, damaged beyond repair. The streets are empty. No dogs bark. No birds sing. No children play in the gutters or ride bikes down the sidewalk.

The sun beats down relentlessly, and I wish I'd worn my tank instead of a full T-shirt. I didn't even bring water. My mouth is starting to feel like the streets, dry and dusty.

"I need something to drink," I say finally. "I'm going to check out that shop." I point across the street to a soda fountain storefront that has no glass in the front window, just broken shards of someone else's dream, ready to slash and cut anyone who trespasses.

The door is cracked open and I push against it, the hinges stiff and squeaky. Bret places his hand above mine and, reluctantly, the door opens for us. Russet-colored leaves carpet the floor and bleached, red vinyl stools stand at the counter. They wait for patrons that will never come. The back of the shop is dark and shrouded in shadow. The store is silent and as creepy as a graveyard on Halloween.

There has to be something liquid here, something that someone has not ransacked yet. The more I think about it, the thirstier I become. Rather than search the little shop with me, Bret sits down on one of the stools. He draws in the dirt on the counter, doodling. It stops me for a moment because it's something my brother Brecken would have done, right down to the way he curves his pointer finger. Weird.

I shake my head, tempted to say something. He reminds me so much of him, and it makes my heart happy. I'm tempted to walk over and hug him, maybe even dole out a Wet Willie, just to show my affection. He glances up then as though he can feel my gaze. He smiles, his dimples creasing in his cheeks. So much like Brecken.

"I'm going to check the back. There's nothing up here."

"Okay. Yell if you need anything." He turns to watch out the front window.

I doubt I'll *need* anything. I'm pretty self-sufficient and skilled at defending myself. I push through a swinging door with a small, round window at the top. It's dusty and impossible to see through. The door opens into a kitchen with a deep fryer, a sink, and dusty, stainless steel pots that hang from the ceiling. I'm tempted to take a few down to take home with us. We need pots and pans. They can be polished up, but I don't want to haul them around all day, so I pass them by.

There are plenty of cupboards to go through. Some are homes to rats. I hold a scream inside when a rat as big as a housecat runs across my shoe when I open the door to his residence. I almost lose it right there.

Mouse droppings are all over the floor and counters, light barely penetrating through the dirty window in the door. Now, I'm no superhero, I know perfectly well that something could be hiding in this dismal kitchen, but why would they? The demons don't anticipate us coming here or even entering this particular store. Especially in the daytime. The odds are slim, but still, I'm wary.

There's a refrigerator at the back, but it's dark and empty. It has been for a long time, although a rotten stench permeates the lining, and I quickly close the door. With a sigh, I head back to the front. When my hand presses against the swinging door, goose bumps sprout along my arms and I freeze, listening. I sense someone else in the room, like the apparition of a ghost. The room doesn't get cold or change in any way, but I feel it. Like an invisible phantom breathing down my neck.

Darting for the door, I push through, huffing in fright. I run smack into Bret's back. He faces the front of the store, his Nephilim sword drawn.

A demon stands before him, possessing the body of an average-looking guy who wears a denim jacket even though it's a hundred degrees out. He's clean cut and nice looking, smelling of aftershave rather than death, so I already know he has more brains than the last demon we encountered.

"We meet again, Bretariel," the demon drawls with a half-smile.

"I don't know what you're talking about. I don't know any Bretariel." Bret's voice trembles, and I glance at him. I've never seen him unnerved, and it makes my heart beat erratically. If he's nervous, a demon slayer without remorse, how much more of a need did I have to be afraid? And who's Bretariel? The name feels strange on my tongue. I've never heard it before.

"Let's not play games, old friend." And then the demon's gaze lands on me. His eyes widen and his eyebrows rise. "Oh, I get it." The demon doesn't look the least bit afraid of Bret or his Nephilim sword. "The Great Undoer is here incognito. Do you suppose *I* will keep your secret?"

Bret is poised to thrust. "I'm not looking for trouble. Just information." He stares hard at the demon, his eyes never wavering. A vein pulses in his forehead, sweat beading along his brow and upper lip. He looks terrified, and I can't get the demon's words out of my head. They know one another? Slowly, I pull my dagger from its sheath and hold it against my leg, prepared to lunge.

Bret circles around a table and I follow, staying at his back. Step by step, he forces the demon to shift position until his back is to the door to the kitchen. He has nowhere to run.

"We're looking for a boy named Dean. All we want is to know if you know anything about it." Bret's voice grows strained and higher pitched than normal. His hand shakes.

"A boy named Dean?" the demon repeats, his smile incredulous. "He must be an important player if The Great Undoer has come looking for him." He laughs, sounding like a cackling witch. His cynical laughter rings through the storefront. Seconds later, Jag bursts through the front door.

"I heard laughing. What's going on?"

We don't answer, keeping our eyes on the demon.

Jag's reaction is lightning quick. He has his dagger out and at the demon's throat before it can even react.

"Wait!" Bret screams as Jag bends the beast over the counter. "You know where Dean is," Bret growls into the guy's face, only inches away. "I can see it in your eyes."

"My, my, you've found me out." The demon doesn't seem to mind the dagger at his throat. Nor does he act afraid of Jag's silly runed knife.

"Let him talk," Bret says, pulling Jag back. The demon straightens and smoothes his clothes with a chuckle. If he has any weapon at all, he doesn't show it yet.

"So, where is he?" I scream, growing desperate and tired. Even though Bret blocks my way, my heart races and the sting of adrenaline coats the insides of my veins. I'm eager to start the battle I know we'll win… before the demon can escape through a back door.

"Fine, fine," the guy answers, his hands up and placating. "I *have* heard of this boy, but what is he to you? A slave?"

Bret takes a threatening step closer, his dagger raised. "Where's the boy? And be careful how you answer. If you've hurt him in any way…"

"You'll what? Kill me? I'm not afraid of you, Undoer." The demon's back is almost to the kitchen door. All he needs to do is turn and dart into its depths. If he knows of an escape route, he just might make it. I don't like the look on his face, like he knows the odds are in his favor.

I quickly grow impatient with this bantering. This idiot isn't going to tell us anything. They never do, not even with torture most of the time. We should just cut him down. The poor human who once inhabited his body is already gone, his soul hopefully dwelling peacefully in heaven.

But still Bret waits, holding Jag and me off with a raised hand. "Stop calling me that. I'm not this Bretariel."

The demon gives us a knowing smile, his confidence abrasive and irritating. I'd like to smack him… or worse.

"I am not afraid of you or your trinket," he says, motioning to Bret's Nephilim blade, but I can see the alarm in his eyes. That blade will end him for good, and I have a feeling he knows it.

"I am the only one who knows where your little friend is hidden," he continues, backing away slowly. "You kill me—you kill him."

Jag roars in fury, trying to push past Bret, but somehow, Bret holds him back without much effort. The expression on Bret's face changes only marginally. A tighter grit to his jaw, a muscle flexing, a narrowness to his eyes. I marvel at his ability to stare the demon down and keep his cool.

"Where is he?" Bret asks calmly. Maybe he thinks he should play *good cop* since Jag *always* plays the bad one. "What do you want in return, Coem?"

"Wait—what?" Did Bret just call the guy by name? This demon that he doesn't know?

The demon's smile widens. "Oops. Whatever will you do now?"

Bret's head drops, bowing in what looks like defeat. The muscles in his jaw clench and when he finally raises his eyes, he wears an expression I've never seen before. Fury mixed with defiance, blurred with impotence. "What do you want, Coem?"

"Ah… you know me well, Bretariel."

Bret doesn't move or even twitch, but Jag does. "You know him?" he asks, gesturing to Coem, finally piecing things together. He arrived to the party late.

"Oh, we're old friends," Coem says. "He and I go way back." His cold gaze never wavers. He watches only Bret, taking in every movement and expression, looking amused and fascinated.

I'm fascinated too.

The look on Jag's face is downright murderous. I'm not sure who he wants to kill first. Bret or Coem. This whole situation is insane.

Again, Bret asks, "What do you want?" His jaw clenches, and the degree of hate in his eyes is terrifying. Something is happening here. Something secret, evil, and dark. Chills prickle along my arms even though it's an oven in here and we're all dripping with sweat.

It's quiet for a moment and Coem crosses his arms over his chest, his smile easy. "I want *you*," he says to Bret. "I want to be the one who finally takes down The Great Undoer."

23

Brecken

The heat of their gazes pin me to the filthy floor, like a wasp in a bug collection. Coem has made no secret of our past relationship, and now Jag and Heidi want answers. She's angry and confused, I can tell. I can't blame them, but I also don't want to explain.

Coem wants me in trade for Dean, but that isn't going to happen and wouldn't work anyway. They'd just keep us both, and I don't have time for that. I should have killed Coem the moment I saw him, but that is a lost opportunity now.

I glance over at Jag. A million different emotions flash in his eyes. Disbelief, horror, disgust, hurt, betrayal. The dim soda shop grows even dimmer with his anger. I realize what a mistake it was to come here, but it's too late to go back.

"I swear, I've never been anything but honest with you," I say.

Jag doesn't even take time to answer. He lunges… at *me*, his body slamming into mine, knocking the breath from my lungs. We slide across the dusty floor and into the rear wall, my head banging on the sharp edge of a broken chair.

Dizziness spins me in circles, and for a moment, I can't focus. That could also be from the fist that keeps pounding my face. It's Heidi who finally drags Jag away, and by then, Coem has disappeared.

Blood flows from my nose and down over my lips, the metallic taste of pennies filling my mouth. I wipe it away, but Jag's animal hatred is still visible in the squint of his eyes.

"I knew it! I've felt it all along. You *are* a demon, and I let you worm your way into the Cazadors. You lied to us… over and over!" He reaches down and grabs me by the shirt, pulling me close until our faces are only inches apart. "Was that your plan, jack-nit? To break us apart and kill us one by one in our sleep? And Heidi…" He gives a strangled curse, running a hand through his hair. "What were you going to do to her, once she felt safe in your apartment?" I don't know why he hasn't actually tried to stab me yet. I don't ask. It might remind him he can. Maybe he wants answers more than my death, but this has gone far enough. I can't keep lying about my identity. It isn't getting me anywhere. They know something's off. It's time to spill my guts, metaphorically, not actually.

"I wouldn't ever hurt Heidi. *Ever.*" I try to wipe the dirt off my clothes. "I love her too much. She's my sister, after all."

She stares at me, wearing devastation and betrayal on her face as well as a dash of confusion.

"It's me. Brecken." I look only at her, trying harder than ever to somehow communicate soul to soul. I reach for her, but she backs away, closer to the counter, her eyes wide and showing only mistrust.

"I mean it. It's me. I was allowed to come back to help in this… demon battle."

"I think she'd recognize her own brother," Jag sneers, scorn staining his voice. He raises his knife, finally remembering he has one, I guess, but I pay him no attention. I look only at Heidi.

"It's true. They made me unrecognizable… so I could do this job without the complication of past relationships." Saying it out loud sounds pathetic and stupid, and I wonder how I ever agreed to those terms.

"Don't move, or I swear I will cut you down where you stand," Jag says with a ferocious growl. I'd been backing toward the door, but I stop. He isn't lying, and even though I'm sure I'm stronger, I don't want to make things worse.

I keep my gaze on Heidi. "Remember my basement bedroom and how you thought it was haunted? Well, it was. Kind of. And remember we ate mac and cheese for lunch every day when Dad was gone plumbing? Sophie climbing in bed with you at night when she got scared? The gum under the coffee table? Your blow dryer that kept blowing a fuse? How would I know all of that if I weren't your brother? It's me. I promise."

She stares at me hard, as though trying to see inside me, to recognize something of the brother she remembers. "You look my age. Brecken would be in his twenties."

"I know. It's just the age of this body."

She squints harder and leans forward.

"He's not your brother!" Jag roars. "Can't you see what he's doing? He's trying to lure you away. You know how demons work. They can't be trusted, Heidi. He's a demon. How would that Coem guy have known him otherwise?"

"That's true. How did you know him?" she asks.

I'll never be able to get through to her with Jag yelling in her ear. When she pulls out her dagger and holds it in her fist, I realize I've lost.

"Okay, so, that's harder to explain, but I promise. I'm Brecken. I was sent back here to help close *The Door to Hell because* I know demons. It goes way back… I mean, eons of time back. Angels and demons both."

"Right," Jag says, moving so Heidi is behind him. "Now you're saying you're an angel?" He inches his way toward the front door of the shop, pushing Heidi toward freedom whether she likes it or not. "I don't really care. Consider it a gift that I'm not killing you this very second."

"You couldn't if you tried," I say stupidly, letting my temper flare. They aren't listening. Heidi is coming around, but Jag isn't about to let her really hear me. He doesn't want me to have her loyalty *or* her forgiveness.

Jag stops abruptly. "What did you say?"

Great. Now he'll fight back just to prove I don't scare him, to prove he can take me… which he can't. He's a storm waiting to happen, and I just gave him the opportunity. The sooner we get it over with, though, the better.

He lunges, and this time, it isn't in a good-natured test, pitting his strength against mine like at the church. He is going to kill me if he can.

My face is still hurting from the beating he already gave me, and I'm not about to let it get worse, but Jag has other plans. He brings his dagger down hard. I twist slightly at the last second, or it would have gone into my shoulder. It nicks me, but it's only a scratch. A scratch that stings like a thousand fire ants burrowing their way under my skin.

I roll away, kicking him in the stomach. He stumbles back. I jump to my feet, and we circle each other. Heidi yells for us to stop, her eyes wild with fear, but she doesn't get involved or try to break us up. She knows better. Jag is single minded, and he intends to finish me. If she accidentally gets in his way… I need to end this now.

I stand up straight and let my dagger fall. "I don't want to fight you, Jag."

He lunges again, his knife aimed at the center of my chest. I twist, lift my arm, and push him past me as hard as I can. He rams straight into the wall, head-first. Stunned, he falls to his knees. I take that moment to slam my fist into the side of his face. He hits the ground, out cold.

Heidi screams and runs over to him, turning his body over. A slash on his forehead seeps blood and a cut over his cheekbone is beginning to swell. He'll have a nasty headache when he wakes up, but he'll live.

She swivels toward me with eyes full of fury. "You're lucky he's not dead, or I'd kill you myself."

"He wouldn't let you listen," I say, pleading. I leave my knife on the floor and kneel beside her. "Everything I said is true. It's me, Heidi. I've come back to help you. I'm so sorry I wasn't here before when things were so terrible, but there were other things I had to do in… in… Oh, it's too hard to explain. And Dad didn't kill me," I add as an afterthought.

At this point, she jerks away from me, slapping me hard across the face. "How dare you even bring that up?" She's shaking, her hands in fists, her lips pulled back into a snarl. "I know exactly what happened. I was there. I saw him attack my brother in the hospital. He had a knife to his throat. I know what I saw!"

"*I'm* your brother. And yes, he attacked me at the hospital, but it wasn't what you think. You have no idea what was going on behind the scenes."

"I would if someone told me," she says finally. Jag moans but doesn't wake up.

"We need to get out of here before the real demons come back. Here, help me." I lift Jag by the armpits and wait for her to lift his feet. She doesn't want to trust me, I can see that, but she also knows I'm right. We can't stay here.

We leave the shop, hurrying down the street and out of the Down Quarter to a bus stop. A few times, we have to put Jag down and rest. Becoming a bit more coherent, he fights us more. When he finally comes to, he doesn't let us carry him at all. He holds his head in his hands, scowling as though he hopes his evil looks will kill me.

I ignore him and try not to take his venom too personally.

Once we stop and get on a bus, we help Jag into a seat and Heidi sits beside him. He lays his head back and closes his eyes.

"We should take him to a doctor. I think you gave him a concussion." She glares at me, but it's more of a little-sister-who-is-pissed-at-her-brother look than the distrusting, suspicious Heidi who thinks I'm a demon.

"He'll be all right. He just needs to rest."

"You could have killed him. You were too rough," she says with bite in her tone. Her eyes narrow, and I can tell she's in the mood to quarrel. I remember this Heidi. She'd follow me all around the house like a shadow, hounding me with her opinions or lecturing me until I cried uncle.

"Let it go, Heidi. I'm not in the mood for one of your tantrums."

"Did you seriously just say that to me?"

Great. And so it begins. I turn to her and level my gaze so she knows I'm not joking. "You have no idea what I've been through since I've been here. I've been given an impossible task with only a bunch of kids to help me." Now that she knows I'm her brother, I don't feel the need to coddle her.

"A bunch of kids? Is that what you think of us?"

This isn't working. "Look, I'm sorry. Okay? I'm sorry I hurt your boyfriend who was trying to kill me."

"You sound just like my brother." She stares at me, her countenance rigid and her attitude frosty.

I can't help but smile back at her. "That's because I *am* your brother, through and through. Is that more impossible to believe than the world falling apart and demons possessing people right and left?"

She studies me, her shoulders still tight and her arms crossed over her chest. She doesn't want to answer and looks the other way, glaring, but I hear her mumble, "I guess not." She turns back to me, the snotty cheerleader look still there. "But how is it possible? If you're really Brecken, then how did you die if Dad didn't kill you?"

I hurry to explain while she seems open to an explanation. "At the time, there was a battle going on in a spiritual realm you don't know about and… well, like I keep saying, it's hard to explain, but someone there needed my help, and I couldn't stay here and let her die."

"Her?"

"Yeah." I can't conceal my smile, and I fight the urge to turn away to hide it.

"The girl you told me about?"

"Yes."

"I can't believe I kissed you."

True to form, she changes the subject on a dime. "Me neither. Gross," I say, shoving her from across the aisle. Could she really capitulate so easily? Oh, I hope so. She's gotten more cynical in the last few years, but my sweet Heidi is still in there, I can tell.

She laughs and hugs me. "It makes so much sense now—how I felt drawn to you, how comfortable I feel around you, and how easily you make me mad."

"Yeah, that's a sure sign."

"It was actually the eggs," she says out of the blue, losing me completely.

"What?"

"You know. When you made me eggs with avocado. No one else cooks them like that. I should have known."

"Yeah, but it *is* unbelievable."

"Yeah."

We ride the rest of the way in companionable silence. When we finally make it back to the church, we tuck Jag into his sleeping bag, and then I go in search of Doug and Owen.

It's time for a Cazador meeting.

24

Dean

Lost and confused, I sit in the dark, my head in my hands. I don't even try to understand my situation. There are no lights on in the hall outside my cell door, and the demons certainly didn't give me anything like a candle. What I wouldn't give for a smidgen of light. I can't even see my freaking hand in front of my face.

For the millionth time, I stumble to the door, press my face against the window hole, and yell for help, for light, for a voice in the dark, for stimulation of any kind. There is no answer and I wonder if they have forgotten me down here. I haven't eaten in twenty-four hours, so maybe they are trying to kill me by default.

I mean, what do they care? I'm a nobody now that they know I can't be possessed. I don't know what keeps them from latching on inside me, but I heard someone sneer the word *inviolable* as I was dragged out of that farce of a party. Three other demons tried their hand at me, and none could possess me. Coem had looked at me like an impossible puzzle he's determined to figure out.

I take that moment to scream through the door again, banging my head against the rough wood in helplessness. Why am I even wasting my breath? I'm hungry, dirty, and only have the corner of my cell to use as a toilet. They don't even given me a bucket. It reeks in here, and so do I.

And then…

A light begins to glow far down the hall, bright enough that my hungry eyes search pathetically for the source. I wait, my breath rasping in excited hitches. "Help!" I scream again, hoarse from lack of water. Again, I lean my head against the door, tears forming at the edges of my eyes. "Please," I whisper. "Please, help me."

"*I* will help you," a voice says happily from the other side.

My head jerks back at the sudden utterance. In the dim light, my eyes struggle to focus. Just outside my door stands a girl. A child really, with red, curly hair, and her eyes… her bright blue eyes… they are so easy to see. They practically glow. She's about seven years old, but rather than relief at finally having someone to talk to, a dark terror grows inside me. This isn't a normal little girl. Not with those alien eyes and that piercing voice.

I back away from the door until my legs hit the cot.

"Can you come out and play with me?" Her voice rises to a whine—a clarion bell of pleading—the sound of a spoiled, lonely child with no friends.

I can't see her, but each time she calls out, a sickening chill prickles my spine. Crawling onto my cot, I push myself all the way to the wall until I'm practically part of the plaster. I squish my eyes shut and cover my ears.

"She's not real, she's not real, she's not real," I whisper, over and over.

"Come back to the door," she calls, her shrill tone growing angry and determined.

A long time ago, when I was very young, I woke in the middle of the night, a terrible fear consuming me. At the foot of my bed, I could see a girl. Formless. Wispy. Ghostly. At the time, I was only five or six, but I remember the terror that consumed me. The ghost hadn't spoken, but she had stared at me with large, soulful eyes, with the saddest expression I'd ever seen. I was so frightened that my bladder released and I wet my bed, too terrified to get up or go to the bathroom. Soaked and smelling of urine, I stayed in my bed for the rest of the night until the sun rose and I could no longer see her. She hadn't hurt me or even said a word. But her mere presence had paralyzed me.

This girl brings that moment back to me with chilling clarity. My heart pounds in my chest and tears threaten to fall. It doesn't matter that I'm almost a man and have been living on my own for so long. Somehow, I'm a child again, alone in my room, unprotected and so afraid.

"You can't hide from me."

She sounds so close. I crack open an eye because *not* seeing is just as terrifying as being able to. She stands right next to me in a blue-and-white gingham dress, her iridescent eyes full of fury. I screech, scratching at the cement wall in an effort to Shawshank my way out of here. Something inside me breaks in that moment. I shatter and dissolve.

25

Heidi

I lie on Dean's sleeping bag, my arms crossed over my chest, staring at the ceiling. The candle that sits on the trunk flickers, making the shadows dance across the bare cement walls and ceiling. I repress a shiver, hating this room, and I think back over the day and all that has happened.

Jag snores beside me, oblivious to my musings. He hasn't quite recovered from Bret's punch in the face. He went straight to bed once we got him home, and Bret left without a word to go back to our apartment.

Now, awake in the quiet, I think about my brother, Brecken. Could he and Bret really be one and the same? My mind races to fill the holes of the last five years after he died. Was he reincarnated? And if it isn't reincarnation, is it possession? Did he take over someone else's body? That sounds too demonic for a benevolent god to do, but I'm not sure. I don't know what to believe. It's all too weird, crazy, and *un*believable.

Glancing at Jag, I study his sleeping form. The skin around his left eye has turned a deep shade of purple, and I wonder if his nose is broken. He has such a pretty face in sleep. So worry free and peaceful.

As though he can feel my gaze, he groans and cracks open his eyes, rolling onto his back, his hand coming up to delicately finger his bruises. "That jack-nit," he groans. "I think he broke my nose."

I don't say anything, propping my head on my hand as I lie on my side. I can't seem to stifle my smile. He's so cute, lying there and complaining, saying the swearword he made up. It's all very

Jag and so endearing. Dean once told me he started using it when they were kids. Jag's mom had washed his mouth out with soap from using a *real* curse word. It was one of the last interactions he had with her before she died in the Rift. He'd never used "bad" words again.

He glances at me. "What's so funny?"

"Nothing," I say, still smiling.

He tries to sit up, but he quickly changes his mind with another groan.

"You want something to eat or drink?" The food I have in my pack runs through my mind. Green tea, two granola bars, a mashed chocolate chip cookie still in its wrapper, and a couple of sticks of gum. Not much in the way of nutrients, but it will fill our stomachs.

"Nah. I'm not hungry." He slowly rolls until he lies on his side, facing me. "How long did I sleep?"

"Only a few hours. It's nine PM," I answer. "Early."

"Good." Pushing himself to his feet as smoothly as the cat he is named for, he loses his grace as he stumbles toward the stairs. He leans against the wall, his head resting against the cement wall.

"Where are you going? You should rest. I think Bret gave you a concussion." I leap up and try to take some of his weight.

He won't have it and pushes me away as gently as he is capable, which isn't that gentle. "It's time to hunt."

I know for a fact he hasn't missed a night of hunting in five years. Why would he skip now when we still haven't found Dean?

He looks up, his gaze heavy, his eyes full of anguish. "I can't stay here knowing Dean's being tortured or worse. I can't rest until I know if… if he's even still alive."

If anyone is being tortured, it's Jag. The rest of us too, but none more than him.

"I know," I say. "I feel the same, but you can't fight like this." I gesture to his whole body, begging him to lie back down.

He shakes his head, making a slow ascent up the stairs. "I can't. I just… can't."

If he goes alone… "Okay," I say, relenting. "I'll go with you."

I don't offer to call Bret for help. I know what Jag's answer to that would be. I strap on my two runed daggers and pull on my jacket. Jag takes a bit longer to get ready. How he intends to get any work done in his condition, I don't know, but I do know better than to argue. Maybe we won't encounter any demons tonight. Maybe we'll just miraculously stumble into Dean. Wouldn't that be nice?

As we walk slowly down the church's darkened street, the stars begin to peak through the clouds. A warm breeze wafts over us, smelling sweet for once, like flowers instead of rotting garbage. I take it as a sign of good luck.

We head to the plaza, which is always Jag's MO, and hide in the copse of trees. The nightlife has already started. Music pulses from the bar across the street and people visit or dance on the grass. You'd think they'd learn to stay home, but no, night after night, they come back to drink and party and get possessed by demons.

No one looks out of the ordinary at the moment, but Jag studies each swaying hippie and beach bum with intense scrutiny. He doesn't trust anyone.

We wait until midnight, but no demons show, and for once, I'm glad. Jag is starting to sway himself, so he reluctantly lets me lead him back to the church. The wretched expression never leaves his face. He falls onto his sleeping bag, exhausted.

"I'm sorry," I whisper, not sure, exactly, what I am sorry for. No demons showing up? Brecken hitting him? Me being here with him? Dean missing? The Rift in general? I am sorry for all of it and wonder if he wants me to leave.

"Me too," he says, turning over and leaving his back to me.

Figuring it's a sign he wants to be alone, I start back up the stairs.

"Don't go," he says. "Can you lay here with me for a while?"

"Sure." I plop back down on Dean's bag, unsure if I should snuggle up next to him or just sit there. I'm not good at this. I don't flirt. I don't play games. If he wants company, I can be company, but I'll need a more specific message if he wants something more than that. Like a huge neon sign above his head with a bright red blinking arrow. Just because he kissed me doesn't mean he likes me, although I hope it does.

"Do you *want* to go?" He rolls back to face me, his eyes glistening. It makes tears spring to my own to see Jag's emotions so close to the surface. I don't think anyone has ever witnessed tears in his eyes before.

"Not really. I just don't know what to do or what you want from me."

He studies me a moment, his gaze dipping to my mouth and then back to my eyes. A flush creeps up my neck, and I can't hold his stare. Taking my hand, he pulls me down next to him, drawing me back against his chest so we're spooning. He pulls me closer, breathing into my hair. I close my eyes, basking in this new feeling. His thighs press against the back of my legs, and I feel completely protected. A wholly foreign experience for me… at least for the last five years.

What are we doing? Is this love? Is this fluttering in my belly the real thing or just a physical reaction to a hot guy who is all muscle? Is Jag my boyfriend? I can't picture being this way—lying in someone's arms, fantasizing about the taste of their lips—with someone who isn't. What if I let myself really give in, and he breaks my heart? Is that a chance I should take?

I inhale, memorizing this moment in case it never happens again. He smells male, earthy, and not at all unpleasant. I hope I smell as nice, although I doubt it, and I can't get it out of my head that the odor of my sweaty armpits is wafting into his nostrils as he inhales, his chin next to my shoulder. But if he doesn't mind my stench and I don't mind his, then why worry? I let the tension go, release my doubts, and let my muscles go flaccid.

I relax… finally.

26

Brecken

I stand before my wall of windows, my chest bare and the moon glowing down on me, but I feel no magic from the slanting moonbeams. Only the cold, slashing truth. I have been here almost two weeks—yet it feels like so much longer—and I'm still not part of the Cazadors. I have failed in my mission to win over the demon hunters, and now they've lost an important member under my watch. So much for becoming a part of their group.

It takes all the self-control I have to leave Heidi at the church with Jag rather than drag her home with me. She is grown up now, and I can't tell her what to do. If she wants to stay with a guy who's sneering and snarky, who only knows how to kill, how can I convince her otherwise? Jag won't try anything with her anyway. He probably won't wake up until morning.

I debate what to do now. Everything is falling apart. I'm sure Michael, the formidable archangel and leader of heaven's armies, is laughing at the debacle I've made of my mission. If it weren't so tragic, I'd be laughing too, but too much rests on my shoulders. I have to get to *The Door to Hell* in Turkmenistan, whether I have a team at my back or not. *The Door* has been burning for a long time, but the Rift did something. It opened it wider somehow.

Running a hand through my hair in frustration, I stomp back to my bed and yank a duffle bag out from under it. I throw in some clothes and every weapon I own. When I'm finished, I look around at my new, awesome apartment that I've hardly lived in and will never live in again. An ache grows in the pit of my stomach, knowing I'll never be back, will never see Heidi or argue with her about who gets to shower first.

In the kitchen, I grab a box of granola bars—the kind Heidi likes—and then count my money. I have enough and plenty more for the job I'm about to do. Silently, I thank my heavenly benefactors and then leave my apartment, locking it behind me.

Four flights of stairs give me plenty of time to debate if I should tell Heidi I'm leaving or not. I don't want a scene and am tempted to just disappear like a phantom, but after the way I left last time…

Jogging, my shoes squeak on the warm asphalt as I make my way to the church. My pulse quickens the closer I get. The church stands alone at the end of the street, a silent sentinel, dark, with its one spire stretching upward like a spike rather than a steeple. Creepy rather than comforting.

At the door, I knock tentatively, hoping to only wake Heidi. It takes a few minutes, and then the door slowly opens, Heidi's eyes are wide and searching. Afraid or just startled? Surely, she knows it's only me or another Cazador. Who else would knock at an abandoned church so late at night?

"Brecken!" She exhales in relief, opening the door wider. "You have no idea how much you scared me! Never do that again!" Her laughter bounces around in my chest like bubbles, and I welcome it.

As I step inside, I know it will be the last time. The heaviness continues to grow inside me. I shake my head, wishing it could be different. Does she even notice she called me Brecken? "I came to say goodbye."

"What?"

"I have to go. I need to finish this mission I was assigned. I have to close *The Door to Hell.* I really wish I could stay and find Dean, but it's almost too late as it is. Too many demons are coming through, and I can't keep… trying to fit in."

She frowns at me, her mouth working in disbelief, her dimples deepening. She's so beautiful, so talented and smart. She deserves a chance at happiness, to get married, to have a family. If I don't close *The Door*, she'll never have that.

I glance intermittently between her and the floor, knowing I'm making a terrible choice… but the correct one. "I'm really sorry." It sounds stupid and won't fix anything, but I have to say it. I need her to know.

"But… you just barely came back."

"I know." The words escape as a whisper. No one is sorrier than I am. I hate to leave, but a pressure builds in my chest and my mind screams that I need to do this or it *will* be too late.

"We'll come with you," I hear from the stairway.

Jag leans against the doorjamb of the stairwell, his hair a mess of tangles, his black eye shining like a dark monster, the bruise taking up most of his face. I'm stunned at how terrible he looks. I appreciate his offer, but he has no idea what he's saying or how far I have to go.

"I'm going to the Middle East." I state it as clearly and precisely as I can, keeping my emotions out of it. This is harder than I imagined. I don't want to say goodbye again. It's too soon.

"That's okay. I have money," Jag says. "Dean would want us to help you finish this. We'll do it for him."

"We do it for everybody," I say.

"You have money?" Heidi asks in astonishment, still stuck on that point. She turns to stare at him. Actually, we both stare at him. If he has money, why would he continue to live in this dive?

"Yeah. I do. Saved. Hidden for a rainy day. It's raining cats and dogs out there now. Can't you hear it on the roof?" he jokes without a smile. There's nothing funny happening, and we all know it. "I have enough for Heidi and me anyway."

"I can pay for Heidi," I say quickly. I could pay for all the Cazadors, actually, but I hold off to see where this conversation will go. This will be dangerous work. More dangerous than anything I've ever faced before, and I'm not sure I want them to go with me. A handful of kids will be nothing against a horde of demons. I don't know what Michael and Raphael were thinking. Kids can't do this. There's no way they can go up against the forces of hell. Four kids against thousands?

"If all the tickets cost the same, what difference does it make who pays for who?" Jag smirks. He has me there, but for some reason, my human emotions—even though I'm not sure if I am totally human—take over, and I want to pay for Heidi's ticket myself. She's *my* sister. *My* responsibility. Not Jag's.

"I guess it doesn't." It was a mistake coming here. I curse to myself and force my mouth to relax. I'm gritting my teeth, and it's starting to make my jaw ache. I can't let them come with me. It's just too dangerous. Even though it felt good, knowing for a moment that I wouldn't have to do this alone, I feel like maybe I need to.

"Give us an hour at least. I need to get ahold of Doug and Owen." Jag is resolute and nods as though it's been written in stone.

And then Heidi asks the question that is on all our minds. "What about Dean?" She addresses Jag, who has already turned away, his jaw clenched and tight. "We can't just leave him."

"He's dead," he answers, still facing away, his voice soft and filled with ache. "We all know it. There's no way they'd keep him alive. It's not how they work."

"Is this true?" she cries, reaching for me for confirmation, as though I would know.

All I can do is shake my head in ignorance. "I honestly don't know."

"Can't you find out? They'll tell you, right? Whoever's in charge?" she pleads with me, holding my hands for good measure. She believes I've been sent here by God. By all standards, I should be able to communicate with Him. She has so much faith in me. More than I have in myself. I don't know what to say. Technically, I *can* call for assistance or information, but I've never felt comfortable praying to the God I betrayed so many times in the past. I'm not sure where I stand with Him… but I can talk to Raphael. "I can try."

She hugs me fiercely and then runs out the door. "I'm going to pack. Don't leave without me!" The front door slams behind her and I am alone with Jag, who looks at me with those dark eyes that deepen into unfathomable depths.

"I think you're full of crap." Jag stares me down as if we're at the OK Corral. "But I'm going along with this… for now… for Heidi. So you better not be leading us into a trap because if that's what it turns out to be, you're gonna wish you'd never met me." He turns and bounds down the stairs.

I walk over to the fire pit to sit on one of the pews, determined to keep my promise to Heidi. Dust has accumulated on the benches since we were all here last, eating pizza and laughing. Darkness shrouds this end of the church, so close to the pulpit, but I'm not afraid of the dark. It welcomes me as though I am a long-lost son of perdition, which maybe I am.

Clasping my hands together, I close my eyes and clear my throat, but rather than speak out loud, I decide to pray in my mind. Raphael will hear me either way.

Okay, so Raph? I need to talk to you. Are you there? Are you listening? I sit for a moment, waiting for something profound to happen or for the angel to appear. He doesn't. Big surprise. *Um, Raphael? I need your help.*

Nothing.

With a sigh, I try a different tactic. *Damn it, Raphael. Talk to me!* My fist pounds on my knee and my teeth grit painfully. Screaming in my mind feels less powerful than using my outside voice, but the results are the same.

A vast silence.

And then… *You are making the right choice. Go to The Door to Hell.*

That's all I get. Short. Simple. Nothing about Dean and nothing about the Cazadors. But chances are, if they go with me, they'll never come home. With my teeth clenching and my heart pounding, I rise and stride over to the door. Taking one last glance around, I say a silent goodbye and slip away.

Despite the fact that technology is at a near standstill, some airports are still working, but only in the big cities, and no flights fly to Turkmenistan. Iran is the closest I'll get. That's fine. It's right next door… except for all that distance in between where bands of roaming thugs live. I'll have plenty of time to find trouble.

Standing at the counter, I pay for my ticket—which is handwritten—and then shoulder my bag. Not many people are here. Not many people have money to fly. Airports don't even bother to use x-ray machines anymore. Why would they? With all the worldwide catastrophes, governments don't concern themselves with global terrorism. Only surviving.

Shaking my head, I walk the long, almost deserted hallway. The carpets are dusty and worn. I search for loading zone B18, where my flight for New York will board… if enough people show up. The wait might be one hour or twelve. You never know. I might be the last one they're waiting for. From New York, it's a straight shot to Spain, where I'll do the whole waiting game again. Then on to the Middle East. I am so *not* excited.

I take a seat in the waiting area, my fingers drumming, *Carry on My Wayward Son*. It's fitting, and it's also one of my favorites. Quite a few people are already waiting, and I count myself lucky… or blessed. How many do they need before they'll take off? I count at least twenty travelers besides myself.

The minutes tick by and my anxiety rises. Not just because my sister could show up and ruin my sneaky escape, but because I hate flying. It's irrational and I know it, but it's my only human weakness. Out of a body, I'm fine. No fears. No problems. But flying? Strap me into a straightjacket and Xanax me for the long haul. I've always been this way.

There are plenty of passengers waiting, so what is taking them so long to call our flight? Airlines don't use large airplanes anymore. They cost too much with not enough people flying to fill them up these days.

We need to get going!

Thirty minutes later, I'm walking down the narrow aisle of the plane with about forty others. It's a fifty seater. Way smaller than feels safe. I stow my bag above my seat and sit down next to the window to gaze out over the tarmac.

The sun will rise any minute and heatwaves will shimmer on the asphalt. Soon, I will be thirty thousand feet in the air in this piece of tin. Even though I understand physics, I still can't believe this metal coffin can fly.

Not two minutes go by before I get that strange feeling—that sticky prickle on the back of my neck, screaming that someone's gaze is boring a hole through my back. Turning, I'm met with the angry glares of Heidi, Owen, Doug, and Jag. Heidi's hands are on her hips, her eyes spitting fire… or maybe daggers. Either way, I'm dead. The others push their packs into the overhead bins above their seats, but Heidi is only getting started.

"How dare you leave us?" she yells, oblivious to the other passengers. "Why did you even come to say goodbye if this was what you were going to do? You knew we'd follow, right? What game are you playing? You're such a damned idiot!" Her voice rises to a deafening pitch, and everyone avoids eye contact with us both.

"Geez, Heidi. Tone it down." I glance at the other passengers and lower my voice also. "You do realize, if you come with me, you're never coming back. None of you. This is a one-way ticket. I can't stand the thought of something happening to you and having it be my fault. I don't want you guys to come. *Please*, go home."

Jag plops down in the seat across the aisle. "Too late, jack-nit, and I think we're all aware of the odds. Plus, we've already paid for our tickets. We're not here for you. We're here for Dean. Don't think for a minute I care about you."

Heidi throws her bag above my head and slams the bin shut. The set of her jaw declares I will not be spoken to for the rest of the trip. Not necessarily a bad thing.

I'd hoped the flight would leave before they could book tickets. I knew they'd follow. The whole situation is stupid, stupid, stupid. I should never have stopped at the church to say goodbye. A hundred other alternatives go through my mind. I could have just left a note. I could have stolen away like a thief in the night. I could have just called from New York to tell them I'd left.

Shaking my head, I berate myself. Once again, I am putting my friends and family in danger just like always. It's because of me that Alisa got messed up with the demons in the first place, because of me that Heidi and Sophie witnessed our father—an angel of protection—trying to kill me. It was because of me that Bas Iblis stabbed Alisa with a Nephilim dagger. I still thank God every day that she was saved from total annihilation.

I know I'm supposed to use the Cazadors for this mission, that they were chosen and prepared, but to go up against so many seasoned demons with this ragtag group of teens leaves me paralyzed with fear for their safety. It shows my lack of faith, I know, but I'm not used to using humans as pawns, and that's what it feel like I'm doing. I shouldn't change the rules now that I'm here, but I'm beginning to seriously doubt Raphael and Michael's plan.

27

HEIDI

I refuse to speak to Bret for the rest of the trip. I still can't believe he actually planned to leave us and go to *The Door to Hell* by himself. And to stop at the church first… what an idiot. Totally something my dumb brother would do.

Brecken was constantly changing his mind at the last second, always second-guessing himself. It was one of those things that used to drive me nuts when we all lived together in our cute house at the end of death row.

He had this insane desire to be absolutely certain he was doing the right thing. He'd go over and over his plan, writing down pros and cons for whatever he was trying to figure out.

I try to put myself in his shoes, with what little I know. It isn't that hard, considering how close we used to be. I know Brecken well. He practically raised me. If I trust anyone, it's him. All of these thoughts go round and round in my mind as we cross the United States in the little plane that bounces around on the slightest breeze.

I turn toward Jag, who sits in the window seat. With one hand on his thigh, his fingers spread, his chin is resting on his other fist, he stares out the window at nothing. This high up, there's nothing to see but outer space above and clouds below. I can't see even a sliver of ground. The light streaming in enhances the gold in his hair and he appears radiant, angelic even. He's beautiful, in spite of the fact he wears a scowl.

I take a chance and place my hand over his.

He gives me a surprised glance, but a smile comes quickly.

"Hey." He moves away from the window and leans toward me.

"Hey, yourself." I can't help the grin that plants itself on my lips. It's automatic, every time I look at him. I still can't believe how all of this has turned around. After the last year of begging to be a part of the Cazadors, of being rejected and criticized, now he looks at me like I'm the next best thing since ice cream.

"You okay?" he asks.

"Sure. Why?"

"I thought that little vein in your forehead was going to explode when you were yelling at Bret." He chuckles and tickles the back of my hand with his finger.

"Yeah. There was a moment there when I wondered the same thing." I glance over at Brecken, whose eyes are closed at the moment. He looks exhausted and so lonely, sitting all by himself on his side of the aisle. I feel a little sorry for him, shouldering so much responsibility on his own, but that's what we're here for—to take some of that weight off him. My heart fills with warmth as I realize I'm on a plane with my brother. We're going to fight evil together. I can't think of anything more amazing.

"Are you afraid?" Jag asks, and my gaze returns to him. He searches my face for any micro expressions I might let escape. He does this to everyone. It's why he's so good at what he does. He's always one step ahead, making people feel like he can read their mind. It's one of his many gifts.

"Of what?"

"Of where we're going. *The Door to Hell.* The demons we'll face. The possibility of imminent death." He says this last part with a sly grin, and I shake my head.

"Yes and no." I turn and face him fully, sitting sideways in the seat. "If for some reason I don't make it, I want you to know something."

He watches me, his smile turning into a frown.

"These last few days with you…" I glance away, unsure how to finish. How do you tell someone who is looking right at you—who you are still shy around—that you love him? That he is in your thoughts night and day? That your heart aches for him, and the thought that he may only be in your life for a few more days is more devastating than anything else you've experienced so far?

He doesn't say anything as he stares at our hands, trying to sort out his thoughts. At least that's what I'm hoping he's doing. And then I realize I don't want him to say anything in case it's something I don't want to hear.

He sighs, glancing out the window and then back at me. "Things are coming to a head?"

"What do you mean?" There are a ton of things that feel like they're coming to a head, but I don't want to discuss most of them.

He exhales and chuckles, rubbing his hands on his pants. A nervous habit, which means he's about to open up and tell me something personal. "To be honest, ever since Bret told us about *The Door to Hell*, I have the feeling *it* is my purpose. It's why I'm still alive. It's why I have this gift. I'm supposed to go there."

"What makes you think that?"

"I don't know." His fingers close around mine, holding my hand tightly as though it will somehow help his words make sense. "It's just a feeling I have. Something is going to happen there. Something big."

I don't know this side of Jag well—the intuitive side. Dare I say it… the spiritual side? Does he have a spiritual side? I don't even know if I do. I have no idea what his beliefs are, and I've never talked about mine. I'm not sure what I believe.

"So you believe Bret?" I ask, hoping we are all finally on the same page.

"Partly, but not like you think. I believe him about *The Door to Hell*, that demons are coming through, that it's some kind of hotspot or something. But I don't trust that we're going there to kill all the demons and close it. Just hear me out," he says quickly when he sees I'm about to argue.

This insane idea that Bret is out to get us is starting to feel like deluded paranoia. It's all too much, and I hate it. I don't even want to think about it.

"Just listen," Jag insists. "If you don't believe me, that's fine. At least I've put it out there."

"Fine," I breathe quietly.

Bret's eyes are still closed and he looks like he's sleeping, but it's pretty quiet in the airplane right now. Maybe he's listening to our conversation. I hope not.

"Okay, so Bret is a demon. I know it. That's not even a debatable point." He hurries to put his hand up as I'm about to interrupt. "The thing we have to figure out is why he wants us to go with him to *The Door to Hell*."

"He doesn't."

A slow smile comes to his lips. "That's where you're wrong, Heidi. He came to the church on purpose. For one reason only, and that was to tell us he was leaving and then act like he didn't want us to come. He knew we'd follow. He manipulated us. But I didn't fall for it."

"You're here aren't you?"

He releases a bemused chuckle. "Not for him. This is the only explanation. Seriously. After everything that's happened so far since we've met him?" He sits back, letting his hands rest on his lap, giving me space.

I recline, brooding over every conversation, every experience, and every word that has come out of Brecken's mouth. It does all seem very coincidental.

"I'm telling you," he whispers. "He's trying to make us think he doesn't want us to come, that it will be too dangerous, but he does want us there. So bad that he's willing to use your dead brother to deceive you."

Brecken wouldn't do that. Or is he just Bret? Could Jag be right?

He must notice my indecision and hurries to add, "One of my theories is this… that there are other Cazadors around the world and the demons are rounding us up so they can get rid of us in one fell swoop."

His whispers can no longer be classified as whispers. Sure enough, when I glance over at Bret, he's watching us, a dejected expression on his face. He doesn't say anything, turning away to gaze out the window.

I release a heavy breath. I don't want to argue. Especially with Jag. He's too hard to debate with, and he always wins. He thinks too fast and too logically. He's too dang smart. I can only think of witty responses the next day. I'm on a twenty-four hour rotation for clever comebacks.

"Just think about it," Jag says as he climbs past me to go to the restroom. "Because what if I'm right?"

28

Brecken

The flight to New York takes years, and the fact that I haven't been spoken to in almost five hours makes the time lapse even slower. It should be a relief. The silence. But it's not. The quiet is heavy, oppressive, and not the way to start out a long trip around the world with a team. The anxiety of being up in the air in this flimsy tin can makes it worse. And we're going to do it again… over an ocean.

Heidi sits across the aisle, mostly staring out at nothing, while Jag whispers to her furiously. Nothing he says is true, and yeah, I can hear their whole conversation. I'm only three feet away, but I'm not going to fight with him. Not on this tiny plane where everyone can hear. I just hope she has more faith in me than Jag does.

We arrive in New York at the LaGuardia airport in the evening, and I'm one of the first people off the plane, rushing to be on solid ground. Inside the terminal, I almost fall to my knees and kiss the stained carpet. We check in for our next flight, and then the wait continues.

I take a seat in the waiting area, a wall of windows to the west. The sun begins its slow descent, and I watch until the very last rays disappear. It feels like a sign, like a portent of things to come. Like the world will grow black until only darkness reigns. I pray it's not true, that it's only my wild imagination and cynical outlook on life.

Owen plops down in the seat next to me, the armrest between us. I'd give anything to lie down. I'm so exhausted. I could fall asleep standing up.

"Hey." He nods, acknowledging me.

"Hey."

"So… what exactly are we going to do in Turkmenistan or whatever it's called?" He flips through a paperback book he brought along.

I snort, unable to stop myself. "The impossible."

"Well, I mean specifically?" When he leans forward, the honesty in his eyes undoes me. He trusts me completely. They all do, really. Except for Jag. It's time to be a leader once again. A general of a teeny-weeny army, but a general nonetheless.

I glance at the others. They're watching and listening, even if it's only with half an ear. "There's a giant, burning crater, two hundred and thirty feet wide and a hundred feet deep that demons have been using to come to this world for at least forty-five years. There was a shift during the Rift that somehow opened *The Door* wider. It's allowing demons to come through at an unprecedented rate. I've been assigned to shut it."

"You mean *we've* been assigned to shut it," Owen says.

Smart kid. Too smart. And he's flying toward his death. He will never see the United States of America again. He will never see his parents again. He'll never find a wife and have kids.

"So, what's the plan?" He's excited, like a kid at Christmas, ready for a new adventure. He really doesn't get it.

"I'm still working that out."

"He doesn't have a plan," Jag says, finally adding to the conversation. "At least one that doesn't involve sacrificing us to the gods." He's sitting across from me, looking totally bored, faced away with one leg crossed over the other. He doesn't want to be here, and he doesn't believe my story. He's here for one reason only. Heidi. And for the sheer chance we might be able to do something about the demons… and maybe to witness my downfall.

"I said I'm working on one, and once it's solidified, all of you need to obey me without question. What we're about to do will have lasting, eternal consequences. We can't mess up." I look hard at each member of the group, making sure they understand. Jag is the only one glaring back at me. He doesn't say anything, and he isn't about to take orders from me.

He's going to be the weak link, and I'll have to figure out a solution or we'll never survive. We have to be able to trust that we have each other's backs. Having Jag in this group is a huge test for me. Maybe it's some stupid game that Raphael and Michael thought up. They probably want to see how much I can take before I lose it. Demons are famous for capsizing quickly, but I'm not a demon anymore.

"I wish Dean were here." Heidi looks off into the distance at nothing. She rests her chin in her hand and kicks her crossed leg. Her shoulders are hunched and tight, tense. If I tell her to relax, she'll probably punch me.

"I'm glad he's not," I say kindly, trying to catch her eye. We gaze at one another, a whole lot of meaning passing in our expressions. "It's not the place for someone like him. Someone who doesn't fight. It's not who he was." Back when we were kids, Heidi and I could communicate without having to say anything at all. With just one look, we knew what the other was thinking. We mostly used this form of communication when our dad was mad and we were trying to protect whoever was in trouble. Not that our dad was mean or violent, but I hated it when he yelled at Heidi or Sophie.

"Jag says he's dead." Owen shakes his head, folding and unfolding his book. By the time we get to Turkmenistan, it's going to be shredded. The thrum-thrum-thrum of the pages has grown annoying, and if he doesn't stop folding it over and over, I'm going to grab it and chuck it into the trash bin myself.

"I don't know," I answer, wishing I could give them something definite, but I haven't gotten any inspiration on the subject. I chalk it up to the fact that we're not supposed to know at this point. My guess is that Dean is in a better place, even though it kills me to admit it.

"He's with his family now," Doug says hopefully, looking at each member of the team. "They died in the Rift." He nods when he glances at me, unconsciously, I think, to spur a yes answer from me.

"Yeah. Probably." I give him a reassuring smile.

"So, let's hear this plan of yours." Jag sits up, a tired sigh playing around his lips. Lips that Heidi can't seem to stop staring at. It's maddening beyond anything, and it takes effort to put the plan I have into words instead of saying something I might regret about their budding relationship.

The flight from New York to Spain goes quickly, thank heavens, as it's during the night. I try unsuccessfully to sleep and ignore Jag and Heidi, snuggling across the aisle. But by the time the sun rises, I am ready to collapse. I stare out the tiny airplane window at the dusty, sunburned city of Tehran, wound up so tight that one wrong move from Jag and I might actually lose it.

Iran suffered severe damage during the Rift. The tall buildings are now piles of rubble, weeds growing through to reclaim their prize. In the distance, snow-capped mountains strain to reach the crystal blue sky, and I'm amazed that such a vast city like Tehran could fall to ruin so quickly.

The plane rumbles as it circles around to taxi, updrafts bouncing us like leaves on rising gusts of wind. The plane rattles and the overhead bins shake. I grasp my armrests, white-knuckled, praying that we'll land soon and that this will all be a distant memory.

I glance over at Heidi, who leans over Jag to see out her window. Owen and Doug visit, looking completely unconcerned, and as usual, I sit alone with only my aviophobia as my companion.

I'm not afraid to die. It's not that. I just don't like strapping myself into a metal container that can fall out of the sky at any moment. I like picturing my destination in my mind and then arriving there two seconds later, like I did in the world of spirits. Instead, I sit here for hours on end, my back cramping and my nerves fraying, at my wit's end, before I even reach my destination.

To calm my nerves, I force my mind to the only thing that will help. Alisa. She's somewhere in the vast whiteness of Elysium, learning and growing without me. Does she think about me at all? I picture her in my mind, her golden hair cascading over her shoulders, her twinkling eyes, crinkling with a smile, and I wonder what she is doing right now. I wish she were here with me, with her snarky comments and dry sense of humor. I miss her so much it hurts.

The things that seem important to us here in mortality are nothing but gnat-like worries—if they are worries at all—in the afterlife. Am I a gnat to Alisa now? I yearn to have this mission over with so I can get back to her. I can't find peace in this world where doubt and fear are constant emotions. It's amazing anyone survives it.

The wheels finally touch down with a thump. My head actually bounces forward. Practically whiplash. I jump up, grab my pack from the overhead bin, and sling it over my shoulder. I help Heidi with hers, and then wait for Owen and Doug to get out of the way so I can hurry down the aisle.

As soon as my feet hit the pavement outside, dry waves of heat slam into me, and all thoughts of flying are erased. I can only think of one thing. Water. My mouth and the inside of my nose feels like I've swallowed sand. Within seconds, sweat drips down my back and the sun is hot on any exposed skin.

Heidi gasps next to me. "Oh, my gosh, I'm going to die here."

I pray her words are not prophetic.

And in spite of the heat, she pulls a scarf from her pack and wraps it around her head. I'm amazed she thought to remember, and my appreciation for her grows. She's so freakin' smart and always has been… except when it comes to boys.

It's late enough in the afternoon that we look for a hotel rather than continue travelling, because I'm so tired that I'll never make it without sleep. I flag down a taxi, asking the guy to take us someplace nice and quiet.

I glance at the others, and they gawk at me. I guess I'm the only on here who speaks Farsi. Heidi's eyes grow wide, and Jag's jaw drops as soon as I start talking.

"Dude!" Doug exclaims. "You speak Iranian? That is so cool!"

"It's Farsi," I say, humbled to have this ability, and I give silent thanks to Raphael for the gift.

The taxi driver nods, and the five of us jostle for space in the backseat. We don't want to split up in two cars and the driver won't let anyone sit up front with him. Heidi sits on Jag's knees. I try not to glower, but she notices my scrutiny. I'm still trying to figure out their relationship. It feels wrong to me.

Jag's hand slides up her waist. It takes all my self-control not to grab it and fling it away. That would get me on her good side for sure.

Doug sits on Owen's lap since he's the smallest and there isn't room anywhere else. Owen doesn't let him forget it either, doling out snide remarks all the way to the hotel like, "I can hardly tell you're there, you're so light… except for those really sharp bones in your butt. Those are huge. It's a good thing you don't have a lot of muscle. I wouldn't want to not feel those butt bones!"

Doug elbows him in the chest. "Shut up, douche-bag."

Owen erupts into peals of laughter and adds a few more derogatory remarks I wouldn't repeat out loud—I swear they're still in junior high—and then the car gets quiet.

We're dropped off in front of the Azadi Grand Hotel, once a five-star establishment, now a rundown, falling-apart, barely surviving edifice. The Iranians keep it as nice as possible, but with dust and sand taking over the city, it seems an impossible task. It doesn't bother me much. We won't be here for long.

"Two rooms, please," I tell the desk clerk. This guy speaks broken English, which is a relief. It feels weird to speak Farsi in front of the others. I'm getting rude looks from Jag.

"Three." Jag slaps down some money.

The desk clerk glances at the bills on the counter and smirks. "Your American dollars will not work here. We only use the rial."

The look on Jag's face is priceless, and it takes all the self-control I possess not to rub it in. Instead, I ask, "Is there some place where we can exchange our money?" I try to be as polite as possible, but the clerk shakes his head. He's lying, but I don't accuse him. Instead, I switch to Farsi and say, "You would do well not to annoy me. If Coem finds out that our treatment here was less than perfect, you will pay a steep price for your insubordination." I take a chance with this threat, hoping he knows Coem, because he *is* a demon. I know this instinctively—we can always recognize one of our own—and it pays off.

The guy's face visibly pales. "My mistake, sir. You can exchange your money here."

"In that case," Jag says again. "Make that three rooms, like I asked before."

I turn to him, frowning. "We'll save money if you bunk with Doug and Owen. There's plenty of room. They have two king-sized beds."

"I want my own room." His expression remains calm, his gaze soft.

I stare at him hard, my teeth grinding. A million reasons why he would want his own room go through my mind. All of them have Heidi's name in bright neon letters.

"Whatever. It's your dime." I'm not going to fight about it here, but if he thinks he's going to share a room with my little sister… The muscle in my jaw actually cramps as I grit my teeth.

We head to the elevator, which miraculously still works, but I take one look and choose the stairs. I can hoof it up four floors. Jag smirks, grabs Heidi's hand, and pulls her into the elevator behind him. He winks at me as the doors close. I just stand there, watching like an idiot.

By the time I get to my room, I'm huffing and out of breath. The hall is empty, so the others must have gone into their rooms already. Doug and Owen's is right next to mine. I walk over and lean close to the door, hoping to hear Heidi's voice. No sound comes from inside. I walk to the next door, Jag's, and hear muffled voices, but nothing distinct.

The urge to knock is almost overpowering. I even raise my fist, but I get the distinct feeling I should let her be. I'm not her parent. And I don't want to ruin everything. Not now. Not at the end of it all, and that's what this is. The end.

I run a frustrated hand through my hair and enter my own room after trying the key card three times. There's a moment when I actually think I'll have to go all the way back down to get a new one. By the time I shut the door behind me, my heart is pounding in my chest. Everything is coming to a head. *The Door* is only a few hours away. My whole purpose for being here is fast approaching. I'll be facing the hardest assignment I've ever had in my whole existence in just a day or two. Suddenly, I feel unqualified and incapable of completing it. I don't even have a plan!

I turn… and my stomach falls to my feet. Where my window should be is a huge, clear sheet of plastic nailed to the wall. One corner flutters, the hot, dry afternoon breeze blowing right into my room. I walk over and peer down four stories. There are at least a dozen other windows like mine. Nice. So much for air conditioning.

There's a queen-sized bed, an old TV that probably doesn't work on the dresser, and a small bathroom. It's a bit dingy, but not bad considering it used to be a five-star hotel.

Just out of curiosity, I pick up the remote and hit the power button. The TV turns on with a buzz, but static is the only thing playing on every channel. I turn it off, toss the remote on the bed, and sit down to kick off my shoes. The only sounds in the room are my breathing, the creak of the bed, and the snap of plastic.

Once again, I'm alone, but this is how I wanted it. This is how it would have been if they hadn't followed me. So what's wrong? I miss Doug and Owen's bantering and Heidi's snarky comments. Truth be told, I even miss Jag. He's a huge presence. When he's not around, something feels like it's missing.

I lie down on my bed, my arms behind my head. Water stains dot the ceiling, and I'm not sure I want to sleep on the sheets… or the quilt. Closing my eyes, I will myself to relax, but I keep thinking about *The Door*, and how much I *don't* want to go there.

29

Dean

Day in and day out, I'm tortured by demons. But it's no longer taking place in that big auditorium where everyone watches, their grins slick in anticipation of my pain. No, now, it's an interrogation room. Just a demon and me.

Today, Coem sits across from me, a sly smile on his lips. He's thinking of something wonderfully evil, some new form of torture he wants to try, or a new demon he wants to pit against me.

After what feels like hours, he opens his mouth and speaks. The sudden echo of sound startles me, and I jump in my seat, pushing myself erect, exhausted, but ready.

"You have been here… what? A little less than a week?" Coem leans forward, resting his elbows on his knees, a pleasant smile on his face. "You seem impossible to possess, and I have made it my mission to figure out why."

"Why does it matter?" I slump back down in my seat, no longer caring what his motivations are.

"Because if I can figure you out, I can figure out anyone." His smile widens, but it never reaches his eyes. They remain arctic and biting. He hates me. I feel the enmity wafting off him like the stench of garbage that rots across the street from the church. Fermenting and sour. He wonders how such a weak, effeminate—his word, not mine—boy is able to resist his horde of demon soldiers. What is it that makes me so different?

I glance around the room at the solid metal walls. I'm not breaking out of here on my own… unless I come up with a brilliant plan… but Coem always seems one step ahead of me. I'm tired, it's cold, and I haven't eaten since yesterday. I don't think they care.

"I'd like you to paint today."

"What?" Coem's comment takes me by surprise because he doesn't do things to make me happy. He always has an ulterior motive, but even so, I feel a frail thumping in my chest, faster than it was a moment ago. Something to break up the monotony.

"Whatever you want," he says with a disinterested wave of his hand. "Scenery, a self-portrait… whatever."

The door opens with a whoosh. A guy I haven't met before brings in an easel, a set of brushes, and oil paints. A variety of colors. I can't help that my mouth starts to drool. Coem is taunting me somehow, but I don't care. The demon bows to Coem, and then leaves without a glance or a smile in my direction.

My shackles rattle as I lean forward to pick up one slim brush. A Filbert. Sable hair. It's beautiful. Expensive. And I raise questioning eyes to Coem. "I don't get it."

"We aren't the bad guys here." He rushes to scoot forward to the edge of his seat, close to me, excited. "This is a peace offering. We can be friends. It's possible to live together in harmony. We just want our chance to have bodies. To experience the world!" His smile is genuine as he throws up his arms, like a child, trying to convince me of his altruistic motives.

"From what I understand, you had your chance and were cast out of heaven." I can't help the snark that sneaks into my voice, but it feels good to say it, and I'm glad I remember my Sunday school lessons so I can taunt him. I enjoy seeing the hard edge come back to his eyes. Score one for me.

Coem shakes my comment off and replaces his snarl with a plastered-on smile. "I can neither confirm nor deny any allegations along those lines. Enjoy your gift." He stalks from the room, the air electric.

I smile at the closed door and glance up at the monitoring camera in the corner. A red light watches me, but my smirk remains.

A few hours later, I set the paintbrush down. My shoulders ache from lifting my arm with the heavy, iron shackles—the kind you'd see in a horror movie—still attached. No, they did not remove them. I'm a fierce creature, and I guess they think I'll attack or escape if I'm not nailed to the wall like a rabid dog.

I assess my artwork, a true masterpiece really, and it gives me the chills just looking at it. I don't have to wait long for the door to slam open. Coem races in, his small frame seeming monumentally huge as he stares down at me and then at the painting. I detect a bit of narcissism as he straightens and preens, a smug smile curving on his mouth.

I've rendered him perfect, from the sharp, dagger-like teeth and red, leathery skin to the black horns that twist back from his forehead. His *true* form, under all that humanness. No matter where you stand, the rage in those black, beady eyes seems to follow you, his piercing gaze burning a hole through your soul. Hate simmers, in oil and shadow, just under the taut muscles of his neck and face, a heathen devil, a satan if I've ever seen one. The painting inspires fear, even in me. Each odious stroke epitomizes who Coem really is.

From his expression, he considers it a magnum opus. "I had no idea that you were so talented," he purrs as he circles the easel.

I shrug. I didn't do this for him. I have my own reasons for rendering him in oils, but it was therapy more than anything.

He stops pacing and crosses his arms, studying me, one hand stroking his chin. "I think it's time for a new adventure."

"Oh? And what would that be?" I can't imagine any kind of adventure I'd like to take with him, although the word—at first—sends a thrill through my heart. It's something my mother used to say before we went camping or to see some exciting national treasure like the Grand Canyon or Yosemite. Just one more sacred memory Coem and his cronies are ruining for me.

"It wouldn't be much of a surprise if I told you." There's a glint in his eyes that I've learned to recognize, which does not promise a favorable outcome. "Have you eaten or bathed in the last few days?" He gestures to my whole body as though he can't tell.

Dirt and grime have become permanent stains on my skin and may never wash off. I haven't brushed my teeth the whole time I've been here, which pretty much sums up my situation, but I did start getting one full meal a day. It's always bland and awful. Oatmeal, with no sugar, milk, or even butter. I feel like I've already lost weight, and I didn't have much to spare in the beginning.

"Charl!" Coem calls.

A guard enters the room—the same one who brought the easel.

"Get this is poor waif some food and a bath."

"Excuse me, sir?" The guard seems genuinely baffled by the request.

"Do you not know what food and a bath means?" Coem asks, his tone condescending and biting. "Is there any reason you should question me?" He spits this last sentence out through gritted teeth, and the guard snaps to attention.

"No, sir." Charl yanks me up from my chair and hauls me out of the room, none too gently, and my chains clank and bang behind me, heavy and cumbersome. At the end of the hallway, he shoves me into what looks like an old locker room and unlocks my shackles, pushing me through the tiled chamber to an area of showers without curtains or any form of privacy.

"Shower," he commands, his arms crossed over his chest and staring. He doesn't look like he intends to leave.

"Can you at least turn around?" I'm not normally shy, but after hardly eating the last few days, I look less like a Cazador and more like a starving refugee. I'm embarrassed, and truth be told, ashamed. I have no reason to be, but I feel broken somehow, and I can't stand to let them see my pathetic nakedness.

"No."

One more abuse in a long line of suffering. "Whatever." I turn away, accepting my fate, and pull my filthy white T-shirt off and slide down my pants. I don't even bother checking to see if he watches. I don't give a damn anymore. Let the perv have his thrills. If a starving, malnourished, half-alive orphan is what gets him off, he'll deserve his place in hell when Jag finds him.

The shower knob squeaks as I twist it, and in slow motion, a stream of water explodes from the head. Cold water runs over my face like a baptism and tears form at the edges of my eyes. I let the water rinse away my misery as well as my stench.

There's a tiny, half-broken bar of soap that someone else has recently used. It's slightly damp and dirty, but I rinse it off, letting my fingers wipe away the mud streaks, and then I slowly slide it all over my body, imagining that this small bar of soap can cleanse my aching heart as well.

It's chilly down here, underground, and this arctic stream of water gives me goose bumps all over my body, but it's worth it. This one small mercy, a *shower*, is more of a gift than anything. More than getting to paint today. It makes me feel like I can go on. Like I just might make it. Like I'm still human.

And that, most of all, fills me with hope.

30

Heidi

Jag and I sit on his queen-sized bed facing one another, our legs folded beneath us. I clasp my hands and stare at my fingers, playing with a tiny, silver ring I wear on my pinky. I remember when I first got it. My last birthday before the Rift. Brecken gave it to me. It wasn't expensive, but was the kind I liked, simple and shiny. Cute, yet practical. Feminine, but durable. All things I strive to be.

Jag watches me with a quirky smile. He reaches out and takes my hand, bringing it closer to him. He studies my ring, my fingers, my nails. It's more for the chance to touch me than to memorize the tiny, childhood scars that pepper the backs of my hands.

"Why are you here?" He lifts his eyes to mine in genuine interest.

"Same reason as the rest of you, I guess. To kill some demons and shut *The Door to Hell*." I can't offer more than a sad smile. My reasons for being here are much more than that. I'm here for Bret, or Brecken, whoever he is in my mind, and I'm here to avenge Dean. I'm also here for Jag. There's more to that than I care to discuss at the moment.

"Do you know why *I'm* here?" he asks, bringing my palm to his lips.

I think I do. We discussed it a bit on the plane, but even so, a lump forms in my throat and I can hardly swallow. He's being especially tender as he rubs my wrist with his thumb, his eyes soft and his mouth softer. There's a look in his eyes I recognize. One I've seen before from other guys. The pounding in my heart is a telltale sign of my panic. This is unchartered territory.

"I have my own plan," he says. "We leave. You, me, Owen, and Doug. We get out of here without Bret knowing. He's going to stab us in the back anyway. We sneak across the border, find *The Door to Hell,* and then figure out how to close it."

This is so far from the train of thought I was on that I can't even answer. I'm still trying to catch up, not to mention trying to ignore the way his thumb is sliding over my knuckles, playing with the skin on the back of my hand.

"If there are demons, there's a God. You can't have one without the other. He led us here… to this very moment… to destroy one of the most complex, wicked demons ever born into this world."

Wait. What? I yank my arm back. What he's doing to my hand is so completely incongruent with his words that I can only stare. "Are you talking about Bret?" Where he's going with this makes me sick to my stomach, and I automatically recoil. Bret is anything but a demon. He's my brother. I believe him about that. On the extensive flight over, I had plenty of time to think about it, to analyze it, to meditate on it. On some very deep level, I know he's telling the truth.

"Of course I'm talking about Bret. Who else? This is our chance to cleanse the world of demons, possibly once and for all." He stares at me in confusion, as though wondering how I could possibly think anything else.

"He's my *brother*, Jag. And the only one of us who speaks Farsi."

"No, he's not your brother. He just wants you to think he is. Have you learned nothing in the last five years? Do you not realize how devious and conniving demons are? Just because we can't see the gray man inside him doesn't mean he isn't there. He's probably a higher-up demon. Higher even than Coem. Remember *that* guy?" Jag jumps up from the bed, running a hand through the strands of hair that have fallen into his face, and then he turns back to me. "He *knew* Bret. Remember?"

I'd forgotten about that, actually. I've been so excited to have my brother back, that the day in the soda shop had completely left my mind. That unnerving feeling comes back now because I can't really argue this point with Jag. It does make sense.

"And don't you think," he continues, "that a demon who could come up with this kind of story would let the only people who know his plan live? Of course he wants to destroy the Cazadors! It's so obvious!"

"But what about Coem's reaction to Bret? They hate each other. They're enemies. *That* was obvious. What if he's telling the truth—that he's on our side?"

Jag hurries to sit back down beside me, taking both my hands in his and peering deeply into my eyes. "I understand how much you want your brother back. I totally get how alone you feel. There's no one who understands better, but Heidi… you can't believe him. You *can't*."

The earnestness in his voice, the desperate clasp of his hands over mine, almost convinces me. Or at least, mostly convinces me. I shake my head, unwilling to let go of my brother completely. Not just yet. I want to believe in Bret so much. I need to believe Brecken is back. What a heartless, cruel joke if what Jag says is true.

He scoots closer, placing one warm palm against my cheek. I sink into it, soaking up the heat, because suddenly, my heart feels so cold. He turns my face to his, and I'm forced to open my eyes. He's only an inch away. The warmth of his body radiates around me, a source of tenderness I crave. Jag is safety. He's security. He cares about me. I know this. It has taken a while to get here, but somehow, I've been able to pierce the military-grade armor he wears around his heart. Dean was the only one who could get through before, but somehow, he has let me inside too.

I search his eyes. His gaze flicks to my lips. In the next moment, he closes the distance. The kiss starts out slow, soft, and warm, just like the rest of him, but it deepens and becomes more intense as he puts his arm around my waist and pulls me closer.

My arms snake around his neck and my mouth parts. That's all the invitation he needs. In one smooth move, his other arm is around my hips, scooting me down on the bed and then he is lying on top of me, all without breaking our kiss.

It happens so fast, I'm not sure what to think of it. Intense heat courses through me. This is no casual make-out session. How far will this go if I let it? Do I want this? Is this what I have to do to keep Jag? What will his reaction be if I want to stop? I'm not sure I'm ready, mentally, emotionally, or physically. It's been so hard to crack his prickly shell that I'm afraid to stop, but is that the kind of guy I want to be with anyway? Someone who gets mad if I say no? But do I want to say no? I'm not sure I do. I love the feel of him, the taste of his lips, and the connection we have. I love the way he holds me and his weight against my body.

These thoughts slam through my mind, rapid fire, and I realize we can't do this now. Not here. Not yet. It feels too rushed, and with Jag, I want it to be special. Not a distraction. I turn my face slightly. "Jag?"

He pauses and props himself up on his elbows with a playful smile. "Is this not a good time? Should I come back later?" His smile widens, and he swipes a strand of hair from my face.

I'm achingly aware that he is still lying on top of me, every inch of him touching every inch of me and it's hard to form words. "I'm sorry," is all I can think of, still not sure what I want.

"It's okay." He kisses the tip of my nose and slides to the side, keeping his arm around my waist. He lies next to me, continuing to play with my hair. I gaze at him, surprised, and a bit confused. I guess I don't know Jag as well as I thought, and the reality of that hits home with slamming force.

I expected anger. When it doesn't come… when I get this loving and extremely patient response, I'm left speechless. I know his fighting technique like the back of my hand. I know his drive and commitment to his goals. I know his love for his friends, like Dean. I know he'll do anything to protect us, and that he can. He's capable and strong. That alone is enough to make me fall for him. But this side… this tender, playful side… I have no idea how to respond to *this* Jag. I have no idea who I am supposed to be around this Jag.

"You can stay with me if you want… to sleep," he says. "If you want."

I put my arm around his chest and lay my head on his shoulder. He's warm and his muscles flex as his arms squeeze me. He stirs something inside me, but I tamp it down. "Can we just lay here for a while?"

He pulls me closer in answer and I lie there, soaking him in. Soaking us in. Until I hear a pounding on the door.

Jag lifts himself reluctantly from the bed. I watch him saunter over to the door, sleek and catlike. He peers through the peephole, giving me a wry smile as he opens the door. My curiosity is piqued until Doug and Owen plow past him and jump on the bed to lie next to me like two rambunctious puppies. Owen props himself up on his elbow, not unlike Jag had done a moment before.

I can't help the giggles that escape me. Doug and Owen are like little brothers, and I can't be mad at them for interrupting us. Exasperated, yes. Angry, no. "What are you two doing?" A twinge goes through me, knowing Dean should be here too. My heart aches for him because, like Jag, I've resigned myself to his death, and I mourn for him every time he pops into my mind.

"Just hangin'," Doug says, grabbing the remote and flipping through all the staticky stations.

"I think we should order pizza." Owen stares at me with pleading eyes, like I am the mother and have the right to veto their ideas. I actually like the feeling and wonder what it would be like to be a mother. Would Jag be a good father? I can't picture him with children, but at the same time, it makes me smile. And then I laugh at myself. I'm picturing things too far in the future. Who knows where this new relationship will go?

"He's the one with the money," I say, pointing to Jag. He stands at the foot of the bed, giving me a mocking grin that is way too sexy for our own good.

"They don't have pizza here." Jag tosses Owen the room phone. "Just order whatever is cheapest."

That's all the leeway Owen needs, and he starts punching numbers into the phone.

"Get something safe," I say, thinking of all the unusual things they probably eat over here, even though I'm not really sure what that would be.

Doug throws his arms in the air. "Hello? Who cares about safe? If we cared about safe, we wouldn't even be here!" He's joking around, but his words cast a serious pall over the room. We all know our situation is life and death, but we need something to relieve the tension. Our playacting does that for a while.

When the food arrives, Doug opens all the cardboard cartons. The smell alone starts my mouth watering, and *safe* goes out the window. Whatever it is, I'm eating it.

The food turns out to be rice, lamb, steamed veggies, and some kind of flat bread. We dig in, sitting in a circle on the bed, moaning over the wonderful flavors. After a few moments, Doug asks me what I've been thinking for the last ten minutes. I've been quiet, methodically munching without conversing, watching these guys who feel like *my boys*. But one of us is missing.

"Maybe we should invite Bret over." I glance at him, wanting someone to extend the invitation. I risk a glimpse at Jag.

Something flashes in his eyes, but it's gone before I can grasp what it is. "Keep your friends close and your enemies closer." He speaks with droll seriousness.

"And that's a yes!" Doug says, hopping off the bed to run two doors down to get Bret.

Secretly, I'm happy. I hate excluding him, but I also don't want to be the only one to suggest he participates. Not with my feelings so topsy-turvy. I don't want to ruin things with Jag, but he's put me in a terrible situation. Like I have to choose. And I can't.

How do I pick between my heart's desire and the brother I've mourned over for so long?

Five minutes later, Bret is sitting on the bed with the rest of us, chewing his food with a wary eye. He keeps glancing at Jag, who never stops watching him. The air is static and chilly. The cold war becoming a simmering boil. Do Doug and Owen sense it yet? I search for something to say instead of cautiously watching the other two.

Surprisingly, it's Bret who breaks the silence. "So, I guess the rest of you have windows in your rooms? Actual windows?"

"Huh?" Doug stops eating with a look of total confusion on his face. "It's a fire hazard not to have a window."

"Oh, I have a window… of sorts," Bret says with a chuckle. "Made out of plastic. It doesn't keep the flies out."

"Seriously?" Owen hops off the bed and holds his hand out to Bret. "Let me see your key card. I want to check that out."

Bret chuckles and shakes his head. "Knock yourself out."

Doug hurries out with him and then it's just Jag, Bret, and me on the bed, staring at one another in the most uncomfortable silence I've felt since I found my dad trying to murder my brother.

"So, how's the rest of your room?" I ask.

"It's good. You should see for yourself."

Jag's eyes narrow at his comment, but he doesn't say anything. His eyes flick to mine, waiting for my response. I don't want to be the middleman here, pulled from both sides.

"Yeah. Maybe later." I smile and dip more rice. Who knows? It might be our last chance at a real meal.

31

Brecken

By four in the morning, I've ripped the plastic down, opting for quiet rather than protection from the elements. I've hardly slept, and I feel like the walking dead. Soon, my mood will need a massive overhaul. Maybe breakfast will help, but I doubt it, knowing I'll most likely have to eat with Jag, who's plotting my demise.

I rise by seven and pack all of my things, not planning on wasting another night here in the city. Shouldering my bag, I head down the hall to Owen's door. After knocking, I shove my hands into my pockets to keep from fidgeting while I wait. It takes a few minutes for him to open the door, and when it opens, it's only Heidi in the room.

"Where are the boys?" I look around, suddenly filled with relief—she didn't sleep in Jag's room. But if the boy's aren't here, I'll have to search for everyone individually just so we can get out of here.

"They already went down to eat." She gives me a tired sigh, and I take in her hair, which is a mess, her pajamas—a gray tank top and plain pajama bottoms, men's, with a fly. Typical. She hasn't changed much.

I sit down on one of the beds, watching her gather up clothes and head into the bathroom. "I don't want to stay in Tehran all day. We need to find a car."

"Okay," I hear from the bathroom.

"It's going to be dangerous from here on out. There are tons of demons here, and it will only get worse the closer we get to *The Door*."

"There were a ton in L.A. too," she answers.

"Not like here. Just wait. It's going to get rough. We need to stay as incognito as possible. They surely know we're here by now, which means we can expect all hell to break loose. Literally." I pull a thread on the quilt. It undoes the entire seam.

When she exits the bathroom, there's a black hijab covering her head. She could almost pass for Middle Eastern except for the bright blue eyes. As blue as mine.

I motion to the shawl. "You look awesome. Glad you thought of it."

"Jag did."

He's smarter than I give him credit for, but I don't admit that out loud. A lot has changed in the world, but culture hasn't. Women in the Middle East still need to be covered up, and with all the devastation in the last five years, it has only gotten worse as people try to hold onto what is familiar.

Heidi grabs her bag, and we shut the door behind us. Doug and Owen are in the cafeteria eating dates, cheese, and some kind of grilled meat. I pick up a date, letting its sweetness explode in my mouth. When I plop down on the bench seat, Heidi slides in next to me. We order a bit more and wait for Jag.

"Do you know where he is?" I ask Doug, who sits right across from me.

"Yeah, I saw him leave."

"Leave? The hotel?"

Owen nods, his mouth full. "Yeah. About a half hour ago. Said he was going to look around."

This is just the kind of thing I wanted to avoid. Did he even bother to let me know where he was going? *No*. Is he safe here, where he doesn't know anyone? *No*. I try not to let it darken my mood further, but I feel a familiar emotion simmering deep in my belly. Jag would rather sacrifice our safety than be controlled. I keep my thoughts to myself, the grit of my teeth the only thing that declares outwardly how I feel.

"He'll be back," Heidi says. "He knows we're leaving early."

I don't bother to answer, because it will only turn into an

argument, which is no way to start the day. The conversation turns to the weather, which is already sweltering and it's only eight-thirty in the morning.

"I don't know if I can stand this scarf all day." Heidi adjusts how low it sits on her forehead, loosening the neck. She's wearing a long-sleeved, white cotton blouse. It's the coolest material here—everyone wears it—but I doubt it's as comfortable as her usual tank tops.

The rest of us are dressed in jeans and T-shirts. Men have a lot more freedom here. We just can't wear shorts. Owen wears a baseball cap, and with that, we look pretty American.

It isn't long before I feel the energy in the room shift, growing sharp and intense, hotter, if that is possible. I glance up and notice two guys staring malevolently at us from across the restaurant. Within moments of catching my eye, they stand up and walk directly to our table. They aren't waiters and their scowls remain fixed as they stride over.

"Can we help you?" I ask when they stop next to our table, glaring down at us. I kick myself for not sitting on the outside edge of the booth. I grab Heidi's hand under the table, hoping she'll keep her eyes down and stay quiet.

"You aren't welcome here," the guy on the right growls. He's tall with a black goatee, wearing black slacks and a black, long-sleeved button-down shirt. Fierce is the only word I can think of to describe him. He's also sporting a shiny new gray man inside and is probably unaware of our unique abilities, but he might sense something different about me. Most demons do… and some demon hunters. He's probably newly arrived. Most seasoned demons don't pick a fight unless they *know* they'll win, but they're also pretty arrogant, so I'm not surprised.

"We'll be on our way in a moment." I hold his gaze. Heidi keeps her eyes on her plate, but I see her hand slide to the dagger in her belt. I nudge her leg.

"Dude, we're almost done," Doug says, scowling up at the guy. He doesn't seem the least bit afraid, but I'm sure he sees the gray man as well as I do.

"I think you should leave... *now*," the second guy says to us, his tone polite and calm. He waits next to his friend, not quite as tall, with softer features. Also wearing black. His long hair is tied at the nape of his neck. He watches only me, conveying something deeper in his gaze, as though he knows exactly who and what I am.

I'm not sure if the others pick up on it, but his message is clear. He doesn't want problems and if we leave now, there won't be any. People are beginning to stare.

Slowly, as though the ticking of the clock has stretched and lengthened, Heidi raises her eyes, glowering straight into the eyes of the tall, angry man. "We're still eating."

The guy looks down to see the tip of her dagger pressed against his belly, just above his belt. She adds pressure, and it digs in a little deeper. His eyes narrow and the muscles in his jaw flex, but he doesn't step back.

"I don't think you want to bother us at all," she says. "I think you want to walk away and mind your own business." She smiles, but it isn't friendly, and I couldn't be prouder or more mortified.

Polite Guy raises one eyebrow, but he seems completely unperturbed. "May I ask who you are and where you're from?" He directs his comment to Heidi now, clearly fascinated.

"We're from your worst nightmare," Jag whispers into the guy's ear from behind. He snuck up so silently that I didn't notice him until the last second. I catch a glimpse of the edge of his dagger pressed to the demon's side. "And if you don't want trouble, I suggest you walk away, and make it fast, because I'm dying to see some demon dust." Jag's lips pull back into a feral grin, like a wolf... or a jaguar.

"Ah. I see. I bid you good day then," Nice Guy says. "I'll be seeing you." He directs this last comment to me, nodding, and then backing away, Jag giving him room. Angry Guy seems torn. He doesn't want to bow down or lose face. He's itching for a fight, but this is not the place, and Polite Guy presses a hand to his arm. They back up until they are far enough away to turn and scurry out of the cafeteria.

"Whew! That was close!" Doug exhales a tension-filled laugh, his eyes wide. "I thought for sure we were going to have to take them down right here." He glances back over his shoulder at the door.

"I wouldn't have minded," Heidi mumbles as she pushes her food around with a fork. "I had it covered. You didn't need to swoop in and save the day," she says to Jag, who's still standing next to the table, mainly watching her eat. There isn't room for him to sit, but since we're all pretty much done, our appetites ruined…

"That's not what I was doing," he says, an expression of dismay flitting across his face. "I saw them threatening you guys, and I just did what I always do."

"Yep. Take over," I say, without thinking.

I wait for a caustic remark, but it doesn't come. Instead, he says, "Whatever," and turns and walks away. Owen takes a breath as though he's about to contribute, but Doug nudges him and his mouth snaps shut.

There's nothing left to do here, so we all slide out of the booth and pay for our meal with newly traded money. Just outside the restaurant is the concierge desk. The same guy who was there last night is there this morning. He looks absolutely delighted to see us with his grim expression and hooded eyes.

"I'd like to rent a car." I try to look as non-threatening as possible, but after our run-in at the restaurant, my nerves are running high. Not to mention my lack of sleep. I'm ready to snap, but I hold it in. I've gotten good at holding things in.

He nods and opens a notebook, searching through the entries. "I'm sorry, sir. We have nothing available." He glances up and gives me a Machiavellian grin. A smile that says he can't wait for us to leave.

"Really?" Jag asks, pushing forward. "Because I was just walking past your rental hub, and I saw a bunch of old jalopies out there." He stares at the man with the arrogance that only he can pull off, and I'm tempted to say "down boy." I wish he'd just shut up and let me handle it. His interference is starting to drive me crazy. I'm not sure how much longer I can keep my mouth shut just to avoid an argument.

The concierge never loses his smile. "Let me check again. I could have missed something." He takes a moment to look through his notebook, pretending to actually read the listings. "Ah, yes. Here's one." He jots my name down and calls a young boy over to take us to our car. "And here are your keys."

The boy leads us outside to a parking garage where a section has been roped off and designated for their rentals. The cars all look like they're ready for the scrap yard. None look completely dependable. He leads us to an old Jeep 4x4 that actually looks better than the rest. It's a five seater and has room in the back for our stuff. I'm relieved and hope it gets us where we need to go. We just might make it.

We pile in and quickly learn that the air conditioning doesn't work. There is only one radio station. It's staticky and in Farsi.

Heidi shuts it off with a smile. "We don't need the radio," she says. "The boys can sing." She winks at Doug and Owen in the visor mirror as she adjusts her scarf and hair.

Jag sits right behind her. His hand is stretched forward, resting on her shoulder. He smiles at me as if he's daring me to say something. I don't give him the satisfaction and act like I never noticed at all.

We drive through narrow streets with all sorts of maniacs weaving their little cars in and out of traffic. There are no rules, and no one to enforce them if there were anyway. The few police I've seen don't seem to care.

Heidi shrieks as I hit the brakes, narrowly missing an elderly man who shakes his fist at my stupidity, as though it was my fault he walked right in front of us on a green light! Slowly, we make our way out of town and into the country where the roads are mostly straight, black, and hot. All around us, the region is wide open, making us easy targets. I felt safer in the city. These dusty hills provide too much cover for demons and gangs.

The afternoon wanes, and we stop at a little vegetable booth on the side of the road. Local farmers are selling their wares. Off to one side, an elderly woman is selling rice with some sort of meat in it. I don't ask what it is because it smells heavenly, especially with my stomach growling. I buy a plate for each of us.

We sit on the side of the road in the blazing sun, shoveling hot rice and meat sauce into our mouths, and I have to ask myself, could this be more ridiculous? We're cooking ourselves from the inside out.

32

Dean

I sit in one of the nicest restaurants in downtown L.A. The Mozza. A posh Italian joint. I've never been here before, let alone in this part of town… in a suit. We have the whole place to ourselves because, yeah, Coem has contracted it for the next two hours. Guards are posted at every door. I'm not sure if it's because he's afraid the Cazadors might find him or that I might try to escape.

That thought has crossed my mind, but at the moment, I'm eating spaghetti and meatballs. Actual spaghetti and meatballs, which I haven't had since the beginning of the Rift. I can't normally afford food like this. There's a salad on the side and the promise of dessert. I'm about to die of happiness.

I should refuse this pampering, but I'm so hungry and I've been starved for so long, I don't say no. The advantages of playing Coem's game far outweigh refusing. I'll bide my time, gaining strength in every opportunity I can.

"Are you enjoying your food?" He's relaxed, his fingers intertwined over his stomach as he watches me devour my ambrosia.

"Yeah. You should try it." I slurp another huge forkful, feeling like this might be my last meal so I better enjoy it.

"I just might." He gives me a lazy smile and takes intermittent sips from a glass of red wine that sits before him. He's quiet for a moment, and then he inhales audibly before speaking. "I want to thank you again for the amazing painting. I have it hanging in my home in Gehenna. Everyone is jealous and clamoring for their own portrait. This could be lucrative for both you and me."

I nod, but I keep eating. I have no interest in making money from demons, but I'm surprised he's never had a picture drawn before. After all, he comes across as pretty vain, but my painting was a surprise, like he was shocked at never having thought of it himself. Idiot.

Abruptly, a strange feeling of queasiness begins to grow in my stomach. It builds, the roiling expanding, until I realize too late that I can't hold the nausea back. I've eaten too fast. A second later, my belly cramps painfully and the hot, acidic taste of bile fills my mouth. There's no way I can keep my lips closed even though I try. My stomach heaves, and all the food I'd been shoveling into my starved innards comes exploding back out… onto the table. I can't even control it. I continue to retch even when there's no food left in my stomach. When it's over, spittle drips from my lip and I wipe it away with horror and mortification. I can't believe this happened. I look up slowly, terrified to meet Coem's eyes.

His reaction is split second. He jumps up from the table and stares in disgust. Wiping off his suit, he closes his eyes, his jaw flexing. I watch him, shrinking back from certain death. Instead, he sighs and motions for the waiter to clean up the mess, and then he sits back down to the vomit-strewn table.

"I'm so sorry. This rich food was too much. You may not believe it, but I feel terrible at how you were treated, and I want to make it up to you." He waits for me to look up again before continuing.

He's right. I don't believe it. He acts as if he weren't the one in *charge* of my mistreatment. Like he didn't know what was happening? It's difficult to hide my sneer—because I totally hate this guy and I think I *could* actually kill him. I'm sure Coem notices my expression.

I stare at the breadsticks, the smell of garlic and tomatoes almost more than I can handle, and I moan, holding my stomach, feeling feel like I might puke again. I have to get away from this table. Why are we still sitting here?

"Have you traveled much?" he asks out of the blue.

Shaking my head, I snort. "Yeah. With my millions, I've

been all over the world." I use a clean corner of my napkin to wipe my mouth, sensing my stomach is about to cramp again.

Coem doesn't respond to my snarkiness, but he nods. "That's what I figured. How would you like to see the world? Eat the best food every country can offer? See the pyramids!"

"No thanks."

"I think you might change your mind when you see what I have in mind."

I place my napkin on the table, staring into those beautiful cobalt-blue eyes that aren't really even his. "I think you misunderstand me. I can't be bought."

"You've already been bought. Look at your clothes. You're clean… well, you *were*. You're eating food you've only dreamed of for the last five years and you didn't say no to any of it."

"I puked it back up." But he's right, and for that, his words stab like a hot needle, straight into my heart.

"How about this? We go back to my home. No more dungeons or dark nights alone in a cold cell. You'll still be guarded because I don't want to lose you just yet, but you'll be able to live in comfort and paint. I have a friend who would like her portrait done. You'll be paid in food and clothes, so you won't feel like you're working for free." His smile is tight and never reaches his eyes. He folds his hands over his stomach again and waits.

What do I say? His offer is hard to resist. The thought of going back to my cell where the stench is overpowering, sleeping on a cot filled with bedbugs and who knows what else is devastating. And having to pee in that disgusting corner… it makes me want die… and yet I feel like I'm selling myself if I accept his proposal.

How many times will I compromise? How many times before it's too late and I'm really theirs? Heart and soul? I stare at my hands in my lap, my stomach still churning and achy. When I shake my head, my tongue feels like cotton in my mouth. It's difficult to breathe or swallow, and everything inside me screams to shoot down his evil proposition—that he has nothing I want.

But I can't force the words from my mouth. I can't make myself say I want the loneliness of a stark prison cell, little to no food, and foul-smelling darkness. Slowly, I lift my eyes to his and give him a nod. That's it. And then I go back to staring at my hands.

Within minutes, I am whisked away in a plush, black limo and transported to a gated mansion in the distance. The black gates slide open and the limo pulls through. Trees and other greenery line the drive, and flowers in all colors bloom in the gardens. It takes my breath away.

It's an artist's dream, and I can't believe a demon would even want to live here. I picture them skulking around, hiding in darkness, the ugliness of their surroundings matching the ugliness in their hearts.

Not so for Coem.

A butler opens my door, and I step from the car to walk up the stone steps into a foyer of marble. A huge chandelier hangs overhead, reflecting rainbows of light into the mirrors and other crystal ornaments. There is nothing in this house or on this property that would suggest any type of *Rift* has occurred.

I walk to a marble table that holds a giant stone flowerpot with magnificent flowers. I can't believe what I'm seeing, and I turn to stare at my surroundings. How can these pigs live like this when so many people are starving and alone, shivering in the night, hiding from the vampiric demons that snatch their bodies away, only to consume them before their time should even be up?

"Right this way, sir," the butler says to me. He walks up a set of gold-carpeted stairs with gilded railings, the best money can buy—without looking back. He just assumes I'll follow, which I do. Turning down a hall, he opens the third door on the left and shows me in.

A king-sized bed sits against one wall, wine-colored satin quilts decorating the mattress. There's a fireplace on one side and tall, bright windows that allow golden light to filter in. It's a room for a king and now it's mine. There's an armoire in the corner and I walk over to it, flinging open the doors.

"All to your taste, I assume." Coem leans against the doorway, his arms crossed over his chest. He gestures to the rack of clothes hanging in the closet. Name-brand jeans, brightly colored, button-down shirts—the kind I love—T-shirts, and two rows of shoes. More clothes than I had even before the Rift.

I have no words. A part of me wants to scream for joy and throw myself on the bed that I know is going to be plush and warm, because I have never seen such lavishness in my life. It's seductive on so many levels. But another part of me screams that this is a trap and that I must run from this room! That Coem is binding me with chains that will drag me down to hell.

"Come. Let me show you your studio." Swirling out of the room in a graceful pivot, he walks three doors down, shoving open the door in a flourish. He stands back, proud and excited, and ushers me in with enthusiasm. Even though I've walked hesitantly down the hall, his eager smile says this room will be even better than my bedroom. That's what I'm afraid of—that the temptation of something even better will be impossible to refuse.

And he's right. Windows line one whole wall, pristine and crystal clear. Easels of various sizes stand in a corner. On the other side of the room is a kitchenette with cupboards and shelves full of paints of all brands, colors, and types. Watercolors, oils, acrylics. Brushes of all sizes, canvases for every medium… everything an artist could dream of and then some.

"Well, what do you think?" He steps to the center of the room, his arms outstretched as he spins in a slow circle.

I'm still not able to form words.

"It's wonderful, isn't it?"

I nod, turning in a slow circle myself. "Why?" I whisper, still unable to grasp it all. "Why are you doing this? I know you don't like me."

"Oh, contraire, my friend! I *do* like you. You are not the first human I have taken a liking to either, and I take care of my friends. I want to nurture your talent." He walks up to me, a genuine smile in his eyes. That's a first. He places his hands on the tops of my shoulders. "Someday, you are going to be famous and I'll be able to say I knew him when." And with that, he walks back to the door. "I'm going to let you rest before my friends come. Say, a couple of hours?"

I nod, feeling extraordinarily confused. I don't understand any of this. Why is he really doing this? Nurture my talent? No way. He wants something from me, so I'll play along for a while until I figure this out. Really, this is awesome, and maybe there is some way I can get a message to Jag while I'm here. I'll think of something. This house can't be that secure.

Did he say friends? With an S?

33

Dean

One of Coem's "friends" sits on a chair next to my easel in a flowing emerald gown, her golden hair cascading over one shoulder. Her demon eyes burn with fire, like the afternoon sun shining through the wall of windows, which creates a halo of light around her.

There's no smile on her lips, but she wears a look of self-assurance and satisfaction. She knows she's magnificent. At least on the outside.

I can easily see who she really is on the inside. *Not* a gray man. So many of the top dogs here aren't, but she's something… else. Her demon skin is pasty white. Her hair is long and gray, slicked back over her head between two short, black horns that spiral back. Her blood-red demon lips are a mirage behind her human ones, smiling seductively.

I've gotten good at perceiving the details of their true selves. Colors, tones, and depth. At first, it took focus, and I had to stare hard, but now—ever since my torture in that underground auditorium—it's easy. I see them both. The human body and the demon body as though they are sitting side by side.

Coem calls her Chumlento. A stupid name if you ask me. She wants me to paint her inner demon self—like I did with Coem, but with the emerald dress on. Her demon body doesn't have any "girl" parts like her human one—no breasts or curves whatsoever. Just leathery, gray skin. Only the contours of her demon face—the high, slim cheekbones, delicate chin, and wide, fiery eyes—make her look female. I try not to look her directly as it gives me the creeps. I swear she can read my thoughts.

She reclines like a cat, sinewy and relaxed, her long, human limbs muscled and beautiful. "They call you Dan?" she purrs, leaning forward, the V in her neckline showing more of her human cleavage than I'm comfortable with. I keep my eyes on the canvas.

"It's Dean."

She shrugs as though she couldn't care less. "And what is the meaning of such a name?"

Rather than snub her or give a snide remark—because I've learned that only gets my face slapped—I shrug also. "I don't know. Probably nothing."

"What kind of human doesn't know the meaning of their name?" She peers at me closely as thought trying to understand me. "Names are important. They always mean something. Your name opens a window into your soul, and I'd like to know who's painting my portrait."

I shake my head, wishing she'd just shut up. Who cares anyway? "Well, I had a plaque on my wall when I was a kid that said my name means *the way of life*."

"In what language?"

I shrug again. "How should I know? That was a long time ago. It doesn't matter."

"Maybe. Maybe not." In a flash, she sits up straight, the flirtatiousness of the conversation coming to an abrupt halt. I flinch, thinking she might hit me, but instead, she stalks from the studio without any semblance of grace. I watch her retreating back, the gown dipping low, showing the soft curve of her buttocks. The attractive, human one.

Once gone, I stare at the empty doorway. Maybe she's upset I didn't ask the meaning of her name too.

I sit in a chair directly across from Coem. He scowls at me, his face uncomfortably close to mine. He hasn't said anything yet, but I'm sure I'm in trouble. At least he hasn't kicked me out of his house yet. I haven't even been here for twenty-four hours. I still have plenty of fattening up to do.

"What is your religion?" he asks, his expression intense and searching.

"Huh?"

"What is your religion!" he screams, suddenly furious for no reason, spittle flying from his lips.

Startled, I jerk back. "I don't have one. What difference does it make?"

He calms down and takes a couple of deep breathes, relaxing back in his seat. "It's important. What religion? Are you Christian? Jewish? Muslim?"

I wrack my brain to figure out his line of questioning. "Uh, I guess Christian."

"Were you christened as a baby? Baptized maybe?"

"I don't remember if I was ever christened. I only have vague memories of ever going to church." I frown back at him, growing worried. Who cares what my religion is now?

"Were your parents Catholic? Protestant? Baptist? Which Christian sect? What is your genealogy? Where do your people come from?" He's back to leaning forward in my face. The intensity of his gaze demands an answer and I try to think back—in my fear and bewilderment—to any stories my parents may have told me as a child. Were we European?

"Uh, I'm not sure. Maybe English or Scottish."

"Any Middle Eastern blood by chance?" Chumlento asks from the door. She has changed from her gown to a pair of tight-fitting jeans and a form-fitting white sweater.

"Uh…"

"As in Jewish, Arabic, Turkish etc…"

"I don't know." I look from her to Coem and then back at her. I'm so lost I can't even begin to decipher their line of questioning.

She sighs and throws her arms down, stalking over to us. Once she's standing next to Coem, she cocks her hip and places her hand on her waist. "He's an idiot. You'll learn nothing from him. Just take a blood test. You have people under your thumb who can analyze blood, don't you?"

I don't know anyone else who can talk to him as she does, like she has no fear of him. Everyone else grovels in his presence. But Chumlento, she's an empress as soon as she enters any room. Everyone bows to her. Even Coem… kind of.

"True." He sits back and threads his fingers together, a smile growing on his face. "Good idea. Very good." He turns to me. "We are finding that certain races are easier to possess than others. Certain names offer protection, depending on the religious rites you've experienced. Genealogy also matters. It's all very interesting stuff." He snaps his fingers, and the guard who's been waiting outside the door comes in. "Take the boy to the lab and have them test for ethnicity."

I rise from my chair as the guard approaches. No sense having my arm ripped from its socket. He takes me to the end of the hall where an elevator is open and waiting for us. Nothing good can come of this, and I almost scream, *hell no, I won't go!* But I force myself to walk into the elevator anyway. They won't kill me yet. Not until they figure me out or give up on trying.

When the elevator doors open again, we're three floors down, in a stainless steel, sterile medical lab. All sorts of equipment is spread out on tables, and at least five guys in lab coats are busy working.

"Coem wants blood drawn," the guard says, gesturing to me.

"What is he looking for?" one of the tech guys asks, walking toward us.

"Ethnicity."

The technician nods and leads me over to a corner where a chair sits with a tray of needles and vials for this sort of thing. How often are they drawing people's blood down here? What are they up to? What are they studying? And then it hits me with sickening clarity. They are studying humans. Like lab rats. Trying to figure out what makes us tick and probably how to keep our bodies working longer. I'm kind of curious about it myself. Will they figure out what makes me different? Is it in my blood or in my soul, or maybe even a mixture of the two, this resistance to the demons?

My stomach turns, and I feel bile rise in my throat. I swallow, refusing to throw up in front of these people… again. I hate needles… and blood. I turn away, not able to watch.

"Okay. We're finished," the technician says after a few moments. "You're good to go. And don't forget to stop by the kitchen for orange juice." He smiles, pulls off his rubber gloves, and spins on his stool to throw them away. The thing that really gets me here is that the guy is human. No demon inside. He doesn't act like a prisoner, which can only mean one thing. He's here of his own volition. Paid to do whatever Coem wants. Traitor.

I glance over and notice three vials of dark red blood, lying on a metal tray. My blood. My magic blood that keeps the demons out. I love that blood and completely rebel at having them steal it from me.

The guard leads me away, and I can't help but wonder if they will ever let me go.

Life in the mansion is an amazing experience compared to living in my little church. I'm never cold, never hungry, and I wear only the most expensive clothes money can buy. Truth be told, I can't stand the feeling I have inside, like I've converted to the dark side by agreeing to all of this. I should be fighting back more. I should refuse their gifts and manipulations, but I don't. I can't. After going without for so long, it feels good to have a full stomach every night. I keep telling myself that I'll figure out a way to hurt them from the inside, but I've yet to come up with any ideas.

I sit at the easel with the painting of Chumlento before me, almost complete. I'm just doing a few touchups. Thoughts of our conversation come back to me, her smug stance and even smugger comments. I picture her condescending smile as she sneers at me, as if I'm a bug she'd like to step on. I hate her. And without thinking, I grit my teeth and smudge the paint on her right eye with my fist, giving it an ugly, sagging slant. The colors smear from a bright, flaming, golden fire to puce-ugly orange. Grotesque, like she is.

The impotence I feel is somewhat assuaged by my rebellious rant and I sit back, not wanting to paint anymore. It's early, and breakfast will be served any minute. I stand up, wipe my hands on a towel, and head toward the door. My heart beats erratically, knowing I'll be sitting with the king and queen of hell—how I refer to them—in only a few minutes.

My guard waits outside the door. There is something about him that gives me the chills. Literally. He's a gray man, but he's *cold*. Where he touches me, I feel frostbit for a moment. It's crazy, and I have no explanation for it. Should he be able to do that in a human body?

The door swings open before I can open it myself. The guard stands there, staring me down, neither of us saying a word. I blink and look away. He wins.

I dart forward before he can touch me. "So, what's your name anyway?" I ask, figuring I might as well get to know him. He doesn't answer; he just keeps walking. I glance over at him, and he's staring straight ahead. Okay, so he doesn't want to be friends.

When we reach the dining room, I'm motioned to the other side of the table to sit next to Coem. Chumlento is already seated directly across from him. I initiate a smile as I sit, but then freeze when I notice her face. Her right eye sags and the hue of her iris is a muted, sickly green color. *Puce* green.

My jaw sags, and she notices me staring. She growls, looking like she might reach across the table and smack me. I hurry to glance away and sit down.

Coem clears his throat and wipes his mouth. "Our dear Chumlento is feeling under the weather this morning, aren't you, dear? I'm sure it will clear up soon."

"Shut up." She glares at Coem and gives me another sneer.

"What happened?" I hear myself ask, as though my mouth has a life of its own. I could kick myself. Why would I ask such a stupid question? It's none of my business and will likely get me slapped.

"We aren't sure," Coem answers. "It happened early this morning. It looks like a palsy of some sort."

"Palsy?" I repeat.

"Oh, for Hell's sake! Shut up. Don't talk about me as if I'm not here. It will wear off, whatever it is. It's probably just an allergy or something."

I stare at her, my hands on the table, the paint stains visible. I snatch them back and hide them below the tablecloth, trying to rub the paint from my fingers. It's just a coincidence. A crazy coincidence. I can't wrap my mind around it, and I can hardly chew, let alone swallow.

There has to be a connection. But how? Why? There's no way I did this. I don't believe in this kind of… what? Magic? Voodoo? Do they suspect me? If they did, I'd already be dead. Chumlento would have killed me herself. I don't think she's big on forgiveness.

I eat quickly and then push back from the table.

Both Coem and Chum look up, surprised.

"Done already?" he asks. "You haven't even finished your coffee."

"I'm… full. Thanks for breakfast," I mumble, stuffing a banana into my jacket, which I always wear to meals now. It has a lot of pockets to hide food in. Plus, I can't keep sitting there, pretending I'm calm and that everything's fine. I have to check my painting and figure this out.

I hurry around the table in time for my nameless guard to shove my shoulder. An icy zap stabs through me, and I feel numb in that spot for the next ten seconds. It wears off by the time we get back to my studio, but the sensation leaves me chilled and yearning for a hot shower.

As soon as I'm in my studio with the door shut, I forget about my guard and his ice cube fingers and hurry over to the painting. I have to check it before I do anything else. But the painting hasn't changed. It looks the same as it did when I wrecked it… on purpose. But it does look an awful lot like Chum's palsy, and I can't help but release a wicked snicker.

It's late and I sit on my bed, sketching a picture of Coem. This will be a notebook will be an experiment. Something I keep hidden. A notebook of every demon I see, hopefully mutated. I can't hide it under the mattress. That would be too obvious. Not in a dresser drawer either. That would be the first place they'd check.

I forget about the stress of finding a hiding place and focus on Coem's likeness. I'm drawing his human face, experimenting on whatever magic happened with Chummy's painting and hoping it will happen in pencil too. I've analyzed and decided I need to try everything. Oils, acrylics, water color, and sketches in pencil. Drawing parts of the demon face over the human one and then vice versa. Does it only work on canvas or can a paper notebook work magic too? Is it because he gave me these items? Are they enchanted somehow, or is it a power inside *me* I never knew about?

When I finish, I inspect my work, deeming it good enough and wondering if I'll see results in the morning.

I start a second sketch. This time of my guard. I do this one in pencil also because it's quicker and easier. I draw the demon inside, gray and smooth, his toothy grin in a grimace. I purposely draw human teeth where the demon teeth should be, and then erase one. Front and center. After examining my work, I fix the shading and search the room for a hiding place.

There's no good spot. Not anywhere… until I turn and study the headboard of the huge monstrosity of a bed where I sleep. Running my fingers along the ridges, I notice for the first time that there are little grooves carved into the wood, running along the outside posts. They aren't deep, but I'm curious and hook one with my fingernail. A long, thin drawer slides out. Like it was prepared just for me. Like God made it happen or something. I bend over and look into its depths. It's easily big enough to hold a rolled up piece of paper.

The drawer slides back in effortlessly and is undetectable from the outside. I wonder if Coem knows about these secret drawers. Slowly, I search the whole bed, opening each secret compartment I find. There are four on each side of the headboard. They are smooth and flat, without knobs, so I'm sure they've been overlooked. I say a short prayer of gratitude and hope nothing demonic will ever suspect.

34

Brecken

Evening approaches, but that doesn't mean it cools down at all. The sun sits at the top of the hills and soon it will set, leaving this valley carpeted in blackness. It's still sweltering. You'd think we'd have a reprieve from the radiating heat. *Nope.*

The windows of the Jeep are down, letting a breeze blow over us. Heidi has taken off her scarf and long-sleeved shirt, and I don't blame her or say anything about it. No one can see her anyway. The boys sprawl as much as they can in the backseat. Doug, with his head back and mouth open, snores. Jag watches the landscape out of his window in silence, and Owen works on something in his lap with a headlamp.

It's quiet, but we're still pretty far from any sort of town, and I don't want to camp out here in the open. I did find a tent at the roadside shop, so we'll camp if we have to, but the hills that dot the countryside don't feel safe and could have anything hiding behind them.

By eleven PM, I'm so tired I can't go on. The others look just as wiped, so I decide to pull off the road. There's a small copse of trees that we can pitch our tent behind, and it's far enough from the road to offer cover. We'll be hidden at least, and that's about as good as I can do. It's safer than trying to drive through this area at night. I know what hides out here in the dark.

Doug wakes up as the Jeep bounces over the uneven terrain. There's no road, but we clear it easily. Behind the trees, I pull to a stop.

"What are we doing?" he asks, sitting up and peering out at

the darkness.

"Stopping."

"Why?" he asks with a yawn.

"Because I'm tired," I answer. "We can set up the tent and get some shut-eye. Since you've slept already, can you take the first two-hour watch?"

"Yeah, I guess." Doug doesn't sound too enthused, but he hops out of the car, grabs the rifle we picked up when we bought the tent and other camping supplies—an old AK-47 with an extra clip—and loads it. There are more guns readily available in this country than I'm comfortable with, and they are all old, from before the Rift, but at least we have protection that works at a distance.

Jag and I put up the tent while Heidi unloads the bags and blankets. Fifteen minutes later, I'm in a ragged sleeping bag and nothing could feel more wonderful. Heidi is a little more vociferous about her lack of comfort.

"I'm sleeping on a rock." She tries to move the pebbles beneath her, but they are also beneath the tent, so she doesn't have much luck. That gives her a reason to move closer to Jag. He doesn't seem to mind.

"Better?" I ask now that she's a few inches farther from me. I can see her face in the dark and her eyes blink.

"Yeah." She smiles.

I close my eyes and let exhaustion take over. I need as much sleep as possible. We can't make any mistakes, and the others don't understand what we are really up against. We need to be sharp, quick, and ahead of the demons at every turn, but I can't seem to make my mind turn off.

I'm not sure who exactly we'll be fighting. Coem is an insidious demon, but he's not the worst and he's back in the United States. They'll have some other general in charge over here, and I worry it's someone I know. Someone who would do anything to see me, not dead, but tortured for eternity. And they'd be able to think of a myriad of ways to make that happen—all of them so terrible that I would beg for death before it was over.

I can only think of a couple of beings who could really do the job. Eligor, demon of murder, genocide, and war strategies, would be more than capable. Mean to a fault, but he's defiant and doesn't take orders well. Thanatos, one of the many demons of death, is pretty arrogant, and has been known to play well with others… at times. He was decent to work with when I reigned at my most powerful among the demons. He's earned his place at the top, so it could be him.

But then there is Mictian, a demon of death and destruction from another realm entirely. He comes here—like a sub-contractor from his world—to wreak havoc, cause war, and other atrocities. He's worse than the other two, and he hates me with a vengeance. He's fierce, unforgiving, and he doesn't quit until the job is done. *Ever*.

Mictian was the highest ranking when I defected—a brigadier general, if a comparison can be made with the human military. They all have different talents and abilities, but are all deadly and powerful. Each one fills my heart with dread.

I review in my mind how they might attack. Their strategies and weaknesses. Then I move on to how they might be coming through to this dimension at *The Door*. Is each demon checked off a list or do they come through in companies? Are they even keeping track of who's here?

Round and round, my thoughts tie me into knots. I toss and turn in my bag, trying to get comfortable and get my brain to rest. My heart races and my eyes scrunch shut, my hands in fists. I can practically hear their demonic laughter. They know I'm coming, I'm sure of it. They're ready for me and waiting—all set up to capture me and kill the others. Or maybe they'll make the others watch while I'm tortured.

Suddenly, I feel a cool hand on my arm. "Are you okay?" Heidi's soft whisper penetrates the craziness in my mind and I open my eyes, finding hers in the dark.

"I'm not sure." I chuckle softly, wondering if I've fallen victim to another kind of treachery. A subtler kind. How stupid could I be? How could I have forgotten something so important? In my defense, I was a demon for an eternity and I haven't been away from them for that long. These things don't come to me naturally, but I want them to for Heidi.

"Create a shield around yourself," I whisper to her.

"What?"

"A shield of protection."

"Why?" I see her questioning expression, her eyebrows pulled down in confusion.

I would think it's basic demon hunting protocol, but who knows if they've been taught to do this. I'll have to explain it to the others tomorrow when they're awake.

"It's easy," I say. "Just visualize. Picture a bright, white shell around yourself that nothing can get through. Nothing evil, that it. No devils, demons, spirit fragments, contracts, or demonic promises. Nothing. Understand?"

"Good grief. Are there really that many things to be afraid of?"

"Yes. Do you have it pictured in your mind?"

"I think so." She closes her eyes, breathing evenly, but a little faster than before. "Okay. Got it. Will it work?"

"Yes, usually." There are exceptions to every rule, after all, but I don't tell her this. I can feel her anxiety, and I want her to be able to fall asleep.

"Why are you telling me this?" she asks.

I hesitate before answering. She's asking, so I should tell her the truth. There's no time for lies anymore. "Because we aren't alone."

Her eyes grow wide and she quickly glances around the tent, searching.

"You can't see these guys."

"They aren't gray men?" she asks, pulling her bag up higher around her neck.

"No. But these beings follow the gray men around. They can inhabit bodies too. They don't need gray men for that."

"What are they?" she asks, scooting closer to me. I guess she thinks I'm the better protector since I'm still awake.

"Just what I told you to protect yourself from. Evil spirits, programs, spirit fragments, and the like. Most people don't know they're there. They are invisible to mortal eyes, but they fill your heart with doubts and fears. Nasty little pricks. They have no purpose other than to make you miserable."

"Just when you think the monsters under the bed aren't real," she says with a chuckle.

"Right?" I roll to my back, forming my own mental shield of protection. It's amazing how well it works when I think about it. The power of the mind is astonishing.

But spirits aren't the only things we'll be up against at *The Door*. We'll be fighting the big wigs who rule the underworld, who want to keep the door open, who are somehow benefitting from this whole catastrophe. They don't yearn for bodies. They have their own already. What is it they really want?

"How long does the shield last?" Heidi whispers.

"As long as you keep thinking about it."

"Okay."

My breathing slows and my mind finally rests. I check the watch on my wrist. I've lost forty-five minutes. If I'm going to sleep at all, I better get to it.

35

Heidi

I listen to Bret's breathing as he falls asleep next to me. I think about what he said—this visualization stuff, the shield of protection, evil spirits that surround us even though we can't see them. It creeps me out and I shiver, trying to ignore the niggling fear that scratches at the edges of my mind.

It's dark. So, so dark. I can hardly see my hand before my face. Owen snores on the other side of Jag, and I'm the only one left awake. I listen to their inhalations like a symphony of drumrolls. I should have brought earplugs.

I'm having a hard time closing my eyes, knowing there are dark souls out there that I can't see. Not that being able to see them would make it better, but I keep searching the shadows, wondering if each trick of the light is a demon coming to kill me. Bret's pep talk has done little to calm my racing heart, and I lie awake for the next hour until Doug crawls inside the tent. He's about to wake Owen, but I get up instead.

"I'll take next watch," I whisper. "I'm awake anyway."

"Okay." He hands me the rifle when I step out of the tent. It's pretty dark out here too, the moon glowing only a sliver. I take a place on the hard ground against one of the trees, praying I'm not sitting on an anthill. Once that thought goes through my mind, all sorts of other creepy crawlies infiltrate my thoughts. Scorpions, spiders, and other insects. I find myself itching and scratching at phantom annoyances for the next two hours. Not to mention the tricks my eyes play on me in the dark. I'm too frightened to even think about how tired I am or of falling asleep.

When I hear something, I sit up straight and listen, but when there's nothing more, I figure I'm just psyching myself out. I don't want to wake everyone up over nothing. I'll just sit here for now, tired and miserable, because I'm being ridiculous.

The night passes quietly. Three-thirty rolls around—when it's Jag's turn to take watch—and I'm so exhausted and stressed out that I could literally weep. My eyes feel full of sand, and I can hardly keep them open. I don't think I'll have any problem falling asleep now.

Jag pops his head out of the tent and then he plops down beside me. His body has a clock of its own. I don't know how he does it, or how he seems completely rested after only four hours of sleep.

"You better get in there," he whispers. "You only have two hours left before we have to get up."

I can only sigh in response as I try to stand on tingling legs that have gone to sleep beneath me. But before I can even get through the tent flap, I hear a scuffling in the distance. It's coming toward me fast. I turn to Jag, but he's no longer sitting by the tree.

I'm alone.

Softly, I move back, one slow step at a time, until I'm behind the biggest tree, my dagger in my fist. I can't see anything, but that doesn't mean I can't defend myself. I'm tempted to call out, but I'd rather take whatever it is by surprise if I can. If we can't see them, they can't see us. It's probably just an animal wandering around in the night, and I'm scaring myself to death over nothing, but we can't take any chances. Jag has probably taken off after it.

When I think it's safe to move, I feel a sudden presence behind me. I swirl around, my knife extended as I frantically peer into the darkness. The air moves in front of my face and I jump back, but not fast enough. Burning slices across my belly, and I grab my stomach in surprised reaction. A warm stickiness seeps through my tank top against my fingers. It's not deep, but it stings like a mother.

I don't bother being quiet now. "Jag! Bret!" I attempt to scream for Owen and Doug too, but my attacker strikes again.

This time, his knife slices through the air like a soft breeze, inches from my face, and I feel it even though I can't see him. I jerk back, tripping over my feet and falling over a prone body. I scream, my mind going immediately to Jag. I don't have the chance to check who it is before my attacker is on me again, pushing me down and straddling me.

Against such a powerful foe, my arms feel weak and pathetic, and I'm tired from lack of sleep. But adrenaline is zinging through my veins, hopefully giving me the edge I need. He pins my wrists with his knees, and rocky pebbles dig painfully into my skin. I buck my hips and he falls forward, his head hitting me in the chin. With his body out of balance, I yank my arm free, still holding my dagger, and plunge it into the guy's neck. He explodes in a cloud of russet ash all over my stomach. Some of him even gets in my mouth. I spit him out, so grateful it isn't blood sliding between my teeth.

Blinking into the darkness, I search out the body I'd tripped over before I killed Dusty. I *have* to know who it is. I just couldn't bear it if it turned out to be Doug, Owen, or heaven forbid, Jag. My toes find the body before the rest of me. Crouching, I run my hands over his still form. From the bandana tied around his face and the pajama-type clothes he's wearing, I know he isn't one of us. A rush of relief surges through me as I rise and search for my next victim.

I hear a struggle behind the tent and make my way, following the edges of the canvas. When I hear someone grunt and fall to the ground, I freeze, listening. And then it's quiet. Shouldn't people be yelling or crying out at the very least?

"Jag?"

He doesn't answer.

"Jag?" I whisper again, moving closer to where the struggle was. My foot hits another prone body and I immediately crouch down, running my hands over the still figure while my eyes scour the dark. I'm panicked and can't focus. I can't tell who this body is. My fingers come away sticky, and I run my hands up the guy's shoulders and then to his head. I'm sure it's one of my boys, and my heart twists, tears welling in my eyes. I should have been protecting them better. I should have been more alert, more careful, more… something. I let a murderer sneak into our camp. I let him get close enough that he could ambush us.

The weight of my failure is oppressive and overwhelming, and when I run my fingers over long, shoulder-length hair, I cry out in anguish. Tear burst from my eyes as I realize what this means. I shake his body, hoping he's only unconscious and not dead. Hoping he'll wake up. This can't be how it all ends. Not for us. The ache is almost too much and when he doesn't move, when I find the slash across his neck, sticky with blood, I throw myself on top of him in abject misery.

I don't even try to be quiet. What's the point? I know what my fate will be when I'm found, and I'm tempted to plunge the knife into my chest myself. All my friends are dead. I never even told my aunt I was leaving. Sophie will always wonder what happened to me.

I let my tears spill.

And then the strike of a match startles me and I jump back, ready—in a millisecond—to fight again. He stands five feet away. My gaze moves up his legs, hips, stomach, and chest, and finally, to his face. His dark eyes search mine and, in a rush of emotion, he dives for me, scooping me up in his arms, pulling me so tight against his chest I can hardly breathe.

I grasp his golden head in my hands, hardly able to form words. "Jag?" I hold him against me, kissing his neck, his eyes, his face, his lips. Never have I felt such relief. One minute, I'm in the depths of despair and the next, I'm flying up to unimaginable heights… in one blink.

"You're okay?" he asks me, my face cradled in his palms. He searches my eyes, but the match he lit is quickly dying in the dirt, and it's getting hard to see again.

I can't believe he's really alive. I turn and crouch down next to the body I was so sure was Jag. "Who's this guy then?" I study his features in the dying match light—long, black hair, smooth skin. He's young, but definitely Middle-Eastern. No one I recognize.

Some hired hitman of the demons.

Still trembling in relief and fatigue, Jag and I hurry to search the tent, finding it empty. Doug and Owen stand over another dead body dressed in black. His cohorts—piles of ash lying close by—are obviously unidentifiable.

Bret comes running back from the direction of the road, out of breath, his Nephilim dagger in his hand. "The guys from the restaurant… they followed us."

"Are you sure it was them?" I ask, finally coming down from my adrenaline high, and my body starts trembling. I need my jacket and feel like I might vomit. I force myself to breathe deeply, sitting down on a nearby rock. We're all alive. But why did I doubt? This is what we do. We're Cazadors. Demon hunters.

And then Bret notices my bloody shirt. "Are you okay?"

The boys circle me, and I lift my tank. An ugly, red gash, about three inches long, stretches across my belly. "It doesn't even hurt." I press my fingers over the cut. Then it hurts.

"I'll get the first aid kit," Doug says, hurrying back inside the tent.

The others stare at me as if I'm some kind of enigma to even still be alive. They rally around me, patting my shoulders, telling me how brave I am, and that they are so happy I'm still safe.

"I'm surprised it isn't worse." Bret examines the wound. "You're lucky."

"Or fast," I answer. "Maybe I'm just a better fighter." I mean it as a joke, but nobody laughs. The situation just isn't funny. It was too close. We all could have been wiped out in one night. "Is anyone else hurt?"

"I am," Owen says, stretching out his arm, showing us a gash on his bicep.

"My shoulder got nicked, but it's not really worth mentioning," Jag says.

"We'll check it anyway." My gaze moves over to Bret. He shakes his head. Every time I look at him, he becomes more and more familiar. More Brecken. I reach out to him and he slips into my arms, hugging me. "I'm so glad you're okay," I whisper in his ear.

"I'm kind of hard to kill," he says, joking, but I think he means it.

I stare into his eyes in the match light. "You've died before."

"That was my choice." He smiles and hugs me again.

Doug comes back with the first aid kit and goes to work on my cut. I try to hold in a hiss as he dabs the wound. He smears some ointment on, and then tapes the bandage to my stomach. "It needs stiches."

The boys all look at one another.

"The next town?" Owen asks.

"The next city with an actual medical clinic is over a day away." Bret shakes his head and grits his teeth—telltale signs that he's worried and doesn't want me to know.

"There's a sewing kit in my pack." Owen glances at Doug. "Jag did your stitches, remember?"

Doug nods. "He's stitched us up a lot of times. We can't afford to go to the clinic, and not many people want to even if they can."

Everyone glances at Jag. This is crazy. I'm tough, but I don't know if I'm that brave. "Uh… I think I'll be okay."

"If it gets infected, you'll be no help to us. At the very worst… you won't be here for it to matter." His bluntness is always a surprise, but I've come to expect it too. It's a catch 22, and I lift my eyes to the dark sky, trying to decide what I want to do… as if Jag will give me a choice.

"Get the lantern," he says. "Doug and Owen will keep guard outside the tent. Let's go inside," he says to me as he thrusts out his hand for me to take.

I stare at him. "Are you crazy? I can't do this. Not without something to numb it."

"You can do it. You're stronger than you think. Plus, you don't want your stomach to fall out." He smiles and shakes his hand at me, demanding I take it. I do and let him lift me from my spot on the rock. He leads me inside the tent, Bret right behind us with the lantern.

"Lie down," Jag orders.

With a sigh of exasperation, I recline on my sleeping bag and pull up my dirty shirt. He threads the needle, and I close my eyes. I can't watch.

36

Heidi

I don't know what I expected, but it wasn't the white-hot sting of the needle going in and out, over and over, in a million teeny, tiny stitches. Jag is meticulous. Every suture is even and straight. He's like a surgeon, and I clutch Bret's hand with all the strength I have inside me. Each time the needle goes through my tender wound, my toes curl in anguish. I try to breathe, panting methodically to control the pain, but it doesn't work. My stomach muscles contract each time the needle pierces my skin.

I can't stay still.

Bret presses my shoulders down, his hands like heavy weights holding me beneath the water, drowning me. I'm sweating profusely as I hold a thick piece of leather between my teeth. Tears leak from my eyes and the seconds tick by, feeling like an eternity.

Scuffling breaks out outside, and then shouts from Owen and Doug. Someone falls against the tent, and I scream out as Jag is shoved on top of me.

"What's going on out there?" he yells.

"Nothing. It's fine," Doug says. "We got him."

Owen pops his head into the tent. "It was another demon, but he's dust. No worries. Just hurry up!"

My eyes roll in their sockets, but I call myself back from the edge, my heart racing. "I can't take it anymore!" I try to push Jag's hands away, but Bret grabs my wrists, holding me away from the needle. There's more shouting outside the tent, but I can't understand what they're saying. I can't concentrate on anything but the burning of my wound.

It's only a second later that Jag sits back on his heels, the bloody thread dangling from the needle. "I'm done." Setting the needle down, he wipes the stitches, and then smothers on antibiotic ointment. He covers the wound with a bandage.

I can hardly breathe. I really feel like I'm going to die.

"It's all good," Doug calls from outside. "No worries here. We'll just stay out here by ourselves, killing one demon after another. No biggy."

"Do you need anything?" Bret whispers to me, ignoring Doug's sarcasm. He smiles, which actually helps. He doesn't seem too worried, and it calms me a little.

I open my eyes, my heart slowing down, but I'm nauseated and my head is pounding, not to mention the burning of the sutures. I need painkiller. Something to knock me out, but we don't have anything like that, nor do we have time for me to be drugged and out of it. I want to sob in frustration. Instead, I shake my head, grit my teeth, and say, "No, I'm good. Thanks."

Bret squeezes my hand, kisses my forehead—which I almost don't notice—and then covers my shivering body with a blanket. Yeah, it's a hundred degrees outside, but I'm shivering. I close my eyes, trying to ignore the whole world.

"What time is it?" I ask as he lies down next to me on his bag.

"It's almost five in the morning," he answers.

The sun will rise in an hour and a half. Not much time to rest because we need to get moving. I sigh and let it all go—the exhaustion and the fear of almost losing Jag.

The enormity of our situation settles uncomfortably in my chest. I'll be no help at all now. I'm the weak link. I'm going to get us all killed. We're a man down and our mission seems impossible. How will we ever close *The Door*? It's too daunting a task, and I'm too tired and in too much pain to figure it out.

It seems like only five minutes has gone by when Bret wakes me, but the sun is bright overhead. I feel dazed and achy; I can hardly move. In fact, I can't get up at all. It hurts to roll to my side, and there's no way I can sit straight up. My stitches pull and sting when I try. I don't want to say anything, as I already feel weak and helpless, but Bret seems to understand. He takes my hand, placing his other hand behind my shoulders and lifts.

I get to a sitting position with tears brimming in my eyes. I would give anything for painkiller. Rolling to my knees, I make it the rest of the way by myself, but I'm sweating profusely, and the thought of pulling my tunic over my head just about makes me break down right there. I'm still wearing my bloody tank top.

I glance down at my clothes and Bret stares at me blankly, as if he knows what I'm thinking but doesn't want to suggest helping. He's my brother though. He has to. "It's not coming off by itself."

Bret grimaces. "Right."

"I'll help you change," Jag says with a devious smile from the tent door, watching our exchange.

"No, it's fine. I'll help her," Bret says, pushing Jag out and zipping the door closed.

"Hey, if you're not man enough…" Jag says from the other side. He laughs, and I can hear him walking away.

I glance at Bret, expecting him to get mad or make a retort, but he doesn't. He presses his lips together and waits for me. "In the top of my bag," I point. "The white one."

He opens my bag, grabs the white tunic and a white tank top. There's a somewhat-white sports bra that he picks up delicately, like he might get cooties from it.

"Seriously, Brecken?"

His eyes go wide, and I realize I called him by his old name. I feel a blush creep up my cheeks, but I don't apologize or say anything about it. He *is* my brother. I know it on the deepest level. I trust him implicitly, and I think Jag is actually coming around too.

Bret crawls closer, and I slowly raise my arms. "It's ruined anyway. How about we just cut it off?" I suggest.

"Right. Good idea."

I turn around as he slips his dagger from its sheath. He slices up the back of the ruined tank top. It separates like butter. Good old magic dagger. I won't be able to wash the bloody sports bra I'm wearing, and it will be a nightmare to take off over my head.

"Just cut it," I say, my face hot and thumping with my pulse. Bret's expression matches mine, so I know he's just as mortified. He averts his gaze and cuts. The straps slide down my shoulders, and I let the ruined material drop to the floor. I lift my arms up and Bret stands behind me, threading the clean underclothes over my hands. He slides the spandex bra down my arms with minimal pain. I adjust it before raising my arms for the tank and tunic. They slide on much easier, like a whisper over my chilled, yet fevered skin. I'd die for a bath.

"All done," he says, surveying his work. "I should be a nurse." He smiles, and I grin back at him.

"Thanks. I couldn't have done it alone."

"I know. Don't worry about it." He turns away, rolls up his sleeping bag, and grabs his pack. "I'll get your stuff in a minute. Come out and sit down."

"Okay." I don't even bother trying to pick up my backpack. I'll need a few days to feel like I can do anything, but I'm afraid we don't have that long. Owen has a bandage around his arm and Jag sports one over his shoulder. Other than that, we were lucky. How none of us died is a mystery to me. Maybe God *is* on our side after all.

The drive starts out hot and only gets hotter. We don't pass any roadside stands, and we're getting low on water. There might be a stream further into the hills, but Bret doesn't want to deviate from our path. He's convinced that staying on the road is safest, and he's probably right.

Every bump in the road makes me feel like I'm being knifed all over again. It hurts to sit up and it hurts to recline. I can't shift without gasping and I'm ready to start screaming… or crying profusely.

The next jostle of the car is the cherry on top. I just can't take it anymore. "Are you trying to hit every pothole in the road?" I screech. Sweat is dewing on my forehead and upper lip. I wipe it away, knowing I'm in trouble. I need drugs. Antibiotics mostly.

Lunchtime rolls around, and the boys eat dates, figs, and cheese in the car. I can't force the food past my lips. I'm too nauseous. The fruit is warm and mushy and the cheese has started to sweat, bending easily in my fingers. So gross.

It's silent in the car most of the way until Doug pipes up late in the afternoon. "Want to play I-Spy?" he asks. "I know it's a stupid game, but I'm totally bored."

I glance into the backseat and hiss, pain slicing across my abdomen for the millionth time. "I'll play with you. I'm bored too." I need something to take my mind off myself. My seat is laid as far back as it will go without totally smashing Jag, who sits behind me. I'm so grateful he'll let me recline. I don't think I could sit up straight and not pass out. He plays with my hair and tickles my neck, and it helps me relax. I'm stunned that he performs such tender acts in front of the others. He doesn't seem to give a crap about what anyone else thinks.

"I'll play too," he says.

Doug starts. "I spy with my little eye… something round, gray, and—"

"A boulder," Jag says.

"Huh. Yep." Doug shrugs. "There's not much to choose from."

The game goes on for ten minutes with things like skeletal shrubs, starving trees, and the occasional bird flying over.

Owen takes his turn next. He looks around, bored, but at least he makes an effort. "I spy, with my little eye, something dark and… uh…" He's quiet while he stares out over the landscape. "Moving." He sits straight. "And it has a gun!" he yells into the tight confines of the Jeep.

"What? Where?" Bret yells back.

Owen points off to the east and we all spot him. Like a tiny ant. He's far enough away that it's a miracle he saw him at all. The guy scurries, low to the ground, behind a hill, and then he is gone.

"Where there's one, there's more." Jag leans forward.

I sit my chair up straighter. I don't want to be in his way. It makes me gasp and hold my breath, waiting for my stitches to stop screaming. I try to keep my focus on the hills and not on my burning wound, but the thread pulls and stings. I lift my shirt up to inspect it. The edges are red and swelling, and it hurts worse now than it did earlier. There's nothing we can do about it, so I keep the news to myself.

37

Brecken

I watch the bandit hurry behind the hill. I've noticed others too, long before Owen said anything, but I didn't want to worry the others. There's not much we can do anyway, and I'm not about to stop the car.

The sightings are growing more frequent though. Soon, there will be a group big enough for an ambush if they all work together. We're almost out of Iran, and for that, I'm grateful, but the land is becoming more rocky and mountainous, filled with thugs with bandanas over their faces. There are also fewer roadside shops with food, water, and fuel.

I press my foot to the pedal, hurrying. We have to get to Mashhad, the next big city, and then go north to Turkmenistan. The topography of this area has changed since the Rift—according to our map—which was a waste of money and is useless. Where there were mountains, there are now valleys. Where there was once a valley, there is now a lake.

It's going to get dark soon, and no way are we going to camp again. Not after last night. Heidi is totally incapacitated. She's been popping aspirin—which hasn't done much good—like it's candy. She needs serious painkillers—but from the dew on her brow and the flush to her cheeks, she needs antibiotics and a visit to the hospital.

"Do you have any water?" she rasps, her head lolling toward me.

She looks terrible and my heart skips a beat. "Yeah. Owen, are there any water bottles back there?"

"Yep." He hands one up and she guzzles it down, then wipes

her mouth, breathing hard.

"You don't look good," I tell her, noticing another thug dressed in black, darting behind a tree about fifty feet off the road.

"I don't feel so good." She closes her eyes, her pale skin seeming even paler in the waning sunlight. Dark circles stain the skin under her eyes and a sigh parts her lips.

"She needs a doctor," Jag says from the backseat, his tone accusing. I can't see his expression, but I can feel the tension rise. He's angry and blaming me. We wouldn't be in this predicament if it weren't for me. I know that and feel the ache of guilt without Jag's condemnation.

"I know, but I'm not sure what you want me to do about it. I'm not a doctor." I flash him a glare in the rearview mirror, which he returns.

"Pull over," he demands.

"No. There are too many demons out there or haven't you noticed?" I shake my head, tempted to tell him how stupid he is for even suggesting it.

"We need to check her wound," he says, his voice rising. "Look at her! She has a fever. It's probably infected."

"We'll stop when it's safe," I bark back. "She'll be okay for a minute." I don't know what he thinks we can do in the middle of nowhere in the dark. "There. See that?" I point off to the east, toward a glow over the hills. "That's Mashhad. We'll stop there for the night."

"Fine," Jag mumbles, and I notice Doug and Owen glance at one another in the rearview mirror. They don't say anything, which is probably smart.

We only drive for a few more minutes when an explosion erupts, fire blossoming outside Heidi's window. The Jeep rocks to the side. She screams and falls against me in the driver's seat. The guys shout from the backseat. It's too dark to see much, so I don't know if another attack is on the way. What was that, anyway? A rocket launcher? A roadside bomb we drove over that didn't function right, blowing us to bits?

I push the gas pedal to the floor, only able to see a few feet in front of us. Men dressed in dark clothing dart into view, throwing rocks at the windows, trying to stop us. No other bombs go off, and for that, I am grateful, but it isn't over yet.

"Why are they attacking us?" Heidi screams.

"They want the Jeep and whatever supplies we have," I say, swerving to miss a guy who tries to jump onto the hood.

"How do you know?" she cries, practically sobbing in pain and holding her stomach. "Just make it stop!"

Jag rolls down his window, brandishing his dagger, leaning out to stab anyone who gets close. Owen does the same on his side, and we race through the winding countryside. More than once, a bandit launches himself at the car and tries to grab the rack on top. Jag never lets them get a grip. Doug yells for Owen to move over because he's not seeing much action, stuck in the middle, but soon, the attack slows and finally stops. Everything grows quiet.

There's no sound in the car but our heavy breathing. Heidi's head rests against her window, her eyes closed.

"Heidi? You okay?" Jag asks, leaning forward and brushing her hair from her face. Her skin is fevered and flushed, her forehead hot, her breathing rapid. "Heidi!"

I can't go any faster, but my racing heart makes me feel like we can. After another half hour, we close in on Mashhad. Lights fill up the night as the city comes into sight. The first couple of exits are for industrial areas, so we keep going until we are passing downtown Mashhad. There's a motel just off the exit, and we pull up to the front office. It's old and rundown, but they all are. I doubt we'll find anything better.

Once we've paid for our room—we share one for safety's sake—and we've laid Heidi on the bed, I gently lift her shirt. The cotton bandage sticks to the incision; the scab is full of pus and sticky. It's definitely infected and screaming red. I glance at Jag, who gives me an expression of horror.

"That's bad," Doug whispers.

"She needs a hospital," Owen adds. "Like right now."

"Well, let's at least put some more ointment on it," I say, grabbing the tube from my pack.

"I'll get directions to the hospital." Jag leaves without even asking if I think it's a good idea. It bothers me, but at the same time, it's a good idea. I'm just jumpy and don't want us to split up. This close to the border, it's not safe. I feel an enormous number of demons in the area—like static before a lightning strike.

Jag is back a few minutes later. "The guy doesn't understand me," he growls. "You'll have to get the directions yourself."

I curse under my breath, but I leave Heidi with the Cazadors and go to the front office. I get directions, scribbled on a piece of paper, and make it back to our room in under three minutes. "Got it. Let's go."

"No," Heidi mumbles into the pillow. "Get Dad."

"She's delirious," Doug says.

I lift one arm while Jag lifts the other. We help her back out to the car with Heidi shouting at us the whole time, crying from pain.

The Jeep races through the streets, Jag yelling out directions. We get lost and have to backtrack twice, and it takes a half hour longer than it should have. When we finally arrive at the hospital, it's just a small, rundown facility. A white, brick building that has seen better days.

We rush Heidi in through the front doors and sit her down in a chair. Even this late at night, the room is full of waiting, sick people. I push my way to the front desk and tell the receptionist that we need to see a doctor immediately.

She doesn't even glance up, only gives me a paper to fill out.

"Seriously?" I say in Farsi. "My sister has a terrible infection. She's practically incoherent." I stare her down until she finally looks up, a white hijab wrapped around her annoyed face.

My glare does not impress her. With a bored expression, she says, "Everybody here is sick and practically incoherent. Take a seat." She motions with her head to an empty chair and then goes back to whatever she was doing before I approached her.

Gritting my teeth, my hands in fists, I stomp back over to where the boys are waiting by Heidi. "It's gonna take more than just asking to get her in before it's too late." Looking around, I know we won't see a doctor until morning at the rate things are going. Half of the room is filled with gray men inside human bodies, hoping to get help before anyone else. They don't care about the average mortal. They'll make sure Heidi is last in line.

That's all it takes for Jag. He jumps up, wearing that devious, totally frightening grin he gets while fighting, and pulls out his dagger. My heart lurches and adrenaline shoots through my body as I attempt to jerk him back, but he's too fast. He pushes through the doors to the emergency room and disappears. Fifteen seconds later, he's back with a doctor, whose mouth is in a grim, frightened line.

"Her," he says, pointing with his dagger to Heidi.

The doctor motions for some orderlies to help her into the back room. We start to follow, but they only let Jag in. He's the one with the knife after all. I go back to our row of chairs and pace, wondering if I should just push my way through like Jag had, but he'll make sure she's given the best care. Either that or more people will need emergency attention.

38

Dean

I throw the covers back and jump out of bed. It's not light yet, but I can't sleep. It takes only thirty seconds to get dressed and five more to run a comb through my hair. Pacing my room, I wait anxiously for the clock to strike eight, when breakfast is served. I drum my fingers against my leg, and then I pace near the windows, counting the seconds as the sun climbs over the hills to the east.

From the colors in the sky, it's getting close. First, indigo, but then it lightens just a tinge to the color of cotton candy. A few minutes later, a gorgeous shade of orchid paints wild streaks across the clouds. Lighter and lighter, the colors fade, until the pink hues diminish into blue, and then, in all its glory, the sun bursts over the hills, bright, bold, and blinding.

That's it. I'm out of here. I shove the door open, and in my enthusiasm, it crashes back against the wall. "Ready?" I say to the stunned guard, already heading down the hall. I know the house now, and I don't need him to lead the way. It takes effort for him to keep up with me.

I reach the dining room and fly through the doorway, propelling myself toward the table… and my excitement deflates like a smashed Whoopi cushion. No one is there eating breakfast.

"Where is everyone?" I turn back to the guard.

"How should I know?" He scowls at me, folds his massive arms over his chest, and then leans back against the wall, consciously ignoring me. And then I see it… between his rubbery lips. He's missing a tooth. My pulse races, like a flash flood through my veins, delivering adrenaline all the way to my fingertips.

It worked.

I'm dying to ask him about it. Did it fall out during the night, rotten and diseased? Did it somehow get knocked out? Did it hurt or just painlessly dissolve into nothing? I'm nearly giggling with glee!

I take my normal seat at the table, which is already laden with breakfast food. Scrambled eggs, pancakes, mixed fruit, coffee, juice—as though we're going to feed an army. I dig in, afraid it will be taken away at the slightest whim.

I slip a biscuit into my pocket, and then keep adding anything that won't leak through my clothes. I'll hide this food in my closet—in case I get hungry during the night—but I could put it in the little drawers in my bed now. My own little pantry. I won't even have to get out of my covers to eat.

I eat in silence, alone, in the dim light of the chamber, the curtains still drawn. Coem is usually the one to open them. The darkness is oppressive and I hurry to finish, to get back to my studio where the sun shines and I can draw another portrait.

Just as I stand, wiping my hands with a napkin, Coem enters. He looks hammered, exhausted, and irritable. It stands to figure since he has green puss oozing from his tear ducts and nostrils. Pustules cover his lips, seeping infection, thick and milky. I recoil, not wanting to catch his germs, if he has any. But the thing that really hits home is… I did this. *I* did it. I gave him the malady. I'd drawn it.

I stand there, trying not to stare in disgust.

"Done so soon?" He smirks. "You don't want to keep me company while I eat?" His eyes squint and I'm not sure if it's out of hate for me, as though he knows I am the perpetrator of the crime, or if it's because his eyelids are swollen. Maybe a bit of both.

I want to refuse because looking at him makes me sick to my stomach, and I can't afford to throw up again. I'm still gaining weight. But maybe I overdid it a little on the drawing, and I don't want to anger him further. A sick demon most likely equates a mean demon.

"Sure. Of course." I take my seat, a bagel in my pocket

smooshing against my thigh. "How is Chumlento this morning?"

"I have no idea," he snaps, placing his napkin over his lap. He rests his head in his hands.

"Are you okay?" I ask stupidly.

"Do I look okay?"

"Not really. Have you ever been sick before?" I ask, sincerely interested. I've never seen a sick demon. Ever. They usually die before they get sick with anything, wearing their new bodies out by getting into fights and thrill seeking, wanting to experience *everything*.

"No. Never." With his head still cradled in his hand, his elbow balancing against the table, he glances up at me through hooded lids. "My head is pounding."

"That's… weird."

"I would say so." He takes a long breath and leans back in the chair, closing his eyes. "I don't know what to make of it. First Chum, and now me. Maybe there's a new virus that has mutated or something. Maybe we are not as immune as we used to be."

Ha! You're not! I yearn to scream. *I'm your worst nightmare, pal. I'm your deadliest virus come to hunt you down!* These words scream through my mind, and what I'd give to sing them out loud, but I cover my delight with a frown. "You should lie down. Get some rest."

"I can't. Have to pack. I'm leaving on a trip."

"Oh?" Where could he possibly be going? We've only been here a few days. Will he make me go too?

And then he answers my question. "You'll stay here. I just need to see to a few things. Keep painting and getting as much practice as you can. You're going to win me this world, Dean. You are the key to securing my place at the top, my… holy offering, so to speak. So be good." He smiles, but I see the weariness in his eyes. "Lamassu will stay with you."

"Who?"

"Your guard," he says like I'm an idiot as he motions to the unfriendly, yeti beast who's missing a tooth and stands by the door.

"Oh. Right. Lamassu." *Duh.* I shake my head, holding my

tongue. There are so many awesome things I could say. So many sarcastic remarks, but I don't think Coem is up for it today. "Well, I hope you feel better soon." Rising, I hurry from the room, hoping I can control the gleeful laughter that yearns to burst free.

Finally, I am a Cazador! Tormentor of demons!

39

Dean

I've had a few days free with Coem gone, and I take advantage of that freedom, keeping my sketchpad with me at all times as I wander around the mansion, drawing each demon that comes to visit. After I give them their pics, they fawn over them as though I've given them a priceless gift. I heard they are paying Coem copious amounts of money for these treasures. I've yet to see a penny.

I have copies of twenty-three demon sketches in my hidden drawers. On each portrait, I've changed some little detail, growing braver with each drawing. I keep the deviations minor for the most part, and it isn't until I hear shrieking downstairs that I think I may have gone too far.

I run to the top of the staircase. Brak, one of the demons that takes care of the grounds, is in the foyer screaming, crying, and bumping into walls. The skin where his eyes should be is smooth and even. No eyes, no eyelashes… nothing but skin. It's chillingly freaky. Three other demons surround him, calling out to him, trying to figure out what happened, but it's obvious it's something supernatural. He had eyes this morning, and now he doesn't.

I swivel back and lean against the wall. This is bad. I shouldn't have done it. I run back to my room and slam my door, hurrying to my secret hiding spot. I shuffle through the drawers, trying to find the sketch of Brak.

A part of me feels terrible and cruel for what I've done, even if he is a demon. Regret fills my heart, and I hate how that feels. This isn't me, causing such fear. I thought it would be funny and kind of horror-movie cool to erase his eyes. I'd pictured *Twilight Zone*, but seeing what I've done makes me sick. I'm not sure I can go through with my plan. Grasping a plain old number-two pencil, I draw a pair of eyes on Brak's face.

Even though these beings are demons, the bodies they steal are not, and I can't get past the human part of it. I'm not a bully. I don't like hurting people. And when I look at my captors… I see *people*. Although there's a voice in my head, probably my own, that tells me I'm a stupid idiot, that these beings don't care about me in any human way, that whatever their plans for me are, they aren't good. I'll end up dead. There's no way to live through this. Demons don't care about people, other than to benefit from them.

I walk over to the window and stare out over the backyard. Brak is out there now, sitting on a stone bench, sobbing into his hands. When he raises his head, I notice his eyes are back. But of course they are. That's my gift. I don't kill demons; I'm their persecutor. Half of me rejoices. The other half recoils.

What is wrong with me? I have an opportunity here. I can seriously wound them and I'm feeling guilty? What kind of Cazador am I? I pace, making tiny corrections to my plan, my fingers tapping my leg as I walk. My sketches are still lying on the bed, scattered, so I begin picking them up, placing them in a pile, when the door slams open.

I jump and freeze where I stand on the far side of my bed, my mouth gaping, the damning evidence hanging limp in my fingers, but Coem doesn't look at my hands. He stares at my face.

"Get packed. Now." He breathes in heavy gasps, his suit askew and dirty. He still looks terrible.

"Are you okay?" He's going downhill fast and will need a new body soon, his skin a sickly gray and his thick head of white-blond hair falling out in clumps. In the two days he's been gone, his body has grown thin, emaciated even… all from my infection? For the millionth time, I wonder how it is that I came to have this gift. I didn't have it before I arrived, so it happened once I got here, but when was that magic moment? I can't put my finger on it. Did God give me the ability to curse the demons? Or did the demons themselves… without knowing it? Surely, they wouldn't endow me with such a weapon intentionally.

No, if they knew about my gift, I'd be dead already. They are just as oblivious to the cause as I am.

"Do I look okay?" he responds, glaring.

"Not really. I'm sorry you don't feel well." I give him a weak smile and he shakes his head, rolling his eyes in derision, sufficiently wiping out any pity I felt a moment before.

He starts to turn away, so I hurry to ask, "Did my blood test results come back?" This is something that has been on my mind. Maybe my gift comes from a virus in my blood, and like Spiderman, I'm now a superhero. It sounds childish to think of it that way, but still cool, and I hope that is what happened.

"The results haven't come back yet, and we don't have time to wait, so I guess we'll never know." He stares at me for a moment as though trying to see inside me, trying to decipher what the results would have told him if we weren't in such a hurry to leave. His eyes fall to the floor, and he heaves a heavy sigh.

I go back to gathering my sketches. "So, where are we going?" I ask in a friendly, nonchalant tone. But he's already gone. There's a bag in my closet, and I place it on the bed. I throw in a few pairs of jeans, underclothes, and some of my favorite new shirts. I have toiletries of all sorts now, like an electric razor and toothpaste that tastes like licorice. I pack it because why not? I'll only be spoiled for a short while longer, until they realize I'm cursing them with my art, and then I'll either be back on the streets or dead.

Within an hour, we're sitting aboard a private jet with white leather seats and all the amenities you could ever desire while traveling. I recline, gazing out over the shrinking city of L.A., wondering if I'll ever be back.

I never had a chance to contact Jag and my heart sinks, knowing I'll probably never see him again. I haven't stopped thinking about Heidi either, and her face floats in my mind, so I decide to do something that will not only pass the time, but will make me happy too.

I begin at the bottom of the page with her feet, drawing her in combat boots, making them black and sooty with thick soles. Heavy and strong, to keep her grounded and balanced. I sketch her legs, long and muscular, her cargo pants form fitting. I mean, hey, she's sexy, and it's my picture. I can draw her how I want. No one else will ever see it.

I pencil in a thick leather belt over her hips, with plenty of weapons hidden in it. She's loaded for bear, totally tough, and superhero sexy. I draw her stomach flat and the muscles flexed, a womanly six-pack. I'm already drooling and I haven't even done her face. When I start on her arms and chest, I swivel my body so no one can peek at what I'm drawing. I have no problem drawing women, but Heidi's different. She's special and beautiful. Perfect and kind. I'm not just drawing her body. I'm drawing her soul. At least, that's what it feels like to me.

It isn't hard to sketch her sleek and beautiful body. I've looked at her for so long that I have every inch of her memorized… at least in my imagination. The curves of her breasts are hidden by a snug-fitting vest that is sleeveless to show her muscular biceps. She holds her dagger in one hand, her arm stretched out as though pointing it like a sword. In the other hand, she holds an AK-47, just for fun. Her body is rock hard and she-woman fierce, a powerful demon huntress, if I've ever seen one.

And then I begin her face. I sit there for a moment, trying to decide what kind of expression I want her to wear. It needs to match the rest of her, so I give her face a hard edge of fury, as though the demons have hurt her for the last time.

Her eyes are narrowed and piercing as she gazes at me from the page, and her pupils follow from every angle. Her full lips are pulled back into a feral grin, but they still look sexy to me, and her teeth are straight and white, true to form. She's ready for the apocalypse.

Her dark hair whips wildly around her oval face as though there's a storm at her back, and I fix the shading, adding a sunset-imbued tempest behind her.

When I'm finished, I can't quit staring at my masterpiece. I don't think I've ever drawn anything so compelling. I ache to see her in real life, to hold her, to kiss her. To tell her that she is the one who saved me. That she is the reason I've held on. She is the reason I find meaning in life or for even wanting to exist.

My heart swells, and an overwhelming surge of love fills me. I'd give anything to hold her just one more time, to feel her fingers threading through mine. If I ever do see her again, I'll tell her how I feel. I'll never hide my feelings again.

Before anyone else sees what I've done, I hide the sketch between the other pages of my art book.

This one's mine, and mine alone.

40

Heidi

My eyelids are heavy and the lights above me are too bright. I'm lying on a hard, cold table, and I try to roll off. Rough hands hold me down as I cry out. I feel like I've been drugged, and my stomach burns so terribly I can hardly breathe.

"She's septic," I hear an unfamiliar voice say.

"What?" Jag asks. I don't hear anyone answer.

Are they talking about me? I manage to peel open my eyelids long enough to see a man with very dark skin and a white, medical jacket leaning over me. He shines a light into my eyes. I bat it away, and then he jabbers in a language I can't understand.

I don't want to be here, and they can't make me stay. When I attempt to roll off the table, pain burns in my arm. Someone jabs me with a needle. I recognize that feeling. They're drugging me! But I refuse to go down without a fight.

"Heidi, stop!" Jag is in my face, his eyes only inches from mine.

I grab his shirt and pull him closer. "They're here, Jag. The demons are here. They're trying to get inside me," I hiss at him. I know this is happening. It's the only way to explain it, the burning, being held hostage, but he doesn't believe me, I can tell. He gives me a worried scowl, but that's it. He's useless.

My head lolls to the side and I see Brecken out in the hall, pacing, running his hands through his hair as he always does. Why doesn't he help me?

"Help," I whisper to him, trying to reach out. He doesn't notice, and I feel the sensation of cold steel against my chest. My shirt is snipped off in less than three seconds. I'm practically naked with boys in the room. What are they doing? I fight them hard, determined to escape before they can do worse, but the room starts to spin. The lights above me swirl like a merry-go-round, and I fight the urge to hurl. I manage to hold it in, just barely.

Jag grasps my hand and brings it to his lips. There are tears in his eyes. Actual, honest to goodness tears. But I don't have a chance to say anything. My eyes are too heavy, my mind too fuzzy. My world goes dark.

The fog lifts slowly, like a dream. I'm alone. The lights are dim, and I'm surprised to feel no pain. I lie in a stark-looking hospital room, trying to figure out exactly where I am, and then I realize… I'm not in pain!

Memories of the night before flash in my mind, and I remember everything. I blink as my heart lurches and adrenaline shoots to my fingers and toes. Jerking to a sitting position, I swing my feet over the side of the bed to wiggle my toes, the hospital gown bunching up to my thighs. I slide from the bed, unsure if my legs will hold me. They do. I'm fine. I feel strong, and still… no pain.

And then I remember why I hurt so badly before. Yanking up the hem of my gown, I lift it up to my chest. My incision is gone. Completely disappeared. Totally healed. Like… miraculously. I run my fingers across the smooth skin of my abdomen and I swear, my stomach muscles look and feel more defined than ever before.

How long have I been here? Have I been in a coma? It would take months for my scar to become so smooth. Did the boys leave me here to deal with the demons themselves? Is it all over? After yanking the IV from my arm, the alarm on my monitor begins to blare. A nurse rushes in and starts babbling, but I don't understand a word she says.

Brecken and Jag push past her, their faces stretched with smiles.

"It's about dang time those drugs wore off!" Jag throws his arms around me and picks me up, twirling me in a circle while the nurse tries to get me away from him. "You had us scared for a minute!"

"For only a minute?" I joke, trying to figure it all out. How long have they kept me drugged? Why would Brecken allow it? Why would Jag?

"Well, for about two hours is all." Brecken waits by the foot of the bed, but he gives me a radiant grin. "They said you'd be out for six."

"What?" Two hours?

"They anesthetized you to prep you for surgery," Jag explains. "You were septic and going into shock, practically unconscious and totally out of it when we brought you in."

I vaguely remember that part, but even I know that if you are septic, you're pretty dang sick, and sick for a long time. Nobody recovers from that in just two hours. "What happened?"

"Nobody knows," Bret answers. "They got you on the table to begin your surgery and your wound was gone. And I mean, just completely gone."

They all stare at me, and then Jag says, "So, what happened on your end? Do you remember anything? Any visions or near-death experiences?" He's smiling like he's joking, but I get the feeling he really wants to know.

"I don't know. I just know I don't hurt anymore."

The nurse stares at me as if I'm an anomaly. Who heals that fast and how? It's unexplainable, but I'll take it. "Well, get out of here, you two," I say to Jag and Bret. "I'm gonna get dressed."

They leave and I go over to the closet, expecting my bloodied, worn-out clothes to be hanging there. I find black cargo pants, combat boots, and a tank top with a black vest that fits snug around my chest. I've never worn one this style, but I like it. It has a ton of pockets. I find a combat belt, which sits low on my hips, and strap it on. Brecken must have put these things in here while I was sleeping, and I make a note to thank him.

These clothes rock. I feel like Wonder Woman.

41

Dean

Coem shakes me awake, and I have to wipe drool from the corner of my mouth when I sit up. "We're here," he says.

I stand slowly, my body aching, and I have a crimp in my neck. Grabbing my art supplies, I shove them into my backpack and follow him out, down a flight of stairs that has been placed at the door of the plane. We walk across the hot tarmac. The first thing that hits me is the wall of heat that immediately dries out my mouth and throat. It takes my breath away for a moment.

A man wearing a white turban and tunic stands next to a running sedan. He opens my door for me, bowing at the waist.

"Thanks," I tell him, but he ignores me and shuts the door. There's a gray man inside him, and I wonder what the guy's life was like before his body was stolen away.

"Where exactly are we?" I ask Coem, knowing we've flown halfway around the world. We were in the air for at least eighteen hours. Will I ever get back home?

"You'll see, my new friend. You will see." He smiles and goes back to flipping through a newspaper. He's back to normal since I fixed his picture before we left on the plane. He was so irritable and grouchy. I had little desire to travel with Cranky Coem—a demon that was growing more and more enraged. I'll make his malady come back later.

My heart has felt heavy ever since this trip started. I'll never see my friends again. It's so unfair, but I learned a long time ago to not feel sorry for myself. Life isn't ever fair, and it never will be. There's nothing I can do about my situation other than to learn as much as I can about these demons and hinder their progress if possible.

The car takes us through dusty streets of rubble and destitute people, but Coem seems completely unbothered by it all. I can't tear my eyes away. Half-naked, alarmingly thin children sit in the streets, not even playing, but seemingly waiting. For what? I don't know.

We pull through some tall, dark gates and up to another magnificent house. How many of these does Coem have? The house is large, but not a mansion. It's white and clean, with greenery along the drive and the front steps.

My car door is opened for me once again, and I step from its air-conditioned interior into the stark heat of the desert. I hurry inside the house, which is cool and comfortable. The interior is open and airy—beautiful.

"This way," a man says. He wears a gray man inside, as well as a black tunic and matching goatee. He leads me toward the back of the house. "Dinner will be served in an hour. You may rest until then," he tells me as he closes the bedroom door behind me.

I set my backpack next to the double bed that is covered in a white quilt and walk over to the windows, pulling the sheer curtains back. It must take a ton of water to keep this place so lush and green. A yard that beckons me. I'll have to sneak out there to draw.

Walking back over to the bed, I sit down and pull my sketchbook from my pack, slipping the picture of Heidi from its pages. I gaze at those fierce eyes, her confident stance, and I can almost feel her presence next to me. She fills me with courage and the fire to go on. I can almost believe I can bring these fiends down. For *her*.

Hiding the sketch under the pillow, I lie down and stretch out on the bed. It's a little on the firm side, but I close my eyes, just for a minute. Exhaustion soon overtakes me, and it feels good to let go.

The dinner table is spread with fruits, breads, cheeses, and wine. I eat very little as I can't stop thinking about those starving children right outside the door. I know what they're feeling, and I can't get their pathetic faces and bloated stomachs out of my mind.

All this excess. What gluttony! It makes me sick. When no one is looking, I hide food in my pockets for those hungry kids… if I can get it out there.

"There are some very important people I want you to meet," Coem says.

"Okay." I take a fig from my plate and bite into its juicy sweetness. I've never had figs before and I think I've found a new favorite.

"They'll want their portraits painted." He smiles and wipes his mouth, watching me while I eat.

"That's fine."

"Good.

"How's Chumlento? Is she any better?" I ask.

He cocks his head as he considers his answer. "I suppose she'll dispose of that body and opt for a healthier one. She'll meet up with us as soon as she's able." He smiles and rests his hands on either side of his plate, one eyebrow raised. "You have an important purpose in being here."

"And what is that?"

"To make me a lot of money." He smiles as though I should already know this, and then he takes a bite of bread with cheese.

"You brought me halfway around the world, or wherever we are, just for money?" I stare at him, dumbfounded.

He chuckles and shakes his head as though I'm very slow and stupid, like a dumb cow. "No. Not just for that, but it's a nice perk. Money rules the world, you know. If you don't have it, you're nothing. How do you think you got here, into this beautiful desert land? With money. Why are you in this house? Money. How is it possible to wear those clothes?" He points to my outfit. "With money. And the food you eat? Money."

I place my hands in my lap and stare at them, noticing how stained and calloused they are… the hands of someone small and seemingly unimportant. But those stains come from something I love, from something that gives me untold happiness. It doesn't cost a thing, but then I realize… it does. I can't afford brushes, paint, and canvas on my own. He's right about money in so many ways, but I'd like to think it's the intention that matters. Coem could spend his money for good, for feeding the poor and creating shelters, but he doesn't. He doesn't help. He harms.

"Money isn't everything. Money won't make you happy, Coem."

"Maybe not. But it helps." His eyes are wide and watchful. The world is his oyster. He could buy and sell countries, or so he says. There is nothing and no one to stop him. He's powerful, and his money makes him more so.

He doesn't comprehend what I'm saying. He can't. His heart is shriveled and cold, evil. He thinks he can buy me, and in a way, he has, but I will stop him. If it's the last thing I do before I die, I will at least stop *him*.

42

Brecken

I have no explanation for Heidi's miraculous recovery. I stare at her in awe as we walk out of the hospital. How is this possible? I've seen some amazing things, but nothing like this. It's magic... and I don't believe in magic. So then, it's a miracle. There's a reason for everything, but for the life of me, I can't figure this one out.

Maybe it's just a sign that we're headed in the right direction. That what we're doing is what we're supposed to do. I send a thank you out into the universe, hoping the correct recipient hears it.

Doug and Owen pester Heidi for answers too. She just laughs it off, wearing an air of confidence I've never seen in her before.

"I told you," she says. "I don't know any more than you do. I just woke up and felt great. More amazing than ever before. Just look at these guns!" She flexes her biceps, and Owen reaches forward to give them a squeeze.

"Dang! Rock hard."

"Yup." She laughs, shaking her head, and glancing over at me. "Remember when you used to call my biceps *pancake* and *syrup*?"

The memory rushes back, and I laugh. I'd forgotten all about that. But that was when she was just a little girl. "It looks like they've graduated to something more." Her shoulders are also more defined, as is every other muscle in her body. What happened to her in that hospital? She was dying and now she's whole. No, *more* than whole.

I drive us back to our motel. And even though Heidi is revved up and ready to go, the rest of us are exhausted. There are two queen beds, so it's going to be tight, but sleep beckons, and I can't hold it off any longer.

I crawl into one of the beds and fall flat on my face. My brain shuts off, and I tune out everyone. There's a discussion going on, but I don't listen. I feel the bed dip and crack open one eye. Heidi sits next to me on the edge of the bed.

"I can't sleep. There's just no way." She smiles down at me. I can tell from her tone that she's informing, not asking permission for anything.

"Okay. Just watch TV," I suggest, mumbling into the pillow.

"Yeah. Okay." She flips on the television that is mostly static. There's one station that is kind of coming through, so she puts her feet up and reclines in the chair. Jag plops down on the other bed next to Doug, which leaves Owen sharing with me. I totally don't care.

43

Heidi

It doesn't take long for all four boys to fall asleep and start snoring in four-part harmony. I smile, knowing my moment of freedom is at hand. Feeling something deep inside that I've never felt before, I slip out the door, completely unafraid. I'll be back before they wake. I have a runed dagger on one hip and Bret's Nephilim dagger on the other. He won't mind if I borrow it.

The streets are dark and warm, even at this time of night. Shadows hide the fact that it's a war-torn, earthquake-destroyed city, but it actually seems quiet and peaceful… unless you look hard enough. A soft breeze blows with the scent of earth, sand, and flowers.

I roll my shoulders and then my head, loosening up. There's no fear inside me. None at all. Not like last night when I was attacked. Was that just last night? It feels like a year ago, and I can't believe I feel so different.

There's no comparison. I'm a completely different person today. The scared, weak Heidi is gone. She doesn't even exist.

Starting out at a jog, I make my way a couple of blocks farther into town. You'd think the streets would be empty, the people sleeping safely in their beds, but not here. There's a nightlife going on, not unlike the one in L.A.

The downtown strip is busy with revelers, all with their very own gray man inside. I start out on the edges so I don't bring attention to myself. A silent slash here, a quiet stab there, and the piles of ash begin piling up.

I'm full of adrenaline and kicking butt. I'm Desmond Miles

in *Assassin's Creed*, taking down my enemy with the silence of a shadow. Shouts of "Nephilim dagger" rise on the wind. And after that, rather than coming at me, most of the demons turn and run, trying to hide from the deadly swipe of my dagger.

I move down the street, a samurai warrior, unstoppable, and it feels so good. Nothing can stand against me. Every demon I face dies. Every single one… until I round the corner.

I come face to face with something I've never seen before. A being at least seven feet tall, with red, leathery skin, black horns, and sharp teeth, like a vampire. I slow my attack and let the victim at my feet—a gray man—scramble away.

I face this new form of demon, a dagger in each hand. A smile comes to my lips as I balance on the balls of my feet. "Come to mama," I taunt.

The demon smiles. "It will be a pleasure, but first, who are you? I've yet to meet a mortal with the courage to stand against me." His lips pull back into a savage snarl, which I think is supposed to be a grin.

"I'm your worst nightmare."

"I don't have nightmares," he growls. "I *am* the nightmare." He steps toward me with heavy clomps of his hoof-like feet. "And you don't scare me, little mouse."

"I don't need to scare you. Just kill you." I begin to circle him, studying his moves, searching for a weakness, which I've yet to find. His shoulders are huge and well muscled, and his clawed fingers flex and contract. Powerful thigh muscles make him strong, but not fast.

"You can try, but it might prove difficult," he says.

"Then let's dance." I don't say another word. I didn't come here to talk. I came here to kill, and now I've been given the ability to do just that. I feint to the right, and he falls for it. He counterattacks, but his movements are sluggish. Weakness number one. I swirl in a circle, my dagger an extension of my hand. It nicks his skin. I expect a puff of ash, but nothing happens, and then I realize I'm holding the runed dagger in my right hand instead of the Nephilim. I would have to stab deeper with that knife to kill him… I think. He's not in a human meat suit, so this is all new for me.

He laughs, robust and deep, like thunder, and throws a meaty fist at my face. I duck, and he misses me by a hair's breath. We circle one another, his fangs glistening with saliva. "You're quick."

"I like to think so." I smile, giving him a wink. I might be playing the over-confident card a bit, but it feels good after how afraid I've felt for the last five years. It's as though my dagger tattoo has finally imbued me with the magic I yearned for. Better late than never.

I push forward, slashing with my daggers, one after the other, until I force him back against the brick wall of a building and he has nowhere to go. "Looks like you're out of street."

He stops and lowers his fists. "It does, doesn't it? I guess I'll have to say goodbye then. Don't want to get pricked by that pretty dagger of yours. One quick question though, before I go."

I stare at him as if he's crazy. Where does he think he can escape to? I have him trapped. If he tries to dart either way, I'll get him, and he knows it. "Okay. One question before you die. Seems only fair."

"Where'd you get the Nephilim, and who taught you to use it?"

"That's classified." The corner of my lip curls up at the same time as his.

"Touché." He inclines his head toward me. And then, just like that, he's gone. Not in a puff of smoke, but gone. Disappeared. Invisible to the naked eye.

I swirl around, fully expecting him to be standing behind me, ready to deal a death blow. He's not, and neither are any other demons. I'm alone on a quiet street that not long ago was disorderly and raucous. This just doesn't happen. Demons like that don't run from a fight, and I keep half expecting him to reappear and stab me in the back.

When he doesn't come back, I jog to the next street, anxious to find more demons to dispatch, but they're gone. All of them… on every street. How disappointing. With a deep breath of resignation, I turn and head back the way I came, all the way to the motel. The door handle turns silently in my hand, and when I push through, the boys are all still asleep and snoring.

My belt slips off, and I kick my boots from my feet. It feels good to have worked my muscles, and I'm now tired enough to fall asleep. From the foot of the bed, I climb up the middle and snuggle against Jag, breathing him in as my eyes close.

The morning dawns and I stretch as the sunlight filters in through a slit in the drapes. "Man, it feels good to be alive!" I slide from the bed to notice Jag studying me with inquisitive eyes.

"Oh?" One of his eyebrows rises in question.

Man, he looks good today. I'm tempted to say that right in front of everyone, to take his face in my hands and lay a passionate kiss right on his mouth, but I refrain. "Yep. Let's get going and kick some demon butt," I say instead.

Normally, I take a while to wake up. It takes copious amounts of coffee and sugar to feel I'm among the living. Today, I don't need a thing. I strap on my belt and tie my boots, grabbing my stuff to take out to the Jeep.

"Jeez, Heidi. Give us a minute," Doug says, rubbing sleep from his eyes.

Jag is still staring at me, taking slow sips of his coffee. "How was your night?" he whispers when I sidle up next to him to pour myself a cup also.

My eyes snap to his, my innards twisting. "Uh… same as yours."

A sly smile comes to those rosy lips I love as he shakes his head. "I don't think so," he whispers, his mouth grazing my ear before he walks away to sit on the bed.

I watch him, wanting to defend myself or say something quirky, but Owen is watching. Doug is in the bathroom and Bret has gone to the office to speak with the desk clerk. So, I bide my time. Jag gives me another knowing look, and I give him one right back. "I'm going to load the car."

"I'll help." He follows me out, still wearing that dang smile.

Yanking open the back, I toss my bag inside and he does as well.

"So," he says. "The big guy eluded you."

I glance up, knowing there's no point in lying. Somehow, he knows I snuck out, and it looks like he followed me. "I guess."

"Did he mention his name?"

"You didn't hear the conversation?" I shut the door and lean against the car, my arms folded.

He matches my stance. "Nope. Wasn't close enough."

I sigh. Why be cryptic? If he's going to get mad, he's going to no matter what I say. "Naw. But he was friendly. I'll remember him."

"So will I."

"You're not mad?"

"Should I be?"

"Well, normally you would be." I turn to face him as he sets his coffee mug on top of the Jeep, taking both my arms and pulling me close.

"Did you not see yourself last night? I don't think we have anything to worry about where you're concerned. But I didn't know that at first, so yeah, I followed you because I heard you leaving. I didn't want you to be alone if you happened to need help."

He'd held back and watched, never once giving his presence away. A sense of pride begins to grow inside me because I'm fully aware of what he saw… a fighter who is equal and possibly better at this than he is. Does that bother him?

"I have to admit, it felt really good."

"It was amazing. I need some of your mojo." He kisses me deeply, as though trying to draw out some of my magic for himself, and then he goes back inside the motel room to grab his stuff. By this time, the others are all packed up and ready to go too. We load up and head out by seven. We're only a couple of hours from the border, and then only a couple of more to *The Door*. I'm itching to get there, so I hop into the driver's seat before Bret can.

He stares down at me as I sit there with my hands on the steering wheel.

"I call shotgun," Jag says, sliding into the passenger seat.

"Sorry, bro. You're in the back." I smile, remembering the old days when our dad was around, and Brecken and I would fight for the front seat. I'd wink at him and gesture to the rear with my thumb, giving him an *I own you* expression—like I do now. Does he remember? When his eyes narrow in mocking defeat, I know he does.

"Fine. Just be careful." He slides in behind me, and I glance at him in the rearview mirror. He's frowning and I'm tempted to tease him about pouting, like old times, but there's nothing more annoying than sibling rivalry in a car when you can't escape.

But inside… I'm smiling.

44

Dean

The living room is full of demons, sitting on the sofas and chairs, visiting. Wide windows line the front wall and lush, soft couches fill the rest of the room. Fans circle above us and everyone socializes as if it's a family holiday.

They're waiting in line... for me. I sit in a corner of the room where morning sunlight flows in through the high windows, creating the best illumination. I have already painted three portraits and I'm tired, but they won't let me rest until it's time to eat. So, I'll get three breaks a day and that's it.

The only thing that makes it worth it is that I'm memorizing each face, and then in the privacy of my room, I'll sketch them out again, adding things on the inside, creating bacteria, viruses, parasites, and other pests that will eat them from the inside out, things that will be highly contagious, but only to demons. I know it will work. It's all about intention.

There's excitement about the demons getting sick and dying. I try not to think of the suffering I'm causing, but it's my only way to even up the odds in this war. I've learned something new, living here with my enemy. Once a demon takes a body, he can't get out of it until it dies somehow.

The demons I'm painting right now aren't the big wigs, but they aren't the grunts either. They're the rooks, knights, and bishops of the demon kingdom. These guys pay a lot for their portraits, and I laugh when I think about it. They have no idea what they are in for. That they are paying me to kill them slowly.

The man who sits before me now reclines with one leg

crossed over the other. His flaming red hair is spiked up and bleached at the tips. He has a gray man on the inside, but he wants me to paint his mortal body rather than the demon one. He visits with his cronies who watch me work from over my shoulder. It's beyond annoying, but the last time I asked them to back away, one of them smacked me over the head with a magazine. I keep my mouth shut now, although when it's his turn…

Red Spikes' eyes turn to me. "How's it coming along, Don?"

"It's Dean."

"Right. How's it coming?" He wears a serene, condescending smile.

I shrug and frown, studying the depiction. "Hmm. Not sure. Something's missing."

"I think it looks fine," demon number two states, looking over my shoulder.

"No, something is definitely missing." I mix some colors and deepen the color of his eyes, adding tiny slashes in the irises. In my mind, I tell these slashes to widen during the night, so that this vain being won't be able to look at himself anymore. He didn't want a picture of his ugly demon body, but one of this handsome mortal man that he stole. That tells me everything I need to know about him.

When I'm finished, the demon behind me nods, his arms folded over his chest, his finger tapping his lips. "Yes. This is good. Very good. He painted you perfectly. You'll love looking at this every day. Where will you hang it?"

Red Spikes comes around the easel to gaze down at my work of genius. "Wonderful! It's perfect. I'll hang it over the fireplace of my new home in Paris."

"You have a house in Paris?" I ask. "And you came here just for a portrait? How did you even hear about me?" These demons have quite the underground network.

He gives me a knowing smile and glances at his friend. A silent message passes between them. "We have our ways."

I take his painting and gently carry it to the other side of the room to dry with the others, a whole wall of demonic faces smiling back at me. I shiver in spite of myself. Red's friend sits down in the chair and I walk back over to him, taking my seat in the sun. I study the demon's mortal face, and then look deeper to his demon visage. He's also a gray man, which makes this easy.

"Which do you want painted?" I ask for what feels like the hundredth time. These demons are all different in what they are hoping for.

"I want you to paint *my* face, but with the body of an angel." He smirks, and I'm not sure if he's kidding or not. With this new gift I have, a portrait like that could have repercussions.

"Are you serious?"

"Of course." He stares at me, unblinking, and I stare back, trying to figure out how to give him a weakness in a picture like that. "Okay. Let's see what I can do then." I smile and get to work.

The afternoon sun dips below the horizon, and my neck and shoulders scream from the abuse I've put them through. I seldom paint this long without a break, and I'm starving. When I think dinner will be announced, Coem slams into the room, the door banging against the wall. The demons in the room jump in fright.

"Everyone! To *The Door*!" He darts back out, and I sit there watching with my mouth hanging open as they scatter like ants.

I have no idea what is going on, but I'll leave them to their drama. I take my brushes to the sink with the intention of rinsing them out and cleaning off all my supplies, but my guard rushes in and grabs my arm. An icy sting zings down to my hand and numbs my fingers. I yank away.

"Don't touch me!" I glare at him, at the end of my rope where he's concerned. "I'm sick of you doing that." I can barely hold my brushes and palette because my arm hurts so badly.

His eyes narrow and his lips twist into a snarl. "It's a little late to complain. You're to get out to the car immediately."

"I'm going too?" And then what Coem said sinks in. *Get to The Door*. What door is he talking about? I wrack my brain for some reference to what he's talking about, but I come up with nothing. Still, I feel the tension in the air, like static before a lightning strike. Something big is happening.

Throwing only my pencils and a sketchpad into my pack, I hurry back downstairs. My heart races with anticipation, and I wonder what could possibly be so important that the demons are running around like it's the end of the world.

45

Brecken

We race to the border without any problems, but then, at the speed we're going, nobody would be able to keep up.

"Slow down!" I yell from the backseat, but all I hear is Heidi's laughter. Jag glances back at me and laughs too.

A sign appears on the side of the road, welcoming us to Turkmenistan. We cross the border as though it doesn't exist at all, and I guess when you think about it, it doesn't. The demons don't recognize borders, and I doubt God does either.

My past is ever present in my mind, and the closer we get to *The Door*, the more I feel the seductive pull, the power and the heat, that comes along with being a demon. Closing my eyes, I pray for the strength and courage it's going to take to face the beings who were once like family to me—or as close as you can get as a demon—and the strength it's going to take to destroy them if I can.

Demons don't feel love, so I'm not sure what these feelings are that I have for them, but something inside me cares. Cares for their souls. I don't want them to perish. I want them to change… like I did. I want them to choose good rather than evil. To choose a mortal life of their own rather than stealing someone else's, but I know most of them won't. Most would rather die than admit they picked the wrong side.

"Dude, are you okay?" Owen asks. He's sitting in the middle of the backseat between Doug and me. "Your face is all sweaty."

"Yeah, man. You look sick." Doug leans forward, studying my face.

"You better not throw up!" Heidi yells from the front. "Do I need to pull over?"

I shake my head. "No," I whisper, bowing my head, feeling defeated before we even begin, which is no way to start at all. "I'm just worried."

"Okay." Jag turns in the passenger seat, so that he's looking at Doug, Owen, and me. "Let's talk about our plan, since we don't even know what it is yet."

My stomach sinks. How do I tell them I *have* no plan? What is a bunch of kids with a few runed daggers going to do against the greatest and most powerful demons that exist? How do I tell them there is nothing we can do to stop them?

Doug pats my back. "Don't worry. We can do this."

He seems to have read my mind, and I look up into his trusting brown eyes. An icy fist wraps around my heart, and I picture him lying dead on the ground. I see it in my mind like a vision, and I look away, shaking my head in denial.

"Seriously, Bret," Jag says. "What's the plan?"

I meet his gaze and his eyes narrow, his lips pressed together. He studies me intently, waiting. "I see." He turns back around and faces front.

"What do you see?" Doug asks, frowning. He glances at me. "What does he see?"

"I know what he sees," Owen states. "That there is no plan. That we came all this way to stop millions of demons, but Bret doesn't even know how to do it himself." He stares forward, his hair flopping over his forehead as if he hasn't combed it in days. Maybe he hasn't. He hasn't changed his T-shirt either, but that's not going to matter in a few hours.

"What?" Doug asks again.

"There's no plan," Jag says, reiterating Owen's words. "But I already knew that."

Doug swirls in his seat so he can get a good look at me. "Dude! We need a plan and you said you had one."

"I'm trying!" I yell back. "I know these demons, and I honestly don't know how to defeat them. I've been wracking my brain for weeks trying to come up with something! And I don't know how to keep you all from getting hurt in the process!"

They all stare at me, even Heidi, in the rearview mirror. It's a few moments before anyone says anything.

"What about a bomb?" Doug asks. "We could blow up the hole."

"That would just make the crack bigger." I shake my head, knowing we need to come up with something else.

"I don't know what else we *could* do to destroy a hole that size." Owen taps his knees, bobbing his head as though he's listening to music. "We don't need to destroy the demons right now. Just shut the hole. We can get to work killing them later."

My head snaps back as I realize he's right. Why didn't I think of that before? I think back to my original meeting with Michael and Raphael. They never said anything about killing demons. Only shutting *The Door*. I let my mind mull over this as my heart picks up speed.

"Owen, you're a genius!" I grab his head and pull it towards me, hugging him fiercely. A mile-wide smile grows on my face. "All this time I've been trying to come up with ways to kill the demons who are in charge of this mess and who are keeping *The Door* open, and all this time, the answer was right before us... and you thought of it."

His lips stretch into a huge grin. "Well, yeah. Now it's doable. We can do this. We just need to figure out how."

"Yeah, how." Jag glances over at Heidi and reaches across, taking her hand.

Because of the Rift upheavals and shifts in the Earth, it takes hours longer to reach *The Door* than I thought it would. Darkness covers everything and night has come to the desert again. I'd hoped to arrive during the day when the demons were still hiding from the sun. Now they'll be awake and alert.

Our Jeep bounces over the rocks and dirt toward a massive

circle that glows in the distance with the radiance of the sun. There are no trees for miles, and desolation covers everything. The closer we get, the colder my heart grows.

It's the energy of this place, I know, but it doesn't change the fact that it's real, and that I'll have to fight my demon tendencies every step of the way. I hadn't anticipated this. I'd figured it would be more like the Idir Shaol battle five years ago, where angels were at my back and the power of God surrounded me. I didn't have to struggle with my demon side then.

I don't want to do this. I hold onto the front seat until my knuckles are white, practically ripping the upholstery from the frame. The closer we get, the more the realization sets in that there's nothing we can do to stop the demon infestation. I won't be able to shut *The Door*. I can't. And I'm taking these kids—including my sister—to their deaths.

"Dude, are you okay?" Owen asks me again.

I swear he asks this every five minutes, and I snap at him. "Of course I'm okay. Stop asking me that!" The words come out like a snarl, and everyone turns around to stare at me. I shake my head and growl under my breath, unable to apologize. I don't even care.

"Dude," Doug whispers. "We're all in this together."

"I know," I whisper back, resting my head on the front seat. But we're not in this together. It's just me. They won't be able to shut it. That's my job. It will take more than muscle. It will take something supernatural, but I'm not sure what that is. I don't want to make this scarier for them, but I can see from the looks on their faces that they are afraid. At least Doug and Owen are. Jag, if he's nervous, has the best poker face of everyone. Heidi… well, I just can't figure her out. She's been so different since the hospital.

Heidi stops the car about a hundred yards from *The Door*. The glow beckons me. I open my door and step out so I can gaze on its beauty with my own eyes and not through a window. The others do the same.

"Wow," Heidi breathes, her arms resting on her door, one foot still in the car. "That's incredible."

"Yeah," I agree. "Get your weapons. It will be your job to keep the demons off me."

"Where, exactly, is the opening?" Doug asks, strapping on his dagger. "At the bottom? We won't have to actually go inside, will we?"

"No," I say. "You'll burn to death if you even try. You'll have plenty to do up top." I can't help the sarcastic chuckle that escapes me as I picture it, and then glance away. This is not good. I have got to get more control over my emotions. The power around the crater is unbelievable, and I feel stretched thin and weak, my knees shaking as I walk toward the fiery glow in the distance. My home.

The others follow, the five of us looking pretty insignificant, walking toward the OK Corral. But I don't feel like Doc Holiday and I doubt the others do either. We're truly walking toward our deaths, but I've yet to see anyone else around.

It's late. It's dark. It's quiet, and the air around us grows hotter.

It doesn't take long to get to the edge and look down into the burning pit—a huge crater, over two hundred feet across and a hundred feet deep, with embers and flames that never stop smoldering. We gaze into its depths in silence until Heidi speaks up.

"This is amazing. I've never seen anything like it, and when you described *The Door*, this is not what I pictured."

"Me neither," Doug answers.

Jag is silent with his hand resting on his dagger. He backs up slowly. "Step away from the edge," he says. "And stop looking at the flames or you won't be able to see in the dark."

"Too late," a voice says from the darkness.

We whirl around. A host of demons stands at our backs. Mostly gray men, shoulder to shoulder, their wide, dark maws cracked and jagged in their glee. They think they've already won. All they have to do is move forward and push us into the crater.

"I knew it would be you, Mictian." I stare my old nemesis down, my hand on the hilt of my Nephilim.

"And I knew it would be you." He stares back at me, his sword tip resting on the ground. He also uses a Nephilim blade, as do a few of the others, but none of the gray men do. They have no weapons at all. Only the fear they try to instill in men's hearts.

"The gray men have no power here," I say to my Cazadors. "Don't let them scare you."

"Create a shield around yourselves," I say. "Like I explained in the car." I try to do the same for myself, but I struggle to picture the bright white glow of power, and my shield fails to appear. I'm not like the others. I'm still a demon, at least partly, and I don't deserve God's protection. I don't deserve to be saved. Even so, I try again as Mictian steps forward, walking toward me with slow, sure steps. His army follows a few paces behind.

"I have missed you, my friend," he says. "Come back to us. There is still a place for you among us. Stop this nonsense of redemption. You are already redeemed in us." He smiles and reaches out to me. For a moment, I think of how easy and appealing his offer is. I'm tempted to drop my dagger and run forward, taking my place beside him.

Shaking my head, I push those damning thoughts away. "I'm on another path now." I glance to my right and then to my left, making sure my team is ready.

Jag holds two daggers. One in each hand. He stands spread-eagle, ready, his gaze never wavering. Heidi is between him and me, the radiance of the crater making her hair glow with fire. She's the personification of a demon huntress times a hundred. Her daggers are poised, her eyes riveted on Mictian. Is she's planning to go directly after him? Not if I have anything to say about it.

Doug and Owen stand on the other side of me. I feel their fear—raw and palpable—but they don't show it. They also have two daggers each. We're ready. We're armed. And we're not leaving here until it's over, one way or another.

46

Dean

We're riding in a limo… off-road. The wheels bounce over the terrain as if we don't have shocks, and the beams from the headlights slice through the dark, showing only gray dirt on the ground for miles and miles. No trees, plants, or anything else. A fiery, red circle glows in the distance and, from what my demon captors say, it is *The Door to Hell*.

A pit grows in my stomach. I'm not sure what is about to happen or what we are up against, but my captors' anxiety also heightens as we gain ground. They know something I don't know, and they won't tell me what it is.

We're still a good distance away when it comes into full view. A steady burn of cinders, flames, and the silhouettes of demons—hundreds of them—blotting out the backdrop of stars.

We pull closer, until we're only a few yards away. "You stay here," Coem orders as the car stops. He opens his door, the smoky odor of sulfur filling the confines of my new prison. Within seconds, I'm sitting alone. Flipping the ceiling light on, I grab my pack and pull out my sketchpad, but after getting everything ready, I realize I can't see through the tinted windows. Not with the dome light on, and I won't be able to see my sketches without it.

Quietly, I pull on the door's handle. It doesn't open. Child locks. I scoot to the other side and try that door. Locked. I sit there a moment, trying to figure out what to do, when I notice the partition to the driver's compartment is still open. *Idiot*! Slipping through without a problem, I unlock the front doors. I hide a chuckle as I slide from the quiet into the chaos.

Gray men are pouring from the crater's edge in a tidal wave. They don't do anything but wail and screech. It's a terrifying sound, and my heart quakes. I skirt around the edge of the crowd, trying to stay out of sight. If I can get to the other side of the crater—the side devoid of demons—maybe I'll be able to see to draw better.

The few that notice don't stop me. Maybe they think I'm one of them now since I've painted their faces. The temptation to run is almost overwhelming, but where would I go? I circle *The Door* and sit down among the rocks and dirt, the glow of the eternally burning pit lighting up the stage for me.

Not sure how to catch each individual demon at this distance, I opt for something else, hoping it will work. I sketch the silhouette as one entity, heads and shoulders mostly, coloring them in as one body. Then I take my eraser and slash through the narrow section of their necks, picturing their heads falling to the ground.

When I glance up, all those gray men are gone! I didn't even get to see it happen! I rip out that page and begin another.

And that's when I see her… her long hair whipping free as she swirls in a circle. My throat catches and I jump up, moving as close as I dare to see her better.

Heidi shows no fear and she moves with precision. She attacks without hesitation. Her daggers slice into the attacking demons as she spins, but they don't die. She only has runed daggers, and they won't kill the demons that aren't in a human body. The moment it registers, it's like someone has cut my feet out from under me.

But she doesn't seem to care. This is not the Heidi I remember. The one who *wanted* to be powerful, but wasn't. The one who yearned to be a Cazador, but who harbored insecurities only shown to a few. Me, for one.

This Heidi… this girl is the one in my art book, right down to her style of combat boots. I can't tear my eyes from her. My heart swells. I want to run up to her and throw my arms around her.

Did I do this? Does my gift work on humans too? And all this time I'd thought only of the demons. I could have been beefing up my friends and maybe even myself!

There's only one way to find out.

Frantically, I switch her daggers to something she needs, drawing Nephilim blades. Long and sharp. Quick and deadly. The moment she realizes something has changed, her whole demeanor shifts. I'm close enough to see the glint in her eyes as her ferocity is dialed up a few notches and the demons start disintegrating at her feet.

I quickly turn the page and search for the other Cazadors. I count them one by one and find that they're all here! I start with Owen and Doug, who have always been joined at the hip. I put them together on the page, twin warriors. Yin and Yang. One dark and one light. One tall, one small.

I sketch with urgency, my lines hurried, but as accurate as I can make them. I draw Owen with height, lean and quick. I draw a fierce look on his face, his eyes piercing and sharp, never missing a demon in his path, his feet un-trippable. He's magical as he spins and stabs. Last of all, I begin the downward slash of Nephilim daggers. Poison to demons. I quickly examine my work, pleased.

The moment my drawing is finished, the shift takes place. Owen stills for a split second and his eyes close, his face raised to the heavens, and then it's as if his lungs fill with an ethereal power. When his eyes open again, he's different. Fine tuned. His movements become precise, quick, and deadly.

His arms swirl in an arc as he slashes through gray men as though they're made of butter. They disappear in clouds of ash so quickly that he's killed the next five before the dust even settles on the ground. Sketching frantically, I make touchups to the blades, making them longer, gilding them with the designs I remember seeing on Bret's Nephilim blade.

I start on Doug, and even though he's stalky, I bulk him up, imbuing him with strength and stamina. I give him Nephilim daggers also. They sit in his grip like fangs, deadly poisonous. Each strike causes a demon to disappear. There are fewer and fewer to deal with as the moments tick by.

I switch to Jag. There isn't much to do for him. He has always been an animal in battle, but I give him Nephilim blades, plus speed-enhanced reflexes—if that is possible—and enhanced vision, so that nothing will get by him. The changes are minor, but I can see the difference as he fights. Does *he* notice?

47

Brecken

I kill mindlessly, without focusing on each demon I slay. If I stop to think, even for a moment, I might not be able to continue. The pull of the crater is so great that it almost overcomes me. I don't want to go in there, and yet, I yearn to jump inside and revel in the energy emanating from *The Door*. I haven't felt these passions in ages. Not since I left the Underworld.

For a demon, these feelings are normal and common. For someone trying to leave his demon side behind, they're excruciating in their seduction. It's power. It's control. It's supremacy. It's evil dominion in its purest form.

And I love it.

I make my way forward, trying to get to Mictian. He isn't even fighting yet, only watching from a distance, just beyond the ring of demons that surrounds us. They have no hope against me, and I wonder why he keeps sending them into the fight. He must be trying to wear us down. I happen to glance at Heidi, who fights on my left, my heart swelling when I see her. She's amazing and strong, and then… I do a double take. What the hell is she fighting with?

Nephilim blades?

How is that even possible? Where did she get them? I'm frozen, trying to figure out the puzzle, when a demon—that *isn't* a gray man—almost takes my head off with his sword. I swirl away, giving myself some distance, and then slash back at the demon's ugly, crimson-colored head. It falls at my feet.

Mictian smiles from just a few feet away. "He's mine!" he

yells to his minions as he swings his broadsword in wide arcs. It's much longer than my little dagger and he'll be able to lunge at me much easier than the other way around. "It's time to end this, my friend," he says.

"That's what I'm here for." I wait for him to come to me. The other demons stay back, watching.

"It doesn't seem fair. You're ill prepared for a swordfight." Saliva drips from his fangs, and he's uglier than I remember.

"I'll manage."

He smiles and steps closer. "I hate for it to end."

"I don't." This *must* end. *I* must end it, but fighting with Mictian, sword to dagger, won't do it. It will only delay the inevitable and might possibly cause us to lose. One scratch from his sword and I'm done. I can't afford to fight him or make any mistakes, but the desire to pit my strength against his is unbelievably irresistible. I can't turn away.

I inch closer to him. He raises his sword, his lips pulled back into an *I've already won* kind of grin.

"You can't close *The Door*," he says, thrusting at me. "It isn't possible. No one knows why it's broken and no one knows how to fix it, not that we want to."

I jump back barely in time, but when I look down, my T-shirt has a nice, even slice through the front. As I glance up, he smiles again. He can't be telling the truth. There must be an answer, and I better figure it out quick.

"You can't win," he yells, slashing at me again. And even though he plods toward me like a slow steer, I know better. I know him well.

"The crater, Brecken!" Heidi calls.

I turn to see thousands more demons crawling out over the edge, and I know it's already too late. I was given a mission, and I've failed a thousand times over. I have no solutions and no ideas…

Until I notice Heidi dashing for the edge. My heart falls to my feet. She can't go in there. She wouldn't survive for five seconds! Not only is there a constant burning flame in the crater, but deadly poisonous gases rising out of it.

"Heidi! Stop!" I scream, turning away from my foe.

But she doesn't listen to me. She's belting for the edge and she's almost there. I give Mictian one last grimace before running for my stupid sister. I was always a faster runner than her, but in the last two days, she's become something of a paradox.

It's a race for the edge and it's going to be close. I'll barely make it before she hurls herself to her death. I push myself, pulling in huge breaths of air, forcing my legs to move faster, my stride to stretch farther.

"Heidi! No!" I scream again, but she either doesn't hear me or doesn't care. She's determined to do something other than kill demons, but killing herself isn't going to do a damn thing. She has no power to shut *The Door*. That's my job… *my* job. Given to me by Raphael and Michael.

With one last burst of energy, we reach the edge at the same time. I throw myself in front of her, my hand slamming into her chest, shoving her back from the edge and into Jag's arms—he's chasing after her too—and in my momentum, I hurl over the edge.

48

Heidi

I know what I have to do. It seems completely crazy and I'm not even sure it will work, but I have to get Brecken to jump into that crater. It doesn't look like he's thought of it, so it's up to me. I don't know how I know this, but it's clear in my mind, as if God himself explained it to me.

I finally understand. Brecken is something different—not completely human—but chosen.

I face my last demon, slicing through him easily, and then I run. Straight toward the crater. Brecken sees me and my heart leaps, because he better hurry. I don't want to die.

He tears himself from his own duel and darts after me, screaming my name. I slow imperceptibly because I'm going to make it to the edge before he does. It's going to be close. Jag shrieks for me to stop, but I'm way ahead of him. He won't make it to me in time. No one can stop me.

The demon horde opens up, making a path for us, as if they know we're about to end our own lives and they're here for the show. Brecken's look of terror almost stops me because I don't want this to be the end. I'm filled with such love for him that I can barely contain it. My brother. My beautiful, bossy, perfect brother… he's willing to die for me and I'm willing to die for him.

He barely reaches me in time.

His hand slams into my chest, throwing me backward into Jag's arms. My breath explodes from my lungs and I gasp, flailing and trying to breathe as I watch Brecken—my best friend, who I don't even get to hug goodbye—fly into the fiery depths of the crater. My heart rips as his dark head disappears over the edge.

I scream for him even though I know he can't come back for me. Jag and I scramble to the edge and peer over. The demons that surround us clamber for the edge also, staring down into the flames. I'm not afraid of them. They can't hurt me and they know it. They seem as amazed as I am at this turn of events.

When Brecken reaches the base of the pit, he slides right through instead of slamming down onto hard-packed ground, as though the fiery crust opened just for him. It closes over his head and then he's gone. That's it.

In a slow, measured motion, I turn and glance at Jag. Both Owen and Doug are beside us, searching the depths of the crater. They gape at me with questioning eyes. I can't answer their questions. I have the same ones. Is it over?

A gray man in a human body gazes at me with a frown. "What does this mean?"

"I don't know," I answer before stabbing my dagger into his chest. He disappears in a puff of ash. The other demons who are close throw themselves over the edge to safety.

I glance at Jag, my lips stretching into a slow, provocative smile.

He grins back at me, pulls me into a one-armed embrace, and plants a kiss full on my mouth. "This is the most fun I've had in ages," he says, drawing me closer.

I wrap my arms around his neck, never happier… or sadder. I lost my brother today, but I have my soulmate. Jag is like no one else. Strong, yet gentle. Fierce, yet loving. I love him so intensely that it makes my heart ache. Those very words slip from my mouth as I kiss him one more time, breathing him in.

He pulls back an inch or two and stares into my eyes, his hand cupping my cheek. "If you're trying to scare me away, it's not going to work." He grins and then releases me, brandishing his Nephilim daggers. "Let's clean house."

49

Dean

I can't believe Bret actually jumped over the edge. Surely, he'll find a way to close *The Door*. My heart flames with happiness… until Jag takes Heidi in his arms and kisses her passionately… like he's done it a hundred times… right in front of everybody. And she kisses him back just as ardently.

My heart—which was burning with happiness—plummets and is dashed on the rocks. I freeze, staring at the heart-wrenching sight. When did they become a *thing*? They can't stand each other. I was the one who constantly brought them together. I helped them work out their differences. *I* love her.

What does this mean?

I have to look away and for a moment, I let myself collapse in the dirt, trying to figure it out. The whole time I was gone, they were together… doing what? It makes me sick to even imagine it, and I feel betrayed. I try to shake it off as the Cazadors go back to work, getting rid of the rest of the demons, but I can't quite pull myself together. I'm shaken, more from that kiss and the expressions on their faces than the demons that surround us.

The battle isn't over yet, and I still have work I can do, so I resolve to think about this later. I can't dwell on it now. My friends are depending on me whether they know it or not. My gaze roams over the demons and lands on Coem. I vowed to make him my first official victim, and I intend to fulfill that promise. I slide the picture I already drew of him out of my backpack. With meticulous detail, I draw a dagger sticking out of his chest and make a few changes to his face to give him a look of horror.

Not ten seconds later, Doug launches himself at Coem, his dagger raised. Coem sees him coming and swirls out of the way at the last second. Narrowing my eyes, and with quick strokes, I draws roots growing out of the bottom of his feet, deep into the ground so he can't move. The real Coem freezes immediately, his feet suddenly glued to the earth.

He looks up with a perplexed expression, and then he turns, searching for the cause. He finds me staring straight at him, my pencil poised, a look of vengeance in my eyes. A shiver of fear slithers over my shoulders and, for a split second, I'm afraid. His gaze narrows, boring into me, and I know he knows. *I* am the one ending his life. *I* am the one who will finish the great and powerful Coem.

I lift my hand, my pencil raised in salute. His demeanor registers defeat the moment Doug plunges a dagger into his chest.

In a poof, he's gone. It's too easy and almost anticlimactic. I'm left feeling deflated, like I missed something, like it should have lasted longer or been more exciting. Maybe I'm sitting too far away to feel it.

Jag works his way through the crowd, and I scramble closer to get a better view. Demon after demon falls by his hand, but then he comes up against one of those demons that isn't a gray man and not as easily killed. The massive monstrosity sidesteps Jag's thrusts and knocks one of Jag's daggers from his grip. The demon carries a long broadsword, but he has yet to use it. My heart twists because I instinctively know this fiend will not be easily killed, even though Jag has been enhanced.

Jag steps back.

I've never seen him do that. Ever. He never retreats. He wins. Always. My heart races as I hurry to get this demon's visage down on paper, but he's moving too much, and it's hard to be meticulous. I scratch down the black horns, the leathery, russet skin, fangs that glisten in the firelight, and then I try to sketch the details of his face.

He's huge—well over seven feet tall—powerful and menacing. He swings at Jag with his fist, but why not use his sword? And then I understand. He's prolonging his enjoyment. He knows he's going to win. He knows he's unbeatable, so I need to make him otherwise, but what will work on a demon of this sort? He doesn't have a human body I can make sick, and something tells me that drawing a weakness for him won't be as effective as it is with the others.

I try anyway.

I scratch out his eyes and then glance up to see if it has any effect. The beast keeps pushing Jag backward, out into the darkness, away from the crater. I turn his fingers into twisted, gnarled sausages, unable to form a fist or hold his sword. I glance up. They are farther away, and I can't even see the demon's hands let alone his fingers.

I pick up my stuff and run for them. "Heidi!" I scream as I dart past the vast crowd she whittles away at.

She glances up, her eyes wide with wonder. "Dean?" She stops fighting and her daggers hang limp from her fingers. Her jaw drops, dragging on the ground as she watches me dart past like a ghost.

I'm running as fast as my legs can carry me, faster than I've ever run before. So fast, my chest aches and my legs cramp. But Heidi catches up to me, stopping my forward momentum and pulling me into her arms.

"Oh, Dean! I can't believe it! You're here! You're alive!" She searches me from head to toe and then pulls me in for another huge hug.

Nothing has ever felt more wonderful. Here she is, my dream come true, the girl I've loved for so long that it hurts to breathe when I gaze at her. But I can't stop. I have to help Jag. I cut the moment short, pulling away. It feels like I'm ripping my heart out with my bare hands, but I manage to do it.

"Jag!" I gasp, pointing out into the darkness. I hear grunting and punches landing on skin and bones breaking. Someone cries out, and it isn't the beast.

Heidi's eyes widen in horror and she darts away from me, into the shadows. I follow in her wake, hoping to be able to help, but not having much faith in my ability since it hasn't worked yet.

They materialize before us, the stench of blood wafting on the sulfuric breeze. The beast hears us coming and turns toward us. Heidi and I stop suddenly, as if we're on the edge of a cliff. Jag hangs in the demon's fist, those meaty fingers wrapped tightly around his neck. His head lolls to the side, but he's not unconscious… yet. Blood seeps from his left ear and also his nose—which looks broken. His shoulder hangs crooked, like it's dislocated, and his jaw is slack and maybe broken, but I can't be sure in the dim light. Only a minute amount of light glows from the crater this far out.

"Jag!" Heidi screams in horror. "Let him go!" She screeches as though her brain is no longer functioning. She races forward, but the demon's sword is longer than her daggers and she can't get close. The realization that the Nephilim blade can kill us, even with a scratch, is all too real.

With a howl of fury, she darts past anyway. Figuring what? That she's invincible? I can't risk losing her, so I grab her long hair at the last second and yank her back. Not a very gentlemanly act, but I'm pretty sure I've saved her life. "No, Heidi." I hold onto her, which takes a monumental amount of strength because she's so dang strong now.

"He'll kill him. Can't you see that?" She falls to her knees and sobs.

"Yes, little butterfly. Listen to your friend," the demon growls in a deep, gravelly voice. "You don't want this poor boy to die. He's put up such a good fight."

"Who… who are you?" she whispers, trembling in my grip.

"I am your worst nightmare. Remember?" His laughter rumbles like distant thunder and she looks up, her eyes widening.

"I remember you."

"And I remember you." He speaks as if he's conversing with an old friend, even as Jag dangles in his grip.

"You're more powerful than the others," she says, still on her knees with her daggers clutched in her fists.

"I am Mictian, and I am a god of immeasurable power."

My stomach twists. There's no way out of this. "Please let

him go." I place my pack on the ground and raise my hands in surrender, my pulse pounding and my heart racing so fast it feels like it will burst.

"And why should I do that? This filthy human came to destroy me. To destroy all of us." He gestures to the whole area of demons, which have dwindled remarkably. Doug and Owen haven't stopped slaughtering them even though the rest of us have. The vast remainder of demons are throwing themselves back into the pit, hoping to escape the Nephilim daggers that wait for them otherwise.

It's pretty much just Mictian and us now. We stare at one another in the dark.

Mictian considers us, completely unafraid.

I hear the pounding of feet growing closer, glancing over my shoulder at Doug and Owen charging toward us, ready to continue the battle. Their daggers are mere extensions of their arms and their voices grow to berserker pitch.

"Wait! Stop!" I yell as they barrel past.

They either don't hear me or aren't listening. With one solid thrust of Mictian's arm, they soar to the side like rag dolls. Owen lands hard and lies unmoving, but Doug moans and rolls to his side.

"Your friends don't listen well," Mictian says to me. "But I sense something wiser in you. Something powerful and... might I say... demonic? My, my. Why is that?"

Heidi glances at me, searching for whatever Mictian can see.

This is the moment where I can fix things. I can save Jag. I can save us all. "I have a gift. One that can benefit you if you let him go." I point to Jag, unable to believe the words just left my mouth. I tremble in this demon's presence, but I have to strike a bargain. It's the only thing I can think of to save my friends.

"Yes," he says. "It is a gift. A demonic gift. They tried to possess you, didn't they? Perhaps more than once? That was very careless of them." The deepness of his voice vibrates through me, leaving me shaken, but his words penetrate to my core. The demons did this to me. They gave me the power to hurt them...

accidentally. And then it all makes sense.

"Yes," I whisper, almost too horrified to say it out loud. "Please," I beg, slowly lowering myself to my knees, submissive, powerless, and pleading.

"What is he talking about?" Heidi stares at me, her daggers raised. She won't let him hurt me. I hope.

Mictian is no ordinary demon. My powers don't affect him in any way, and if he can completely incapacitate *Jag*… He studies me, his eyes narrow and piercing. He looks me up and down as though with the ability to see right through me, to see through my lies. "Come," he commands, his hand outstretched.

Before I move, my gaze flicks to Jag. His eyes are locked on Heidi. He doesn't say anything. I don't think he can, but I see something pass between them. Something I've never seen before, but it's plain and obvious. She aches for him, her heart bared and bleeding for all of us to see. Jag's eyes scream the same thing. They're not just a thing. They're in love.

But they hated each other. Jag couldn't stand Heidi.

The way he looks at her now though, the longing in his eyes… One lone tears drips down his cheek and I'm frozen.

My hand reaches for Mictian's and my heart skips a beat.

I've been gone for what feels like a year, but in reality, it's only been a couple of weeks. Feeling like my own heart is ripping in two, I realize I'm too late. Can I live beside them, watching as their love grows? I'm not sure I can.

Mictian scrutinizes me, a knowing grin on his feral lips. His eyes dart between Heidi and Jag, who grows more lifeless as the seconds tick by. "Aw… young love. So precious, so tender, so… fleeting."

My gaze rises to his, my agony evident in my devastated expression. But this changes nothing. I love them both. I'd give my life for Jag, my brother, and I'd also lay down my life for Heidi, who is still the love of my life.

I take Mictian's hand. He wraps his fingers around my wrist and my hand disappears inside his grip. Jag's tries to loosen the demon's grip on his neck, but he isn't getting away until Mictian is good and ready to let go.

"Please, let my friend go," I plead. "Please."

"And you would give your life for his?" the demon asks, amused.

"Yes! In a heartbeat, I would." There's not much more I can do but beg with my whole heart. Every cell in my body is beseeching him for Jag's life. There's nothing more I can give.

Mictian looks from me to Heidi, and then at Doug. He ignores Owen, who is still unconscious, and then his gaze comes back to me. "I don't think so." And with a flick of his powerful fingers, he snaps Jag's neck. The sound cracks like thunder and the world around me stops turning, moving slower and slower as Heidi shrieks and darts past me to grab Jag's limp, falling body.

I can't think. I can't feel. I'm under water where all sound is muted and dark. My heart stops beating in my chest, and the twist inside my gut pours icy poison through my veins. My mind can't grasp what just happened. He didn't really kill Jag right in front of us. It's unthinkable.

And now he is dragging me behind him like a rag doll, the clomping of his hooves bringing sound back to me with slamming clarity. My friends are growing smaller and smaller in the distance, scrambling around Jag as I yearn to do. I try to get to my feet, but I stumble over and over as Mictian continues to tow me. We're closing in on the crater, and it registers what he's about to do.

I'll kill myself before I let him drag me to hell as his puppet.

With my free hand, I reach for my pencil, which is still in my back pocket. It's deadly sharp as I haven't used this one yet. Holding it tight in my fist, I plunge that yellow number two into Mictian's back, right where his kidney should be. I push it all the way through his skin with all the strength I have, screaming out my heartache for the abuse I've suffered and for the friend I've lost.

Mictian stumbles, but catches himself, then stumbles again, falling to one knee. My hand falls from his grasp, and I use that split second to scuffle away from him. Dirt and gravel dig into my wrists and the stench of sulfur fills my nostrils, but I'm free and I don't stop moving.

Mictian doesn't rise. He stays slumped over, balanced on one knee. He slowly turns, glancing over his shoulder at me, and then, as though time is holding its breath, he tips forward and falls headfirst into the flaming depths of the pit.

I scramble back to the crater, terrified, but I have to see. Peering over the edge, relief bursts in my heart. He lies on the bottom, his once powerful body burning and turning to ash.

And then a heart-wrenching wail erupts behind me.

50

Brecken

Heat wafts up around me as I sink through the floor of the crater to the actual door, which is framed by polished obsidian pillars. The scent of sulfur, like a sweet perfume, fills me. Like a comforting blanket, I'm surrounded with the warmth of a thousand unseen worlds. I can go to any of them from this place.

I see where the Rift has broken the foundation, and all around the base of *The Door*, magma boils up like a river to anywhere, but it's not supposed to. It escapes through the cracks and creates pathways into the darkness in every direction. It truly is the door of possibilities.

For one moment, I yearn to hitch a ride away from this place. I don't have to be here. I can start over again with my brothers. I feel them at this very moment, inviting me back into the fold. I can be powerful again. I can be a general in the armies of Hell. I can be *Bretariel, The Great Undoer* again.

The pull is magnetic and pulsing, and I can picture that life ahead of me. A life of limitless power.

I reach for *The Door*'s knob, a clear, white crystal of the most beautiful workmanship, and I remember, instantaneously, that it can only be turned by a demon. No one can enter through this gate unless they are fully committed to evil, and the temptation to actually turn that knob is crushingly potent. Would I be allowed to enter or would I die on the spot for even trying? How much of the demon still remains inside me?

My heart races. I can't believe I've even gotten this far. Like any other human being, I should have burned to a crisp as I passed through the crater. But I didn't, and now I wonder why. Although, I know why.

I'm a demon.

I always have been. Like Jag said, a tiger can't change its stripes. How could I think I was redeemable? How could I even think to escape the grasp of the underworld and why would I want to?

I place a hand on each pillar and close my eyes. They hum with the energy of a thousand ages. They've been here forever, a doorway to and from Hell. Their power emanates through me, a thrilling experience. I stand there long enough that when I once again open my eyes, I can't seem to remember why I'm standing here. My mind draws a blank, and I yearn only to turn that handle. To be The Undoer.

I turn back to the door.

My fingers tighten on the crystal, the edges digging into my skin. The knob begins to turn under my grip, but a strange, sudden awareness surrounds me. An uncomfortable sensation that makes my skin itch, that fills me with anger and frustration. It holds me back from my destiny. My calling.

When this strange, painful energy has coursed through my body and finally enters my heart, I cry out in anguish, the agony unendurable. I lose my strength and fall to one knee as a phrase forms in my mind. Solid. Loud, and unmistakable.

Close the door.

I'm confused. The door is already closed. It stands before me, solid, black, and unyielding.

Close the door.

"What do you want?" I scream out, my second knee smacking the stony ground. "It's already closed!" Conflicted emotions battle inside me, warring so powerfully that I can't even move or comprehend what is happening.

And then I do.

It's clear, as though I'm looking into a crystal ball. I *know*.

It's me. It has been me all along.

When I snuck away from the demon world and crossed over,

I created a fissure between the world of gods and demons because I never truly let go of my demon heart. Not completely. I'd always left a piece of my soul open, a piece of The Undoer alive.

Close the door, the words scream in my mind again. *Now!*

They are coming. I can feel it. Just on the other side, millions of demons, no, more than that, on the threshold of this world. They've been called by Mictian. And now, I know what to do, as though I'm reading a script. I have to play my part. For Heidi, for the Cazadors, but most importantly, for myself.

Lurching away from the door, I close my eyes and use the same visualization I taught Heidi. Could it really be this simple, this obvious an answer? I had it with me all the time?

Clutching my chest, I say, "I am a demon, but I purposefully let go of that life. I give it up. I give it away. I no longer want it. It has no hold over me. I choose to be a free soul in the universes of man. I embrace my destiny and my future. I embrace eternity and the chance to be forgiven of my wrongdoings. I close this door in my heart, this rift I caused that has damaged the whole world and allowed evil to come through so rampantly. I offer myself as a sacrifice to close this door."

A whirlwind of air whips around me, fiery sparks flying. The ground rumbles, an earthquake of power. The rock around the door groans and churns at my feet, shifting and collapsing, sealing the cracks. The demons roar on the other side, their screeching and wailing cut off as the fissure heals.

The moment it happens, I *feel* it. Something inside me shifts also. Like an old wound that has been seeping, it closes. That leaking out of my soul—that I didn't even know was happening—stops. A feeling of wholeness fills me, and my heart swells. I've never felt anything like it and there are no words to describe the lightness inside, like I could lift right off my feet.

I turn back to the crater that burns and crackles just over my head. I only have to close my eyes and visualize being on the other side and I'm there, the golden embers sparking and popping around me.

I crawl to the top, amazed that I don't suffer any burns.

Not even my clothes are singed. I roll over the edge, breathing in the sweet scent of Earth and sky, and while I'm rejoicing in my newfound happiness, I am met by the most grief-stricken sound I have ever heard.

The sound of abject sorrow.

51

Brecken

I can't seem to make my feet move. I'm frozen, staring and astonished at the scene before me. Rising at the crater's edge, I stumble toward Heidi, who kneels on the ground, Jag's lifeless body enfolded in her arms. Her wails of grief pierce the air, and her three brothers-in-arms stand as sentinels behind her.

All is quiet, but for the breaking hearts of the Cazadors, and I can't stem the tears that threaten at the edges of my eyes also.

What I'm seeing can't be real.

Jag is not dead, even though my eyes tell me it's so. I'd come here knowing it was a one-way trip, that none of us would make it home, so the fact that only one of us has lost our life should be a comfort, but it's not.

I kneel beside her, placing my hand on her shoulder, my chest filled with ache at the agony I see in her eyes. I have no words. There *are* no words for something like this. And even though I know this is not the end for Jag, I can't stop feeling as if I have failed my new friends. I should have saved him. I should have been quicker at closing *The Door*.

Hugging my sister, I whisper how sorry I am, and how much I love her.

She hugs me back until all is silent in that barren wasteland, including her tears. "We should bury him here," she says finally. "Next to *The Door*."

"Are you sure?" I whisper.

"He sacrificed his life for this. He knew something… something was going to happen. I think he'd want this."

Leaving him buried in the dirt in this desolate wasteland doesn't feel right to me, or like something he'd want, but then another thought comes to me. "I can take him into the crater." As soon as I say it, I know it's the correct thing to do.

Heidi gazes into my eyes, the fiery light reflecting in those deep pools of sadness. She nods. As one, we lift Jag, all four of us bearing his weight back to the crater. At the edge, I slide over, cradling his body in my arms.

The crater's fire sparks and pops around me as I make my way to the bottom, gently laying Jag's body down on the embers. Even still, I am unharmed as I stand there, gazing down on his face, now smooth and at peace in death, all frustration and annoyance for this lost boy dissolving into admiration and love.

When I step back, the fire consumes his body. Our tears fall uninhibited until it's over.

And then, something unexpected happens. The flames burn down to nothing, and then go out completely, the crater becoming dark and cool as smoke tendrils twist and spiral into the night sky, Jag's spirit rising with it.

Epilogue

Brecken

"You tricked me." I sit across the desk from Raphael in his bright, white office in Elysium. My heart is healed and I am a completely new person, yet I feel such heartache and sorrow. How is it possible to have succeeded in my mission and at the same time, feel like I failed? "You could have told me these things in the beginning. And then everything would have been different."

"It's not supposed to be different," he says, his expression gentle and sad. "Plus, you wouldn't have believed me. It had to be *this* way. You had to figure it out on your own. You had to be the one to realize that the cracks in *The Door* were caused by you. You were the only one who could fix them."

I shake my head, not able to meet his gaze, all the memories of the last couple of months drifting through my mind—the first time I met the Cazadors when I watched Dean and Jag eat candy in the plaza. The first time I saw Heidi, sitting on the front steps of the church. Doug and Owen bantering back and forth, eating pretzels. The ache of loss, of what they have all lost, is such an incredible weight in my heart. "And what if I'd failed?"

"But you didn't."

This outcome doesn't seem right and though I understand it now, the pain I went through—that everyone went through because of me—is difficult to let go of.

"Tell me what happened after they all got home," Raphael says, although he is perfectly aware already. He sits back, his fingers threaded over his stomach, and waits, his expression loving and patient, like always.

With a heavy sigh, I begin, picturing the events in my mind as they occurred. "It was terrible. I've never seen anyone so... broken."

"Heidi will recover," he says sadly, "But it will take time." He nods for me to continue.

I shake my head in denial, staring out the windows at nothing, picturing her face. The way she held Jag's ruined body in her arms, the tender way she smoothed his hair from his face, the gentle kiss she placed on his lips for the last time.

Something twists in my heart, and I have to fight back tears as I relive it all. The memory is still too raw, too painful, and I look away so Raphael can't see my sorrow.

"And Dean?" he asks me as though he doesn't already know. "How is he doing?"

Raphael is trying to get me to talk. To get it out. To have closure. It's a compassionate gesture, but I don't want to talk about it. I want to hide in some corner of heaven and cry. A lone tear glides slowly down my cheek. I don't bother to wipe it away.

"He's okay. He sat with Heidi the whole way home. He never left her side, and I don't think he ever will. He loves her." That is the only consolation that allows me to be here rather than there with her. I couldn't have left her otherwise. "I took Heidi and Dean back to my aunt's house to grieve and heal. They'll be okay there, surrounded by family. Dean's gift went away."

"Yes, I know. That kind of power doesn't belong in the hands of a mortal. He had it for as long as was needful."

I nod in agreement.

"And Doug and Owen?" Raphael asks. "They're incredible boys. I really admire their dedication and grit." He smiles and chuckles to himself. "I don't think there are two other companions I'd rather have at my back."

I picture their faces in my mind and smile. "Owen suffered a concussion, but he'll be all right. The boys are back with their families, safe and sound, healing and dealing with what we all went through." The Cazadors are no more. They aren't needed. The demon problem has been handled. Everyone can go back to living a normal life… if that is even possible. "We're lucky to all be alive really. Well, they are, I mean."

Raphael doesn't respond out loud, but he concurs with a dip of his head. "I'm sorry, Brecken, for everything difficult you've had to go through. It was necessary, but I'm sorry all the same."

His words touch my heart, but they refresh the pain I carry. I need to be someplace where I can heal. I lean forward to let him know we're finished here.

He gives me a sad smile and sighs. "You'll move forward now. You've made amazing strides and Alisa couldn't be happier."

My head snaps up. "She knows?"

"Of course. She's never stopped watching over you."

My heart skips a beat as I picture her face. If only we could be together now. I don't see that happening. She's way ahead of me. I still have too far to go to even dream of being with her. But to someday be at her side… I'd go through *anything* for that.

Raphael rises, a stupid grin on his face. "I have a surprise for you."

"What?" I ask, suddenly suspicious, but a part of me already knows, and hope pushes me from my chair. Rushing to the door, I fling it open. She's there, a wide, beautiful smile spreading across her rosy lips, her golden hair tumbling over her shoulders. Her eyes crinkle as she lifts her arms to hug me, and her laughter bubbles around us like music.

I take her in my arms, pulling her close and inhaling the scent of cinnamon.

Her soul melds with mine.

This. This is why I went through hell… and now… it's totally worth it.

Acknowledgements

I have to admit, The Undoer is my favorite so far, and as every author knows, it takes a lot of blood, sweat, and tears to bring a book to life. This one was no different. I want to thank my awesome beta readers first off—Renae Mackley, Rebecca Jamison, and Janice Sperry—for slogging through the first drafts and pointing out all my holes and inconsistencies. You guys rock!

A special thanks to Jenny Bynum for being my first official reader and for being so excited about this book that she wrote her review before I'd even sent the manuscript to my publisher!

A huge thanks to my publisher, Clean Teen Publishing—Rebecca Gober, Courtney Knight, Marya Heiman, and Melanie Newton—for taking another chance on me and loving this book as much as I do! Thanks for your patience and encouragement and for being there to answer my every question. Thank you, Marya Heiman, for the gorgeous cover and for graciousness when I was picky, picky, picky.

Thank you, Cynthia Shepp, my editor, for correcting my mistakes and helping me polish this into a work of art!

There aren't enough thanks I can give to my husband and kids for their constant support. I couldn't do this without them. On those days when I want to throw my hands in the air, give up, or bang my head against a wall, they are there, telling me to keep going! I love you guys so dang much, it hurts!

And last of all, thank you, fans and readers! You're the ones I love to drag into my world of madness! Enjoy the ride!

About the Author

Melissa Cunningham (also known as M.E. Cunningham) was born in Oregon but grew up in Utah, where she was raised on a steady diet of fine literature from Charlotte's web to the The Trumpeter Swan, and then plenty of romances in her teen years. She now lives with her husband on a little farm in northern Utah where all she can see out of her back door is miles of pasture and stunning sunsets. Not only does she raise horses, dogs, cats, and chickens, but her five kids also. When Melissa is not writing you can find her spending time in the outdoors with her family or dancing wildly to rock music in her living room. She loves running, camping, and all things fiction—scary, mind-numbing stories preferred.

CHARACTER PLAYLISTS

Brecken
Safe.... by Westlife
Blow Me Away.... by Breaking Benjamin
It's Not Over....by Daughtry
Savin' Me....by Nickelback
This Means War... by Nickelback
Enemies.....by Shinedown
Come With Me Now....by KONGOS
Carry On My Wayward Son.....by Kansas
I'd Love To Change the World.....by Jetta
Savin's Me....by Nickelback
Angel.....by Digital Daggers

Heidi
This is Where I Belong....by Bryan Adams
The Voice Within.... By Christina Aguilera
Ashes and Wine....by A Fine Frenzy
Near To You....by A Fine Frenzy
Lost.....by Within Temptation
What Have You Done....by Within Temptation
Don't Leave Me Behind....by We Are The Fallen
Close Your Eyes.... By Digital Daggers
Still Here....by Digital Daggers
Heaven of Hell....by Digital Daggers

Dean
Jungle....by X Ambassadors & Jamie N Commons
Over You....by Daughtry
I'm Not Alright....by Shinedown
Paint Me Black....by Ben Hazelwood
Brother....by Need To Breathe
Keep Me Watching....by Jason Walker
Creep....by Radiohead
Congratulations....by Blue October Feat. Imogen Heap

Also in the Ransomed Souls Series:

Be sure to check out Melissa's other series,
The Into Terratir Series

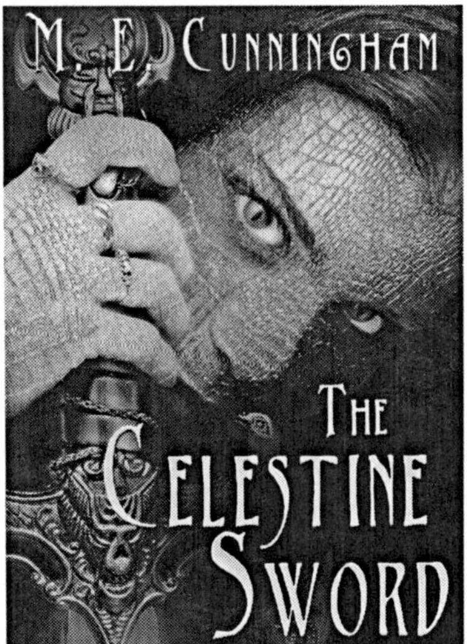

You can find all of Melissa's books on her website:
http://www.melissajcunningham.com/#!books/cnec

CPSIA information can be obtained at www.ICGtesting.com
Printed in the USA
LVOW08s1928240716
497224LV00001B/7/P

9 781634 221993